D0974443

Lani Wendt Young was born and raised in Samoa. She completed her tertiary education in the USA and New Zealand before returning to Samoa to teach high school English for ten years. She now lives in Auckland, NZ with her husband and five children. Lani's award - winning short fiction has featured in collections published in Samoa, NZ, Australia and the United Kingdom.

Her first book – "*Pacific Tsunami*" was published in 2010.

"*Telesa: The Covenant Keeper*" is her first book of fiction. Readers worldwide are calling it "the Pacific Twilight."

ALSO BY LANI WENDT YOUNG

Pacific Tsunami – Galu Afi

"An informative, most sensitively articulated and beautifully woven
story that records with colour and feeling, a significant moment in
Pacific history."
*His Highness Tui Atua Tupua Tamasese Ta'isi Tupuola Tufuga Efi,
Head of State of Samoa.*

"Lani's style of language keeps the story moving fast with excitement,
curiosity and interest. She has done a marvellous job in weaving
together the stories from hundreds of survivors and tellers."
Prof. Albert Wendt. Novelist, Playwright, Artist

Telesa

The Covenant Keeper

Lani Wendt Young

Cover Design: Tim and Efi Rasmussen
Tirza Laughs
Additional Photography: Jordan Kwan
Cover Models: Ezra Taylor, Flora Rivers, Faith Wulf

To Darren.
Who teaches me daily how to love with fun, faith and fire.

"No ... please ... how to stop it? How can I stop it?"

I burst into useless tears. Tears that fizzed and hissed in a heartbeat of heat. No amount of crying would help now. I wrung my hands, no way out of it. It was hopeless. In a few minutes I would be a mass murderer. A killer. In my mind's eye, I could see it now. People on fire running in circles, frantically beating at the hungry flames. The smell of flesh scorching, peeling off ashy bone. Screams. Pleas for help. I sank to my knees, drained dry of strength. Unwilling to watch the carnage but unable to take my eyes away. I was drowning in a sea of fiery despair. Suffocating in a red night of terror.

A clear, calm voice spoke from beside me. "Leila. Call it back. You can do it. Call it back. Call it back NOW."

I looked up, eyes glistening with molten tears. He stood as close to me as he dared, shielding his face from the heat with his hands, the edges of his clothes singed and charred.

"I can't." Abject despair in my voice. "I don't know how."

"Yes you can. You have the power. You know you do. You spoke to it before. It listens to you. Call it back now before it's too late. Please."

It was the 'please' that did it. That snapped me out of the depths. He wanted me to call the fire. He believed that I could. And I wanted him to believe in me. Slowly, I raised myself from the ground, closed my eyes and willed that fiery beast to come home.

To listen to me – its mistress. To return and feed instead on my molten core. I trembled at the very thought of the blaze finding its way back. How could I possibly summon it all when it had grown so exponentially as it fed? But this was my fault. I had to find the strength from somewhere. I opened my eyes and shuddered at the majesty of the sight before me.

*Directly ahead of me was a massive wall of fire. It had stopped advancing across the field and now it stood waiting; the beast waited for my command. **Now** – it asked – **what would you have me do?** Opening my arms, every ounce of my being quivering with fear, I summoned it home.*

I burned. Inside and out. I burned. There was indescribable pain and the knife edge of pleasure. It was ecstasy and hell all at once. Then, as swiftly as it had begun, it stopped.

I was empty. A dried husk scorched beyond belief. Withered and dead. I fell.

The steaming darkness claimed me.

ONE

What was I doing? On a plane thousands of miles away from everything familiar, going to a land I had never seen? Well, a land I didn't remember seeing, I corrected. Clenching my palms tightly, I pressed my head against the window, staring blindly out at the motionless clouds. The engines of the 747 were a dull roar and the flight attendant a vapid chatter behind me as I tried to block out the images that threatened to bring tears to my eyes. Flashes.

Dad. Weakly trying to clasp me close as he lay on his hospital bed. Trying to push aside the oxygen mask so he could whisper in my ear. "Leila – very important – I love you – whatever you do, don't go back there, don't let them send for you. Please stay here. Please don't go back."

"Excuse me, here are your arrival forms to fill in. Do you need any help, Miss?" The flight attendant was a slender woman with hair swept up in an effortless swirl. Her eyes were concerned as she looked at my tear-stained cheeks.

Cringing under her gaze – and resenting the assumption that I, a world-weary eighteen-year–old, would need help filling in a simple form – my reply was abrupt.

"No. I certainly do not need any help from you."

I regretted the belligerent words as soon as they were out of my mouth, but it was too late. The woman pursed her lips and walked away up the aisle stiffly.

Great. Just great Leila. Way to go. What are you gonna do? Yell at everyone who's nice to you? I turned back to the window with a mental sigh of resignation. Hoping for a glimpse of my destination and yet wishing I was a million miles away.

Back home. In D.C. With Dad. In my own room with its tropical print bedspread, walls covered with Dad's black and white portfolio photos, shelves strewn carelessly with shells and coral from one of our trips to the beach. French doors open onto the balcony that was filled to overflowing with my plants. Some gently dug from the rich earth of the forest reserve at the end of our street. Others, exotic greens brought back from my father's many trips to Africa and the Middle East. Each one nurtured and cared for with innate skill. Each one a friend. And now each one probably dumped in a landfill somewhere as the new house owners cleared out the leftovers of my life. Oh, I had tried to take my plants with me to grandmother's house. But of course the old lady would have none of it.

"Don't be ridiculous child. We have no space for your sticks and leaves. Besides, we have a beautiful conservatory where you can have more than your fill of plants. They are all very expensive and rare, mind you, so I won't have you fumbling around in there damaging things. I shall speak to Manuel and see if there is some small task you can be entrusted with – perhaps watering?" The last was added on with a gracious nod of her perfectly coiffed silver head as Elizabeth Folger bestowed what she viewed as a comfort upon her far from satisfactory granddaughter.

"Forget it. I'm not interested in that ridiculous collection of hothouse plants" I muttered under my breath.

"What was that child?" an imperious tone as my grandmother displayed her uncanny knack for perfect hearing exactly when you didn't want her to.

"Nothing grandmother. Never mind." How I wished the old lady would stop calling me a child. I was eighteen for heaven's sake. And she needed to look in a thesaurus and find a new word to replace 'ridiculous' because when it came to talking about me, she couldn't seem to escape ridiculous.

Thesaurus. That brought a smile to my thoughts as I remembered how Dad used to insist I carry one around with me everywhere. Even to the dinner table. So that when we discussed the meal, my day, I would have to use new adjectives every time.

"This meal, I mean this 'repast' is absolutely superb father."

"Really, oh light of my life, how and why is it superb?"

"Umm, because the French toast wasn't burned to a crisp this time! I mean, because the French toast was oh-so-delectably soaked in a confection of whipped eggs and cream, sprinkled with cinnamon and then indulgently browned in a daub of creamy butter, is that good enough for you?"

And then we would erupt into peals of laughter. And eat our French toast. And toast each other with a can of Diet Coke. With a twist of lime. Our 'after dinner cocktail' my dad would call it.

It shook me to realize I was smiling at the memory.

Smiling. Something I hadn't done for weeks now. Smiling about French toast and cokes with my dad. How lame. I didn't know whether to laugh or cry.

"The captain has turned on the fasten seat-belt sign. We are approaching Faleolo Airport and will be landing in a few minutes."

The announcement crackled over the headphones, breaking into my thoughts. A few minutes. That's all that separated me from the rest of my life. I gave myself a mental shake, turning away from the window. Away from where I had come. Must look ahead now. Need to be ready for this. A leap into the unknown.

Samoa.

The one place my father had NOT wanted me to come. The place he had pleaded with his dying breath for me to stay away from. And now six months later, here I was. A traitor to the last wishes of the only person who mattered to me. I closed my eyes as I took the final step off the plane, sending him a silent plea for forgiveness – wherever he was.

The sweltering heat embraced me, smothering me in its heavy wrap as I walked out. Sweat already trickling down my back; I slowly made my way across the tarmac and into the arrival building. People jostled and shoved trying to get in line for immigration check-in. For the first time, I took a good look at the people around me.

Lumbering ladies in floral print dresses sweated beside me in the line, carrying shopping bags stuffed with chocolates, plastic flower wreaths and shiny keys that read 'Happy 21st!' There was an ancient Elvis look-alike to my left, resplendent in flared pants and a half-buttoned shirt. Clutching a duty-free bag chock-a-block full of bottles of vodka that was making almost as much noise as his layers of gold chains. A little old lady in a sequined red dress stood beside him.

I was feeling seriously under-dressed in my white cotton tee and favorite faded denim jeans, with only a backpack for hand luggage. As the seasoned traveler, Dad had always emphasized to me the importance of traveling light – and dressing for the climate of your destination. The one time he took me on assignment with him to Nigeria we had squabbled for days over what items in my suitcase were actually deemed 'vital necessities.' My shampoo, face wash, and iPod had all lost the battle for inclusion. The shampoo and face wash because according to Dad's philosophy on personal hygiene - a bar of soap would do for everything. And I had a sneaking suspicion the iPod had lost out because Dad wanted there to be no excuse for me *not* to listen to him. It had been an amazing trip, the last we had taken together.

An explosion of gangsta-style swearing startled my thoughts. Three hulking boys wearing baggy jeans that dragged on the ground and huge t-shirts that would fit a whole extra person were complaining angrily at the back of the line about the long wait. I shook my head, with a shiver of disgust at their rudeness.

The immigration official at the desk contemplated them with a sardonic expression and then returned to lazily stamping passports. It *was* a long wait for them to check my passport and an even longer one for the bags to appear through the conveyance belt. That gave me time to study my surroundings even further.

I had been to several countries one could only classify as VERY hot but this sauna-like heat was different. It was wet and heavy. I struggled to find pockets of oxygen to fill my gasping lungs. Only a half hour landed and I was longing for a cold shower, wishing I could peel away these sweat-soaked clothes.

A floral shirted band played for our listening pleasure – four men with a ukulele, guitar, wooden drum, and another unknown string instrument.

My mood lifted at their song – a cheerful melody of Samoan words.

It was the first time I had heard the language of my mother being spoken and I was fascinated.

The words flowed and rippled in a rhythmic flow that tried to tug me along with it. I was almost sorry when my one suitcase appeared and it was my turn to pass through the security detector.

I emerged into the waiting area tense again with suspense. I had written to my aunt, Matile, and her husband Tuala, using an address I had found in one of my dad's old fragmenting notebooks. Remnants from his time as a US Peace Corp volunteer in Samoa. Unsure how reliable the Samoan postal service was, I had followed up my letter with a phone call, leaving a message with the young girl on the line about the date and time of my arrival. Apparently, both my aunt and uncle had been at church.

I was nervous. What if they didn't show up? What if they did show up and I walked right past them?

I had no clue what they looked like and for sure they wouldn't know me from a bar of soap.

Passengers jostled past me, anxious to greet their waiting relatives. Families. Loved ones. A small child in pink rompers called out "Mama!" and ran on unsteady feet to hug the old lady in the red sequins. Elvis was met by a crowd of people, as if an entire village had come to welcome his return.

Even the unsavory gangsters transformed to sheepish, smiling teenage boys as aunties and uncles swept them in a warm embrace.

Not for the first time, I felt my 'alone-ness' keenly emphasized. No parents, no brothers or sisters. A distant grandmother. Kind but distracted uncles. Several cousins way older than I and already busy with raising families.

That was about the full sum of my family. I hardly dared hope – even in the darkest recess where I admitted my deepest secrets – that this alone-ness would change, that my desire for a family to belong to had been my real motivation for coming a thousand miles to this unknown land.

I bit my lip as I scanned the waiting crowd anxiously. Would they show up? Someone spoke from behind me.

"Leila Folger?"

I turned eagerly and was stopped short by the sight of a slight woman dressed in navy, gray thinning hair drawn into a tight bun. Her eyes were deep-set pools that stared at me unblinkingly, her mouth set in a frown. Behind her hovered an equally stern-looking, heavy-set man formally dressed in a long-sleeved shirt and black *lavalava* skirt.

"You are Leila." It was a statement of fact, not a question. "I am Matile. This is your Uncle Tuala."

The old lady did not smile in answer to my hesitant greeting. Indeed, if anything, her face darkened even further. She did not move to hug me or even offer her hand. It seemed to my tired brain that she took several steps backward, as if loathe to get too close to me.

I tried to break through the awkward painful silence. "Umm, hi. Thanks for having me."

My aunt only shook her head slowly. Then she spoke six words that dashed to pieces my hopes for a family, for welcome – and set the tone for my homecoming.

"You should *never* have come here."

With that brisk announcement, she swung on her heels and began striding towards the car park. I was so stunned that if Uncle Tuala hadn't picked up my suitcase and set off after her – I would have stood and watched them walk away from me. He looked over his shoulder and motioned impatiently for me to catch up. I hovered for a moment, looking back at the refueling 747. Surely I could buy a ticket out of here with my precious credit card and be winging my back to D.C., back to what?

My grandmother who would be exultant with her '*I told you so*'? The summer school program she had chosen for me with the vain hopes that I could get enough makeup credits so a decent college would want me? No. There was nowhere else for me to go – but forward.

The drive from the airport was painful.

Uncle Tuala silently loaded my bags into the boot of the double-cab pick-up truck while I climbed into the back seat, Aunty Matile ignoring me from the front. The silence continued through the long bumpy drive to the main township, which I knew from my internet tourist reading was called Apia. The road wound its way along the coast, villages on one side and diamond blue sea on the other.

I was aghast at how slowly the traffic moved. Uncle Tuala never went over 30 miles an hour and the rest of the traffic was no exception. How on earth did people stand driving so slow? I knew Apia was about twenty miles from the airport and had imagined it would take us only a few minutes. I was dying to get out of the oppressive unfriendliness of being trapped in a car with two people who had made no secret of their dislike for me.

Stifling my impatience, I uneasily studied the villages as we passed through. My sightseeing was interrupted by Aunty Matile's heated exchange of words in Samoan with Uncle Tuala. The unfamiliar words rose and fell in the car. I didn't need a translator to figure out that they were surely arguing about me. Being the cause of conflict had me squirming and so, never one to shy away from confrontation, I jumped in headfirst, adopting a fake cheery tone.

"I want to thank you both for letting me come visit. I've always wanted to see my mother's home and meet her family."

They both halted their tirades at my words. I hastened to reassure them that I wasn't here *forever* and certainly wasn't going to be a financial burden. "I'm hoping to visit here for three months. I have a return ticket for the end of August. I have my own money and would be happy to pay for my room and board."

There was a horrified look on Aunty Matile's face as she turned to answer me roughly.

"Don't be foolish girl! You are our *aiga*, our family, and we would never expect you to *pay* us!"

I hated to remind her that *she* was the one who had made it clear that a loving welcoming family they were NOT.

Uncle Tuala spoke. "Leila, what your aunty is trying to say is that while she doesn't think it's a good idea for you to be here, we of course are *happy* to meet our ahem, niece, and, of course, you will stay with us as our daughter until August."

Such a long speech seemed to go against the grain with him as Aunty Matile threw him a sharp glance. Or was she reacting to his use of the word 'happy'? However, they both seemed to find comfort in the thought of this being only a temporary visit, grasping hold of the promise of my departure in August with relief. Matile spoke now with weary resignation.

"Well, yes, as your uncle says, you will be our daughter while you are here. We do have plenty of room and of course you must go to school. We are both working and I don't want you home alone idle for so long."

School?! I had not contemplated *that* possibility. I was no stranger to the angst associated with starting at a new school mid-year. I had done it before and I definitely didn't want to even attempt trying my hand at a Samoan high school. No way. When I had walked out of the National Cathedral after graduation it was with the firm resolve that I was done with high school.

I had come here to find out about my mother and her family (*however unsavory they may be*, I thought darkly), and I wasn't going to waste any time with school, thank you very much. Before I could point all this out reasonably and politely, Uncle Tuala spoke pre-emptively.

"We know that children in America are raised differently from here. We are sure that our ways may seem a bit strange at first to you. But we must make it clear that while you stay, you will be our daughter, and so you will have to behave a certain way. Ahem, we have seen those types of young people that come here from America with their styles and their language and their disrespect. We hope you will not be like that."

He spoke firmly from the front seat, his gaze never wavering from the winding road and I had the sneaking suspicion that he was trying to be nice by warning me that what I probably took for granted as 'regular' behavior would be considered horrifying by Aunty Matile. I almost felt like, in him, I just might have an ally against the indomitable Matile who continued to sit straight backed, shoulders rigid.

I thought back to the teenagers on the flight from L.A.X. and cringed inwardly. Well, if *that* was what they were comparing me with, then I would have to allay their fears ASAP. I thought about Grandmother Folger and her strict expectations and how well she would probably get along with my Aunty Matile, and I hid a grimace. A deep breath.

"Please don't worry, Uncle. I want so much to learn about my mother's culture and her family. I'm certainly not here to cause trouble or to bring any disrespectful attitudes from America."

My tone was earnest. I wanted to find a place here. And I certainly didn't need any conflicts with the two people who – let's face it – were being very generous allowing me to stay with them – even though they didn't have the slightest clue about me.

If that meant enduring a new school in some third-world education system, then so be it.

There was a slight relaxing of the tension in the front seat at my words. Feeling better about the next three months, I settled back in my seat to enjoy the sightseeing ride.

Samoa was unlike anywhere I had ever been. Nigeria had been beautiful – in a stark, dry kind of way. Rolling hills and red earth. But the tired desperation of so many of the people we had met had gone a long way to obscure the land's promise. It had been difficult too, to accept the appalling poverty of so many – contrasted with the sleek high-rise wealth of the cities.

But here, while many of the houses were humble, there was an unabashed cheerfulness about the scenery.

There was green everywhere. Every house surrounded with multi-colored bushes and flowering trees. We passed a pool of fresh water, encircled with rocks where half-naked children splashed and waved at us as we passed by.

Further along the road, a group of women swept cut grass into piles with long-handled brooms – scattering chickens and shooing gamboling dogs. People walked alongside the road as if they owned it – not the cars that frequently slowed to let them cross, or swerved to avoid clusters of youngsters sitting on the tar-seal. I was starting to realize why Samoa needed such a slow speed limit.

Grateful for the cool escape of the air conditioning, I closed my eyes, allowing the tiredness of eighteen hours of non-stop travel to lull over me. I awoke with a start at the sound of the car door slamming shut.

We had arrived.

Uncle Tuala was struggling with my suitcase at the back of the pick-up while Aunty Matile was shooing an enthusiastic canine. It had to be the ugliest dog I had ever seen.

Splotchy black and brown fur, missing half his tail and one ear ripped to shreds but his coat was sleek and shiny and he was far too fat to be a stray. I watched fascinated as Aunty Matile bent to embrace him, ruffling his fur and hushing him with half-muttered endearments.

Aha, she can't be that bad if she loves such a hideous beast! I thought to myself with some triumph.

I alighted from the truck, stiff muscles aching for a stretch, and examined my new temporary home.

It was a solid brick box house with faded orange paint and a green tin roof. A steel rail encircled a verandah overflowing with pot plants. Exuberant bougainvillea trailed from hanging pots, vivid orange and flame red. A row of tiger orchids danced in the afternoon breeze.

The garden was a riot of color and texture, so many different plants that even I couldn't identify them all. Gracing the front yard was a sweeping frangipani tree thick with fragrant white blossoms.

I took a few steps closer to its hanging branches and was assailed by the sweet scent of my dad's favorite. I wasn't prepared for the wave of emotion that swept over me. I fought the tears that threatened to spill. Struggling for control of my emotions, I hastily turned my back on Uncle as he took my bags to the front door.

This was the land of my mother. This was the home of her sister. This was the place where my dad fell in love with the woman who would captivate him long after her premature death.

I took a deep breath and reached with trembling fingers to pick a single white frangipani from the boughs above me. Aunty's stern tones startled my reverie.

"Frangipani, we call it *pua* in Samoan. You like plants." It was a statement, not a question.

I nodded, unwilling to trust my voice. As if sensing my fragility, Aunty's voice softened. "You have come a long way. To be with people you know nothing about. That, at least, took courage."

I was taken aback by her compliment. Kindness would only loosen my hold on the floodgates though, so I simply shrugged, not trusting myself to respond.

"Come inside. You must be tired. And thirsty."

Aunty Matile beckoned for me to follow her, snapping sternly at the dog as he made a cheerful lunge for me as I walked past.

"Terminator. Halu! Shoo!"

I loved dogs. Even ugly ones. We could never have one since Margaret our long-suffering housekeeper had been allergic to them. It was a thrill to kneel beside Terminator and hug his wriggling body.

"Hey boy, you're so beautiful, you gorgeous thing, you wanna be friends? Huh?"

He licked my face, his pungent fishy breath wrinkling my nose. "Eww ."

For the first time, a smile cracked the rock expression on Matile's face. "He's a very naughty dog. Don't give him too much attention or he'll expect you to adore him all the time."

Uncle Tuala's guffaw held disbelief. "Ha! As if he isn't spoiled enough as it is by you, Matile!"

She only pursed her lips and marched into the house, Uncle following with a gleam of satisfaction in his eye. I, too, hid a smile as I walked in slowly behind them. Clearly, Aunty wasn't such a dragon and she did have her soft spots. My steps lightened.

The front room was a spartan affair. A sofa set, the obligatory television, a woven mat on the floor. It was the pictures lining the walls that stood out. Christ looked down at me from every angle – all the sober, suffering pictures of Him. Dying on the cross, praying in the garden, breaking bread with His disciples. Clearly in this house, Jesus was a serious matter. Past the living room, through the kitchen and down a bare hallway was my room.

Four walls. A bed draped with a mosquito net. Drawers. Another woven mat. A mirror. Windows overlooking the backyard where chickens roamed and a cluster of baby pigs snuffled happily under a breadfruit tree. Thankfully, I noted the ceiling fan as Aunty pointed further down the hall.

"The bathroom is down here. It's best to shower early because the water usually goes off in the evening. We have a water tank but the pressure isn't strong enough for a shower. You'll have to use a bucket and bowl if you bath late. Once you get settled come and have something to eat in the kitchen."

With that invitation, she left me to unpack. I sat gingerly on the bed, looking around my surroundings.

Funny, the room didn't look lived in. The sheets crackled with newness and the mat was pristine. There wasn't a cobweb or speck of dust anywhere. Some effort had gone into preparing for my arrival and I was touched by the thought. It lessened somewhat the awfulness of my airport welcome. My travel weariness faded, replaced with an eagerness to explore.

I showered, gratefully replacing sweaty sticky clothes with knee-length shorts and a cotton tee, pulling my long hair up into a ponytail. I paused for a moment in front of the mirror, tilting my head to one side at my reflection.

I was a ramshackle collection of 'too's. Too tall. Too broad. Untamable dirt brown hair that was too bushy, and only redeemed itself slightly by having gold highlights in the sun. Too wild, Brooke Shields eyebrows to match. Dark eyes set too deep into a forehead too wide. Lips too thick – lips that my dad had called "luscious," but who was he kidding? Legs too skinny and gangly that loved to run but didn't do too well in high heels. Too brown to be white but too white to be brown. *Ugh.*

I rolled my eyes at myself, wondering why I even bothered with mirrors. It's not like I was going to look any different the more I looked! With a parting wrinkle of my nose, I went out to the kitchen.

Uncle Tuala sat reading a newspaper while Matile bustled around with dishes and serving spoons. They both looked up at my hesitant entrance.

"Ah Leila, come have something to eat. Your aunty was cooking all morning. She wasn't sure what American children like to eat. Sit."

I pulled up a chair as Aunty Matile put a plate in front of me, overflowing with food. Steam rose in tantalizing swirls and the aroma had my mouth watering. I had only nibbled on the cardboard airplane meals, and I realized I was famished. Picking up my fork, I dug into the most recognizable item on the plate – fried rice – and took a huge mouthful, burning my mouth in the process. Aunty smiled at my enthusiasm.

"You are too skinny, Leila. So skinny. *Oka!* Does nobody cook good food for you in America? Your grandmother - what does she cook for you?"

I choked on a piece of chicken at her words and paused to take several gulps of ice water. No-one had ever called me too skinny. And the idea of my elegant, Vogue magazine, grandmother actually *cooking* anything was enough to make anyone who knew her hysterical.

"Umm, no. My grandmother doesn't cook. But she has a very nice lady – Maria – who made our meals."

"So why are you so thin, then? While you're here, we need to make sure you eat good food and put on some weight. Need to get healthy. Here, try some of my chop suey."

Aunty scooped a pile of noodles onto my plate. I started on the other unfamiliar foods - chunks of grey potato-like stuff covered in a thick white sauce. Gingerly, I took a small bite and was surprised by the rich creaminess.

"This is good!" I exclaimed, and was answered with a beaming smile from Aunty.

"That's *kalo,* taro. In coconut cream. Makes our Manu Samoa boys big and tough." Uncle Tuala offered helpfully.

I smiled with a mouthful of rugby player food as I made a mental note not to eat too much taro – I certainly didn't need to grow any more.

Aunty handed me a steaming mug of thick black liquid that I regarded with some mistrust. It looked like engine oil, thick enough to harbor state secrets. But the aroma of roasted chocolate made me bold. The first sip confirmed for me what I had always suspected. White people drank dirty water. Brown people? Now they knew how to make cocoa.

"This is amazing stuff, Aunty. I've never tasted anything like it back home."

"*Kokosamoa.* Made from the roasted coco bean. I make it myself from our tree out back." Aunty spoke with pleasure, as if unused to receiving compliments on her cooking. "Plenty of sugar to make it sweet. I put five spoons in your cup. Is that enough?" She looked worried.

I spluttered on my mouthful of *koko.* Five spoons of sugar!? *Hello – this stuff was diabetes waiting to happen.*

Uncle Tuala spoke. "Your grandmother would like you to call her. To let her know that you have arrived safely and are settled."

Only a tremble of my hand betrayed my shock at this unexpected news. I took a deep breath to steady myself, anunciating each word carefully to emphasize my calmness.

"My grandmother? You spoke to my grandmother?"

Uncle sounded surprised. "Well yes, of course. She called us, a few days before your arrival. While we have never met, we were in complete agreement about the foolishness of this visit of yours. However, she seemed resigned to the fact that young people will do what they want to. Especially one as strong willed as you appear to be."

A slight smile softened his words somewhat, but I was still reeling at finding out that, far from being an independent force taking on the big wide world on my own, I was, in actual fact, on a journey that had been somewhat 'sanctioned' by Grandmother Folger. How deflating. Thinking of the old woman sitting in her Potomac mansion, reaching out with money-driven tentacles to control me, even now. Even here, thousands of miles away in Samoa. I began to seethe.

Aunty chimed in. "Your grandmother and I agreed there must be some rules for your stay with us. Rules that will ensure your safety."

My dad would have seen my exceptionally polite tone for what it was. An indicator of my raging inner storm of anger.

"Really? Rules. Rules you discussed with my grandmother. And what might these rules be?"

Aunty was pleased with my apparent acquiescence. "Well, both Tuala and I work all day at the church offices so you will need to be responsible and trustworthy. My cousin Falute comes every day to help with the house and the cooking so you will not be alone here. Also, Tuala has a nephew, Kolio, who works in the yard and he will help Falute to keep an eye on things around here when we are at work. It's not decent for a young woman to go around unsupervised in this country. You will take the bus to school and back. But you will not venture anywhere else. School and home. Oh, and church on Sunday, of course."

"Of course." I reiterated dryly, clenching my palms tightly under cover of the table.

"You can enroll at school under our last name – Sinapati – it will make the process easier. We would rather keep your visit here as low key as possible. Oh and please, you will refrain from discussing your parents with anyone outside this house."

"Excuse me?" The first few rules I had expected, but this? This was insane.

Uncle shifted his feet awkwardly and stared out the window as Aunty Matile continued. "Leila, you must try to understand. There are things you don't know. About life here. And it would not be a good thing for your presence here to become common knowledge. It could be awkward."

Matile halted, as if unsure how to proceed. "Oh, I wish you would reconsider staying here. This can't end well. It won't end well. This place is too small. Oh, how can we possibly keep this quiet?"

Her voice rose one hysterical notch and for one awful moment, it looked as if she were about to cry. Uncle took over, placing a comforting hand on hers.

"Leila, what your aunty means is that you are here in a strange place that you know nothing about. There are different customs and ... and expectations here that may seem strange to you. We are responsible for your safety. And your behavior will be a reflection on us – your *aiga*. We wish to ensure that your stay here is as uneventful and peaceful as possible. That means working hard at school, going to church on Sunday like a good girl, and not roaming about like some manner-less child with no parents."

I winced at his phrase. *A child with no parents.*

My rage seeped away, my body wilting in the late afternoon heat as I mulled over those words.

What else had Grandmother Folger told him? About my fighting at school? My nightmare-filled nights? The psychiatrist the school had insisted I go to after my dad's death? The medication I had refused to take? The long days filled with crying? The failing out of most of my classes? I thought I would escape all that, here in this tropical paradise. But who was I trying to fool? Even here, I was Leila Pele Folger. A child with no *real* family. No friends. An anger management problem.

I refused to cry in front of these strangers. I pushed my chair away from the table and rose to my feet. "Uncle I totally understand. And I promise you both I will be no trouble. If you don't mind, I'm very tired. Can I call my grandmother later, after I've had a rest?"

Aunty rushed to reassure me. "Of course, Leila. Of course. You go have a good sleep. That's what you need after your long trip. We can talk again later. Tomorrow we will go to town to get your uniforms for school on Monday. And any other supplies you might need."

Great. A uniform. Just what I always wanted.

My steps were unsteady as I made my way back to the little room, turning on the fan before tumbling face down onto the bed.

The threatening tears, however, did not come. But blessed sleep did instead.

I woke the next morning unsure of my surroundings. The fan whirred overhead and traffic rattled and roared past on the road out front. I must have been asleep for at least ten hours, but instead of feeling refreshed, I only felt sluggish and hot.

Ugh. Gathering my things, I slipped down the hall to the bathroom where a cold shower went a long way towards waking me up and lifting my mood somewhat. Once clean and dressed, I ventured out to find my 'family.'

The kitchen was empty, but, on the table was a still-hot kettle of *kokosamoa*, and underneath a netted dome covering was a platter piled high with little round pancakes. Breakfast. I sampled them hesitantly but needn't have worried. They were delicious. Crunchy on the outside and sweet with ripe banana on the inside. And perfect when dunked in sugary sweet koko.

However prickly and unpleasant staying with these people would be, the food, at least, would never be a disappointment. When I was done washing up my dishes, I knew I couldn't put off the call home to Grandmother Folger any longer.

I took a deep breath, before hitting speed dial on the pink iPhone she had given me as a farewell gift before I left. The one loaded with limitless credit *"so you can keep me updated via email and direct calls every day on where you are and what you are doing. I want daily reports Leila, do you hear me?! If you do not agree to this condition Leila Folger, then I will have my lawyers make your trip to Samoa very difficult. I can put a freeze on all your accounts. And you don't even want to know what good lawyers and a disgusting amount of money can do to your trust fund if you take this too far young woman! Don't you dare push me Leila, I can't stop you from going, but I can make sure you have no money when you're there!"*

Yes, Elizabeth Folger had been scrambling for ammo when I announced my decision to come to Samoa. It was driving her crazy that, as of my birthday a few months ago, I was legally an 'adult.'

And she was going double as crazy that my dad's life insurance policy had given me a substantial amount of money immediately that was *separate* from the Folger trust fund I would inherit when I turned twenty-one. As the executor of the trust, she had been counting on the fund to control me and had been most displeased that the death money gave me the freedom to fly halfway round the world. Away from her.

Elizabeth Folger wasn't used to people defying her. Especially not her own family. But a month after my father's death, she'd had a mini-stroke and her health was now a barrier to enforcing the kind of control she liked to have over everyone and everything. I had never seen her so frail as the morning I had said goodbye, and it was that frailty more than her threats that had made me agree to accept the phone and now, to use it.

As the line rang, I was rehearsing my replies for all the possible questions and attacks she would have ready for me. So much so, that when she did answer, I was taken off guard.

"Hello."

"Oh, Grandmother Folger, is that you?"

"Well of course it's me, you foolish child. Who else would be answering my personal line? Leila? I've been expecting your call, you were supposed to call yesterday. Where are you? What is it like? Where are you staying? Is it safe and secure? Do you have privacy?"

I tried not to let my exasperation show in my voice as I replied.

"Hello Grandmother Folger. Yes, it's me, Leila. And yes, everything's ok here, I mean, alright here. I'm sorry I didn't call last night but I was really tired from the trip. Aunty Matile and Uncle Tuala met me at the airport and they've given me a lovely room in their home to stay in. It's very clean, very safe. The property is fenced. Nobody else lives with them. Aunty Matile is a wonderful cook and made tons of food to welcome me. We've already discussed the rules and guidelines for my stay with them – including the fact that I'm just to go three places while I'm here. Home, school, and church." I could totally imagine the satisfaction that last bit would give her.

"School in a third-world country, harrumph. What an incredible waste of time, Leila. When you could be working on getting valuable credits at the private summer academy I went to great lengths to arrange for you. Honestly! Your stubbornness serves you no good at all when it is so misdirected. When are you going to shake off this ridiculous mood you've got yourself in and start facing up to your responsibilities? Your commitments here at home? The longer you delay college, the more difficult it will be and dallying about in some wretched little island in the middle of nowhere will do nothing for you – not to mention *blah, blah, blah.*"

I automatically zoned out as she continued on a much-worn path of brisk recriminations, knowing that she wouldn't take a breath until she was done with having her say. She was starting to wind down though, just as I saw Tuala's truck pull up at the front of the house. Quickly, I interrupted her.

"Grandmother Folger, I have to go now. Matile is taking me to town to get uniforms for school on Monday and I can't keep her waiting. It was lovely to talk to you. I'll call you again tomorrow – or maybe just send you an email. Bye."

I hung up before she could protest, and put the ringer on silent before going to help Matile carry in plastic bags of shopping. She nodded appreciatively.

"Thank you, Leila. Tuala and I went out early to do some shopping at the market. We didn't want to wake you but I left you some breakfast – did you eat?"

"Yes thank you. And those were the best pancakes I've ever tasted."

A stiff smile was my reward as Matile moved about the kitchen putting her groceries away. "Was that your grandmother you were speaking to on the phone earlier? Is everything alright?"

"Yes. I checked in with her, let her know I've arrived. I told her I would be enrolling in school on Monday."

As if a lecture from thousands of miles away wasn't enough, Matile then proceeded to speak to me sternly.

"Good. It's important that you keep in contact with your grandmother. I know you haven't had much exposure to your Samoan culture, but here in Samoa, a young woman would never disobey her elders and travel around the world by herself this way. We are very sorry for your grandmother. She must be so worried about you and frustrated about your trip. I hope that while you're here, you can learn many more useful customs and traditions, about what it means to be a *tamaitai Samoa*, a Samoan woman. Now come, let's get you to Carruthers store in town for those uniforms. *Blah, blah, blah*."

I took a deep breath and followed her out the door to the car, reminding myself *stay calm Leila, be polite, you're a guest here, she's your aunty, be patient, nod and smile and agree with everything.*

Thankfully, Aunt Matile's lectures were substantially shorter than Grandmother Folger's and the ride to town was punctuated only by Tuala's attempts to be a helpful tour guide as he pointed out places he deemed to be of interest along the route.

Places like the church headquarters on the main Beach Road where he and Matile worked. The Police Station. The Mulivai Cathedral. The weary courthouse where a sniper had shot a protesting Mau leader. The government building of offices on a stretch of reclaimed waterfront land.

I looked around with great interest. Apia was small. Dusty. Hot. And colorful. I loved the abundance of flowers everywhere and the view out to the golden blue harbor was breathtaking.

We stopped first at an ATM so I could withdraw some cash, the Samoan *tala* notes feeling strange in my hands. At the clothing supplier, buying the uniforms was painless as the first one I tried on, fit perfectly. It was the colors that had me reeling – bright orange pinafores and sunburst-yellow blouses.

"Ugh, Aunty, this uniform is hideous. Who dreamed up this combination?"

She only pursed her lips at me as she took our purchases to the counter. "Samoa College is the oldest and finest high school in the country. Young people are proud to wear these colors. And they try their best not to disgrace them."

O-kaaaay. I repeated what was fast becoming my Samoa mantra. *Breathe. Be polite. You're a guest. Be nice. Be patient. Be quiet!*

I tried hard to sound meek. "Yes Aunty Matile. I will try very hard not to disgrace the uniform or you and Uncle Tuala."

She looked at me suspiciously as if she could read the falseness hidden in my words and I struggled to keep a straight face that spoke only of reticence and humility.

"Harrumph, well then. Let's get going. Tuala will be wanting to get back to the house in time for the rugby game that's coming on this afternoon. Come along, I think we have everything."

Laden with uniforms we made our way back to the car and the short drive home. Passing a cemetery where frangipani trees dropped their petals on moss-covered graves had me thinking, and, back at the house, once the shopping was all safely stowed away and Matile was preparing dinner, I took the moment to ask her for directions. To my mother's grave.

The silence was ominous. Both Tuala and Matile froze and looked at each other. My gaze went to first one and then the other, waiting for the answer. Uncle Tuala spoke first.

"Leila, your mother is a sensitive topic in this house. Your aunty Matile does not like to speak of her."

"Oh. I see."

But I didn't. The woman was my mother, surely I of all people had every right to ask where her grave was?

I persisted. "I'm sorry if it's painful for you, Aunty. If you could just tell me where I can find her grave, I can get myself there?"

Aunty Matile turned her back on me and vigorously stirred the pot on the stove, throwing her answer over her shoulder. "Your mother is not buried in town. Now let us talk of something else."

I took a deep breath. "Aunty Matile, the main reason I came to Samoa is so that I could learn as much as possible about my mother. My dad didn't tell me a lot about her. I've never even seen a photo of her." I quickened with excitement. "Do you have some pictures of her I could look at, please? It would mean so much to me to be able to know what she looked like."

Matile dropped the pot she was holding. It fell with a crash, splattering boiled taro everywhere and bringing Tuala abruptly to his feet.

"Matile! Are you alright?"

Matile was trembling as she shook her fist at me. "Leila, no more questions about that woman. No more."

My confusion made me ignore the warnings. "Why not? I don't understand? What's wrong with talking about my mother?"

"That woman is, was none of your business." was her taut reply.

"How can you say that? I'm her daughter, she was my mother. How dare you tell me she's none of my business!"

"You are too Westernized, too *palagi* to understand. You are too *palagi* to show respect to us, your elders? To us who have taken you in when your own *palagi* grandmother cannot handle you anymore? *Tapuni lou gutu.* Shut your mouth now!"

Aunty Matile's tirade abruptly halted as Tuala moved to place a warning hand on her shoulder. He squeezed her arm gently before turning to me.

"Leila, as long as you are staying here in our home, you will speak with respect to your aunt. You will show *fa'aaloalo* to us, your family. And you will accept that there are some things we do not speak of. Ever. This is a God-fearing house. This land does not belong to the spirits and myths of the past. We are Christians and we will not have anything to do with such beliefs here."

I turned and fled to my room, unwilling for anyone to see me dissolve in a tearful emotional mess. All the while though, questions screamed in my mind.

I don't get it. I want to know about my mother – what does that have to do with his stupid spirits and myths? What the hell is he going on about? I came to this awful place to find my family, to find out about my mother and instead I'm stuck in a house where they won't even allow me to talk about her?

For the first time, I considered the dreadful possibility that coming to Samoa had been a huge mistake. Exhausted from the emotional rollercoaster ride of only my first day in my new home, I fell asleep clutching a picture of my dad. The one person who had loved me. Laughed with me. And left me. I had never felt so alone in my life.

The rest of the weekend passed in subdued politeness. Matile and Tuala said no more about the confrontation in the kitchen and I followed their lead, maintaining a distant civility as they took me to church with them, introducing me to people as their niece, "here for a very short visit from America."

Church was followed by a sumptuous lunch expansive enough for at least ten more people, and I did the dishes before going to my room to surf the net, sending a silent prayer of thanks for Grandmother Folger's forced gift. I shuddered to think how I was going to survive my stay in this house without a lifeline to the outside world. And so it was with unusual niceness that I drafted an email to Grandmother, telling her about my Samoan experience so far. I left out the part about my disagreement with my new relatives though. Grandmother had never tried to hide her distaste for the mere mention of my Samoan mother and I had a feeling she would be right on the same page as Aunty Matile and Uncle Tuala.

As I lay in bed late on Sunday, I could see the southern sky splayed in all its majestic diamond glory from my window but my heart was a million miles away. In Potomac. Where my dad was buried. Not for the first time in the past eight months, I cried myself to sleep.

Would I ever stop hurting this much for my dad?

TWO

Monday morning dawned fresh and clear with a light sprinkle of hot rain. I lay for a while in bed just listening to the sounds of life outside my window. Dogs barked, growling at passersby on the dusty front road. Birds – so many birds chattered in the lush richness of the backyard. A cat yowled in protest as someone threw a splash of water from the cook house in the neighbor's back yard. A bus roared past, gears grinding, wooden seats rattling. Children laughed as they walked by the roadside on their way to school.

School. I sat bolt upright. That's right. It was my first day at school in Samoa. I grimaced with disgust at the school uniform hanging next to the bed. Could it get any more outrageous? Oh well. I didn't want to be late on my first day so I had to swallow my revolt and dress quickly. School started early in this country. I had to be there at 7:30 for assembly – or so Aunty Matile had informed me.

Breakfast was hunks of hot bread with slabs of butter melting onto the plate. A pot of thick, sweet *kokosamoa* that burned the tongue. Licking the butter drips off my fingers, I mused – no wonder most Samoans were overweight and built like football players. If they ate carbs like this every day.

Hmm ... I would have to do something about making changes to the household diet if I wanted to stay the same size. Because this hot bread and *koko* thing was way too tempting to refuse every morning. Grabbing another piece of bread to savor in the car, I made sure to thank Aunty Matile for breakfast and wish her a 'lovely day' – and was rewarded by a fleeting smile from the usually sour-faced old woman.

Uncle Tuala was giving me a ride to school – at least until I figured out the bus routes myself. I didn't know how I was going to be able to do that since apparently there was no regular bus schedule ... or any printed timetables ... or even proper bus stops.

"So, how do people catch the bus to school on time?" I asked, thoroughly puzzled.

"Oh, you just look out for the right bus on the road and when you see it coming you wave at it and it stops. Then when the bus goes past where you want to go, you pull the wire and it stops."

"How can I be sure it will go where I want it to?"

"Because. Everyone knows the way the bus goes. There's not many different roads you know, Leila."

Okay. So catching buses would be one thing to add to my list of 'what to learn if you want to live in this country.' In the meantime, I would be suitably grateful to Uncle Tuala for taking me to school.

Unbidden, a memory flashed of my car at home. The thoroughly-unlike-me, red Mazda Miata that Dad had bought for my last birthday. Completely shocking me. And terrifying me. How was I supposed to hold my head up high driving such an obviously wannabe preppy car? But he had insisted.

Taking me for driving lessons on deserted roads so I could get used to it. Blasting the stereo with his country songs and deliberately embarrassing me by singing along to the music. Especially whenever we had pulled up next to cars with boys in them and Randy Travis soulful voice warbled through the trees.

"Oh Dad, puh-leeeze stop that. You're killing me here! You really don't want me to have a social life at all do you? You want everyone at school to think I'm totally ridiculous with a country singing dad singing off key AND driving a pukey cheerleader car."

I'd hated that car. But oh how I had sobbed when I sold it. Stood at the car lot and sobbed as if my heart would break. Cried so hard the dealer looked worried and offered me more money in an attempt to console me.

"Here little lady, you want a better offer for it? Don't cry, I can go up a little if you want."

His awkward attempts to comfort only adding to my grief. "No thank you, I don't want more money. I want ..." I wanted my dad to come back. I wanted him alive so badly that it hurt to think about him. To whisper his name. My sigh was so heartfelt that Uncle Tuala looked over at me with concern.

"So, you look nice in your uniform. I'm sure you will like this school. It's the best one in Samoa." Forced cheerfulness was nothing new to me. *Heck, I wrote the book on it.*

"I'm sure it will be great, Uncle. Thanks. I'm only here for a short while anyways. Only until I get what I came for. Until I find out about my umm, about my heritage, you know? That kind of stuff is important for a young woman to discover."

Uncle Tuala ignored the almost-reference to matters better left unspoken and focused on swerving to avoid a three-legged dog strolling in the middle of the road. I felt an insane urge to giggle. It reminded me of Harry Potter and He-Who-Must-Not-be-Named – this whole forbidden topic of my mother. It was ridiculous.

No. Standing at the front entrance of my new school I realized *'ridiculous'* was the absolute contrast of Samoa College with Washington Girls – my old school back home. Was it possible to find a more different place of learning in the world no, make that in this solar system?

I stood and tried not to gape at the crowds of teenagers walking through the front gate, resplendent in their blaring sunrise colors. Even the huge cement walls lining the entrance were painted orange and yellow. Just in case you missed the turn-off in the dark, perhaps?

A sloping driveway lined with coconut palms led to the main building – a double-storey block of classrooms. On the right of the drive was a traditional Samoan *fale* with groups of students leaning on its wooden posts. There was so much color it hurt my eyes. Scarlet hibiscus bushes dotted the campus.

Clumps of yellow leaves swayed in the morning breeze. Boys with no shirts on chased a rugby ball on the green fields to the left, sweat glistening already on brown skin and lean muscle.

Boys. There was something else you didn't see at my old school back home. Half-naked boys. Hot, sweaty boys with dark eyes and loud shouts of laughter.

I smiled against my will as I imagined what my uptight grandmother would make of *that!* I almost laughed out loud as I then thought of the reaction of girls back home if they could see this. A private all-girls school in the heart of D.C that catered for the daughters of the rich and richer – certainly didn't get many shirtless Polynesian males running around the campus.

Shaking my head at the thought, I gripped my backpack a bit tighter and made my way through the front gates. I reminded myself that having to endure boys in the same classroom would probably be the least of my worries as I tried to adjust to a new school in an alien place.

Uncle's directions to the office were easy to follow. Seeing as how there were only three buildings in the entire school and one of them wore a sign that read OFFICE.

Finding the office was one thing. Getting someone to help me with a class schedule was a totally different story. A frazzled-looking woman with hair pulled back so tight she probably gave herself headaches told me to "sit there and wait for the Principal. He's busy right now."

Nobody paid the slightest attention to me as I perched on a bench outside the staffroom. I looked around, interested in finding clues about this, the supposed 'number one school in Samoa.'

It certainly didn't look like much. Paint peeled from the corridor walls. There were no window panes – just chain link wire all along the length of the hall. Better for catching the breeze in this humidity I guessed. But not so great at keeping out the rain I thought, noting the slick puddles of water from the morning showers.

The staffroom doors were wide open. A set of shabby tables dominated the room with an odd assortment of broken chairs arranged around them. Open shelves overflowed with textbooks and planners, here and there a chipped coffee mug.

The raucous clang of the bell halted my inspection. Great, now I would be late to my first class, wherever it was, and stick out even more. Where was the Principal? And wasn't there anyone else in this place who could give me a timetable for goodness sake?

I stood and walked to the window hoping to catch a glimpse of someone, anyone who looked vaguely Principal-like. The entire student body seemed to be gathering for an assembly at the head of the long driveway. I had to admit the sea of orange and yellow wasn't *that* bad. It was kind of eye catching and complemented well the fiery colors of a sunny morning in 'paradise.'

I observed with interest that select senior students rather than teachers seemed to be in charge of the assembly. Staff stood in a row in front of the school and waited until everyone was settled and quiet.

A short stocky girl with thick braids down her back, led the school in a hymn. The singing was beautiful – unlike anything I had heard back home. A prayer followed the song and then the girl relinquished her spot to a boy who strode forward with confident ease. I was puzzled – surely he couldn't be a student?

He was tall and broad, built like some kind of body builder – his yellow shirt doing little to disguise his finely toned physique. With his back to me though, I couldn't make out his features.

He spoke at length to the school – I caught fragments on the morning breeze *"reminder about school code of conduct...a reputation to uphold."* He had everyone's rapt attention – it was obvious he held a position of some authority. Even from this distance I was impressed by his assurance and poise with speaking to such a large crowd of his peers. There was no hesitation or nervousness in his demeanor. *Hmm, definitely not your average loopy teenage boy.*

At the end of his address, the school dispersed and the staff began making their way back to the staffroom. *Yes! Surely now I would get some help.*

Help arrived in the form of the Principal, Mr. Raymond. He hadn't heard of me, and of course had no records of my educational existence or background. None of that seemed to faze him – as if he was used to total strangers showing up at his school every day, expecting to get admitted.

He was a broadly built man with a smiley face and a dented nose that looked suspiciously like it had been broken several times, almost like a teddy bear that had been beat up one time too many - I thought absent mindedly as he explained my schedule.

It seemed straightforward enough. They didn't need to see any of my grades since I was from an overseas school (the assumption being, that guaranteed I could at least read and write with some degree of skill) There was no vocabulary or maths skills testing because there was only one level of English and math class to go to. I had to choose an option for my subjects – and that was easy since there were only eight to choose from, three of them compulsory. English, Math and Samoan language.

I wasn't too happy about the Samoan language but Mr. Raymond assured me that I would be "put together with the other *palagi* kids who don't know any Samoan and the teacher will go easy on you."

The entire exercise took all of five minutes. Mr. Raymond spent more time reciting the school rules to me. Some of them were routine – no alcohol, drugs, smoking or profanity.

Others had me raising a mental eyebrow. Things like – no iPods, no makeup, no jewelry, no strange hairstyles and only yellow jandals allowed. What the color of one's jandals had to do with one's learning I had no idea but again the mantra *breathe, smile, nod, agree, you are a visitor here.*

Once done, Mr. Raymond summoned a passing student, a tall skinny boy, to take me to my first-period class, wishing me all the best in my new school.

My tour guide regarded me with frank interest. Mr. Raymond introduced him as Simon – from my new form class – but as soon as we were out of the Principal's range, 'he' hastened to set the introduction straight, with an airy wave of his hand.

"What-everrr! I'm Si-mone. You're in our form class and Ms. Sivani is our form teacher. Come on, she hates latecomers."

I quickly realized that Simone was what my uncle termed a *'fa'afafine.'* On our shopping trip to town for my school uniforms, we had stopped to buy bread and the cashier had been a man in a tight red tank top and floral mini skirt. Pink fingernails and expertly applied makeup had completed the ensemble. I guess I hadn't expected full drag queen attire in a Samoan dairy on a Saturday morning.

Reading my mind, Uncle Tuala had waited until we were back in the car and then gave me a one-word explanation.

"Fa'afafine."

"A fa'a – what?" I had asked, completely befuddled.

"You know – a boy who wants to be a girl? A boy who acts like a girl? *Fa'afafine* translated loosely means umm, like a girl, in the ways of a girl."

Aunty Matile put a stop to the conversation in her usual abrupt manner.

"Leila, in Samoa we have three different genders if you will – men and women and *fa'afafine*. It's tradition. Don't stare. Don't be rude. They don't like it."

Fa'afafine – another new concept to put on my list of things to understand. Very conscious of Aunty Matile's directive about not staring and not being rude, I walked beside my tour guide with my head down, hesitant about what to say. However, Simone didn't seem too fussed about Ms. Sivan's supposed abhorrence for latecomers as he strutted along the corridor with all the studied ease of a runway model, stopping often to greet passersby.

"Daahling, how was your weekend? No way. *Nupi*! Was he there? Ohmigosh, you're kidding, I hate you! Tell me all about it at lunch. Oh, girlfriend wait up, how was Friday night? I heard about the V-Bar hmm, you wicked girl! I know, I was busy at home with our *fa'alavelave* and doing all the chores, going crazy I couldn't get out. See you later. Yoohoo daaahling! "

Like the Queen of England acknowledging her humble courtiers, I thought ungenerously, with a mental groan as I realized there was no way I would avoid a late entrance to class on my first day.

Indeed, I had a sneaking suspicion that my tour guide welcomed a late entrance – the more dramatic the better. I studied Simone out of the corner of my eye as he preened next to me.

Almost as tall as me, skinny, beautiful liquid black eyes (was that a hint of forbidden eye liner?), glossy coal black hair combed in an Elvis style bouffant and carrying a shiny red handbag on one perfectly bent arm. (Don't ask me how he fit any text books in that tiny thing.)

Noticing my scrutiny, he stopped mid-wave to look me up and down, one hand on his hip, Kate Moss style.

"So where you from?"

"D.C. - I mean, the States. My mom was Samoan, but this is my first time here."

"Oh, I see. What did you do?"

"Huh? What do you mean, what did I do? What did I do where?" I was confused.

"You know, how did you screw up? You U.S. Samoan kids get sent here all the time when your *aiga*, your family, can't handle you over there. We get lots of juvenile delinquents here, so what did you do?" Simone seemed bored with my inability to answer his question.

"I didn't do anything. I mean, I'm just here for three months, summer vacation, visiting my mom's family and they thought I would enjoy a Samoan school."

Simone raised an eyebrow in disbelief and pursed his perfect lips. (I'm sure that was lip liner – no boy could have such a perfectly defined cupids bow.) He sniffed and waved his hand airily.

"Fine. *Pugi.* Don't tell me the truth. I can handle it. Now, come on. We're late."

I stumbled along after him with a pained half smile, hoping I hadn't just made enemy number one at my new school. *Great, maybe I should have invented a litany of felonies and misdemeanors just to make him happy.*

We came to an abrupt halt outside a particularly shabby classroom. Through missing window panes I could see the teacher at the board, who stopped her reading of the novel in her hands to confront our late entrance. She was a petite woman wearing a rich purple and gold sari draped gracefully around her slender frame.

"Simon, you are late. Do you have a late pass?" Her tone left no room for argument. Simone, however, was clearly unimpressed.

"Ms. Sivani, the Principal asked me to bring this newcomer to our class. She's transferred here from the States. Her name is Leila."

The room was crammed full with students, orange and yellow sardines in a can. Over thirty curious faces peered at me in all my newcomer glory, looking even more unpolished and unglamorous beside supermodel Simone.

I gave Ms. Sivani a perfunctory polite smile and resumed staring out the window, wondering where on earth I would find a spare desk to sit at in this mob. His duty complete, Simone abandoned me to my fate, sauntering to find his seat beside another suspiciously beautiful boy.

"Oh. I see. Welcome to our class, Leila is it? We were just starting our reading of Macbeth, we had better find you a seat."

A broadly built boy with a ducktail haircut and prominent ears, leapt to his feet, a huge smile on his face.

"She can have my desk Ms. Sivani. I'm happy to go looking for more furniture."

His tone was hopeful and I was suspicious that the search for furniture in this school would not be an easy or speedy errand. Ms. Sivani must have harbored similar suspicions because she shook her head and pointed to her desk at the front.

"That's very kind of you Maleko. But I wouldn't dream of making you miss our reading of Macbeth this morning. You can sit at my desk and at first break you can acquire some extra furniture for our new student."

Maleko scowled with disappointment, the hopes of a chance to escape from English class dashed. Great, another potential enemy I thought, taking the seat he vacated. Ms. Sivani handed me a tattered copy of Shakespeare's Macbeth and resumed her reading.

Macbeth had been the topic of my final English essay three years ago in Freshman year so I was sure it wouldn't hold any surprises, but I dutifully turned the pages so I could follow with the class. Vaguely aware that the entire class was finding the arrival of a new girl more captivating than Shakespeare's masterpiece, I hunched my shoulders even more than usual and slunk down in my seat, aiming for invisibility.

I hadn't been the new kid twice in two years without picking up a few tips about the best way to deal with curiosity and zoo animal watchers. Be as boring and non-descript as possible and the fascination usually dies. Stare at the ground, keep to yourself, don't speak up too much in class. Stay away from the class 'elite' and don't rock any boats. I had only ever been trapped in girl's schools but heck, I was sure a co-ed one wouldn't be much different.

My first morning passed swiftly, the only real struggle being the oppressive heat. There were no fans in any of the rooms and while the coconut palms outside constantly rustled in a tropical breeze, little air found its way into the square blocks, crammed as they were with students.

By second period my orange blouse was sticky with sweat and I felt like I had spent two hours in a sauna. It amazed me that anyone could live in this heat – let alone work or study in it. *Ugh*. Remembering Tuala's gruff advice about avoiding dehydration, I kept taking furtive sips from my water bottle.

It was a relief to find that every lesson was conducted in perfect English. Several of the teachers were Indian and so I had to listen carefully to get accustomed to their accented nuances. But all the teenagers around me spoke with faultless grammar. Indeed, it was a little unnerving that English in Samoa was more English than in America. A throwback maybe to the colonial days? And of course, the absence of slang and profanity made for more 'civilized' conversation.

I had been dreading the possibility of cliques openly talking about me in rapid-fire Samoan, but thankfully, the school had a 'No Samoan speaking' rule for in the classroom, so that put those fears to rest.

English was followed by Math. The only surprise being how far ahead I actually was. Another cause for celebration because Math was not my strong point. I could do the day's worksheet in my sleep so that meant one less subject I would actually have to study for.

In Biology, the class was sitting a test that the teacher, Mr. Matau, graciously exempted me from. Instead, I got a ragged textbook to read through at the back of the room, giving me a golden opportunity to study my classmates.

Real, live Samoan teenagers.

How did they stack up compared with American ones? It didn't take rocket science to figure out that Samoan teens functioned in a classroom according to a markedly different code from those in the States. Here, the teacher's word was law and the students addressed them with deferential respect, even the 'naughty' ones like the burly boy, Maleko.

Students raised their hands when they had questions and nobody argued with the teacher. Another difference was their dress. Back home it had almost been a sign of one's status to be as sloppy and disheveled as possible.

Here, there were no extreme haircuts, no makeup, and definitely no jewelry. Girls wore their hair in neat braids. All the boys except Maleko had hair cut above the collar and Mr. Matau sternly reminded two of them to tuck their shirts into their *lavalava*.

The bell ringing for lunch was a huge relief, dying as I was to get out of the oppressive confines of the classroom and into the fresh air. Everyone else seemed impervious to the glory of the green and gold day, the way the wind ruffled the coconut palms overhead. Washington Girls had been stately grey and regimented cobblestones. Samoa College was a haven of color and light.

I studied everything, but all while trying hard not to stare. Boys played rugby again on the expanse of field. A cluster of girls were shooting hoops on a grass court – netball – Simone explained airily at my puzzled glance. There was another sport I would have to Google, especially since there didn't seem to be any nets involved anywhere?

Other students grouped on the wooden benches lining the driveway as they ate their lunch. I had no idea where the lonesome newcomers were supposed to go but, again, Simone came to my rescue, calling to me impatiently as he walked past me,

"Well, come on Leila, what are you waiting for? Let's go get some lunch."

Awkwardly, I tripped after him as he continued calling out with the same graceful ease to all and sundry. At the canteen (which only seemed to sell carbs and more carbs, all drowning in generous amounts of oil), I refused a burger explaining I wasn't hungry.

Simone then proceeded to lead me to sit underneath a tamarind tree beside the rugby field and subject me to the third degree.

"So, whereabouts in the States are you from? Any brothers and sisters? Do you drive? Do you smoke? Do you party? Do you wear makeup to school back home? Why are you here? How long will you be here? Are those highlights natural? Why do you bite your nails so bad? When was the last time you trimmed your hair – your split ends are shocking. Did you have a boyfriend back home? Why not? Have you had sex? *Nupi*! Get out. Have you kissed anyone? Have you … "

It went on and on. I was painfully relieved when the bell rang for class. Not only was I not used to answering such personal questions, I was especially uncomfortable with the fact that it was a boy asking them. Even if he was the most graceful and feminine boy I had ever seen.

I sighed as I followed Simone to our next class. I had tons of questions I wanted answering but I would have to put them aside for another day.

The rest of the school day passed in a sweaty haze and I was grateful to see Uncle Tuala's car pull up at the gate when the last bell rang. I was tired, hot and thirsty. But I was also mildly triumphant. I had done it.

Survived my first day at school in Samoa. Nobody hated me – I think. I didn't hate anybody. The work had been manageable. The people vaguely likeable. I even kind of had a 'friend.' A boy who was for all intents and purposes – a girl.

Already this school was scoring higher than home. Yup. Fingers crossed it kept on this way. My good mood continued enough that I was even able to speak politely to Grandmother Folger when she called to check on me that night.

Yes, I was fine. No, I didn't need any money. No, there hadn't been any trouble at school that day. Yes, I was fine.

Asleep almost as soon as my head hit the pillow, my final drifting thought was – *I'm fine*. I could almost believe that.

Day two at Samoa College started the same as the first. Morning assembly, only this time it was led by the stocky girl with thick braids.

Simone whispered – *that's Manuia the Head Girl. The prefects lead assembly every morning.*

As the first two periods slid into each other, I fast realized the value of having Simone as my self-appointed tour guide. He shook his head with pursed lips when I went to sit down at the back of the class in Math.

"No. Mr. Michaels hates people who sit in the back. He picks on them extra hard. Sit in front and he'll ignore you most of the time."

In Biology, he rolled his eyes when I took out a text book as Mr. Matau told us to use the hour for study.

"You're kidding right? I know that you've done this stuff already, don't tell me you think you need to study the circulatory system? Here, let's swap iPods. What music you got?"

The last thing I wanted was trouble on my first week, but Simone was difficult to brush off. As discreetly as possible I dug out my forbidden iPod and handed it over. Looking around furtively, I then realized half the class had earphones on. At the front of the class, Mr. Matau took out his iPod and promptly went to sleep.

Okaaaaay. I shrugged and scrolled through Simone's playlist. We spent the rest of the period comparing the merits of Coldplay versus Bob Marley. It was thoroughly relaxing and I was buzzed to be moving on to English with Ms. Sivani. At the door of her room though, everyone stopped short because we were combining with another sixth form class. Ms. Sivani spoke in her short clipped tones over the chatter of the class.

"Today we will combine with 6M for an impromptu debate" a collective groan from the class "and there will be no sounds of angst, thank you very much!"

The class moved quickly in spite of their complaining to make room for the others and there was an undercurrent of excitement as everyone seemed to relish the idea of a change to the usual routine.

We had to cram even closer in the already crowded classroom and I was busy trying to squeeze myself into a gap between Simone and a girl called Sinalei when *he* walked in.

The boy from the assembly yesterday morning. He paused in the doorway for a moment as he surveyed the room searching for an empty seat.

Against my will his beauty took my breath away. He was tall enough that I was sure even my 5'11 height would have to crane up to look in his startling emerald green eyes. Red and gold in the morning sunlight with thick raven brows, one of them flecked with a slight scar, his tousled burnished red-brown hair another startling contrast in a school full of brunettes.

He was broad but lean, like a rippling basketball player, the orange *lavalava* tied loosely to tapering hips. But it was the tattoo adorning the length of his left arm that caught and held my gaze captive. I had never seen anything like it before – it curved down his arm, peering from where his sleeve ended. Intricate patterns of black stamped down to his forearm.

I was so intent on studying his tattoo that I failed to realize he was staring straight at me, a crooked smile on his face as if he found my fascination amusing. Our eyes met and in that fleeting moment, it was as if all the air had fled the room and the madness of fifty students crammed into a room meant for twenty faded to a distant blur. Try as I might, I couldn't tear my eyes away from his, even as my radar screamed a warning,

Leila stop it. This meathead is way used to girls staring at him gaga eyed – stop it!

Thankfully, the ever-timely Maleko broke our locked gaze with a whoop.

"Daniel! *Sole* man, are you ready to have your butt debate kicked by 6T?"

As quickly as it had begun, the moment ended. The demi-god called Daniel turned to Maleko with a huge grin, shaking his head as he replied,

"Aww you know nobody here has what it takes to take me and my mouth down."

The two continued their teasing as they made their way to seats on the opposite side of the room. I bent my head to hide my flush of embarrassment, but not before noticing that Daniel and Maleko had no problem finding space in the gaggle of giggling girls.

Like the parting of the Red Sea, I thought derisively, and made a conscious mental note to ignore the overly beefy and overly adulated Head Boy.

Obviously he was the Samoan counterpart to the American high school quarterback, the preening point guard, the freakishly good-looking jerk who would break hearts left, right and center and then graduate to a life of mediocrity. *Or maybe crime*, I thought with a brief smirk of satisfaction. I resisted the temptation to ask Simone for details on him and instead christened him 'Chunk Hunk' in my mind.

My thoughts were interrupted by Ms. Sivani's call for quiet. Once again I was impressed by the respect Samoan teenagers had for authority. Ms. Sivani was slight, her voice a thin reed in a forest of battering oak – but one call for silence and you could have heard a pin drop.

"Alright thank you sixth formers. You've all been working very hard on your drama projects, so I thought we could come together for a little break. A debate break. Now you know the drill, two teams, only one person speaks at a time. When they sit, anyone can stand and take the floor. They get to keep the floor until they have nothing useful to say, so make sure you remember that particular instruction, Maleko."

Ms. Sivani smiled to soften her words as the boys in the corner laughed uproariously and thumped a grinning Maleko on the back. She turned to write the debate topic on the board. There was a collective groan as she wrote the last word with a flourish.

FOREIGN AID IS GOOD FOR SAMOA.

Ms. Sivani divided the class in half with a expansive gesture."Your half is negative and this half with the new student Leila – you're affirmative."

Hearing my name, I instinctively cringed and slouched in my seat. Did she have to draw attention to me?

"Thanks a lot, lady," I muttered, but not before noticing from the corner of my downcast eyes that the Chunk Hunk had turned to regard me with open interest.

Ms. Sivani continued. "The debate may begin. Remember, please keep it civil, Maleko."

Another hoot of laughter from the crowd of boys around the Chunk Hunk. Laughter that had Maleko jumping to his feet and giving a grandiose bow to the class before launching into his negative attack.

The relaxed atmosphere in the room wasn't something I was used to. I was fast realizing that having boys in a class added another dimension that was quite foreign to me.

Boys were loud. Boisterous. And occupied so much physical space. They pushed and shoved. And laughed. Joked continually. They were impossible to ignore. Especially when they were obnoxious.

As I zoned out Maleko's speech which had everyone around me in hysterics, I wondered idly – were all boys like this? Or was this just because these were Samoan boys?

Hmm, food for thought. I gave myself a mental shake to pay attention as Maleko finished his diatribe and a short, stocky girl from our side jumped to her feet to replace him on the debate floor. I zoned out most of her argument, however, as I was fighting the insane urge to stare at the Chunk Hunk.

When she sat down, our team clapped while the other side of the room began chanting.

Daniel ... Daniel!

Our team began booing as Maleko roughly nudged the Chunk Hunk with his shoulder.

"Come on man, your adoring fans are calling for you."

The jeering died away as the Chunk Hunk lazily stood. Like a tiger unfurling from its treetop perch, he moved with relaxed grace, seemingly unaware of the impact he had on his surroundings.

The afternoon sun glinted off his messy hair, catching on red fire as he turned to smile at his team before addressing the rest of us. I tried hard to remain unaffected. To view him with disinterest.

But I was fighting a losing battle. There was something about this boy that had every particle of my being on edge. I tensed with exasperation, did this arrogant idiot have to be so beautiful?

Don't worry Leila, I comforted myself, *just wait for him to open his mouth and once you hear how brainless he really is, this stupid fascination will evaporate in a puff of smoky reality.*

I was wrong. He spoke with calm assurance. Reason and logic flowed from him with the rich sweetness of coconut milk, and the entire room was swept away by it.

"My fellow orators, our ever stunning and wise judge, Ms. Sivani, ours is a society plagued by a relentless array of social ills. Drug abuse. Unemployment. Youth crime and delinquency. Not to mention a vast array of non-communicable diseases like diabetes, obesity, high blood pressure, kidney disease. And who do we have to thank for these? Our Western neighbors. Those who come here bearing gifts but they are gifts we should never have accepted.Why, from the very first Western visitors who came here seeking to pillage our land of its natural resources to those countries who give us money – just so that we will support them during international proceedings – we have been fighting a losing battle with our Western neighbors. There can be no doubt that foreign aid is a plague on our beautiful island nation. There's a saying – there's no such thing as a free lunch. Well, Samoa has been well and truly overeating on supposed 'free' lunches, breakfasts, and dinners for too long."

His team erupted in cheers and he smiled, holding up a hand for silence so he could continue.

"Let's take an example, one of these supposed aid organizations – the US Peace Corp. They come here to volunteer, but really, aren't they here to disseminate their foreign ideas and values? To convince us of their supremacy in all things?"

At his mention of the Peace Corp, I sat upright and my eyes narrowed. Where was this boy headed with this? He continued, pointing out flaws in other volunteer groups from Japan and Australia before sidetracking to criticize the impact of "intermarriage" on the "purity of our Samoan culture."

He assumed a sorrowful façade as he discussed the decay of traditional values due to the country's increased "infiltration" of foreign influence via aid. His closing statement had everyone in the class laughing, "Where is the pride and purity of our Samoa? Take a look around these days, we're surrounded by mixed-up mongrels!"

What the hell?! I was furious, my anger burning so wildly that I could hardly breathe and my heartbeat was reverberating in my head like a caged creature. I hadn't planned on taking part in this debate exercise, but I couldn't contain my rage.

I thought of my dad. My wonderful dad who had given up his law scholarship at Harvard University to serve in the Peace Corps, driving the first immovable wedge into his relationship with his family. I thought of the years of taunts and snide remarks I had endured about my mixed race and heritage and I was shocked to think that here in Samoa, I might be subjected to the same sort of measurement and be found wanting.

In that moment, I hated that gloriously beautiful boy with every fiber of my being. As soon as he sat down, I was on my feet, my chair a harsh grate against the cement floor. I couldn't see myself, but I felt murderous and I knew I looked it. The room went quiet with a hush as I launched into attack mode, completely forgetting all debate decorum.

"What absolute rubbish you're spouting. Not only do your remarks reek of flawed logic, but they also border on outright racism. How dare you pass judgment on volunteers and organizations that dedicate their lives to serving others? Just who in hell do you think you are?"

Ms. Sivani started at my expression and tried to interject but my tidal wave of words was unstoppable.

"I am totally offended by your reference to people like me being 'mixed up mongrels.' I hate racist bigots like you. People of mixed ethnic backgrounds have the opportunity to build bridges between communities, families and nations. It's people like you, people who think the same way you do, who carve chasms of hatred and ignite conflict wherever they are. You disgust me."

The silence was expectant as I came to an abrupt halt, my hands trembling. I had barely sat down before the Chunk Hunk was on his feet. I steeled myself for his attack. Which didn't come. At least not in the manner I had supposed.

He stood with that same lazy, casual ease, running a hand through his tousled hair. I gritted my teeth – *not the red gold hair again.* This boy was driving me insane with his posturing.

He spread his arms expansively and again it was impossible not to be in awe of his toned strength. He smiled. A delighted smile filled with splendor that had all the females – and, as I heard Simone sigh, some of the males – in the room melting. *Pulili.*

Everyone except for me. It set my teeth on edge, my irritation with him so huge it was physically painful.

"She wounds me." One rugged arm placed on his heart. A sorrowful expression on his face. Betrayed by laughing eyes. "My esteemed and lovely opponent rushes to attack my character, my intellect, my person yet neglects to address the essence of today's topic. Perhaps because she is new to our shores, therefore she does not yet have a full appreciation of the uniqueness of our culture. The importance of preserving our traditions and standing strong against assault – whether it comes in the form of money with an expectation. Or in the form of foreigners who come to steal the hearts of our beautiful Samoan women."

Ms. Sivani interjected dryly, "I think that will be quite enough on the subject of intermarriage thank you very much. Let's all try to remember what the topic is today and stay on track."

The Chunk Hunk bowed his head slightly and flashed his brilliant smile at the English teacher, "Your wish is my command Ms. Sivani. I'm sorry I went astray but this young woman's unprovoked aggression really cut my Samoan identity and pride to the core."

He sat down, but not without another grand bow to his audience. There were ripples of laughter through the room. Like everyone was in on a delightful sweet joke that only I was unaware of. I wanted to stamp my feet and throw a full-fledged tantrum.

Another boy from my team took to the floor when he was done. Then a tall Amazonian girl from the Chunk Hunk's team went on the defensive.

Back and forth the debate went with hoots and jeers while I sat and fumed. And clenched my fists. Wanting desperately to smash something. Or someone. Someone with dancing forest eyes.

When the bell rang, there was a cheer from the Chunk Hunk's team – as if they already knew they had won.

Ms. Sivani, held her hand up for silence and again the class went still immediately.

"Now, thank you – that will be enough of that riot. You all did very well today and I was pleased to see a good range of points covered. Apart from a few small digressions, you all stayed on topic quite well."

"But Miss – tell us who won!" Of course it was the exuberant Maleko again who alone had the impetuosity to interrupt the unshakeable Ms. Sivani. But instead of frowning she only gave him a patient smile.

"Alright, alright Maleko, of course there has to be a winning team, so I have to concede the Negative team takes the win today."

The last words were barely out of her mouth before they erupted into whooping cheers and those sitting around me groaned collectively. I stood to throw my bag over my shoulder, dying to get out of the room and breathe before I imploded. But the teams seemed in no rush to vacate the room, gathering instead in clusters to laugh and discuss the highlights of the morning's debate. With my head down, I was pushing my way through the stifling pack of orange when there was a voice behind me.

"Hey wait up. Leila is it? Wait!"

It was the last person I wanted to talk to right now – the Chunk Hunk. I pretended I couldn't hear him and redoubled my efforts to break free of the crowd. But he didn't let up. I felt a hand grab hold of my backpack.

"Leila, hang on a minute, please."

With a sigh, I turned, making sure to compose my features into the blandest expression possible.

"Yes?" my voice was clipped but my emotions were a swirling mass at the sight of him. I was angry. I hated him. But did he have to be so superb to look at?

He stood behind me, with Maleko at his side. Both smiling. Maleko spoke first, as usual.

"Great debate, ay Leila? I bet you don't get such smooth talkers back where you come from ay?" A puzzled frown had him furrow his brow. "Hey, where DO you come from anyway?"

I didn't want the Chunk Hunk to know anything about me, but it was impossible to be rude to Maleko – his eager smile and barely restrained enthusiasm for everything almost puppy like. I directed my reply to him.

"The States. Washington D.C.. Well Maryland really." I self-corrected. And for some unknown reason, I continued, unwilling for them to assume, like Simone had, that I was some teenage delinquent sent here for straightening out. "I'm here for the summer holidays to visit my aunt and uncle."

The Chunk Hunk smiled warmly at me, an easy smile that flecked his green eyes with gold highlights in the sun. "Great, well welcome to SamCo. I just wanted to say, nice debating. And I hope you didn't take any of it personally. Are we ok?"

His mention of the debate had a wall of coldness crashing down, slicing off any desire I may have had for a conversation with them.

"No. We aren't. You know some of us are products of exactly that exploitative union you referred to. We aren't all pure Samoans steeped in cultural richness and we happen to be proud of that mixed heritage. I don't care if this was just a 'fun' debate, you shouldn't go around saying stuff like that which can be so derogatory and offensive. Especially for those of us who have mixed parents."

My voice rose several octaves as I neared the end of my spiel and several students around us turned to listen. I didn't realize I was trembling until I finished and I felt a huge weariness wash over me.

What was I doing? Why was I wasting my time and effort arguing with this idiot? What did his opinion matter anyway?

"Oh just forget it, you don't have a clue what I'm talking about anyway. You're just another pure Samoan steeped in high and mighty cultural richness."

The Chunk Hunk looked confused and Maleko let out a surprised whoop as I turned away from them and pushed my way through the crowd and out the classroom door. I could hear people laughing as I half ran down the corridor, errant tears threatening to spill. I didn't stop my rush until I was in the safety of the girls' bathroom, where I threw cold water on my face. I felt like a fool, a marked woman and all I wanted to do was go home.

Back in the hall and under control of my emotions, I gripped my bag tightly, resolving not to let anyone else get under my skin. *You've handled worse, Leila* I reminded myself. *You can do this.* So intent on my own private mental pep talk I almost bumped into the graceful Simone preening in the hall. He was alone. Waiting for someone. For me?

"Leila, there you are."

I was in no mood to be gracious. "What?"

"What was that all about back there?"

"What was what?" deliberately obtuse.

Simone pursed his lips and shook his head at me, one manicured hand on his hip.

"Back there. That debate. Your attack on Daniel."

I was so used to calling him the Chunk Hunk that I only looked confused.

"Huh? Who?"

"You know, Daniel the Head Boy? Tall, GQ model beautiful, *dop* – as we would call him?"

I grimaced and shrugged my shoulders, unwilling to concede I made the connection. Simone continued.

"You got kind of upset back there, don't you think you were taking things a bit too personal? Don't you have debates back home?" He looked impatient with my seeming ignorance. "I don't know why you got so psycho at Daniel for."

I stared out the window. Boys were on the field chasing a rugby ball. Girls stood laughing under a palm tree. It was all so alien to me. I was very much the foreigner here. And I felt it. A wave of homesickness swept through me. I shrugged at Simone, wishing he would just leave me alone.

"I guess so. I just didn't like what he said about Westerners coming here to exploit people you know? I mean, I get so much crap from people back home about being mixed that hearing it here was just – I don't know – I couldn't handle it."

Simone considered me thoughtfully before answering. "Well, maybe you should know something. The reason why we were all laughing when Daniel was going on about that was because he was talking about himself there. *He's* mixed like you. Like a lot of us. It's no big deal here. We make fun of ourselves all the time. Daniel's dad was *palagi*, white. And his mom wasn't even full Samoan, she was mixed Tongan, so I guess that makes him even less of a pure cultural product than you."

I couldn't believe what I was hearing. The cold dread of realization washed over me as Simone continued.

"Maybe it's different back where you come from, but here we're all *afakasi*, mixed and it's no big deal. Daniel gets teased about it all the time, especially since he's part Tongan and historically Samoans and Tongans hate each other. Today, back there, he was talking about himself, which is why everybody was laughing."

"Oh no." I groaned, putting my head in my hands as it hit me that, once again, I had jumped in to attack mode on the pure assumption that I was being picked on. Humiliated.

How many times had my dad warned me about this? How many times could I have avoided a conflict if I would just listen, take a breath and get my facts straight before I rushed to kill people?! I had wanted to reinvent myself, yet not even a week in this new school and already I had committed the same fatal error that was a classic Leila move. Glumly, I sighed.

"Thanks Simone for clearing that up. I appreciate it. I thought something else entirely was going on in the classroom back there and I kinda jumped too quickly. Everyone must think I'm a total freak now. Ugh. What an idiot!" With slumped shoulders I sat on a hall bench. Suddenly it occurred to me.

"Hey what do you care anyway? Why are you explaining this to me? What's it to you?" My tone was suspicious and my eyes narrowed. What was this boy-girl's agenda anyway?

Simone raised a perfect eyebrow at my burgeoning hostility.

"It's not about you, trust me. I just don't like to see anyone go off at Daniel like that. He doesn't deserve it. So consider this a heads up or a warning, whatever way you want to take it. Next time you want to get aggressive, take it out on some other boy. Goodness knows there's tons of others who are stupid enough to deserve it."

A sigh as Simone paused and continued, this time without any of his usual exaggerated mannerisms.

"Leila, I've known Daniel since primary school and he's different from a lot of the others. I know. I used to get picked on, you know, for being so 'unique'," a smile, "and Daniel looked out for me. Thanks to him, I made it through primary school in one piece. So, go easy on him okay."

With that quizzical remark, Simone turned and flounced away. My audience with royalty was clearly at its end.

I shrugged, clutching my backpack close as I made my way down to the open courtyard for what was left of lunch period, hoping I hadn't just lost the only friend I had made so far in this place. I thought about what Simone had revealed about the Chunk Hunk – Daniel – I amended in my mind.

Somehow, after being mean to him when he hadn't deserved it, made it wrong to keep calling him a brainless lout. *Oh well,* I conceded, *it didn't really matter what I called him because, after today, I was sure that I wouldn't have to worry about ever speaking to him again.* For a reason that I couldn't name, that thought made me, regretful?

The rest of the day was uneventful. There was some whispering and laughter when I walked into history class, but I steeled myself against it with the reminder that people had far more exciting things to talk about than me and it was highly doubtful that I would be the source of their animated conversations.

Last period was Library, which meant lots of time to sit and think, or – in Maleko's case – lots of time to throw paper at the girls in the front row and fluster the fresh-faced young librarian with his generous smiles. If nothing else, having boys like Maleko in the class meant an hour of Library was never boring.

When the final bell rang, I was in a rush to get to the front bus stop, unwilling to run into any more people who wanted to remind me about the morning's fracas.

Standing at the main gate, a cluster of girls called out goodbye as I got on the first bus to arrive. Surprised, I surveyed them with a hint of suspicion but there was nothing but friendliness in their faces as they waved.

"See you tomorrow, Leila."

Sitting on the bus, I could see the rugby team at practice. The now familiar shape of my debate nemesis clearly obvious as the bus pulled away from the school. Slumped back in my seat, I had mixed feelings about my emotion-saturated day. So I had embarrassed myself by attacking the school's beloved demi-god Head Boy. An attack that had been somewhat unwarranted. But nobody seemed to be holding it against me.

After all, Simone had said – most of the students were 'just like me', mixed-up teenagers. More than anything else, that gave me a shot of positivity.

Maybe there would be a place for me at this school. Maybe, this place wouldn't be so bad after all.

The next day I was resolved to be nice. Positive. Open minded. Heck, I was even willing to try smiling. *Or not. Maybe that was pushing it a bit...*

The morning classes passed uneventfully. An ever-jolly and somewhat annoying girl called Sinalei shadowed me from class to class, filling my personal space with her chatter. Apparently she had decided that we should be friends.

In another world, I would have sent her packing with a snarl, but I had promised. To be good. Nice. So, quite unlike me, I kept a smile that became more and more plastic as the day went on and the temperature began to soar. By lunch, I was ready to send myself to solitary confinement – just to escape her, but it was the heat more than anything that contributed to my building discomfort.

It had been getting hotter each day but today was unbearably humid. Uncle Tuala had warned it meant there would be a storm later on, but that offered me little comfort now as I sucked in the wet, steaming air, trying to find a pocket of coolness.

I groaned when I checked the schedule and saw my first Physical Education class would be after lunch. How could anyone stand to exercise in this weather?

Dragging my feet, I changed into the requisite uniform with the rest of the girls, and then slouched along behind them down to the far field, clutching my water bottle. I had already finished two liters of water but it didn't seem to be doing me much good.

Just walking to the field had my yellow shirt sweat soaked and sticking uncomfortably to my back. I was too hot to even stress about the stupid sports uniform, which should have been outlawed by any and all fashion police.

A yellow cotton tee and an orange skirt over skimpy shorts. It was the shortest thing I'd ever worn and I still couldn't reconcile such a revealing outfit with the strict Samoan dress codes. I was painfully aware that my legs were even skinnier in all their non-tanned glory, especially when standing beside the other girls.

Mr. Otele the PE teacher was an ex-national hurdler. Or so Sinalei whispered. Which meant half the girls were simpering at his instructions. It also meant that he was an enthusiastic teacher who believed in getting involved in the day's sports. Meaning I couldn't hide behind a tree and go sit in the shade until the class was over. Nope. This teacher meant business.

"Right, let's start with five laps around the field." A collective groan. "Then bring it together and I'll put you into teams for a game of touch."

Touch? Okay, that sounded vaguely indecent.

These people and their contradictory standards had me confused. Shaking my head, I joined the rest of the class as they started their lap around the field.

I noticed that Simone was nowhere to be seen. Clearly, PE was not something that he did.

Running in the blazing sun was a first for me but I resisted the urge to quit and slow to a stop like the others. The memory of my dad and I running our last 5k kept me pushing as, one by one, the others slowed to a stroll.

Into the third lap, and the only people still running were me and a pocket of boys led by Mr. Otele. There was an admiring glance from Maleko as I increased my tempo and easily overtook him on the last curve. He called out after me with a whoop.

"Hey Leila! You're not supposed to overtake the Running Man. Hey!"

I could hear him gasping and puffing behind me as I accelerated at the last fifty meters. I threw him a smile over my shoulder as I sprinted to the finish of my last lap. Slowing to a walk, I was exultant as the adrenaline coursed through me. It had been months since I had last run. And it felt amazing. Even while wearing a ridiculous orange skirt. Mr. Otele called us all in and several of the boys complimented me as we gathered under the mango tree.

"Nice run there Leila."

"Yeah good to see a girl beat Maleko the Running Man."

The class erupted into good-natured laughter as Maleko took a bow. He took a swipe at a teasing boy standing behind me before turning to flash me his smile.

"Awww, I was just going easy on you Leila, you know, being nice to the new girl. Don't want you to get scared off us Samoan boys ay?"

Mr. Otele gave out directions for our game of touch rugby but I wasn't listening. I was exulting in this new sensation. Is this what belonging felt like? Is this how it felt to fit in somewhere? I wasn't sure. I had never been just one of the crowd. No different from my peers. People teasing each other. Laughing.

I had spent so many years looking at life from outside the window that it felt strange to actually be in the room with everyone else. Mr. Otele's call for the touch game to begin forced me to put my thoughts aside. The touch game was fun. It seemed to consist of throwing the ball around and then running like crazy whenever it came to you, trying not to get touched by the opposition.

It also involved a lot of screaming from the girls whenever one of the boys pretended to tackle them. And, of course, the requisite showing-off theatrics from Maleko. I was fast realizing that not only was he the class clown, he was also the life of the group, his energy and enthusiasm infectious.

I was sorry when the bell went. Tired, sweaty and hot, but wishing we could play on. Back in the changing rooms Sinalei's prattle wasn't as annoying as it had been and I even fielded questions about Washington D.C. from some of the others. I had dreaded curiosity about my background, but it proved to be easier than I had thought it would be.

No, I wasn't here for good. Yes, I liked it here. No, I didn't have any brothers and sisters (that seemed to generate some disbelief – solo childness being an oddity I supposed). No, I didn't miss my school back home and yes it was very different from SamCo!

I deftly deflected questions about parents and, once I emerged from the girls' room, it was with no small sense of achievement.

I felt like I'd passed through an inquisition and come out okay. And walking to last period with Maleko and a tall quiet girl called Leone was nice. Except for the ongoing trash talk from Maleko about my running skills. He wanted another chance to prove he could outrun me and was determined not to let up until I set a time.

My ease came to earth with a splat when I got to my next class. Geography. With Mrs. Jasmine, another Indian teacher. And sitting in the back row was Daniel.

Suddenly I was painfully aware of how little attention I had paid to my hair. My face. My rumpled uniform. I felt like an ungainly, sweaty beast. And that annoyed me because it felt like it was his fault that my looks were coming up short. There was an automatic scowl on my face as I took my seat at the opposite end of the room, hoping he wouldn't notice me. But Maleko ruined that possibility with his loud blow-by-blow account to the entire room of our 'race.'

It had now assumed mythic proportions and involved us sprinting to a photo finish with Olympic glamour – and he, deciding at the last instant to pull back and 'let me take the hairs-breadth lead.' Since I was a girl. And new. And he was being an honorable gentleman.

I groaned, hiding my face behind a textbook and sending up a prayer of relief as Mrs. Jasmine walked in to the room, putting an end to the clamor. The next forty minutes were devoted to the monsoon rains of India, which suited me just fine. Attention, even the positive kind, made me squirm, and I hoped that Maleko would have moved onto his next hare-brained idea by the end of school. It was not to be, because as soon as the bell rang, he was at my desk. With Daniel right behind him.

"So, Leila when do you want to have our race ay? Daniel here can be the ref. I was thinking that it should be something short distance you know? Like say 100 meters, that way it won't be too you know? Like say 100 meters, that way it won't be too draining for you. I'm sure it must be waaay hot here for you and I wouldn't want you to get heatstroke or anything. How about we go race now? It'll be over in a few seconds. For me anyway!"

His face was eager but I had to laugh at his proposal. I well knew that my strength and his weakness, was endurance. I was fitter than this bubbly wired boy but there was no way I could take him on in a speed event. I shook my head at him as I stood.

"Nope. Sorry Maleko. This isn't a good day for me. And there's no way I would race 100 meters with you. I will take you on in a 5k any day though."

Maleko looked questioningly at Daniel who's eyes had widened slightly at my reply.

"5k? How far is that?"

Daniel spoke before I could. "About fourteen laps of the track."

Maleko's expression was comical. His face fell and his shoulders slumped. I had to smile; he was so transparent. He knew he was beat.

"Oh." He looked thoughtful and then wrinkled his nose. "Girl, I don't want to run that far. Are you sure we can't try something a little shorter? I know, how about we throw a few rugby tackles into the challenge? I'm sure I can take you on those."

Even I had to laugh at that one. Walking to the hall with the two of them felt like the natural thing to do, Daniel leaning forward to open the door for me, "Go ahead."

Once in the hall, Maleko took off after a lithe girl with a braid that fell to her hips.

"Hey – Malia! I need help with the Math homework, Malia!"

Without quite knowing how, I was walking down the emptying hall with the Chunk Hunk. With Daniel. Without knowing why, I was almost paralyzed with trepidation.What should I say? What does one say to a Chunk Hunk? One that you wanted to obliterate from the planet the day before? And now? Now, walking beside me, deliberately shortening his stride to keep pace with me, I felt nothing but breathlessness, my mind aswirl with rapid-fire conversation possibilities.

Should I apologize for the debate? Or pretend like it had never happened? Should I talk about the Geography homework? Ask his opinion of the monsoon rains on the delta plains? That had me rolling my eyes. *Oh, get a hold of yourself, Leila. So he's handsome. Well, make that magnificent. So what. Big deal.* I took a deep breath to plunge in to a question but he beat me to it.

"So, you're a runner?" His tone was light. Casual.

I strove to match him.

"I run a bit. Nothing too awe inspiring. I don't think you should take Maleko's version of events too literally. I may be the new girl, but I think I wouldn't be far wrong to say that he tends to exaggerate things a little."

Daniel laughed. "A little? I think you mean a lot. As in, Maleko is the master of exaggeration! We *never* take anything he says literally."

Our eyes met in perfect agreement, which had me flushed again. So much so that I almost walked straight into the willowy girl standing at the head of the stairs.

"Oh sorry!" My apology was relaxed but the hardness of the answering look in her eyes instantly had me on the defensive.

What was wrong with this girl? I remembered seeing her in my Biology class. A stunning brunette who fit all the brochure pictures of tropical island beauties, she moved with a practiced grace. The same grace that was clearly evident as she put one hand on Daniel's arm, a half pout on her face.

"Danny, I've been looking all over for you guys. My dad is waiting for us... " her voice trailed away suggestively as she half inclined her head towards him, a deliberate attempt to shut me out?

Daniel groaned and rapped his fist on his forehead. "Agh that's right. Sorry Mele, I'm coming." He looked around over his shoulder. "Maleko was just here. "

Nimbly, I quickstepped past them both and dashed down the stairs, throwing a hasty goodbye over my shoulder. I didn't wait to see whether the Chunk Hunk had heard me. I didn't need to. I didn't need any antagonism from possessive girlfriends either, I told myself as I walked down the palm-lined driveway towards the bus stop.

I was almost to the gate when a rush of heat brought me to a standstill. The light turned a hazy red and a wave of dizziness descended on me like a blanket. I swayed.

What was happening? I was hot. So hot that there wasn't enough air to breathe and I felt like I was drowning in the wet humidity. Panic clawed its way up through my constricting chest as I struggled to stay upright. Before I met the ground face first, a hand steadied me and a voice was asking.

"Leila, are you okay?"

I grabbed the hand with relief, trying to steady myself. It was Sinalei at my side, concern on her face.

"Not really. I'm so hot. I think maybe the heat today and PE just got too much for me. I just need to sit down."

Cautiously I walked to the grass and sat down. Sinalei kneeling beside me was rifling through her bag.

"Here." She was triumphant as she handed me a bottle of water. "I knew I had another bottle here somewhere. Go on, you're probably dehydrated. Too much running at PE class."

Eagerly, I gulped down the water, taking deep breaths in between each mouthful trying to slow my racing pulse and attain calm. There were a few curious glances as the school continued to stream out of class and down to the bus stop but, after only a few minutes in the shade, I felt better enough to stand.

"I think I'm okay now. Thanks Sinalei, I guess I'm still adjusting to the weather here." A rueful grin. "And I should take it easy in PE. I won't be in such a rush to humiliate Maleko next time."

She laughed with me and pretended mock horror.

"No way – are you kidding? That was the best PE class ever, watching that show-off get outrun by a girl was classic timeless memories stuff. You have to keep doing that."

She accompanied me to the gate to wait for the bus. I laughed off the whole heat flush incident but secretly I was worried. Where had that come from?

Once back at the house, I took a cold shower, standing under the deluge until my fingers were wrinkly and my face was numb from the spray. Only then could I shake off the heat wave from earlier. I soothed away my worries. It was nothing, just a little too much running in PE. It would be an early night for me.

A quick dinner, another cold shower and then I tumbled into bed with the ceiling fan on full blast.

That night, the dreams began.

She stood in a forest – lush, living, breathing rainforest. A canopy of green, hung with vines and trailing with white orchids.

It was night. A flying fox screeched nearby, startling her. She wore a woven mat-like cloth wrapped around her like a bath towel. So finely made and so worn with time that it fell in soft folds around her knees and caressed her skin softer than silk. A band of brown feathers fluttered at its hem. Her feet were bare on the moist earth.

Her skin glistened with coconut oil, catching the fire of the moonlight as she raised her hands to feel the necklace made of pointed boar's tusks at her throat.

Where was she? Why was she dressed like this? She could hear water rushing nearby. A waterfall?

The sound made her acutely aware of the burning thirst in her throat. She had an overwhelming urge to submerge her body in the rushing falls. Drink deeply of its cool freshness. Lie in the liquid moonlight, awash in its swirling embrace.

Turning towards the sound she started making her way cautiously through the trees. Bushes scratched at her legs. Ferns tugged at the hem of her dress. Leaves entangled in her hair. Her raging thirst grew, the closer she got to the falls. With relief, she parted the leaves and there it was. A small waterfall splashed from a rocky rise in the land, falling gracefully into a circular pool, edged with smooth rocks and trailing ferns. The water sparkled like black diamonds at the base of the falls.

She walked forward to the edge of the pool and hesitated. She hated to wet the finely woven mat but she had nothing on underneath. Oh well, it was only her in the night. Flushing with embarrassment, she quickly shrugged out of the woven cloth and slipped into the welcome concealment of the water.

The cold was a shock. A jolt of refreshing coolness that had her shivering in the warm wet night. She slowly swam towards the waterfall and was pleased to find that she could stand at its base. Cupping her hands to the silver froth, she drank deeply, glorying in the clean sweet taste. She drank again and again, like a water-starved nomad in a desert. Finally satiated, she leaned forward to let the rushing waters sweep over her hair and down the length of her oiled body.

Then she felt it. A chill down her spine that had nothing to do with the night air. A prickling of unease. She was not alone.

Slowly, she turned.

A woman stood at the end of the pool. She was hauntingly beautiful and yet terrifying at the same time. She was tall, with a length of sandy brown hair that fell to below her waist. At her throat was a boar's tusk necklace identical to that which Leila wore. She was half naked, her woven dress clinging to her hips, feathered hem skirting her ankles, full breasts covered by her thick hair adorned with vivid red flowers.

She held a polished bone-carved knife in one hand, the blade gleaming whitely in the darkness as she raised both arms to the night sky.

A dreadful smile lit her face as she exulted,

"Yes. Pele, my beloved daughter, finally you return to me!"

THREE

I woke with a startled gasp, sheets a tangled mess around me, my shirt soaked through with sweat. Pulse racing, I tried to calm my ragged breathing but the room was so stifling I needed to get out. Hoping Aunt Matile hadn't woken with the sounds of my nightmare, I slipped silently through the sleeping house and out into the garden. Sitting on an upturned plastic bucket under the fragrant branches of the frangipani tree, I breathed deeply in the night air.

What did it mean? Where had that dream come from? Was I losing my mind? Was all the pressure of being in this alien land, searching for information about a mother that no-one wanted to talk about finally getting to me? Fluffy chickens roosting in the breadfruit trees rustled and clucked close by and Terminator strolled over to snuffle hopefully against my fingers. *It was just a dream, Leila, just a dream.* I kept repeating to myself as I quietly crept back to my room. But sleep was a long time coming.

The rest of the week was uneventful. I was slipping into a routine with Matile and Tuala. I didn't ask any more questions about my mother. They were kind and careful. I was polite and helpful.

I washed dishes. Matile smiled with startled surprise. I helped Tuala sweep up the cut grass. He brought me an ice cold Diet Coke back from the corner store. I gave Terminator a much-needed bath. Which he hated me for. And which made Matile laugh.

I had not given up on my search for information about my mother though. I risked Matile's wrath and asked Kolio about her when he came to weed the banana patch at the back. He must have been warned by Tuala and Matile not to say anything though – because he only looked uneasy and shook his head,

"I don't know anything. I don't know anyone like that."

Falute was the same. I went outside to help her hang up the laundry, and in-between pegging up lemon-fresh sheets, I asked,"So, did you know my mother?"

At first she acted dumb. "Who? I don't know anything about that subject. No, I know nothing."

"But you're part of the family, you're Matile's cousin, surely you must have known her? You must have at least heard something about her?"

She only shook her head vehemently. "No. I don't want to talk about her."

She turned to walk away and then stopped to look back and consider my crestfallen expression. She sighed, looked around to make sure we were alone and then leaned forward to whisper,

"Leila, your mother was a bad woman. It was good your father took you away from here. It's better you don't ask about her. Better you don't know about her. I'm sorry, that's all I can say."

And with that she bustled back into the house carrying an empty laundry basket on her hip.

I stood there in the yard in disbelief. *Your mother was a bad woman.* I felt cold in the tropical sun because I could no longer ignore what was glaringly obvious.

Matile and everybody else weren't being cagey about my mother because she was too sad or emotional a subject for them to handle. It was because the topic of my mother was too unpleasant. Falute even looked afraid just to speak of her.

But why?

School in Samoa was satisfying.

I was attentive and studious. I smiled at all the right times. And tried hard not be rude with Sinalei when she insisted on keeping me company every interval. I had never had friends before, so wasn't used to how they occupied one's space and time. Even when you didn't want them to. But I was learning.

Simone was still gracing me with his presence and I had to admit that I found myself more relaxed with him than with anyone else. He seemed to have bestowed his approval upon me and regularly called me to sit with him and his group of girl-boys. Flawlessly beautiful, graceful supermodels all of them. All fiery with confidence, loud and exuberant. I laughed to think what my dad would say about my new 'clique' of friends. In fact, everything seemed to be going fine in this new place.

I kept my distance from the Chunk Hunk. Every time I saw him, I did an abrupt about turn and went in the opposite direction. He always stood out, so that wasn't difficult. We only had one class together so it was easy to ignore him. It wasn't as easy to stop thinking about the green eyes and the tattooed arm. But I persevered. I reminded myself he was in a different stratosphere from me. And I wasn't here to get to know the opposite sex. Or to explore this new-found edge that one in particular inspired in me.

No. I was here for three months to find out what I could about my mother. And to get to know my Samoan family. And to have a break from my *palagi* family. Which, let's face it, was really made up of one grandmother. The slight unease Daniel inspired in me was the only complaint I really had about my new school. Samoa College wasn't bad.

If it weren't for the nights, I would have been almost content.Yes, if it weren't for the nights, Samoa would have been more than bearable. Because every night was the same thing.

I slept. I had the same nightmare. I woke up burning hot and couldn't stop the shaking. The gasping for air. The dream was the same every night. But the heat seemed to be getting worse. I slept with a fan. I slept in the bare minimum. I drank copious amounts of ice water. No improvement.

I was trying my best to keep it hidden from Matile and Tuala because I was terrified that I had some sort of disease and it would give them an excuse to send me back to America. I bought a cheap thermometer from the pharmacy. Every night before I went to bed I would take my temperature. 36.5 degrees. Completely normal and textbook perfect. By midnight I would be burning up with some kind of fever. 42 degrees. I took illegal amounts of painkillers. Nothing. According to the textbooks, I should be practically comatose. I stopped taking my temperature. It only increased my agitation.

The weeks passed. I had been in Samoa for four weeks and my nights were taking their toll on my days. At school I was exhausted. I found it hard to concentrate. Ms. Sivani was giving me her stern eyes. The ones she reserved for Maleko on his worst days.

I was finding it harder to be patient with Sinalei – looking for more and more excuses to spend my lunch break in the library. Where I would pore through Science textbooks and Google 'unexplained fevers.' I ignored Maleko's teasing invitations to run in PE class, choosing instead to cut class and risk detention rather than an overheating episode in front of everyone. The Principal shook his head tiredly at me in detention as he reminded me that "we are not a school for teenage delinquents from America you know."

By the fifth week, I was afraid to go to sleep. When I woke up with strange singe marks on my sheets like burnt holes, I sobbed silently into my pillow. That's it, I had to get out of there. I left the house in the dead of night, slipping through the broken fence at the back of the house and into the green trees.

Stars hung heavily in a black velvet night. The cool air was bliss against my skin and I walked almost blindly through the bush. I should have been afraid. Of the dark, the strange surroundings, the possibility of danger. But I wasn't. I felt oddly at ease. Like something outside, out there had been missing from inside me.

I walked and, as I walked, I started to cool down. The dizziness eased. The rising tide of fever burn slowed. And then, there it was.

A pool of silver water that tumbled over a low rocky drop into another larger oval pool below. Ringed with glistening black rock and olive green ferns. Just like in my dream. Only, unlike my dream, there was no darkly beautiful woman waiting there for me.

I breathed a sigh of relief. And ignored the rational voice inside my head that demanded to know how I could possibly have dreamed of this place before I ever visited it?

Without even stopping to think, I stripped off my shirt and shorts and slipped into the water. I caught my breath with happiness at the coldness, the relief it gave me from the heat that had plagued me for so many nights. It was as if this exact water had been waiting for me, calling to me. Again and again I ducked my head under the water, cooling every particle of my being. Every feverish fiber.

I stayed there as long as I dared before heading back home to my still room, grateful that Matile and Tuala were heavy sleepers. And, for the first time in weeks, I slept without dreaming. And woke without a fever.

I went three wonderful nights without a heat attack, enjoying the luxury of a full night's sleep. At school I was almost myself again. Just when I thought maybe I had imagined the heat flushes, they started again, waking me with their fire. Again I went to the pool, praying Terminator wouldn't tell on me and wake Matile with his howling at the moon. And again, the water was exactly the antidote I needed.

As the nights improved – so did the days.

I stopped spacing out in class, falling asleep in Math to the drone of Mr. Michael's voice. I still didn't think it safe enough to try doing sports again though, so I kept cutting PE.

Which landed me in detention. Again.

Detention in Samoa was a universe of difference from America. Like the stark contrast between maximum security and a 'retreat facility' for white collar criminals.

Here, you got detention for coming late to school three times. Or late to class one time too many. Wearing sunglasses. The wrong color jandals. Speaking Samoan anywhere but in Samoan class. Or daring to put on lipstick. (It was tribute to Simone's skilful application of 'natural-looking' makeup that he never got busted. Or maybe it was because he seemed to be best friends with all the girl prefects.)

Here, instead of sitting in a room doing homework or extra assignments, detention was picking up trash. Weeding the garden. Cleaning the bathrooms. Which were disgusting – before and after clean-up. Sweeping every classroom with coconut frond brooms and washing windows.

If you got three detentions then you went on Hard Labor. I kid you not – that's what they called it. This was my fourth time skipping PE class. My fourth detention. So my name was called out for Hard Labor .

Sinalei gave me her saddest look of commiseration. Tinged with puzzlement. She couldn't understand why I – a girl who could outrun Maleko the Running Man – would want to cut PE and go on detention. I shrugged as I gathered my stuff and headed to the staffroom to meet with the duty prefects.

I was the only girl on Hard Labor. Most females here didn't do anything bad enough to merit the extreme punishment. Three other students were waiting under the tree beside the staffroom. Two were juniors. Fresh-faced boys with pimples who were chewing gum and throwing rocks at the stray three-legged dog that liked to visit and forage for lunch scraps.

My other fellow inmate looked considerably more threatening. He was a large, broadset sixth former who (according to the Entertainment Channel, Sinalei) was repeating for the third time. Which made him about twenty years old. Or more.

I had no trouble believing that. He had a snake tattoo on his neck, arms like tree trunks and an angry expression to match. Sinalei also said he'd been in jail for beating a man to death, but I didn't take *that* seriously. Still, I chose to sit beside the irritating third formers. No point testing the borders or anything.

It was with a sinking feeling of dread that I saw the duty prefect of the day walk towards us carrying the detention clipboard. It was the Chunk Hunk. Daniel – I mentally corrected.

 I wanted to shrivel up and die. Just what I needed. To spend an hour doing whatever Hard Laborers did under the watchful eye of the demi-god. Was there no mercy in this world?

I turned my head away, wishing I could make a break for it, skipping over my options. I could plead sickness and ask to be excused? Have my detention moved to another day where some other prefect could tell me what to do? But the thought of having to appeal to this know-it-all, annoyingly perfect freak made my pride rankle. Casting myself on his mercy would mean that I would have to talk to him. Nicely. Humbly. Beseechingly. And then if he excused me, I would be beholden to him. And have to say thank you. And be nice again when I saw him next.

No. I was stuck. And my feeling of constriction was only intensified when he turned bemused eyes on me.

"Hey Leila. Hard Labor? What have you been doing to deserve the worst SamCo has to offer?"

I shrugged and tried to emulate his light-hearted tone.

"Nothing." I lied. "Just a few too many late arrivals."

"Really? It says here, you've been cutting class umm, PE class?!" there was doubt in his eyes this time. "Why? I thought you were supposed to be Maleko's running nemesis?"

I gritted my teeth at the third degree. I was certain that other people didn't have to endure extra scrutiny for their class-cutting shortcomings. I gave Daniel a dark scowl and turned my head to regard the green field, hazy in the afternoon heat.

The two juniors had been listening to our exchange with interest, glad someone else was distracting the Head Boy from their own misdemeanors. The other senior, however, looked bored. As if he had better things to do. Like getting more tattoos. Or looking for people to smash. Just because he wanted to.

Giving up on getting any answers from me, Daniel half sighed and turned brisk and businesslike. "Right people, let's get started so we can go home. Mr. Raymond wanted the grass around the tennis courts cut."

There was a groan from the juniors.

"There's some bush knives here but Leila, maybe you could weed instead?"

I prickled immediately at the assumption. "Excuse me? Why can't I cut the grass too? Why should I do something different?"

The group of boys had turned and were already beginning to walk towards the tennis courts. They stopped to look back at me with raised eyebrows. The juniors in particular looked flabbergasted.

Daniel looked like he was struggling to find the right words."Umm, it's just that usually the boys do the grass cutting. You know they have to use a *sapelu,* a machete?"

One hand on my hip, I bristled defiantly."Yeah, so? Why can't I do that too?"

"It's a bit dangerous, especially if you're not used to using a machete."

"Of course I know how to use a machete." The lies came thick and fast. "I'm sure it's none of your concern anyway. This is supposed to be Hard Labor and all of us are in it, so why don't you let me worry about my machete skills?"

Daniel's easy shrug and crooked smile had me momentarily dazed. He was just so gloriously beautiful, even when he was supposed to be my temporary jailor, that it took my breath away.

"Hey no problem. " he raised both hands in supplication. "You want to cut grass with them, then you go right ahead. I'm just here to supervise and make sure you serve your detention, that's all."

"Fine." my retort was sharp. I walked over to the pile of knives and picked up the first one in the pile. "So where do we start?"

Daniel took up a spot under the mango tree behind us. I ignored him. There were muffled sniggers from the juniors as they came and selected their machetes, shaking their heads at me. I strode over to the nearest clump of tall grass that hugged the tennis court. Once I got there though I halted as I considered the black blade of the knife in my hands. Great. Now what the heck was I supposed to do with this?

I snuck a sideways glance at the three boys spread out along the length of the court. They had stripped down to shorts only in the wet heat and I was envious of their relaxed gear. I hadn't even started cutting grass yet and already I was sweating. I prayed a silent prayer to whatever gods might be listening. *Please don't let me heat panic attack...*

I stood and studied the others as they swung their blades rhythmically back and forth, felling swathes of grass with each horizontal wave. It looked easy I thought. You had to half bend your knees and bend at the waist to reach the grass, sweeping the blade along the top of it. Cut too low and your blade would meet the earth. Or some rocks. Which is what happened on my first swing.

"Yow!" The startled yelp was out before I could stop it as my blade cut into rock and there was a flinty sound of protest.

The three boys paused mid swing to grin at me. Even the senior Mafia-killer. I debated giving them all the finger but decided instead to settle for a haughty smile. Like I was having the time of my life. And I cut grass with a knife all the time. Back in Washington D.C. *Where people were civilized.* I muttered under my breath as I took another swing.

This time I swung too high. The knife slid along the grass with lightning speed unimpeded, and almost came to rest on the side of my leg.

"Damnit!" Because I had nearly sliced through my own leg, I was even madder. I took a deep breath and braced myself for another attempt. But a voice from behind me stopped the swing.

"Hey, hey! You're going to hurt yourself there. Why don't you let me show you how to do it?"

Daniel stood beside me, with a slight frown.

"I said I didn't need any help and I meant it. Thank you but I'm fine." Exquisite politeness.

"No come on, at least allow me to show you how to hold the blade properly? Just a little help before you chop your leg off. Or somebody else's."

A wide gesture to the boys alongside me.They hooted at that. The Mafia gangster straightened from his cutting to speak. Loud and authoritative.

"Don't be such a knowitall, girl. He's right. You don't know what you're doing. Listen to him."

I was outnumbered. And in danger of hurting myself. I held the knife out to Daniel.

"Alright, fine. Go ahead. Show me."

His fingers brushed mine as he took the blade, sending a chill through me. I moved several steps away in case he noticed.

"Right. The important thing to remember with the machete is a firm grip and a relaxed stance. Bend at the knees and lean forward a little. Then let your arm swing loosely. You want to just start off lightly until you learn to gauge the proper distance. Too far down and you'll hit the ground. Too far up and you won't cut any grass."

He leaned to expertly cut the still-untouched section of grass with several easy strokes. Even with his shirt on, I could clearly make out the tense and release of his muscled arms as he hacked at the grass with graceful ease.

I swallowed and tried to find something else to look at. The birds in the tree maybe?

"Leila!" his tone was irritated. "You're supposed to be watching so you can figure out how to do this, now come here. Your turn. You try."

I was tensed with shyness. All four males were watching. Waiting to see what I could do next to make their afternoon interesting.

They would probably love it if I cut myself, I thought darkly, *give them something to talk about tomorrow*. I gritted my teeth and tried to copy the stance Daniel had shown me. I leant forward to take my first swing but again his command stopped me.

"Wait – not like that, like this."

He moved closer to my right side, angling his body to stand beside me, so our arms were in alignment. I tried to ignore his nearness. But it was difficult. I could feel the heat of his arm, the brush of his shoulder against mine. His voice spoke too close to my ear for my liking. I caught a flush of his breath on my cheek as he spoke.

"Bend your knees slightly, lean forward a bit, and let your body follow the swing of the blade. It's not meant to be full force every time, every swing, you'll tire yourself out too fast that way."

His hand was on mine as he swung our arms gently in an arc, mimicking a cutting swing. I could smell his nearness; green grass, sweat and sunshine. It was sending my heat levels spiraling dangerously high. So, of course, the threat made me brusque and rude. Well, more than usual.

"I got it, I got it!" I stepped away from him, but carefully tried to follow his instructions. Painfully aware of his scrutiny beside me, it was a relief when he nodded approvingly after several tries.

"Hey, that's good Leila, I think you've got it. Just pace yourself and remember to focus so you don't hurt yourself."

I wanted to poke my tongue at him or toss him a well chosen curse word, but I thought I better not stop concentrating on the grass. The rest of the half hour passed swiftly in a rhythmic swaying and scything. Dimly I was aware of Daniel, taking off his shirt and joining us in the line along the tennis court perimeter with a knife, making our group five.

I hated to lose my rhythm so I fought the desire to sneak a glimpse of his half nakedness. Instead I gave myself up to the pleasurable burn of exertion, my whole body at work, cutting long green grass on a golden afternoon.

It was a shock when Daniel called for everyone to stop their work. Time already? I halted mid swing with the others and straightened my back with a groan.

Ugh, I knew I would really be feeling it tonight. My back muscles were protesting as I shook my shoulders to loosen them, walking back to the shade where I had left my bag.

Daniel was dismissing us all. Again I envied the boys their freedom as the slight breeze danced over their bare skin and they threw water over themselves at the gushing tap.

I felt like a sweat-stained oil rag and knew I looked it too. I wanted nothing more than to get the heck out of there and home to a cold shower. Daniel's voice beside me, startled my thoughts of Aunty Matile's freshly made sweet lemonade pouring over chinking ice.

"So I bet you're glad that's over." He stood too close to me. Still only in black Nike shorts, a shirt slung over one shoulder.

There were beads of sweat on his arm, the curve of his hip tensed as he bent to pick up his schoolbag. When he shook his head slightly, a faint scatter of water came my way.

"Oops sorry!"

His smile was too genuine, too open to go unanswered.

There was a smile in my voice as I replied, "That's alright, thanks. For your help today. I probably owe you my still-intact leg."

He laughed. It was a warm, rich sound. "Actually all the boys are relieved they still have their legs to walk home on too, they were a bit worried when you started swinging that thing around."

Beside him, the hulking senior heard him and agreed. "Ay Daniel, I thought this girl was going to cut us all in pieces. Should never let a girl loose with a bush knife ay?"

They both broke into laughter. Which had me on auto attack immediately. I hated being laughed at. And I hated walking beside these boys when I was a smelly, disheveled mess. Especially not beside Daniel's perfection. I tensed and shut my face down with a frown.

"I don't know why you thought I wouldn't be able to handle it. I may not have ever used a machete before but there's no reason why I couldn't figure out if given the opportunity. There's no reason to be such sexist jerks."

The words came out colder than I'd planned, but they were already knifing through the afternoon before I could reclaim them.

The senior whistled long and low. "*Sole* man Daniel, I don't think this girl likes our jokes?"

I had quickened my pace to get away from them and Daniel had to place a hand on my arm to get me to look at him. My scowl was armed and ready, where he only looked exasperated.

"What is with you Leila? We're just kidding, don't you ever relax and just chill? I mean, first I'm a racist pig and now I'm a sexist jerk? Can't you ever stop expecting the worst of people? You don't even know me!"

His eyes were jade stones of accusation, his face stormy.

I shook off his hand, jutting my chin defiantly as I replied. "No. I don't know you. And you can be sure that I have no desire to. Now, if you'll excuse me, I have to get home."

I turned and strode away, rigid with anger as I headed down to the bus stop. *Ha. Boys. Even beautiful ones, who needed them?*

I missed my old school. At least I knew where I stood with girls. At least my annoyance with them didn't war with an unwilling attraction to the glory of perfectly defined arms and a crooked smile.

At home, a cold shower didn't do much to cool the heat of my afternoon grass-cutting session. With a sinking feeling, I realized I would need to visit the pool tonight if I wanted to pre-empt a heat attack. All through dinner with Matile and Tuala, I could feel the heat gathering, making it difficult to breathe in a kitchen drowning in the sweetness of Matile's pineapple coconut pie. As soon as it was polite enough, I excused myself to go to my room. Another shower would be required before bed for sure.

I worked on homework while I waited for the sounds of evening to subside. Matile and Tuala were watching television and it seemed an eternity before they finally went to bed. By then I was breathing in huge gasps, the steam rising like a pressure cooker in my chest as I fought the waves of hot panic.

Stay calm Leila, just breathe, you're going to be alright, it's okay. Stay calm, breathe, come on take deep breaths.

It was midnight when I slipped from the house, armed with a greasy mutton bone from dinner for Terminator. He was a wriggling bundle of glee at my gift and I whispered my pleas for quiet as I climbed over the back fence and ran lightly through the forest. I knew the path so well now that I could have found my way there blindfolded.

It was a relief when I broke from the trees and into the clearing. Quickly, I stripped down to the basics, leaving my clothes hanging on a branch with my towel and walked into the water, accepting its wet embrace with pleasure. For a short while at least, I would keep the heat at bay.

It was always a surprise how quickly the water worked on me. A few minutes submerged, floating in the murky night, and I would be me again. Leila. Not the girl who felt like she tiptoed on the edges of an incendiary explosion all the time. Just Leila. Just me.

There was calm solitude in the pool. There was reflection. Here, there was safety. Sometimes, there would be tears as I sat in the pool and cried for my dad. Awash in the midnight, I would talk to the stars overhead. I liked to think that somewhere, somehow, my dad was listening.

Tonight was different. Tonight, my thoughts were filled with green eyes and skin that glistened with sweat, a tattooed arm, the laughter of a boy who towered over me in annoying splendor. I wondered what my

Dad would say if I told him about the Chunk Hunk and how he alternately irritated and fascinated me.

"Leila, you're too hard on people, too quick to condemn them. You need to give people a chance, try to understand where they're coming from," was his advice after a particularly excruciating visit with Grandmother Folger.

"But Dad, she's so rude to you. And to me. I don't know why she even bothers inviting us over for dinner when all she does is tell us how horribly inadequate we are."

His laugh, the way he would yank at my thick braid and toss an arm around my shoulders. "Leila, how could we possibly be inadequate? Look at us, who could find a more perfect pair? You – the friendliest, cheeriest, perkiest cheerleader I know – and me – the dream dad who's never home, who in a year earns, oh, probably as much my brothers do in a week? We're perfect, what could your Grandmother Folger possibly have to complain about with us?!"

I stood in the pool and walked carefully over the rocks, deeper towards the splashing waterfall. I was so caught up in my thoughts that I did not hear the stranger come into the clearing.

"What are you doing here!?" the voice was harsh, stridently breaking into my peaceful reverie. Startled, I missed my footing on the smooth rocks below and slipped backwards, my head going underwater. Spluttering with a mouth and nose full of water, I surfaced with a choking gasp, terrified by my momentary blindness.

"Who is it? Who's there? Get away from me!" the last was a shriek as I felt a hand grab my arm.

"Get off of me! I said get off! I know kung fu, I mean karate. And I have a weapon. I do. Get away!"

My threats were interrupted as, in an attempt to push the hand away, I again slipped and went under. Strong hands reached under my shoulders and heaved me up, dragging me kicking and splashing to the poolside. A coughing tangled mess, I pushed myself over to confront my attacker head on. Only to be brought up short by the sounds of someone laughing.

"So which is it? Karate or kung fu? Either way, I'm reeeeeeally scared." The familiar voice had a rich deep timbre and his laugh rang out through the forest night.

Wiping the clods of sodden hair out of my eyes, I looked up with my angriest expression. The one my father called the "*I'm gonna eat u alive and spit out the pieces and make u wish u had never been born*" face. Apparently, I had mastered it from the tender age of three. I turned it on full blast and looked straight at Daniel.

He towered over me, amusement crinkling his eyes, a half smile on his face as he surveyed my disheveled state. He wore only a ripped pair of shorts that sat precariously low on his hips. Moonlight played on the tattoo snaking its way over his left shoulder as he put his hands on his hips and shook his head.

"And so this weapon of yours? Just where exactly would you be concealing that?" His eyes speculatively surveyed the length of my wet body clothed only in its skimpy black Bendon underwear and bra top.

Furious and horribly self-conscious, I grabbed my towel from the rocks and hastily covered myself before turning to confront this arrogant idiot with the full measure of my rage.

"What the hell do you think you're doing? Creeping around in the dark, sneaking up on people like that and then scaring them?! And how dare you put your hands on me. You – you – horrible creep!"

His smile was quickly replaced with a cold hard look as he folded his arms, his entire body tensed at my tirade. "Excuse me? Oh I get it, we're going for a three count – racist, sexist and now I'm a potential rapist. Great. Is there nothing you won't accuse me of? Leila, last time I checked, this pool didn't belong to you. I have every right to come swimming here. And when a clumsy female falls over in the water and looks like she's drowning in only two feet of water – it's considered gentlemanly behavior to pull her out. In fact, most girls would then say, *thank you* for helping them." His voice was low but full of venom as he spoke, slowly emphasizing each word.

I withered slightly at his response. "Oh." I scrambled for defense. "Well, you shouldn't have scared me like that. That wasn't nice. I mean, it's the middle of the night out here in the middle of nowhere for goodness sake so of course I was gonna think you were attacking me … or something."

He arched one eyebrow questioningly. "I don't know what you were thinking being out here alone anyway. Are you crazy? Yes, this is Samoa and we don't have the same amount of psycho killers running around like you do back in the States but still, it's just stupid for a girl to be out swimming in her underwear by herself. What were you thinking?" His tone was derisive.

From outraged offensive, I found myself struggling in defensive mode. "I know, I mean – I didn't think anybody would be out here so late. And I've come here a few times now and never seen anyone. And I didn't think I was trespassing, so I didn't know it would cause any trouble, and back home you wouldn't catch me out by myself in a forest in a million years, but this place is different and it's just so hot and I can't sleep and nobody cares what happens to me anyways, oh why am I telling you anything?!"

I came to an abrupt halt as tears pricked my eyes and threatened to spill over in my voice. I felt an awful hollowness in my chest as I realized the truth of my words. Nobody did care. I could get abducted by aliens, hacked to pieces by an axe murderer and my aunt and uncle would probably be relieved to be rid of my pestering presence. My grandmother would pay for the funeral, and shower my grave with lots of ridiculous flowers. But tears and actual loss? I doubted it. And there was definitely something wrong with me and it was getting worse every day and I didn't know how much longer I could handle it by myself. I was sick. Frightened. And tired. In that moment, a wave of self-pity threatened to drown me. I turned my back on him and took a deep breath to steady myself, steeling for further attack.

There was a heavy pause, then his words in the dusty velvet night surprised me. "Hey, look, I'm sorry, okay? I come here a lot and I was kinda surprised to find anybody else here. And I didn't mean to scare you." His voice was gentle and soothing like someone trying to hush a skittery colt.

I hated myself for falling apart in front of him. Willing myself to be calm, I shifted into my artificial cheerfulness. Turning to face him again, I smiled brightly and waved a hand casually.

"Oh, don't even worry about it. I over-reacted. It happens. Look, I'll get out of your way. Thanks for your help in the water. Have a nice swim." I grabbed my clothes from the ground and started backing away, ignoring his confused expression. *Just smile Leila,* I thought to myself. *Just smile. Go home and cry like a baby there where nobody can see you. Just keep it together a few minutes longer.*

My plan would have worked too. If I hadn't tripped over a clump of ferns behind me, falling down hard on my overly bright and cheerful backside.

"Owwww!" Once again my outraged shriek pierced the night. Sitting in a bruised cluster of bushes, my feet covered in mud, wet hair plastered to sticky sweaty skin, I (not for the first time) cursed my stupidity at coming to this island. I was painfully homesick. Which didn't make sense because I didn't have a home. I didn't belong here. But then, I didn't belong in D.C either. I was a half-caste disappointment to my grandmother. A disturbing reminder to my aunt of a woman it seemed everyone would rather forget. *Face it Leila – you're an in-between nothing and nobody wants you around.* Head down on my knees, I gave in to the crushing sobs within. I didn't care if this stupid boy laughed at me, yelled at me. Or even if he ran a mile. I cried the bone-shattering kind of cry that shook to the very core.

"Hey, it's okay. You're gonna be okay." Daniel knelt beside me and then after a hesitant moment, huge arms swept me up out of the mud, carrying me the few steps back to the pool. Too upset to stop, even with the shock of being carried, I just kept sobbing and hiccupping, dimly aware of being gently set down on a smooth rock and of him sitting beside me.

Side by side, shoulders touching, we sat by the glistening waters as I cried. Several months worth of anguish rocked my body as I sat hugging my knees. He didn't try to make me stop or even try to talk me out of it. He just sat there beside me and let me cry. I don't know how long the storm of emotion ravaged me, but it felt like hours. Finally, the tears slowed and the sobs receded. Wordlessly, he handed me something to wipe my tear ravaged face. It was my dirty t-shirt. I looked at him questioningly.

He gestured to his ripped shorts with a wry smile. "Sorry, I didn't come equipped to comfort a damsel in distress."

In that moment, with eyes swollen beyond belief, scratched muddy legs and arms, and with a sodden towel draped around my thin frame – I had never felt closer to another human being. Well, at least not since my Dad had died. The night sky stretched overhead, swallowing us in its velvet vastness; the forest breathed us in.The tension within slowly seeped away, replaced by a liquid calmness. Looking into smiling eyes, I felt for the first time in a long time – at peace. Home.

The moment seemed to last an eternity as we gazed at each other. His smile faded, replaced with a look of quiet regard. His eyes studied me intently, as if trying to stare into my soul. If it had been anywhere else, any other time, I would have flushed red with embarrassment and looked away. But out here, with the rainforest breathing all around us, it seemed perfectly normal to sit and stare into a strange boy's eyes, feeling the warmth of his tattooed shoulder next to my skin.

As the moment stretched, I became acutely aware of his breathing. The rise and fall of his perfectly contoured chest. The rip of his muscled arms looped casually around his knees. The curve of his hip resting comfortably beside my own.

My calmness faded, replaced with something else. A rising flush of heat that started deep within. A rise that boiled and surged, threatening to overwhelm my calm exterior. I had an insane urge to reach out with trembling fingers and trace the pattern of his tattoo, wanting to feel for myself the patterned cut in his skin.

How badly had it hurt, I wondered? Had there been much blood? Why had he done it? At the thought of his pain, I felt a twinge. Bemused, I realized why – *it hurt to think of him hurting.* This stranger. This painfully handsome boy, striding strong through the school with confidence and yet, sitting here beside me trying to give me comfort. As if sensing the shift in my thoughts, he smiled. This time, it sent a jolt of pure electricity through me.

The smile crinkled his green eyes and revealed a dimple in his left cheek. He reached tentatively, as if unwilling to break the moment, and gently brushed a strand of wet hair away from my eyes.

His fingers were surprisingly cool on my hot face. I had to bite my lip to stop an answering smile from overwhelming me – trying to downplay the swirling heat of emotions. I was terrified he would sense I was struggling with a serious attack of physical attraction to him. His earlier words echoed in my mind.

Of course, that's how he thought of me. I was a 'stupid' girl who did weird things like go swimming in my underwear by myself in the middle of the night, scream at people who surprised me and then cry all over them at the drop of a hat. I was mortified by my weakness.

I took a deep breath and smiled weakly, breaking our locked gaze to look at the forest around us.

"Boy, you must think I'm such an idiot, crying like that. Whew, I'm sorry."

"Sorry for what?" his eyes were puzzled.

"I didn't mean to fall apart like that. Thanks for being so cool about it."

He shrugged his shoulders, moonlight dancing on his bicep muscles as he reached toward me again, this time to casually brush an ant off my leg. This time his touch burned and I had to struggle for control so as not to gasp at his closeness.

"Hey, don't worry about it. I've been there. Why do you think this is one of my favorite places to come to?" This time, he didn't meet my gaze, staring instead into the depths of the pool.

I was curious. I sneaked a look at his chiseled profile and tried to envision him coming to this pool to be alone. To seek solace. To cry? What could do that to him? I had been wrapped up for so long in my own pain, that it had not occurred to me that possibly others could experience such despair. For a brief instant, out of nowhere, an image of my grandmother flashed into my mind. Ramrod straight and still at the graveside, silent tears streaming down her lined cheeks. Her shocked face at my announcement that I was leaving for Samoa.

"I'm your grandmother's biggest disappointment Leila, not you." My dad would say cheerfully, every time we psyched ourselves to go for our ritual weekly visit to her Potomac mansion, and I would complain about grandmother's endless criticisms. The way I dressed, my grades, my vocabulary, my untamable hair – and my lack of interest in doing anything to tame it.

How I hated those visits. The stilted conversations. The unsmiling welcomes and farewells. But always, Dad would joke and laugh. And tease a smile from somewhere out of the old lady. He would regale her with tales of his latest travels, deliberately excluding all the dangerous and grimy bits of his job that she loathed.

And grandmother would shake her head. And purse her lips. But her eyes would soften at his touch. And surely that would be the hint of tenderness when she hugged him? Dad was the youngest in a family of corporate lawyers, company directors and a brain surgeon thrown in for good measure.

Born in the autumn of his parents' years and then raised by his mother when his father died of a heart attack shortly after. The golden favorite last child who then decided to go against the Folger grain – refusing to join the family business when he finished at Harvard Law, choosing instead to join the Peace Corps, and then adding insult to injury, bringing home a brown baby for a grandchild.

Upon his return to the States with me, my dad had pursued a career that combined his love of photography with his passion for travel and exploring native cultures. He had taken me with him to many of his destinations when I was younger, but then once I reached high school, Grandmother Folger had convinced him of the need for me to 'be more settled,' to focus on school so I could get into a college befitting of a Folger. Meaning I had to endure long periods without him. With a housekeeper and a coldly formal grandmother watching over me. Dad, I miss you.

The chitter of a flying fox brought me back to the present. Daniel was staring at me with that same intense regard as if trying to pierce my thoughts. "Where were you just now?"

"Nowhere. I mean here. Right here. With you." My words faded to a soft breath as once again he turned the full majesty of that amazing smile on me.

"You were not. You were a thousand miles away. Come on, you can't possibly think of keeping any secrets from me *now.*" He gestured at the two of us in our muddy state of companionship.

I felt a laugh ripple forth against my will. "Okay, you're right. I mean, what could the girl who has weapons galore concealed in her underwear possibly have to hide from you?" I joked.

His laugh rang out through the forest night. It was a rich golden sound, resonant of sunny, sandy days. It felt glorious to laugh together. Almost as good as staring into his eyes.

"You're right, I don't know if I'm brave enough to find out!" he teased, eyes dancing with laughter.

My only reply was to poke my tongue out mischievously, wrinkling my nose – a favorite tactic when being teased by Dad. Abruptly, my laughter halted at the reminder. It stunned me to realize that this was the first time in months that I had laughed together like this with another person. And that the last time I had poked out my tongue like this had been at my dad. Oh, how I had missed it. He was so in tune with me now that he pounced on my shift of mood.

"See *there*. You're doing it again. You're miles away. Something sad has got you wrapped up so tight it won't let you go!" his tone was triumphant as he leaned forward in his eagerness. He smelled delicious. Earthy, clean, with a hint of coconut and pineapple. "What is it?" He wouldn't take no for an answer this time.

"Alright. I was thinking of my dad. He died. Eight months ago. He was on assignment in Afghanistan. He had a headache and collapsed. They rushed him home but it was no use. Doctors said he had a brain tumor. Inoperable. He only regained consciousness once before. Before…" I took a deep breath, willing myself to say the words without hurting. "Before he died." The last words were a rush as I waited for the pain to hit with that gut-kicking blow that would knock the breath out of me. It came. But funnily enough, with Daniel sitting beside me in the night, it didn't hit as hard as usual. I didn't realize how tightly my fists were clenched though, how taut my body had gone, until he placed an arm around my shoulders again and almost automatically, I felt myself wilting into him.

"Hey. I'm here. Breathe. There you go. Just breathe." He was calm and assured. His eyes were soft with concern. I could see an errant eyelash quivering on his cheek as I breathed deeply. His closeness was so distracting that I dropped my eyes from his, only to be confronted by the sight of his lean hard chest tapering into clearly defined abs.

Oops. Definitely not helpful. I gulped, shutting my eyes to avert the flood of fire that threatened again to overwhelm me. *What the heck is wrong with me? One minute I'm crying – the next I'm hyperventilating over this boy's naked chest!?* I bit my lip to stifle the hysterical giggle that was bubbling to explode. Mistaking my silence for sorrow, he placed a hand under my chin, raising my face to his.

I could scarcely breathe. Our faces were so close, I could almost taste his breath. There was nothing but concern in his eyes.

"Are you ok? I'm sorry I made you talk about it. I didn't mean to upset you."

Mutely, I shook my head. "I'm okay. It's okay. I haven't talked about it to anyone. It's hard. But I want to talk about him as well too – even though it hurts so bad, you know what I mean?"

"Yes. I do." The confidence in his voice threw me. It was my turn to be puzzled.

"My mother died when I was very young. I never knew her really, so it's different for me. Talking to family about her makes her come alive for me somehow but still it's tough because it reminds me how much I miss having her."

I felt a surge of relief at his words. "Exactly. Nobody loved my dad the way I do, nobody loved me the way he did, so I feel so alone in the way I miss him. I wrap it all up inside – and it's like choking me, killing me. Tonight, crying like that, it felt awful, but really a relief at the same time." I halted, afraid that once again I had revealed too much.

"How about your mom? Can't you talk to her about it?"

"My mother died when I was a baby. I never knew her. That's one reason I came to Samoa. So I could get to know her family and maybe know her. Some stupid idea that's turned out to be." My tone was harsher than I had planned as I thought bitterly about my aunt's welcome reception at the airport several weeks ago.

He swatted away a buzzing mosquito before replying."So Samoa isn't exactly turning out to be what you planned. And your family here? Who are they?"

I smiled. Only on an island with a population less than two hundred thousand people would someone ask such a question and have every intention of knowing who the heck I was talking about when I answered."My aunty Matile and uncle Tuala – they're the Sinapati family. We live just round the corner from the stadium, Apia Park."

He nodded, confirming suspicions. "So, do you have tons of random cousins living with you? Our extended family living must be kind of a shock for a spoilt only child like you." His teasing grin softened his jibe.

"Hey watch it, I can still take you on you know. Spoilt only children are infamous for their tempers. Actually, they don't have any children of their own and nobody stays with them but me. There's always cousins coming over though from next door, round about meal time. Aunty Matile is a major grouch but she's an amazing cook. Especially when you're used to living on fast food. Me and Dad, we weren't much for cooking. But we had the Chinese takeout number on speed dial."

This time he laughed with me, the sound quickening my heartbeat, giving my pulse a hop, skip, and jump. Did this boy even know how gorgeous he was when he laughed?

"Glad to hear that at least the food is to your liking. And how are you finding SamCo?"

I wrinkled my nose as I tried to sum up the contradictory experiences of the first month at Samoa College. "It's okay. I thought I would hate it but it hasn't been too bad. I went to a girls' school back home and so having boys around has been an adjustment. I can honestly say though that this school has been the least painful to be the new kid in. Teenagers here are so respectful compared with back home. Everyone is polite and listens to the teachers – it's a little freaky – but it does make life a bit easier when you're new midyear." I shuddered, remembering some of my long-ago horrible first weeks at Washington Girls. "It's nice not to be the only Samoan in a school. Back home, I got a lot of crap because of my mixed parentage." I paused and took a huge breath before continuing. "Which is why I was a little sensitive about the whole 'pure' Samoan thing in the debate and maybe kind of overreacted to your comments a little bit." I said the last part cautiously and he smiled in return.

"Why Leila, if I didn't know better, I would say that almost sounded like an apology. Damn, that fall into the pool must really have shook you up because I *never* thought the most hostile girl in school would ever say anything remotely nice to me. Maybe I should throw you back in – when I pull you out again I might even get an apology for the sexist attack in detention today."

I grinned ruefully. "Okay, okay, you got me. I was a little rough on you that first day in English. "

He interrupted incredulously. "You think?! And today? How about today? Come on, don't stop now. Let's keep this confession ball rolling. You were unnecessarily mean to me today, especially considering I was only trying to be helpful. Admit it, I was right, you had never used a bush knife before. Come on, say it!"

Shaking my head and laughing at his eagerness to catch me out, I conceded. "Alright, so you were right. I had never used a machete before, but that didn't give you know-it-all boys the right to laugh at me, or to assume that I couldn't learn to use one."

"The only reason we were laughing at you, silly girl, is because you were so stubborn trying to fake that you knew what you were doing when you had no clue and then to take that stubbornness to the point where you were willing to risk chopping your own leg off just to prove your point, argh! Leila, you're lucky I took pity on your beautiful legs and stepped in to give you a grass-cutting lesson, *in spite* of your meanness."

His reference to my legs had me tucking them in further underneath my wet towel but he seemed oblivious to my self-consciousness.

"But I'm willing to forgive you, as long as you promise never to pick up a bush knife in my vicinity again. Oh, and the next interclass debate we have, I want to be on your team. There's no way I want to face you on the debate battlefield again."

Again, we laughed together in the forest night and I had to shake my head at the ridiculousness of it all. Here I was sitting in the mud in the dead of night with the Head Boy, Chunk Hunk from school, wearing nothing but my underwear. And a wet towel, I amended. Yup. Definitely heart attack material for my grandmother if she could see me now. I smiled to myself and was rewarded by an answering grin.

"I like that." He said quietly.

"What?"

"When you smile." His face was serious now.

His words set my pulse racing again. Suddenly, the humidity seemed overpowering, the air so thick that I couldn't find enough air to fill my lungs. I looked away, tugging my towel closer and sitting up a bit straighter.

"I haven't had a lot to smile about lately, so I'm a little rusty."

As if sensing my need to create space between us, he stood and walked a few steps into the water to bend and wash water onto his forearms before turning to throw me another dazzling smile.

"So, Samoa isn't exactly making you feel the love?"

"Oh it's alright. I've dreamed about coming here for years and the reality is a little different from the fantasy you know?"

"What are you finding the hardest to deal with?"

"Where shall I start? My family here isn't exactly thrilled to have me. Then, there's definitely the heat. I thought I could handle it, but lately, I don't know, I feel like I'm constantly running a fever or something." I shook my head thinking again of the panicked heat attack that had driven me to this pool in the first place.

"That would explain the midnight swim then?"

"Yeah I come here every night now, once I'm sure the house is asleep." I sat bolt upright as I realized that I had to have been gone for well over several hours now.

Standing hurriedly, I gathered up my shoes and clothing. "Ohmigosh, I better get back. My aunt will *really* deport me if she finds out I'm roaming around in the bushes like this and having a rugby chunkh – I mean, a boy in the area won't help." I stumbled over the words as my first inclination had been to call him what I'd been calling him ever since the first day I'd seen him at school.

He didn't seem to notice my slip up. Rather he had a speculative look on his face as he stood in the pool, water midway up his thighs. "So, I guess I'll see you at school then, Leila." He smiled one more time, before turning to dive into the water, the diamond splash leaving me feeling a little deflated.

That was it? I watched him lazily stroke his way towards the falls and then I turned away to stumble through the forest back to the house. My excitement faded, replaced by a hollow disappointment. *We talk, we share stuff. What was that anyway? I cry all over him. He comforts me. We seem to connect and then a casual goodbye?*

Shaking my head, I crept into the bedroom, thankful that Aunty was a deep sleeper. I was sure I wouldn't be able to sleep after the night's events, but once changed into dry clothes, I was out as soon as my head touched the pillow.

And thankfully, it was a sleep unplagued by strange dreams.

The familiar rooster woke me early the next morning. Thinking back to the night before, it still seemed so surreal,especially in the light of day. I was distracted as I dressed for school. I took far more care with my appearance than normal but then how much care can one take with a school uniform after all? The strict rules about makeup and jewelry left me experimenting with 101 different ways to tie back my difficult-to-manage hair.

I kept mulling over my conversation with Daniel. There was no denying it, he had surprised me. I had written him off as a brainless jock. Arrogant and brazen in his demi-godness but last night? He had been kind. In my limited experience, most boys would have run a mile at the sight of a girl falling apart in a tears-fest. But he had kept me company through it. He had been sensitive. (I almost cringed using that word to describe him – it was so at odds with his seeming abundance of testosterone.) And then after, when we had stared at each other like that. Had he felt it? That electricity? That same breathlessness? Somehow I doubted it.

I didn't know many boys but I was pretty sure that ones who looked like he did never had trouble with feeling overwhelmed in the presence of a girl. But at least, he didn't seem to be repulsed by me and my far from perfectly made-up state last night. I held onto the memory of him telling me he liked my smile. I was aching to find out what he would do when we saw each other at school. It wasn't the largest campus so it would be unavoidable.

And we did have Geography class together. I was nervous. What would he say? What would I say? A sick pit opened in my stomach as I wondered, what if last night was just an unusual diversion from his usual? What if he wasn't really like that at all? What if he was only talking to me because he had felt sorry for my pitiful state?

What if … the pit yawned wider into a gaping chasm- he made fun of me today? Regaled the entire First XV rugby team about my breakdown? My awkward body in all its semi-nakedness? What if everyone at Samoa College already knew what a joke Daniel thought I was?

The bus lurched to a halt at the school gates. I was frozen in my seat. What had I been thinking last night? Opening myself up to a total stranger like that? I had been stupid. So stupid. There was no other explanation. I steeled myself within and stood up. I knew with dead certainty that this day would not go well. But I had endured worse. If I could take on the finest teenage crap that Washington D.C. had to offer, then I could surely take on what I was sure was waiting for me. Head held high, face set in stone, I got off the bus and walked straight and tall up the long driveway.

Sinalei called out my name, "Leila hey! Wait up."

She ran over to me, breathless and smiling. "Hey. You walk so fast! What's the rush? Bell won't go for ages. Did you do the Math homework? I hope Mr. Michaels doesn't want to check it today, because I didn't finish. The last two problems were crazy hard. " Her voice chattered on and on.

I relaxed a little with relief. This one person at least wasn't waiting to discuss my Daniel episode last night. Together we walked the rest of the way to the school block, Algebra being the only topic of conversation. That is, until we came in sight of the rugby field. Sinalei broke off mid equation to heave a long sigh. "Ohhh boy. Don't you just loooove the way Daniel dresses for training - or rather, undresses!" she hid a giggle behind her hand.

I didn't want to look. I wasn't sure what to expect. But against my will, I turned.

The team had training every morning at 6:30am, before the day heated up. Right now they were doing lineout drills. They had their backs to us but it was easy to see which bronze body was Daniel's. He stood at the sideline, holding the ball high above his head with the others lined in front of him. Once again, he wore nothing but a ragged pair of drawstring shorts, hanging low on his hips.

 The sun glanced off the gleaming dips and hollows of his muscled back, the swell of his shoulders as he tensed and threw the ball. His target missed the throw, players scrambling everywhere after the ball. Shaking his head ruefully at their clumsiness, Daniel turned away from the field for a moment, in time to catch sight of us … looking at him.

I froze. This was not what I had planned. I didn't want him to know I was obsessed with looking at him for goodness sake! I was furious with Sinalei but before I could turn angrily and stalk away, Daniel threw us a huge grin. And waved. Before turning to chase after the team and the errant ball.

Sinalei squealed, "Did you see that? He waved at me! Oh, he is sooo hot."

I mumbled something about needing to get to class and took off, Sinalei having to skip to make up the distance covered by my much longer legs. I didn't want to hear her rave about Daniel. The last thing I wanted was to hear someone else obsess about his perfect body.

I was doing enough of that lately in my mind already. I didn't want her to see my flushed face and suspect that he was anything more to me than morning eye candy. She must have sensed my lack of interest in pursuing a conversation about Daniel because she cheerfully changed the topic somewhat.

"So, Leila tell me, what are the boys like back home? Huh? Did you leave a boyfriend behind?"

I rolled my eyes at her in answer, trying unsuccessfully to hide my look of disgust.

"No." my tone was short. "Remember I told you I went to an all girls school, Sinalei. The only boys I ever came across were the jock heads from the brother school across the road when we had combined sports activities."

"So you *didn't* have a boyfriend then?" her dogged persistence had me suspicious.

"No. Why?" I almost glared at her. She looked taken aback at my hostility.

"Just asking. We watch a lot of movies about dating in America. You know – stuff like going out on real dates … and those wild parties where everyone seems to be taking their clothes off … all the proms and balls." Her eyes took on a starry look. "We don't have those here. And forget about going on dates. No Samoan father's gonna let his daughter out of the house with a boy alone like that!" The mere thought of it had her pealing with laughter.

I smiled back, relenting my earlier hostility. I needed to ease up. I was so used to being on the defensive, to being the butt of jokes and rumors that I was out of practice just having a regular girl conversation.

"Oh, you shouldn't believe everything you watch." Waving one hand airily. "Sure, there are some wild parties – but not everyone goes to them. And as for the whole dating thing. It's highly overrated." I didn't want to admit that I had never been on a date in my life. Far better to let her think I was a world-weary seasoned professional at the dating scene.

My step lightened as we made our way into Math class, Sinalei taking the seat next to me as the bell rang for first period. I was thankful the US Math curriculum was light years ahead of Samoa's as I hadn't even glanced at my homework the night before. It wasn't a problem, however, to skim the questions and be prepared with an answer when

Mr. Miachels called on me. He was a constantly sweating man who breathed with great exertion as he mopped his brow with a dirty rag every so often. He hated it when anyone asked a question, so there was never any discussion in his class. Math period would consist of him telling you what pages of the textbook to read, what problems to solve and then dead silence while he walked around the room holding a long stick to monitor our progress. A fly buzzed loudly in the corner while we made our way through a page of Algebraic functions. I sent Sinalei a sympathetic look as she struggled with the problems that only took me a few minutes. I made a mental note to offer to help her after class. The new re-invented me was nice to people.

There was a collective groan of relief as the bell rang for next period. I gathered my books slowly, dragging my feet, unwilling to face what lay ahead. I had Geography class next. With Daniel.

I whispered his name in my thoughts, dreading being in the same room with him, unsure as I was about his take on the previous night. So he had smiled and waved this morning. Big deal. He was probably exulting in the juicy gossip he had to share with his teammates, several of whom would also be in Geography. I wished I could cut class. But, unlike back in the USA, there was nowhere here to cut class *to.* This school had no shopping mall nearby. No maze of busy streets to get lost in. Just tennis courts and rugby fields. And I really didn't want a repeat of yesterday's hard labor punishment. Nope. There would be no escape for me today.

I said goodbye to Sinalei, who had Chemistry next, and made my way to Mrs. Jasmine's class. She hated it when students were late so I quickened my footsteps. Last thing I wanted was for her to pick on me today of all days. I was sure I would have enough mocking eyes on me already. My tension grew as I walked to the door, steeling myself so determinedly for whatever lay ahead that, by the time I entered the classroom, I was raging mad. From many years of experience, I knew the best defense was often offense. I strode into the room, emanating hostility into the furthest corners, a thunderous look on my face. Mrs. Jasmine looked taken aback as I pulled out a chair to sit at the front of the room.

"Alright, class, come to attention. Let's begin. Take out your notes from yesterday on the delta plains of India …aaah, Daniel, you're late."

Rather than being annoyed at the late arrival, Mrs. Jasmine's accented voice softened as she smiled at the doorway.

"Sorry Miss, I just came from a quick meeting with the Principal." I seethed as the familiar voice prickled at my back. Even the Geography teacher wasn't immune to this boy's charms?! I was so irritated I could have scratched bare fingernails on the blackboard. *Ugh.*

"Come in, come in. You haven't missed anything important. Quickly, take a seat. We are looking at yesterday's notes ... " Mrs. Jasmine beckoned him in.

"Ah, you mean the delta plains of India? A fascinating topic." There was a smile in his voice as he came and pulled up a chair at the desk right next to me. I froze. I was prepared for mockery and whispers – not for his closeness. I tensed as if for battle, staring straight ahead as Mrs. Jasmine favored him with a huge smile.

"Yes, the delta plains has always been one of my particular favorites too." Mrs. Jasmine was beaming now as she turned to the blackboard to continue with the review of yesterday's notes. I was determined not to look his way, but was distracted from my goal by his whisper.

"Hi Leila. Did you get home okay last night?" I couldn't stop the answering smile as I turned slightly to face him. It was a relief to see him wearing the full school uniform – I counted on that being less distracting for me.

He was waiting for an answer. I swallowed nervously, unsure how I would respond. What if this was a trick of some sort? A lead-up to the free-for-all mock fest that would take place later, once the team saw he really did know me? I hazarded a glance behind me where the other six rugby boys sat in a group at the back of the room. They all had blank looks on their faces as they listened to Mrs. Jasmine's technical explanation of the monsoon rains.

I turned back to face Daniel, giving him a brief, cool nod of acknowledgement before looking down to studiously peer at my notes. I would not give him any further ammunition, I promised myself. No matter how badly I wanted to talk to him.

He didn't speak to me again for the rest of the class. The period passed in a daze as I struggled to concentrate while being uncomfortably aware of his nearness. The bell rang and I stood quickly, packing my books with my head down, avoiding his very presence.

He still hadn't moved from his seat when I turned to go. Most of the class had emptied now and I wanted to be on my way in the corridor as far away from him as possible. But he stopped me.

"Are you ignoring me, Leila?" His voice held no recriminations. No mockery. Just quiet statement of fact.

I turned slowly to regard him, still seated, hunched awkwardly at a desk that seemed way too small for his frame. He cocked his head to one side and his eyes never wavered from mine. He waited for answer.

"No. I … uh … I don't want to be late for my next class." It sounded feeble – even to me.

He raised one eyebrow and looked at me quizzically. He was still waiting. I stumbled around further, wading deeper into a murky mire of duh-ness.

"Uh … ah … um … I wasn't sure if … " I cut myself short, biting my lower lip to stop the tumble of words.

"Sure if what?"

"If you … if we … if I … well, if it would be a good idea to talk to you." There I said it. Let him cut me down with that, I could handle it.

He looked mystified. He stood, swinging his backpack over his shoulder.

"Why wouldn't it be a good idea? I don't get it?"

Before I could respond, a voice cut through the room.

"Yo, Danny – coach is looking for you!" It was Maleko. "You coming?" He looked expectantly at Daniel, and then turned an appraising eye on me next to him.

Daniel sighed. He ran a hand through his hair distractedly.

"I gotta go. We have an away game today so we're leaving school early. Right after lunch. I don't suppose … " his voice trailed off as he looked at me speculatively. "I don't suppose you wanna come watch?"

My voice was a squawk. "Me? Watch a rugby game? No." I shook my head firmly. "No, I can't. I don't have a car. I wouldn't know where to go. I don't know the first thing about rugby. I have tons of homework to do. I have to go home … I …" My litany of reasons ran out as he chuckled and shook his head at me.

"Leila it's okay. You don't have to give me an entire book of excuses here. I get it. You don't want to go. I'll catch up with you later." Still shaking his head ruefully, he started walking out of the room.

I watched him go with a lump in my throat, watching the color of the day leaving me with black and white. The day stretched ahead of me, achingly plain and predictable. Class, lunch helping Sinalei with her Math while listening to her babble about boys, the bus ride home to an empty house, an evening of painful pauses and stilted conversation with my aunt. Bed. Feverish dreams and restless sleep.

"Daniel! Where's your game at?"

He turned at the doorway, a huge smile lighting the room.

"It's at Malifa compound. We're playing Leifiifi College at 2:30pm." He seemed about to say more but Maleko pulled at his bag impatiently, so he threw me a half wave instead. I watched him go with a watery smile. What was I thinking? How stupid was that idea? Of course I couldn't go to a rugby game. Just because the Head Boy suggested that I go. For what? So I could join the masses of adoring females who cheered him at every game, I thought spitefully. I was late for next period. Great. Get a move on Leila. Way to go with the reinvention. Tardy hardly fit with the new me.

I squared my shoulders to meet the rest of the day head on. It passed in a blur. I was still getting used to the new teachers, the different way subjects were taught here compared with back home. I had to hold myself back in several classes because I had already noticed that making comments and asking questions was not something that teachers liked here. They seemed to find it a personal attack if you couldn't understand a topic or if you had the audacity to question something they taught you.

Lunch was spent helping Sinalei with Math. Although I couldn't help thinking that she would understand it far quicker if she didn't spend so much time discussing everybody's business. I let most of her chatter wash over me – until a name that quickened my pulse came up.

"Hey, did you hear that Mele's going out with Maleko now? Of course she would have *preferred* to have Daniel – but he's not into that." She sighed regretfully.

"What do you mean? What's Daniel not into?" I deliberately kept my tone light.

"Oh, you know. Going out. Girls. He doesn't go out with any." She shrugged as if this was an obvious detail.

"Why not?"

"Well, Daniel's not like the others. Heaps of girls have been after him. But no deal. He just started back at school this year you know. He's actually meant to be a year ahead of us. He took the whole of last year off after his grandfather died so he could manage the family business. Now he's back, but he's not quite the same. He works – so you'll never see him apart from school and rugby games. He lives with his grandmother who's really old and it's just them two, so I think he kinda looks after her as well. He was offered two different full rugby scholarships to schools in New Zealand when he was only in fifth form, but he turned them both down because he can't leave her. Or something like that." Sinalei waved her hand dismissively, obviously unimpressed with Daniel's commitment to such 'serious' stuff.

I was intrigued. That would explain why he seemed so much older, more mature than any other teenage boy I'd ever seen. I wondered how he made the time to study *and* work a business. What kind of business was it? What did he do? What had happened to his parents? Why did he live with his grandmother? I knew his mother had died when he was young – but he hadn't mentioned anything about his father. Questions swirled through my brain. Questions that I longed to find answers for. I glanced at Sinalei eating her sandwich. I bet she could answer some of them, but I hated to alert her to my interest in Daniel. Best to leave it be. I shrugged and re-focused on the math problems at hand. Sinalei interrupted.

"So, are you coming to the game today?"

"Oh I'm not sure. I don't have a ride and I'm not sure how I'll get home after."

"Oh, that's no problem. You can ride with us in Mele's car. Her dad is the coach, so her mother always comes to the games. They have a van and we all ride with them. I'm sure she won't mind another. Where do you live?"

"Faatoia." I tried not to stumble over the unfamiliar word. I was trying my hardest to not sound like the ignorant newcomer that I was.

"Heaps of buses go that way after that game. It'll be done by 4pm, I can help you catch the right bus."

I was grateful for her friendliness. It was not something I was accustomed to where I had come from. Sinalei called out to the pretty girl she had indicated earlier.

"Hey Mele!"

Mele walked over to us – or rather she flowed languidly. She moved with a grace that I had never seen in another person before. Close up the full impact of her beauty hit. She was a stunning girl. Tall and slender – she made me feel like a stack of bricks. Sure I was tall, but next to Mele's slender frame I felt like a bulky she-hulk. She turned deep brown eyes my way and smiled politely in answer to Sinalei's introduction.

It was a smile that didn't quite reach her eyes as she looked me up and down as if appraising the newcomer to her territory. The look confirmed what I had suspected. This may be an island in the middle of the Pacific Ocean – but I had certainly met Mele's kind before. They had been blonde with ample chests overflowing out of their skin-tight cheerleader tops, but the look was the same. Mentally, I gritted my teeth.I smiled at Mele and waited while Sinalei finished asking her if I could join them on the ride to this afternoon's game.

"Sure – no problem – Leila, is it? So you're interested in rugby?"

The question was casually phrased and I was careful to be equally casual with my reply.

"Oh I've never seen a game of rugby. They didn't play that back at home. It should be a more interesting way to spend the afternoon than studying for Mr. Michaels' test."

"Tell me about it!" chimed in Sinalei.

Seemingly satisfied with my response, Mele drifted away back to her crowd of friends while Sinalei and I packed up for the next class. I felt a quickening of excitement as I thought about the upcoming afternoon. My very first rugby game. I had no idea what to expect, which added to the thrill.

FOUR

Bodies crunched with a sickening thud. There was an answering jolt in the pit of my stomach as I stood in shock and watched the game unfurl in all its bone-crunching madness. What the hell kind of game was this? Were these people insane? Spectators screamed all around me as an orange-garbed player made a break with the ball.

"Go Maleko. Run.Yes!" Beside me, the graceful Mele was jumping up and down in a frenzy as the SamCo player ran the length of the field to score a touchdown – no, that wasn't right. A try. That was it. I shook my head in disgust, wanting to cover my ears as the crowds of SamCo supporters celebrated Maleko's score.

"We're in the lead. We're gonna win this one Leila. Isn't this exciting?" Sinalei's face was flushed, her voice hoarse with screaming.

I gave her a frozen smile in answer, when really my brain was screaming a different story.

It was the last half of the game, and I had just endured an eternity of watching half-grown men inflict the most vile range of torture upon each other in their mad quest to get their hands on a ball. And take it to the try line. With no padding or any other protective gear of any kind, they ran headfirst into each other – a particularly stupid part of the game called a scrum.

Pushing and grunting to try to shove the combined weight of the other team further over into their territory. The ball would get passed along a line of waiting players until it got to the outer edges where one unlucky wretch got the chance to make a break for it. He would then dash for the score line, weaving and maneuvering his way through the opposition. More times than I could stomach it, the unfortunate runner would get tackled, taken down in a shattering rush by one or more of the others. Then everyone in the vicinity would get into the swing of things – by jumping headfirst into the pile up, again and again. Until I was sure the player on the ground must be trampled to a bloody pulp. I even saw players kicking those on the ground with their spiked shoes. Rucking, the others called it. And apparently it was tolerated by the ref, as long as they didn't go "overboard."

"Are they nuts? Look at that guy kicking the other one's head with his shoes. How can they allow that? And look at that one – I swear I just saw him punching the guy underneath him. What the hell?!" I was bewildered and asking so many indignant questions that even Sinalei was getting annoyed with me.

"I told you Leila, that's what happens in the tackles. Ohmigosh look, there goes Daniel. Yes Daniel. Woohoo!"

I shut my eyes briefly, wishing for this horrible game to end. How I wished I hadn't come. And I was furious at Daniel for asking me to. I barely knew him – but I hated watching him smash into people at full speed. I had spent the last half dreading every play, hoping that the team wouldn't pass him the ball. If nothing else, I understood now why he was so hugely built. It was a small measure of comfort though as I couldn't fathom how even his rock-hard body could handle being jumped on by eight gigantic Leififi players. Time and again, I watched him make a break for it with the ball. Even my untrained eye could see that he was one of the lead players on the field. The entire team rallied to him and moved in unison to his instructions.

He was surprisingly fast for someone so big. I held my breath as he sprinted down the field, sidestepping players with a grace that defied his size. Reaching the try line unscathed this time, he dived with the ball. The thought of the impact had me wincing. It didn't seem to affect him at all as he rolled to his feet, hands raised in the air jubilantly while the crowd went crazy.

I was so disgusted with the whole spectacle I didn't even clap. I couldn't wait to get out of here. I felt a sweeping wave of homesickness come over me. I thought of sports at home, where at least they wore helmets and gear. Where people didn't get so ... so emotional at a game. My more reserved *palagi* side was definitely coming to the fore. And I was strangely sad. At the distance between me and the rest of this crowd. Between me and Daniel even. More than ever before, I knew we were worlds apart. I didn't belong here. I shouldn't have come. My father was right.

Lost in thought, I didn't notice the final whistle had blown. The game was over. There was no doubt who had won, as everyone in orange was still hyped and high-fiving each other. Mele preened as people congratulated her on Maleko's game. Sinalei was totally pumped – in her element. I wished that Simone had come but he was playing netball at another interschool game. I wondered if maybe he would have been more understanding of my first reaction to rugby. I looked over at an excited Sinalei – she wouldn't even notice if I slipped away right now. Turning, I started making my way through the crowd towards the busy street where I was sure I would get a bus. I was startled when kids around me started pushing and shoving forward, calling out excitedly, all jostling for a better view of something happening behind me.

"Fight! Fight!" someone chanted.

Oh no. I swung around, in time to see a huddle of orange and blue uniforms. A fight had broken out between supporters from both schools. It was a tangled weave of at least twenty to thirty students, people screaming as others punched and wrestled with each other. Teachers and rugby officials were running towards the fracas, blowing whistles agitatedly. They were outnumbered though, so I didn't hold much hope for their success. I shaded my eyes with my hand and looked around anxiously for Sinalei.

"Leila! Leila! Over here." Her voice was high and thin and came to me over the crowd. She was still standing on the sidelines, far too close to the action, waving at me wildly. I ran over to her.

"What are you doing standing here? We're gonna get hurt – come on." I pulled at her hand.

"Oh Leila, I was looking for you. You disappeared." Her voice was accusing and I felt bad that I had tried to leave without even the courtesy of a farewell.

"Come on, lets go." We started half running, half walking towards the road, as far as we could get from the fight, Sinalei still talking non-stop.

"It's those Leifiifi boys, they're always causing fights. You should have seen last year, they fought with Avele and St. Joseph's College and then they kept looking for people in uniform in town and beating them up. It was awful. And then today, that one Leifiifi kid threw a Coke bottle at Daniel when he came off the field. There was blood everywhere and then Maleko jumped in and … "

I came to an abrupt halt.

"What did you say? What happened to Daniel?" My voice was tense with fear. All I could focus on was Sinalei's words resounding in my mind. *Blood everywhere … blood everywhere … blood … Daniel's blood.*

She looked at me curiously. "Didn't you see it? That's how the fight started. Someone threw a bottle at Daniel, then everyone jumped in and …" she broke off, confused, as I backed away. "Wait, where are you going?"

"I'm going to get something. I forgot something. You go on ahead. I'll catch up." I ignored her puzzled face as I turned and started sprinting back to the still-struggling crowd.

I pushed and shoved my way through the outskirts of the mainly male crowd. Most were fascinated spectators, all shouting in Samoan at the centre stage of the action. I'm sure I could identify mainly swear words. For once, I was grateful for my height and solid build as I pushed through.

"Excuse me. Excuse me. I said, excuse me, let me through." It was no mean feat to carve a path through the pack. Sweat trickled down my back as I struggled to make my way closer to the center field where I could see teachers trying to assert some control over the crowd. I thought I caught a glimpse of a familiar figure in the throng.

"Daniel! Daniel!" It was hopeless. Nobody could be heard over this madness. I pushed further forward and finally broke through to the field, where I came to an abrupt halt. Now that I had front row seats to the action, I realized how dumb I was. Punches were being thrown. Several boys were on the ground while others stood in a circle kicking them.

What was I thinking? I looked around wildly, hoping for someone familiar. There was nothing but a sea of blue uniforms … and several orange ones being stomped on. I turned to push and shove my way out of there and a boy in blue tripped over my feet, turning to swear at the source of his fall. His tirade stopped short when he saw I was a girl. In orange and yellow. Unmistakable in a crowd. He smiled. It wasn't friendly.

My heart thudded over the yelling around me. I felt the now familiar heat flush growing within me. *Oh no. Not here. Not now.* I needed to get out of there. Now. Before the day turned red with fire and I couldn't breathe with a heat attack. I took several steps backward and bumped into more blue uniforms that shoved me forward again so that I half-fell onto the smiling boy. I tried to push him away from me as the first wave of dizziness came. The world was spinning dangerously and the air in my chest was so hot that it felt like a furnace. But the boy didn't release me. Instead he leered.

"Hey beautiful, where you going?"

He had a face pitted with acne and his school shirt was torn. Frantically, I tried to shake loose. "Please, let me through, I need to get out of here, please."

My voice sounded frail even to me. I wanted to run but the heat attack was now in full swing. My vision turned hazy red. I couldn't breathe. The panic rose in tidal wave proportions within me. This heat was way worse than any I had yet experienced. My legs gave way and I wilted against the stranger as others crushed against me in the still-hyper crowd. From far away I heard the boy laugh as he grabbed hold of me.

"Hey, are you drunk?"

All around us was shouting and frenzy. The thought of passing out and then being trampled in this crazed crowd only heightened my terror and I shouted, trying to force out some of the steam trapped inside me.

"No. I'm sick. Please, let go." I whimpered. "I have to go. Please, let – me – GO!"

He was holding me in a suffocating bear hug against him and I focused on his arms, willing the vice-like grip to ease. Suddenly, the boy's eyes widened - in fear, in pain? Instantly, he dropped his arms and pushed me away.

"Aargh! What did you do? You burned me." Wild eyes filled with confused anger, he raised his other hand and before I could react, he backhanded me on the face.

No-one had ever hit me before. Pain exploded in my world. I tasted blood in my mouth. I swayed, but the press of the crowd kept me standing. Strangely, the blow seemed to dispel some of the hazy fog that dizzied me. Rage built. It warred with the whimpering pain in my face. I screamed again – only this time, with an anger so overwhelming it seemed the madness around me faded and all I could see was this vile … creature who had dared to strike me. I reached out for him, wanting somehow to wipe the smile from his face, when it happened. So fast that I barely registered it. A red flash of heat seemed to jolt from my body, straight for the boy's face. He reaction was instant. A scream more agonized than my own. His face in his hands, a hissing spitting sound like fat on a fire, tendrils of smoke curling around him.

I stood still in shock. Stunned. What had I done? What was happening to him? To me? It looked like his face was burning? But that was impossible, wasn't it? I felt cold. Like all the fire had gone, leaving me shivering in the blazing sun on a field full of warring students.

"Leila. Leila!" The voice came to me from a faraway place. "Leila."

Strange. Daniel stood beside me in the crowd, but his voice was eons away. He had a fast-drying trickle of red on his forehead. I tried to smile. To make my mouth form words. To tell him I was glad that he was alright. But that boy, that boy running screaming through the crowd with his face in his hands, he was burning. Burning. And somehow I did that. I shook my head, trying to make the fuzziness clear.

Daniel bent to peer into my eyes. "Leila, are you alright? Leila?"

He looked around and successfully shielded us both from several scuffling students. "What did that guy do? Where is he?" He shook his head. "Come on, let's get you out of here."

Without waiting for a reply, he took my hand in his and began pulling me along with him through the crowd. Numbly I allowed myself to be taken, clinging to his hand, the one thing that was giving me strength. Daniel didn't stop, even when we broke free of the crowd. He kept my hand firmly in his but, all the while, his eyes were searching the field as he muttered.

"Where is he? Where did he go? I swear, if I find him..." He brought us to a halt beside a battered green truck parked by the roadside and studied me anxiously. A cloud of anger darkened his face as he surveyed me. He swore under his breath, "Leila, are you okay – your face, dammnit. I'll kill him. I'll find him and I'll kill him!" Abruptly, he turned away and smashed his fist into the side of the car. I was too startled to be afraid. Students walking past turned to look at us. A girl with a bruised face and a boy with bloodied knuckles, trembling with rage. Daniel stood still for a few moments, head hung low, his face averted from me, a slight tremor to his body.

Instinctively, my hand went up to touch the side of my stinging cheek, which is when I noticed the tips of my fingers were blistering red, like they had been burned? But that didn't make sense. None of this was making any sense. With my mind still reeling, I appealed to the boy who stood beside me. "Daniel, please don't be angry. I'm alright. Honest."

Daniel sighed and ran a hand through his hair, taking a deep breath before replying. "Leila – I'm sorry – I'm not mad at you. I'm sorry that I asked you to come to the game. And then didn't make sure you were alright. I'm so sorry." He gently raised his fingers to delicately dance them along the vivid red welt on my cheek, pausing at the swell of my cut lip. The throbbing pain in my face was forgotten as I looked up at him. He looked tired. And dirty. Dried blood crusted his forehead. And he smelled of stale sweat and mud. I wrinkled my nose.

"Eww, you smell awful. And you look worse. Never mind about me, what happened to you?"

His face lit up with that earth-stopping smile.

"Well, don't try to spare my feelings or anything! Let me think - I've just played a rugby game, gotten a bottle smashed on my head, been punched at by a couple of sore losers and then almost lost my mind trying to get to you."

Then his voice changed. "Leila, what were you doing there? When I saw you in the middle of that crowd, I almost went nuts trying to get to you. What were you thinking? I was sure you would have been with the other students by the road. You know, where it was *safe?*" his tone was accusing.

"I ... I was ... " too chicken to confess I had been looking for him, I resorted to lying. "I was confused about where to run. I got mixed up and couldn't get out of there." Better that he think I was a ditzy idiot than know I was slightly obsessed with him. "And then that Leifiifi boy, he got a little carried away with everything." My voice died away as I remembered the burning and I quickly clenched both my fists closed, unwilling for Daniel to see what state they were in. He was more intent on the state of my face though and didn't notice.

"We need to get you some ice. Before that really starts to swell. You're going to look like one of David Tua's opponents after a fight."

I smiled ruefully. "Thanks. What a comforting thought."

He returned my smile and opened the truck door. "Come on, get in. I'll give you a ride home."

We were driving out of the Leifiifi School compound when a thought occurred to him and he turned puzzled eyes towards me. "Hey, Leila there's something I don't get. After that jerk hit you, what made him run off like that? I wasn't close enough to see it all, what happened to him?"

"I don't know. It all happened pretty fast and there were so many people crowded around us. One minute he was there and the next he took off." I shrugged, anxious for something to change the subject. "So do fights like that happen a lot after rugby games?"

With his eyes on the traffic, Daniel spoke grimly. " There's been a lot of inter-school violence in previous years. In fact, there was a bad incident a couple of years back where one school went on a mini-rampage through town looking for students from another school they'd been fighting with. They threw bottles filled with gasoline at some students and one girl was seriously burned. Several of them ended up going to prison and so the government banned all inter-school sports. I was only able to play club rugby since the school didn't have a team. This is the first year we've started up again. So a fight like this one is not going to go down very well with the authorities." He threw me a quick glance.

"I really didn't think it would be dangerous for you to come to the game today Leila. I'm so sorry."

"Hey, it's not your fault. It's mine for being such a space head. Besides, you probably saved me from getting stomped on ruck style by those psycho spiked boots." I shuddered as I remembered the violent rucking during the game and how often I had despaired of Daniel getting up from one of the tackles.

I was grateful when we turned down the main road through Faatoia. My head was throbbing, my cut lip didn't feel much better and my hands were really starting to hurt now. Not only that but I was sticky with sweat and longing for a cool drink. I pointed out the driveway and breathed a sigh of relief as I got out of the truck. Who would have thought I would ever be so glad to see this house?

Daniel came out to walk me to the door but I waved him aside, worried that Aunty Matile would be home any minute. If I hurried, I could get cleaned up and dream up a suitable explanation for my bruises before she arrived. And make sure Daniel was way out of the picture of course. I hadn't talked to my aunt and uncle about boys, but I was pretty certain that they wouldn't like the idea of me showing up on the doorstep with one in tow. Even one as assured and mature as Daniel. We stood side by side in the drive, awkward and unsure now that it was time to part. He spoke first.

"I better get going. You make sure to get ice on that cheek right away. I guess I'll check out your bruises tomorrow at school." He backed away and then stopped hesitantly, "Leila?"

"Yeah?"

"I'm sorry. Again. For everything today. Really."

I tried to smile without moving my face too much. "Daniel, it's fine. I'm fine. Really. See you tomorrow."

Once inside, I let my façade of well-being drop. I felt like a ton truck had rolled over me, or like I had been at the bottom of one of those almighty rucks.

I took a closer look at my hands – definitely burned. Little blisters were popping up on each fingertip. Where had they come from? How had it happened? I had no clue.My mind danced along the edges of possibilities I didn't want to consider.

That fire I felt within me. That awful furnace burning me up inside, had it been real? Had it come out somehow and burned my fingers? Even worse, had it burned that boy?

I popped painkillers with an entire jugful of water, before hitting the shower, forcing my swollen face to endure the cold spray in a vain attempt to hasten its healing. As I showered, I gave myself another mental talk. *Stop it Leila. Just stop it. You're not going crazy. You've had a rough day – but that's all it was. You were in the wrong place at the wrong time. Nothing else is happening here. You get hot because you have heat stroke. You're not fully acclimatized yet. That's all it is.* I muttered to myself throughout my shower, relishing the tepid water on my skin, wishing it was the deep coldness of my forest pool that I was submerged in. That always seemed to work better at quenching the fire within. But now that Daniel had surprised me there, I wasn't sure I could use that pool as my retreat anymore. I sighed at the thought of Daniel. It was clear he felt responsible for what had happened today. But was that all I wanted? His guilt? Remembering how gently he had touched my face got my pulse racing. This was not good. Not good at all. Only six weeks in Samoa and here I was weak at the knees over the school Head Boy? I groaned with the confused mess I found myself in as I fetched ice from the freezer for my face. I fell asleep with the makeshift ice pack still resting against my cheek.

I awoke several hours later to a dark, quiet house and a soggy wet cloth on my pillow. I could hear the radio playing in the far-off distance from the neighbor's house but of my aunt and uncle I heard nothing. I felt vaguely better after my sleep, well enough to acknowledge the pangs of hunger gnawing at my insides. Without turning on the light, I tiptoed to the kitchen in search of something to eat. The clock announced it was 1am. I had been asleep for over eight hours.

Shaking my head, I made myself a clumsy sandwich with the ever-present chunks of bread, devouring it in a few hasty gulps. My lip ached a little but the swelling seemed to have gone a bit. Enough for me to hope that Aunty Matile would believe I had tripped and fallen down the stairs at school? Hmm…I grabbed more ice.

My hunger satiated, I wandered into the living room, wide awake now, my mind still dancing over the memory of Daniel – his touch, his anger at the source of my pain. On the dining table was an envelope propped against the salt shaker. Grandmother Elizabeth's elegant handwriting screamed at me. My good spirits instantly deflated as I tore the letter open with dread. Oh no, what could have prompted the old lady to write me snail mail?

"My dearest Granddaughter,

It is my fondest hope that this letter finds you well. I can only think with dread of what manner of living conditions you must be enduring on that island. Please know that all you have to do is call and we can arrange for your return. I cannot pretend to understand your motivation for going to Samoa. I know you are grieving – as am I. Perhaps, you are finding solace in the land of your mother. I want you to know that I love you. And I loved your father very much. I am worried about you so far away in a primitive country with primitive traditions. Please be careful. Please come home soon. I was going through some of your father's papers and found this photograph. I thought you might like it.

Yours truly,

Elizabeth Folger

There was a photo in the envelope. A couple sat side by side on a doorstep. Each holding a baby in their arms. The man was my dad. Painfully young and joyously handsome, he held one little baby in the crook of his arm. He wasn't looking at the camera. Instead, he gazed consumingly at the woman beside him. She stared straight into the lens, unafraid and defiantly beautiful. Long hair hung past her waist. Her deep-set eyes dared the photographer to find a single flaw. She too held a baby. Casually. Half slipping off her knee. I was stunned. That was my father. And the woman with him must be my mother. I had never seen the photo before. But I had seen the woman. Many times. In my feverish, adrenaline-racing nightmares. Wearing a finely woven mat cloth, carrying a carved knife. The woman who every night was searching for me. The woman who's exultant smile terrified me. *No, this can't be right. I last saw this woman when I was only four months old. How could I possibly remember her well enough to be having nightmares about her? What's going on?*

Questions screamed in the night. Drowning out the bush crickets and the snickering lizards. Why had my father never shown me this photo?

He had always apologetically explained that there hadn't been many cameras around in his early Peace Corp Samoa days and what few pictures they had taken had been destroyed in the cyclone that had killed my mother. And yet here it was. A photo of my parents and me. But who was the other baby in the picture?

I stumbled back to my room with the letter and shoved the photograph into the bottom of my suitcase. Sleep was a long time coming.

Thanks to my being up half the night, I was almost late for the bus the next morning. I dragged a brush through my hair with one hand, while grabbing my backpack with another, books falling out on the hall floor as I bolted out. I was relieved to see in the mirror that a slight bruised cheek was the only relic of my previous day's adventure. I could hear the familiar grind of the bus gearbox as it made its usual u-turn at the end of our street. Uncle Tuala was reading the newspaper and didn't even look up as he said goodbye to me. Aunty Matile was nowhere to be seen as I opened the front door and frantically waved the bus down to a stop. I had put on a pair of dark sunglasses and, unused to the darkness, I almost fell over the step as I climbed up, sending the two school kids in the front seat into peals of laughter. I poked my tongue at them, which made them laugh even harder. Sitting on the bus, heart pounding with my near miss – I couldn't believe it had been so easy to escape detection with my bruised face. Thank goodness, because I would never have been so lucky if it had been my dad.

The ease with which I remembered him was a welcome relief. The raw edges of my grief were slowly softening. I could actually think of him now without the gaping chasm of pain. Sitting in the sun as the bus bumped and grated its way along the pot-holed road, I felt peaceful. Almost. I had been so focused on getting out of the house unseen that I had forgotten the photo. And as I remembered the picture in my suitcase, again the same cold unease wound its way around my heart.

I didn't think the morning could get any more disturbing until my eyes were caught by a headline on the back page of the newspaper that a wizened old lady on the seat in front of me was reading.

'Boy burned in inter-school violence!' There was a photo of a boy lying in a hospital bed, his face heavily bandaged. I read on with horror.

'Parents and school officials alike are gravely concerned about the extent of school sporting violence. Yesterday, a massive brawl broke out

during a rugby game between Leifiifi and SamoaCollege. Several students escaped with mild injuries while one young man suffered second-degree burns to his face. It was unclear how the boy was injured as he was also mildly concussed and could not remember what had happened. Doctors expect a full recovery and say that, luckily, the burns are only surface burns and the boy will not require any plastic surgery. Members of the public are calling for a ban on inter-school sports until the safety of our young people can be ensured.

I felt sick with shock. That poor boy … his face. My only solace was knowing that he wouldn't be scarred, he would be alright. Stifling a panic-stricken sob with my aching hands, I tried to calm my raging thoughts with deep breaths. Questions screamed at me - what was happening to me? First the heat attacks, the raging temperatures, now – zapping people with fire? Burning their flesh? What would come next? And how would I stop it? All the golden peace of the day drained away. I felt like a killer on the run as I slunk off the bus.

I was so caught up with the craziness of it all that I almost walked right past him. Daniel. Standing at the gate, leaning against a cement post. "Leila! Wait up."

I wasn't the only one to turn, incredulously, at his voice. There seemed to be a hush in the crowd of students around me as people craned their necks to see who Daniel, the school superstar, was calling out to?

I stopped in my tracks, surprised but delighted to see him. Here was someone who could put reason into this insane day.

"Hi." Suddenly I was shy. Even after all the madness of the day before, what we had shared together.

"I've been waiting for you – I wasn't sure if you'd come to school today. I called your house last night to check on you, but a lady said you were sleeping. How are you?" He peered closer at my face, as if trying to establish for himself whether I was recovered enough to be at school. "Hey – that doesn't look too bad, you heal fast."

Hearing him admit he had been waiting for me – watching for me – that he'd called my house, even, to ask after me – sent me into a tailspin. Stunned by it, I almost swayed in the morning sunlight. If this boy was motivated by guilt, or some misguided sense of responsibility for my safety, then he was *really* outdoing himself.

"Fine. I'm fine. I slept for hours yesterday when you dropped me off and I feel so much better this morning." I was anxious to reassure him, so that he could retreat back up into his demi-god heights, leaving me alone on the plane of mere mortals, to catch my breath.

He didn't seem in a rush to go anywhere, walking alongside me up the driveway towards the assembly area. "Are you sure? Here, let me carry your bag." Without waiting for a reply he took my bag off my shoulder, leaving me with no defenses, nothing to hang onto, nothing to hide my confusion behind. All my senses were screaming a warning now. Why was he being so nice to me? People were looking at us. At him rather. Talking to the new girl, walking beside her, *carrying her bag!* The tall, chicken-legs girl with the bushy hair and eyebrows. I felt hot as I imagined the whispers and hushed comments. Heat was the last thing I wanted to feel right now though, so I quickened my pace, hurrying us towards the assembly.

"You shouldn't worry about me Daniel. I'm okay. Really. I am. And I don't hold you in any way responsible for what happened yesterday, just in case you felt that way." Eager to dispel his guilt but then wondering if I had overstepped my bounds by *assuming* he actually cared either way. Oh – it was so frustrating this teenage boy-girl thing.

He shook his head at my words, about to answer when the shrill ring of the bell pierced the moment. "Oh – I gotta go – I'm doing the assembly today. I'll see you later?" He handed me back my bag, turned to walk away and then stopped as if forgetting something. He reached into his pocket, pulling out a star-shaped piece of paper. "Just something I made for you. Catch you later."

He left me then, a swirl of conflicting emotions. The paper shape was an intricately folded origami star. Written in blue ink on the center *For* and on the five points were the letters

L E I L A.

It was beautiful in its delicate symmetry. I slipped it into my pocket – but kept caressing it with my fingers throughout the morning assembly. Daniel was conducting and it was difficult to stop a ridiculous smile from lighting up like a beacon on my face as I watched him lead the morning hymn and prayer. He needed no microphone to hold everyone's attention, his voice ringing out strong and clear as he addressed the school. It assumed a cutting edge as he spoke to the gathered students about the fight with Leifiifi college. His eyes were ice as he reprimanded the rugby team and spectators for reacting to Leifiifi's bottle-throwing assault, reminding them of the school honor code. There was no sound from the school body, several of them hanging their heads as Daniel spoke. When he finished, it was the Principal's turn before we were all dismissed to class. Sinalei grabbed my arm excitedly as we drifted with the slow-moving crowd towards class."Ohmigosh – Leila what happened to you yesterday? Are you okay? Check out your face!" She ogled my bruise, agog with the excitement of it all. "Wow, how did it happen? Last I saw you were running back to the fight. I couldn't figure out what you were doing." Her face was sharp and curious, her eyes questioning. I knew I would have to defuse her immediately, before she ferreted out details that I surely did not want made public.

"Oh this is nothing. I tripped over one of those rocks on the other side of the field and banged my face on the road, talk about clumsy idiot. "

She persisted. "But why did you run back there anyway? Me and Mele were wondering what happened to you."

"Oh I was writing in my notebook when the fight started and I dropped it. It's kinda important to me, my journal you know, so I had to go back for it. Don't want the secrets of Leila Folger leaked out all over school." My excuse sounded pitiful but Sinalei had to be satisfied with it. Like a dogged terrier that never lets go, she jumped to another topic of attack.

"And this morning, was that Daniel walking you to assembly? Did he give you a ride to school?" Her bated breath was full of awe at the possibility that I had actually caught a ride with the demi-god.

Happy to tell the truth on that one, I replied emphatically. "No way. I caught the bus this morning as usual and I almost missed it too. I got up late and had to run to catch it and ..."

My voice trailed away as Sinalei's eyes glazed over. Clearly this was not a fascinating topic. Relieved, I hoped she would back off now for the rest of the day.

First period was dull and predictable. Mr. Michael's equations were a welcome distraction for my overwrought brain. English with Ms. Sivani was a pleasure. She had a way of making poetry come alive. Today was a favorite of mine. 'The Highwayman.' She had a taped reading of it for us to listen to. The lyric tones of Sean Connery ensuring everyone's rapt attention as he resounded throughout the classroom ...

I sighed at the end of the reading – did all great love stories have to end in tragedy? Were we that obsessed with sadness and twisted outcomes? Again, my thoughts were filled with Daniel. *Focus Leila! Stop daydreaming and get to work.* I turned my attention to the poetry worksheet and the rest of the period flew by. "Don't forget your essay assignment class, and I won't accept less than two pages – you hear me, Maleko!" Ms. Sivani snapped warningly as the duck-tailed boy swaggered past her.

"Ms. Sivani, that hurts. Of *course* I wouldn't dream of leaving you hanging like that, you'll get two and a half pages from me on Monday. After all, I am a hotter and smarter version of the Highwayman." Maleko laughed as he struck a pose with an imaginary sword, sending it swishing down – right on top of the books in my hands, sending them flying.

"Oops, sorry Leila. Wait, I'll get them." Maleko ducked eagerly to gather up my notes, while I stood there shaking my head at his antics. My amusement turned to panic, however, when his hands closed around the paper star that had fallen to the floor with my books.

"Hey, what's this?" he read the words out slowly. "For Leila. Ooooh, this looks interesting."

My heart pounding, I tried not to betray my panic – or else for sure Maleko would refuse to give the fragile star back. I had a feeling there was more writing contained in its folds and I had been savoring the anticipation until I could read it undisturbed during lunch. "Give that back, Maleko – it's nothing – just give it back." My voice rose an octave as Maleko held the star up to the sunlight curiously.

"I think it's a letter, let's open it up and read it ay?" His eager face turned to scan the classroom looking for some more of his teammates to share the joke.

Before I could threaten him with death and mayhem, a perfectly manicured hand snatched the star from his grasp and a flippant voice reprimanded him. "How dare you, Maleko. Stealing this girl's private correspondence."

I sighed with relief as Simone flicked the paper star back into my hands, quickly tucking it into the pocket of my blouse while Maleko transferred his teasing attentions onto my rescuer.

"*Se* Simone, I'm just having some fun, don't be jealous cos I'm not playing with you."

"*Nupi*. Whatever, Maleko I wouldn't play with you with a ten foot stick. Unlike Mele, I have good taste." Simone sniffed derisively and turned to flounce his way along the corridor, Maleko's team mates whistling after him and roaring with laughter.

Eager to remove myself from the scene of near humiliation, I swiftly gathered up the rest of my things and walked after Simone. "Simone, wait up."

"Yes, dahling?"

"Thanks for that. I appreciate it." I fell into step beside him as he sashayed along.

"Oh, don't worry. Maleko's an idiot. What's in the star anyways?" Simone gave me a sideways smirk, as if he already knew the answer.

"Nothing. Just origami shapes. Something I like to play around with. You know. Keeps me busy during a boring class."

"Yeah right." Simone arched one eyebrow at my response. "Funny, there's someone else here who likes to do origami too, someone who's better known for his footwork on the rugby field rather than his paperwork. You two should get together and share designs some time. Keep you both busy during a boring class." And with those cryptic words, Simone flounced off after another flamboyant boy-girl. "Daaaahling wait up!" Leaving me speechless.

Shaking my head at his exit I looked around for a secluded spot to open my note, having to be content with a seat inside the library. With careful hands I unfolded the paper edges, trying to memorize the creases so I could be sure of returning it to its original shape afterwards. Yes. I was right – it *was* a note, but a confusing one.

Leila.

'She moves in mysterious ways.' U2.

Trying to figure you out.

Daniel.

I read over the words several times ... *she moves in mysterious ways*? What the heck did he mean? I knew the song by U2 but wasn't familiar with all the words. Urgently, I dug out my iPod hidden in the depths of my bag, glancing around furtively for teachers and prefects. I knew somewhere in my playlist I had an album from U2. Funny – but I hadn't figured Daniel would be a candidate for a fan of an Irish band. Somewhere ... somewhere ... my fingers tripped over each other as I searched the playlist. Yes. I was right, there it was. I slipped on one earphone and pressed play, letting the rich power of the song wash over me. *She moves in mysterious ways...*

So Daniel thought I was a mystery? A puzzle? Oh well, at least that sounded better than thinking I was a weirdo. A misfit. Which is what I was more accustomed to being. I almost laughed out loud in the studious silence as I thought of my gangly surliness moving 'mysteriously.' Flushed with pleasure, I refolded the note and put it safely in my pocket, then went in search of Simone.

I was walking in so much of a daze that the bell ringing for the end of lunch startled me into dropping my books. Bent to retrieve them, I heard a now familiar voice greet me.

"Hey there you are. I've been looking for you. "

Great. It was Daniel. And here I was on the ground scrabbling for books like the proverbial klutz. Quickly, I rose to my feet, wishing that I had taken the time to check my hair, my face, my anything during lunch. Like a regular girl. Instead of spending lunch in the library. Unsure of myself, I must have scowled even more darkly than usual because the smile on Daniel's face faded uncertainly and the question on his lips died.

"Ask me what?" I tried not to sound ungracious. Which was difficult for someone without a gracious bone in her body.

"If you read my note ... and ahem, ... if you were doing anything today after school?"

"Oh. No. I mean yes. I mean – no, I'm not doing anything after school. And I mean yes, I did read your note. Thanks. I ... uh ... it's not what I expected."

He looked quizzical. "What do you mean? What did you expect?"

"Nothing. I just didn't expect anybody here to listen to U2. It's not the usual choice of music for the usual 21st century teenager."

"I guess I'm not your usual 21st century teenager then." His eyes danced and his mouth smiled that smile that kept catching at my heart strings. And sucking the air out of my personal space. Or something like it. Because it immediately had me struggling for breath. While trying not to show it. I mentally tried to slow my pulse and took a deep breath before answering.

"No. I guess not."

Wanting to put distance between us so I could get a handle on myself, I turned and started walking down the hall.

"Hey, where are you going? You didn't let me finish."

I stopped mid-step and half turned to see him looking after me with a confused expression.

"Oh. Sorry. Did you want something?" I was trying cluelessly for an air of sophistication but sure that all I was getting across was loutish grouch.

"Yeah. I wanted to make it up to you. For yesterday. For what was probably the worst day of your school life. I thought maybe we could go somewhere. Do something. Give me a chance to show you a better side of Samoa? Umm, of me?" His last words died away and he looked hesitant as if unsure of my response.

If his smile had me breathless, then his request definitely had me gasping for air. He wanted to hang out with me? He took my silence for unwillingness.

"Hey, if you don't want to, that's okay. I get it. You didn't exactly have an amazing first time out with me, I mean, asking you to come to a rugby game that turns into a brawl where you get beat up is not really the ideal way to impress a girl is it?" His crooked smile lightened his words, but still my mind was reeling. *He wanted to impress me? Are you joking? Is this boy for real?*

"No – I mean yes. I want to. Sure. We can hang out. Today. I'll do it. No problem. I don't mind." I shrugged casually, but my hands were clenched tightly on my book bag.

His answering smile was a light that lit up the entire hall. "Great. I'm parked at the back by the tennis courts. I'll meet you there after school. You remember the green bomb right?"

Without waiting for a reply, he turned and sprinted lightly down the now empty hall. Leaving me shaken. And late for class.

After school, in the car, he produced a red cloth. "Here. Blindfold. Put it on."

"Excuse me? Are you nuts?" My voice rose several octaves. "Just what kind of afternoon did you have in mind?"

He laughed, shaking his head at me as he changed gears, the car slowing as we made our way up the steep incline. "No. It's nothing like that. I don't want you to know where we're going. It's a surprise. Please. Trust me?"

The thought of what my grandmother's reply would be was enough to get me tying on the blindfold. "Okay. But it better be a good surprise. And don't forget, I'm the girl who knows how to kung fu kick your butt outta here."

His laughter was my only reply. We drove like that in companionable silence for a few minutes, the car grating over potholes and still going uphill. The suspense was killing me. I tried more questions, "So where are we going?"

"Patience, patience. You'll see. We're almost there. You'll love it. Trust me."

"Why the blindfold? You know I'm new and have no idea where anything is, so anywhere would be a surprise."

He laughed softly. "I just don't want you to know where we're going. Enough with the questions already."

I wasn't sure why, but I felt a sense of peace sitting beside this red and gold stranger. Instinctively, I knew that the boy who had sat and held me in the weeping night was not a threat to me. Rather, there was an indefinable closeness, an intimacy that I could not explain. Could not capture with mere words. I knew him. Somehow. And I knew that I would always be safe with him.

The truck grating to a sharp halt broke my reverie.

"We're here. Wait, I'll come over and help you out. It's not time yet to take off the blindfold."

The sound of the car door opening and closing had me tensing. The darkness was comforting. But only when he was right beside me. Thankfully, I only had to sit alone in the front seat for a few moments and then he had my door open and his hand was on mine. "Here, take my hand and I'll guide you. There's a few rocks to get through. Watch out."

His hand on mine burned my skin and had my pulse pounding again. Feeling very exposed without my sight, my tone was sharper than I planned it to be. "Well, I can't watch out can I?" I sniffed the air, listening intently to my surroundings, trying to find some clues as to our location. The air was ... cooler? Quieter. There was no sound of rushing traffic. Only the rustle of leaves and grass in the wind. And birds calling. And ... far away, very slightly, was that the ripple of water?

His body next to me, slowly walking me through the grass distracted me from my detective work. He was so close to me that I could taste his scent, the warmth of his skin against mine. He had one arm on my shoulders, the other holding my hand. His voice was a hot breath against my cheek as he replied.

"You can snap all you want but it's still not time to take off the blindfold. Now, I'm going to have to carry you here because there's too many rocks. Hold on."

Without warning, I felt myself swung up and into his strong arms. I shrieked in protest. "Hey! Wait up – noooo you never said anything about this bit, put me down Daniel."

Being carried when you can't see anything is terribly disconcerting. You can't tell where up or down is and you have no concept of how far off the ground you are. I clutched my hands around his neck tightly. "Daniel – put me down. Daniel – that does it, I'm taking off the blindfold."

Before I could carry out my threat, he placed me back on the ground, steadying me with his hands, a gentle touch on my waist. "There you go. We're here. Quiet. Listen. What can you hear?" His voice was a hushed whisper against my cheek and I shivered involuntarily at his closeness. In my darkness I could 'see' him standing behind me, his hands on my waist, his head bent to whisper in my ear.

He had to repeat his question before I could focus. "What can you hear Leila?"

I wanted to reply. *I can hear my heart singing. I can hear your voice filling my world and I never want it to end.* But I didn't. Instead, I stood poised in the darkness and listened. "Water. I hear water. On rocks. And grass in the wind. And birds. And what is that heavenly smell?"

Overwhelmed with curiosity I ripped off the blindfold and gasped at the sight before me.

We were standing in a green blanket. Tall grass blended with darker green bushes. Branches heavily laden with white flowers formed a circle around us. In front of me was a stream of clear water that danced over mossy black rocks, forming a small pool before trailing away through the grass. Spangled above us was the deep blue sky but the scorching gold sun was sheltered by a mountain rise. We were standing somewhere in the mountains, nestled in a green room. Nothing but sky, forest, the white ginger plants, water, and us. It was so achingly beautiful that I hated to breathe. But the fragrance of the white flowers enticed me to breathe deeply. I took a step forward and picked one startlingly white blossom, and savored its perfume.

"Daniel, it's perfect. Perfect."

With eyes only for me, his reply was quiet.

"Well ... now it is."

I was too flushed with the beauty of the surroundings to try to decipher his reply.

I turned to face him, a foolish smile on my face.

"Where are we? Surely we're not still in town? We must be high up – it's cooler here and the water ..." My voice trailed away as I carefully made my way to the water's edge. Kneeling on slippery wet rocks, I leaned over and trailed my fingers in the rippling shimmer.

"Yikes! It's cold. Yes!" I couldn't stop the bubble of laughter that pealed. For a girl used to Washington winters and the temperate air, it was pure heaven to escape, even so briefly, the sauna-like humidity I had been stifling in for the past month. Without thinking, I took off my shoes and waded into the cold stream, taking several steps before sitting down on a rock jutting from the center.

I motioned to the water. "I wish I'd brought something to swim in – the water is so cold. I love it."

Standing across the water from me, his eyes flashed with laughter. "As I recall, that didn't stop you the other night …" his voice trailed away suggestively.

Remembering my outfit the night he had come across me unawares had me flushed with embarrassment. I narrowed my eyes at him. "And as I recall, I warned you what would happen if you gave me any hassle about that. I was hoping you would forget about that, thank you very much."

He held his hands out in supplication. "Okay okay … I'm backing off Oh-Miss-Jet-Li-Supreme-Kung-Fu-Maestro." the same golden laugh sending heat up my spine. "But I gotta warn you, there's some things a guy can't forget."

I didn't think he was talking about my death and mayhem threats but I deliberately misunderstood him. With my legs dangled in the delicious water, I yelled back at him.

"I'm happy to give you a demonstration of my Jet Li skills if you need more reminders!"

"Nope, I'll take your word for it thanks." Shaking his head, he bent to sit on a rock directly opposite me across the silver water, arms hugging his legs. For a few minutes we sat in companionable silence. Just rippling water on rock, wind through rushing grass and the occasional bird call. I felt myself relax, every tense fiber unwinding in the peace of a perfect Samoan afternoon. There had never been a person that I could just sit and be with. Without the need to talk. Fill the gaps. For some reason, there didn't seem to be any gaps between me and this strange boy full of contradictions. I stole a glance at him. He had his arms leant back against the bank of the stream now, head facing the sun, eyes closed. He had taken his uniform off in the truck and a white singlet hugged the curve of his chest, the tattoo boldly curling down his arm. Black rugby shorts only covered the top of his thighs, leaving the tattoo on his calf muscle clearly exposed. I craned my neck trying to decipher the symbols that ran down his leg. Just then, he opened his eyes and crinkled them in amusement as he saw what I was trying to do.

"What are you looking at?"

Caught, I flushed guiltily.

"Nothing. I was just thinking."

He sat forward, his grin unconvinced with my answer.

"Okay, so what were you thinking about then?"

I scrambled for a credible answer. "Umm … you." I winced as I heard how raw that sounded. "Your note said you were trying to figure me out but you're kinda difficult to figure out yourself."

His furrowed his brow. "What do you mean?"

"Well, like – you're this sports machine – built like the Terminator but at the same time you're focused on your schoolwork. And you're like a … demi-god to the other boys at school who all want to be you, so you should be brash and rough and trample all over feelings and stuff but the other night, at the pool, you were so … umm … so kind and you know how to listen to people which hardly anybody knows how to do and look at this place, it's so beautiful and you bring me here blindfolded and it's a lovely surprise and … I just can't figure you out …" My voice trailed away as I realized I may have revealed too much. I looked away, fearful of what his response to my confession might be.

"I guess thats makes two of us then." His tone was light but then it took on an incredulous turn "okay … Terminator? And demi-god? Not sure what the heck is going on with those descriptors there. And about me being 'brash and rough and trampling all over people' – that's what you've been accusing me of ever since you arrived. I didn't even get a chance to show you how horrible I could be before you had decided that I was racist, sexist, oh and let's not forget – potential rapist."

I cringed. "That sounds bad, really bad. I guess I have been a bit quick to classify you." I snuck a glance his way.

He grinned.

"You think? I've never met anybody so defensive, so ready to launch into offensive mode. Are you used to getting trashed back home or something?"

The conversation had swung back too far into my personal space. I was confused how we had gone from my observations of him to all of a sudden delving into my patchy past. The last thing I wanted was to dim this outing by talking about my horrible American school nightmares. I shrugged and tried for smooth evasion.

"Nah, just prickly I guess. Hey, I think there's crayfish in here. Look at that."

Daniel stood to navigate over the rocks and join me. Together we bent to peer into the sparkling diamond water. Spidery translucent shrimp scuttled for safety as we reached to shift pebbles and grass.

"Yeah they're kinda cute. Maybe we should catch some, do you like to eat shrimp?" Daniel's smile was catching even as I shook my head resolutely.

"No we can't eat them. You just said they were cute."

"That doesn't mean we can't eat 'em. There's heaps of cute things that get eaten all the time. Besides, then you can add mean cruel animal abuser to your list of my sins."

I groaned as I sat back down on the warm rocks. "Okay, okay enough with the list of sins already. I'm sorry, I'm sorry! I promise I won't jump to conclusions about you anymore. I will only ever think something bad about you if you make it impossible not to."

He laughed again as he sat beside me. This boy seemed to be happy all the time I thought fleetingly. I wonder what it would be like to be so happy. He interrupted me.

"There you go again, thinking."

"So I'm not allowed to think now?"

"No – I mean yes, I mean you get that look on your face like you're thinking of something far away and you're not really here. You get that same look during Geography sometimes."

I didn't know how to respond. Especially not to the revelation that he had been looking at me during Geography. Another shrug.

"Oh, well hey, Mrs. Jasmine can be boring sometimes."

He feigned mock horror. "How could you say that, Geography isn't boring!"

"You're just saying that because you're Mrs. Jasmine's pet. She totally adores you, it's disgusting."

He was quick with a retort, "You're just jealous cos she doesn't love your map calculations as much as she loves mine."

And that's how the rest of the afternoon went. Sitting on the rock in the middle of shimmering water, we talked. About school. About sports. About books. And TV shows. And music. And we laughed. And he kept teasing me. And I laughed some more. He made it easy. Comfortable. To be happy. To feel light hearted.

It was with unwillingness that I took stock of the time. Quarter to five. Matile and Tuala would be home soon and wondering where I was. And what I was doing.

"I have to get back. We better go." I looked around for one more lingering look at this magical pool. This haven of happiness. Who knew when I would be here again? Daniel stood, giving me his hand to help me up. It was the first time he had touched me in the entire two hours we had been sitting there and it sent a rush of fire through me, so powerful that I worried he would feel it.

He didn't see my nervous expression as he turned to find a foothold through the dancing waters. Still he didn't release my hand. As heat waved through me, I should have pulled away, but didn't want to. I loved my hand in his. It felt … right. Like it belonged there. I took several deep breaths as we waded through the water and up the bank. *Stay calm Leila*. The grass was slippery and his grip tightened on mine as he pulled me up after him. At the top I almost fell into him and for a brief instant, we were breathing in the same breath, the length of his body against mine. His gaze was searching as he looked down at me, intent and steady. I couldn't breathe as I looked up at him. Green eyes were chiseled emeralds cut into his profile. But as quickly as the moment started, it passed. He smiled and released my hand to reach in his pocket for the blindfold.

"What? What do I need that for? I've already seen the surprise." My hands on my hips.

"Yes, and now I want you to put it back on for the return trip. That way, you won't ever know where I brought you. It will stay an unknown, hidden place. And you – and I – will know, that the only way you can come back here, is with me."

His eyes danced, but he was perfectly serious. I flushed at the sweetness of it all. His intent – so unexpected – had me speechless. I stood passively while he secured the blindfold and took my hand in his again to guide me back to the car. I was quiet as I slowly followed his lead through the grass. Forever now, there would be a hidden, special place. That only he and I had experienced together. A secret that only he and I would share. A niggling thought crossed my mind … *as long as he didn't bring another girl here* … or maybe he already had. The thought left grimy paw prints on my happiness and I was quiet on the ride home. Once back in town, he gave me permission to remove the blindfold. Noticing my silence, he queried.

"Hey, are you okay? What are you thinking about?"

"Just wondering, Daniel, how did you know about that place?" I battled to keep the suspicion out of my voice. His uncensored, swift reply went a long way towards stilling my unease.

"My grandmother. She goes there to pick the ginger plants – she says they're better because the water is so clean there. And there's less pollution in the air. She used to take me with her when I was younger. I had to carry the basket while she picked the plants. I gotta say, I didn't much enjoy trailing after her. Not half as much as I enjoyed hanging out there today." His eyes were trained resolutely on the traffic ahead of him, oblivious to my singing joy.

"So do you always take your friends there?" Stumbling over the term friends, hesitant whether or not we were even that

"No. I've never taken anywhere there before."

"Oh." The shortness of his reply had me stumbling for thought. I felt him steal a glance in my direction. I bit the side of my lip and wished I had more experience with talking. To humans. My dad was the only person I had ever been comfortable with. Him and plants had been my sole conversation. The car drew up to Aunty Matile's box house too soon for my liking. I got out reluctantly, shutting the door with a finality that I hated.

"Thank you. I had a nice time. With you." The polite words seemed to stick in my throat. After the ease of the afternoon, I felt strangely awkward with him. But his smile had my tension seeping away.

"Me too. You're welcome. And you didn't even snap at me once. There must be hope for me. I just might be a decent human being after all." This time we laughed together. And the flush of happiness was a good kind of heat that warmed me as I watched him drive away before turning to go inside the house.

That night I was content. For the first time in forever, everything was starting to come right in my universe. I was fitting in. I wasn't the freak outsider anymore. A pathway of possibilities was blossoming in front of me. And all of them involved Daniel. I couldn't understand why it was that I felt so at peace when I was with him, but I wasn't going to question it. Everything was going to be alright … was my final thought as I drifted to sleep.

How wrong I was. This wasn't the beginning of happiness. It was the first step into the inferno of a living nightmare.

FIVE

It was a rushed start to the next day. I slept in and missed the bus. Which meant I had to take a taxi to school. And still got there midway through first period. Too late to steal a glimpse of Daniel at rugby practice. Too late to watch him lead the morning assembly. And hope for a chance to talk to him before class. But all that was forgotten when I felt the earthquake. It happened at the end of third period. Ms. Sivani had finished giving us a quiz and everyone was making their way down the corridor preparing to endure 40 minutes with the droning sound of Mr. Michael's voice in Math. Walking along with one hand full of books and rifling through my backpack with another, I felt a wave of nausea sweep over me. I came to a standstill, causing a traffic jam in the milling crowd of students behind me.

"Hey what's up?"

"Move on, come on girl, get a move on."

Sinalei looked back at me, "Come on, Leila, we're going to be late."

Books spilled from my grasp as a cloud of dizziness fogged my vision. I reached out to steady myself on the wall only to find the wall was moving. The ground was moving. Rocking and heaving beneath my feet. A scream tore from my throat as I tried to stand. Everyone was staring now with confused, some amused, faces. I was terrified. Couldn't they feel it? The earth was moving. The entire school was uprooted and felt like it was about to tumble down around us. I turned, searching to find some means of escape from the destruction that was sure to ensue, only to find my way blocked by a crowd of puzzled people, all staring at me. Again the ground shook violently, taking me with it. I fell to the floor, hands raised to shield my face, landing painfully on my arms. Still the ground moved. I felt nauseous again and then thankfully, everything went black.

"She's coming round." A voice spoke from a far-off distance.

"Leila? Leila are you alright?" It was him. Strong and sure. I clung to that voice with a whimper of relief in the black fog that surrounded me. Something that made sense. Something I trusted.

A cool wet cloth was placed on my forehead and a clicking fan whirred somewhere overhead.

"Tell me again, what happened?" Ms. Sivani sounded puzzled. Sinalei's eager voice answered her.

"We were all walking to Math class when she just started screaming that the building was moving and shaking. Then she fell down and passed out. It was sooo weird." I could tell that Sinalei was thrilled to have been a spectator at the morning's drama. Her voice took on a worshipful tone. "Then Daniel came and carried her here to the staffroom. Thank goodness you're sooo strong Daniel."

In the blackness, I winced at the thought of Daniel carrying me like a sack of potatoes through the school for everyone to gape at. *Ugh.* I didn't want to wake up now, for sure. Someone was holding my hand though and I wanted to see for myself if it was him. I tried opening my eyes, afraid the dizziness and shaking would still be there. The light had me blinking. My vision settled and I looked around dazedly.

It *was* him. He sat beside me, holding my hand in his, his head bowed. For one sweet moment I savored the sight of him, the feel of his skin, the thrill of his nearness. Then Sinalei pounced.

"Miss, she's awake!"

I had worried he would let go once he knew I was conscious, but at Sinalei's words, his grip on me tightened and he leaned forward, blocking out everything and everyone else in the room.

"Leila, are you ok?" His eyes scanned me. "Does anything hurt?"

Ms. Sivani cleared her throat and interrupted him, pursing her lips disapprovingly as she surveyed how closely he was positioned over me. "Ahh, Daniel that will do. You've done quite enough for Leila today and I'm sure you're needed back in class. You run along and we'll make sure that Leila gets home alright." I hid a grin. The way Ms. Sivani spoke, you would have thought that Daniel had knocked me out on the ground himself, instead of being the one to stagger to the office with my inert body.

Daniel went rigid at her words and a familiar angry look came over his face. I was sure he was going to say or do something completely unbecoming of a Head Boy, so I jumped in.

"Ms. Sivani can Daniel please help me back to the classroom? I'm feeling much better now and I don't want to go home. I don't want to miss the Biology test this afternoon." I looked at the teacher with what I hoped was an angelic expression, trying to impress her with this life-or-death commitment to my studies.

Ms. Sivani harrumphed with a disbelieving snort, but she only motioned for Daniel to help me off the bench. "Daniel, you and Sinalei see if Leila feels up to going back to class then. I'm sure we can count on you to keep an eye on her for the rest of the day. And Leila, try not to have any more dramatic episodes in the corridors please?" Ms. Sivan spoke dryly as she moved towards the staffroom door.

I felt weak with relief at the close escape. The last thing I wanted was for Uncle Tuala to come pick me up in the middle of the day, brimming with uncomfortable questions about what had happened. I took a deep breath and went to swing my legs up only to be brought short by Daniel's sharp tone of disbelief.

"Ms. Sivani, I don't think that's a very good idea. Leila passed out in the hall. She fell down and could have hit her head badly. She needs to go home and rest, maybe even see a doctor." He spoke with the assuredness of one accustomed to being obeyed.

I glared at him furiously. How dare he presume to take over like that? I did not want to go home. And while I had no idea what had happened that morning, I was sure that I was fine. The last thing I wanted was for the whole school to have more to gossip about.

The new girl Leila had a wacky spazz attack in the hallway and fainted. The new girl got carried to the office by the dreamy hunk Head Boy. Leila had to go home sick ... brain damaged ... at death's door ... petrified with humiliation ... No way was I going home.

To prove it, I swung my legs over the side and stood up with gusto. "See! I'm totally fine ..." my voice trailed as the room spun and a wave of nausea threatened again. "Ugh, I don't feel so good." Head spinning, I sank to my knees on the floor, reached for the trash can by the bench and promptly threw up in it.

"Eeeew!" Sinalei's shriek of disgust could be heard several classrooms down the hall.

I groaned in self-disgust, grimacing at the sour aftertaste in my mouth. Tears welled at the total humiliation of throwing up right in front of Daniel. If I had any hopes of him pursuing our friendship, they were surely dashed to pieces now in this room that reeked of vomit.

"See Ms. Sivani. Leila is not ready to go back to class. I'm going to take her home myself right away. If that's alright with you." The last phrase was added on as an afterthought of politeness.

Ms. Sivani had a hand to her nose as she gesticulated wildly in acquiescence. "Fine, fine. You go take Leila home. Right now." *Before she throws up on my shoes* were her unspoken words. "Sinalei, take this rubbish can to the incinerator right now."

I caught a final glimpse of Sinalei's look of disgust as Daniel swept me up in his arms once again and was stalking halfway down the hall before I could even get a word out. "Daniel put me down now!" My demand was an urgent whisper, unwilling to draw any more attention from the students bent over their work in the rooms as we passed by.

His only reply was to lengthen his stride towards the green truck parked under the sweeping mango tree by the tennis courts.

"Daniel, I said, please put me down now. What the heck is wrong with you? How many times today are you going to throw me around like a ... like a blob? It's not like I'm the lightest thing around you know." I was indignant, trying to hide my shame at the throw-up episode.

There was no reply. I stopped squirming and stole a glance at the rugged profile so close to me as he strode towards the car. He wasn't smiling. He wasn't looking down at me. He wasn't speaking. He had a grim expression on his face – as if he was planning on tackling someone on the field. Very, very roughly. I swallowed and took a deep breath. This was it. He was thoroughly disgusted with me now. Sick to bits of my hysterics and drama. Tired of picking me up out of yet another scrape. He probably couldn't wait to be rid of me. I felt an awful sadness, contemplating the thought of this being the last time he would hold me. The last time I would feel his warmth against my skin. I sighed, laying my head softly against his chest, wanting to burrow into his safety and security. No one could describe me as petite and yet he carried me as effortlessly as if I were a tiny porcelain doll. His stride never faltered.

He wasn't even out of breath as he finally reached the car and set me down on my feet so he could unlock the door, still supporting me against him with one muscular arm. He cursed under his breath as he fought with the lock. I could feel the length of him against my body as he held me close, worried I would fall. He wore his sports uniform. Orange drawstring shorts and a yellow cotton singlet that did nothing to conceal his physique. I remembered what he looked like that first night beside the pool – moonlight gleaming on the curve of his chest, shorts barely clinging to his hips – and a dizzying weakness came over me again, this time totally unrelated to before and everything to do with the fact this impossibly beautiful boy was standing here with me, his body pressed against mine under the shade of a mango tree that whispered in the breeze.

He finally wrestled the door open and turned to help me in. For a moment he paused, raising my face to his with a hand softly under my chin. His eyes were anxious, his brow furrowed as he surveyed my troubled expression. Before I realized his intention, he leaned forward and placed a single hot kiss to my forehead, his lips barely grazing my skin but leaving a burning mark where they had so briefly lingered. My knees turned to jelly and my already dizzy head spun even further as I leaned into his firmness.

"Hey, let's get you home. I knew Ms. Sivani was wrong, you're not well, you need to rest."

He put me into the car and hurried to the driver's seat. He didn't speak again until we had reversed and were safely out onto the main road. Then the questions began.

"So what really happened today?"

" I'm not sure. I was walking to my next class when I felt sick and dizzy. Then it was like the ground was shaking. Like there was a huge earthquake. It was so real. But nobody else was feeling the same thing and I freaked out. I couldn't figure out what was happening. Then I lost my balance and blacked out. Maybe I was just really desperate not to go to class?" my weak attempt at a joke didn't even rate a smile from him.

"Has anything like that ever happened to you before?"

"No. Never." I must have betrayed some of the fear I was feeling because he glanced my way.

"Don't worry Leila. You're safe now. We'll take you home, you can shower, have a good rest and you'll feel heaps better. Maybe it's the heat, you reckon?"

I grabbed onto that possibility with relief. "Of course that must be it. I'm really finding the heat a killer. I guess my *palagi* blood isn't liking the weather." This time he threw me a half smile.

"Well it suits *my palagi* blood just fine. Just give you some time and you'll be sweet."

I felt a huge tiredness settle over me like a lethargic blanket. That whole earth-shaking episode this morning had taken its toll on me. My brain still felt foggy, I wasn't even up to asking myself searching questions … like, what really happened to me? I didn't want to admit it, but I was frightened by what had happened and grateful that Daniel was taking me home.

All I wanted to do right now was sleep. I settled back in the seat, struggling to keep my eyes open. Sensing my tiredness, Daniel stopped giving me the third degree and switched on the radio, humming along under his breath to the sounds of Bob Marley.

I smiled. What was it with this country and Bob Marley anyway? Everybody and anybody seemed to have his songs on their radios. I was drifting into delicious slumber when the song was interrupted by an announcement. I caught the words 'tsunami watch' and 'earthquake' and sat bolt upright, my heart pounding.

"An earthquake occurred just over an hour ago, measuring 7.9 on the Richter scale off the Tongan islands. There is a tsunami watch in effect. Residents of low-lying areas are urged to be on the alert. Stay tuned to this radio station, as we keep you posted on any further updates from the tsunami watch center in Hawaii. We repeat …"

I turned panicked eyes to Daniel beside me.

"What's happening?" my voice trailed away, reluctant to put into words the fearful possibility that was racing through my mind. An earthquake? So strong it triggered a tsunami watch? But an earthquake so far away that nobody could feel? Nobody, that is … but me?

"Hey don't worry about it. We get these tsunami watches all the time.   And nothing ever happens. Ever since 29/09, the disaster management people like to keep us on our toes – you know, be prepared and all that. It's just a precaution. If it was anything more serious, then they would have announced a warning and schools would be evacuating by now." He placed a reassuring hand on mine beside him on the seat. It was obvious he thought I was freaking out about the possibility of getting swept away by a giant wave – and hadn't made any connection to this morning's incident. I didn't speak again until we pulled up in my front drive. There was a sleek red car parked behind Aunty Matile's truck, blocking the path. Daniel whistled long and low.

"Sweet! That's a nice car. Who's is it?"

I could only shake my head, as clueless as he was but anxious to get inside before Aunty came out and gave us the third degree. Daniel was out of the car before I could move though, out and round to my side, opening the door and trying to help me out.

"Are you ok? Can you walk?" His face held nothing but tender concern. I tested my balance tentatively before nodding slightly.

"Yup. I'm good." I looked up at him, wanting to memorize the closeness of him. "Thank you. Again. For helping me. This is getting to be a habit with us. I'll have to work on my resilience so you don't have to pick me up off the ground anymore."

He brushed a stray strand of hair off my face and I trembled at his touch. Concern colored his eyes again. "Are you sure you're alright? Can I walk you inside?"

That was the last thing I wanted. I waved a hand nonchalantly. "No, no. I'm alright. Honest. Just tired now. My aunt is here, she must have a visitor. If I need anything she'll be home to help me. You better go back to school. You know, before Ms. Sivani gives you detention or something."

He grinned back at me. "Who me? Nah never, you know all those teachers adore me, you said it yourself. Well, I'll see you tomorrow hopefully." His voice trailed away and still he stood beside me, one arm cradling the open car door, looking down at me, somewhat unwilling to leave.

I couldn't decipher the look in his eyes. Was it indecision? Longing at war with doubt? Before I could decide, he leaned down and left another swift, light kiss, feather soft on my forehead. Over before I could even be sure it had happened. He turned and walked back to the driver's side.

Swallowing a gulp of much-needed air, I closed the front door and walked to the house, turning once to smile shyly and wave as he reversed. I felt like I was swimming through cotton candy. Thick, blissful sweetness, clouds of wonder. Daniel cared about me. Daniel had kissed me. Twice. On the forehead to be sure, but still, a first touch from the boy whose very nearness had me scrambling for rational thought. All thought of my strange collapse a few hours earlier were erased. Replaced by the thrill of ... bliss? I couldn't be sure what this was. It was all new to me. I had a foolish smile on my face as I opened the door.

Only to be met by a coldness. Of dread. I should have known better. Happiness is only ever a transient thing. Like fluff in the wind. Worthy only of derision because it only made what came next all the more awful. I stood still in the corridor. There was something, someone in the house. Something that shouldn't be there. Something had me loathe to step further into the house. There was a woman in the kitchen with my aunt. I could hear her voice.

"You can't stop me from seeing her, Matile." She sounded disturbingly familiar. I had heard that steel tone before. But not in my waking world. I felt the air rush to pound through my chest. The hairs on the back of my neck prickling with unease. I shook my head in denial, mouthing a silent NO to myself. This could not be happening. I took one unsteady step back. Back into the sunlight. Back into the world I knew was real and true. But still the voices assailed me. My aunt's furious whisper.

"You – you have no right to be here. You gave up that right eighteen years ago! If there was any justice you wouldn't even be walking free, you should be dead."

"Silence woman." No one could disobey such a command, uttered with such power and restrained fury. "You speak of things you know nothing about. Of things forbidden. Foolish Matile. Still denying your birthright. Spitting on your heritage with your ignorance and pseudo-Christianity. Enough of this! I am not here for you. I am here for the girl."

It seemed my blood turned to ice at her words. There was no mistaking what girl this woman referred to. I was taken aback by Aunt Matile's defiant reply.

"She is not here. She won't be home for hours. And when she does return, Tuala and I will see to it that she is on a plane. Tonight. Far away from you."

I was touched by her attempt to cover for me. I would have thought she would be the last person to sacrifice anything for my well-being. Maybe, I thought in the midst of my dazed thoughts, maybe there was more to her and Uncle Tuala's anger at my coming here. At their obvious state of unease at my presence. Maybe there was more to their insane rules and strict living conditions than I had previously imagined. Maybe, just maybe, they had been protecting me? But from what? From who?

The unknown woman in the kitchen laughed. It was the laugh that confirmed what I already suspected. It was low and cruelly musical. It was the exultant laugh of the woman in my dreams.

"No." I muffled my words with my hands. I was desperate to escape from the house before they sensed my presence. But it was too late. The hall door opened and there she stood. The woman I knew all too well. The woman from the photograph.

My mother.

Her long hair was coiled in an elegant bun at the nape of her neck, accented with the familiar red hibiscus. She was even more stunning close up, dark deep-set eyes and lush full lips, a gleaming silver shell necklace drawing your eyes to the low neckline of her startling red fitted dress.With her black stiletto heels, chic Armani clutch purse and a Blackberry in one hand, she was the epitome of style, a corporate executive on her way to a board meeting, rather than a threatening spirit woman of the night who had assumed mythic proportions in my mind. A smile lit her face.

"Aaaah and here she is! My daughter, Pele." Arms outstretched, she clearly expected me to rush into her embrace. There was a choking gasp behind her from Aunty Matile as she realized that I was home.

I stood my ground. I would not give in to the hysteria that threatened to suffocate me. I was my father's daughter. He was a good man, a wonderful father who loved me more than life itself. I was sure of it. He told me my mother was dead and I believed him. I hung on to this truth, this rock of certainty would be my anchor through this madness.

"My name is Leila Folger. Who are you?" my voice was calm and unruffled. This woman might scare the daylights out of my unflappable Aunty Matile, but I would not be so easily intimidated.

The woman dropped her arms and pouted. On her it looked sensuous. I could easily imagine her using it on some unsuspecting male with devastating effect. Some man ... like my dad? The question came unbidden to my frozen mind.

"Oh Pele. How cruel to have been parted for so long. It pains me that you do not recognize me, that you do not know your own mother."

"My name is Leila. My mother died when I was a baby. I've never had a mother. My *father* raised me. You must be mistaken." My tone brooked no arguments.

"Pele." her voice dropped an octave, eyes glistening with unshed tears. "Oh Pele, you have been misled all your life. By people who surely did love you, but who wanted to keep us from knowing each other. As you can see, I am very much alive and now we have found each other."

I shook my head, raising my voice over and above hers. I didn't want to hear this. My voice was ice. It was perfect Grandmother Folger delivery.

"I think there's been some mistake. Thank you for stopping by but I think it best if you leave now. Matile and I – we would both like it if you left this house immediately."

The woman pouted. "Pele, you speak without thought, without consideration. Don't make me get all legal on you and drag up the necessary paperwork to prove to you I am your mother." A pause, a tilt of her flawless face to the side as she considered my rigid stance, "You know in your heart who I am, and so does Matile."

I looked at my aunt with searing questioning eyes. She refused to meet them, standing there in the hall, shoulders slumped as she cried silently. I hated this red nail-polished woman for hurting my aunt, a woman who had taken me in – in spite of all her reservations, who sang songs from 'Mama Mia' to her ugly dog when she thought no-one was listening and insisted on cooking arrays of food every night in an attempt to fatten me up. Even while she sourly complained that she was tired of having me here. I clenched my fists and stepped away from the still-open doorway.

"You need to leave. Now. We don't want you here."

The beautiful woman smiled but her eyes were cold and hard. "No matter. We will talk again." She took two graceful steps past me then paused to turn and reach out, holding my chin in her hand. "You are as beautiful as I always imagined you would be Pele. These people, they will tell you many things about me, but all I ask is for you to remember – why did you come to Samoa? Why are you here? We all want to know the truth of our beginnings and, as your mother, I can answer your questions, I can give you what these people cannot. Remember that. We will speak again."

I stood straight and tall, without words. Watching as the woman walked out of the house, down the drive and into her sleek car. Both Matile and I watched as she reversed and drove away. A soon as she was out of sight, Matile was on the phone to Uncle Tuala, telling him in hushed, frantic tones what had happened, begging him to come home at once. I waited calmly for her to finish. I had waited eighteen years for this moment after all. What were a few more minutes?

Sitting on the creaky sofa in the living room, I waited for Aunty Matile, my mind a swirling mass of questions. The silence was expectant as Matile walked in to sit on the opposite chair.

"Aunty Matile, that was my mother." It was a statement not a question.

She nodded. In her eyes there was sorrow and fear? What was she afraid of? "I don't understand, you have to explain to me – why did my dad tell me that she was dead? Why did he keep me from her all these years?" I wanted to scream and rage all at once. But I refused to give in to the torrent of confusion that was raging within. I wanted, I needed, the truth.

"Leila, there are many things you do not know, that you do not understand, please."

I interrupted, my voice raising several octaves as my control began to erode. "Obviously. Which is why I want to get some answers, I'm tired of being lied to."

Matile tried again. "I'm trying to explain Leila, but you have to understand, there are many things that even I do not understand, that I do not know. I did not know your father well, remember, so I cannot speak for him or try to explain his choices. But I will try to explain some of what happened." She took a deep breath before continuing. "First, you must know, your mother, Nafanua, is not my sister. We are not closely related. We are many years apart. She is a great aunt of mine."

I was impatient. What did I care about their familial relationship? This wasn't about Matile and her 'maybe' sister, this was about me and my parents, and why my mother, who was supposed to be dead, was in actual fact alive and well. Sensing my irritation, Matile hurried on.

"Your father came here as a Peace Corp volunteer many years ago. He stayed with us for a short while, we were his host family when he first arrived. Before he went to teach at a school in the outer village of Gagaifo, Lefaga. Which is where he met your mother. Your mother was, is, a certain kind of woman. She is *telesā*. Difficult to resist. They are powerful. And when they see something they want, they always get it. She wanted your father and he – everyone could see – he was very much in love with her. Those who knew what kind of woman she was, well, we were sorrowful. Because we knew it could not end well. But what could we do? She is *telesā*." Matile started crying again, sobbing into a handkerchief.

I was more befuddled than ever. "What the heck are you talking about Matile? What is te –le – sa?" I stumbled over the unfamiliar word. "What are you trying to say about that woman? About my mother? Speak English for goodness sake."

Matile only shook her head. "No, it is forbidden. I can't speak of it. She is *telesā*."

Frustration made me cruel. I jumped to my feet. "Maybe that woman was right, maybe she's the one I should be talking to for answers. I'm wasting my time talking to you about this, You've been evasive ever since I got here. You know why I came to this country, after all I've been through, why can't you just tell me the truth?"

"I'm so sorry Leila, I'm so sorry." Matile was almost incoherent with sobbing, and cold shame at my attack on her cut through me like a knife. "She is *telesā,* that is all I can tell you about her. Your father, he loved her so much. They were married in the village and she stayed with him for a short while. For a while she acted like a wife. Then she was pregnant. Your father, he was so happy. We would see him going home early from work every day, taking her special food … she always wanted to go swimming at night. He would take her down to the beach. People would talk and stare. We all wondered what kind of child she would have." Matile's eyes took on a faraway look at the memory. "She gave birth to you on the beach, you know. It was late at night, under the moon. Your father ran to get the *taulasea,* the healer, to help. It was difficult because there were two of you."

I was reeling with shock, holding my breath, unwilling to make a sound that might halt Matile's recollection, but those words hit me like a blow to the solar plexus. "Two of us? You mean twins?" My mind raced to the creased photograph hidden in my suitcase.

Matile nodded, the tears still streaming down her cheeks as she looked up at me. "Yes, two of you. The *taulasea* told us you were born first. She said she had never seen such a strong newborn before. Your mother pushed you out onto the wet sand and already you were trying to hold up your head. Your brother didn't come for several minutes."

My words were a whisper. "My brother? I have a brother?"

For some reason, that seemed to jolt even more crying from Matile. "Not anymore. He died. When you were four months old, there was an accident and your brother died. Your father left the country with you the next week. Right before the hurricane."

"What happened? How did he die? Why did my dad take me away? Why didn't my mother go with us?" The questions tumbled out over each other, eagerly running after slippery eels of elusive truth. But Matile just shook her head.

"I don't know. Your mother is *telesā*. I don't know. He died. Your father left, taking you with him. He never came back here. Your mother went back to her life. After the bad hurricane. It was so bad. Many people died. I remember the wind tearing the roof off our house. We had to break a hole in our cement water tank and hide in there to be safe."

Matile shivered as if somehow the horror of the hurricane was again in the room with us. Again, I was impatient with her reminiscing about things that didn't seem even remotely connected to my life story.

"Aunty, I don't understand any of this. My dad told me my mother was dead. That she died in a hurricane. He said he loved her very much and he wished I could have known the woman he fell in love with. He never spoke a single bad thing about her. This doesn't make sense. How could she be alive? My dad loved her, I know he did. If he knew she was alive, he would have been here with her. He wouldn't have taken me away, he knew how much I wanted a mom. He wouldn't have kept me from her, he wouldn't ..." my voice died away as the cold facts tripped me.

Because that's exactly what my father had done. He had taken me thousands of miles away to Washington D.C. Told me my mother was dead. Told me it was just us two against the universe. Yes, he hadn't talked about her much, but I always understood that to be because thinking about the love of his life was painful for him.

When I was little, I used to pester him, *"What did she look like? What did she sound like? What food was her favorite? What kind of mom was she?"* I remembered the sad smile he would give me. The comfort of his answers. *"She was beautiful, Leila, just like you ... she was an amazing dancer, so graceful ... she liked eating marshmallows. Your grandmother would send me some in my care packages and your mother – she had never tasted them before. She loved them! And she adored you, Leila. She really did. She had eyes for no other child. In fact, she didn't even like me to hold you, she said I couldn't understand the bond between you two, that it was going to be you two girls against the world, together.* No. None of this made sense. I wanted to scream and rage. Smash things. Mirrors, vases, plates and glasses. Wildly, I looked around, but the silent sobbing of Aunty Matile stilled my emotions. The somber pictures of Jesus gazed down at both of us. I walked over to my aunt and awkwardly put an arm on her shoulder.

"Aunty Matile, I'm sorry that woman came here and upset you. You and Uncle Tuala have been so good to me since I got here. You don't deserve to be upset like this. I know that you don't like to talk about ... my ... mother. You never have. I don't understand what's going on, but I want you to know that I'm grateful for all that you've done for me. You and Uncle."

My words only seemed to provoke more tears from her. I was not good with emotional drama. Or closeness. I was hugely thankful when the door slammed open and Uncle Tuala came in, panting out of breath like he had been running. Eyes full of worry that turned to soft relief when he saw Aunty Matile sitting there on the couch. Two big strides and he was beside us.

"Did she hurt you Matile? Are you alright? What happened?"

Matile shook her head and kept crying. I answered for her. "No, she's just upset by things that woman said that's all. But she's gone now. We're fine. You are alright aren't you aunty?"

My every fiber screamed for answers but I knew this was not the time to push the issue. This was not the person to push for explanations. The person I most wanted to talk to was dead. And the only other person with the answers I needed had just walked out the door. Uncle Tuala took Matile to lie down in the room. After fetching her some ice water, he came to sit across from me in the living room, clearing his throat awkwardly.

"Leila, you must be very confused. Very upset. I understand if you are angry at us for keeping your mother's presence from you. But you have to know, that we were only following your father's wishes. Many years ago he took you away from here, away from that woman, Nafanua. He had his reasons. I am sure they were reasons that he shared with your grandmother because the first time she called us about your visit here, she too was very upset that you had chosen to come here. She said that what you were doing was against your father's wishes, isn't that right? Leila?"

Shadows wrapped me in a cocoon of comfort, hiding the red flush of shame that burned my face. I hung my head, my reply was muffled. "Yes. She's right. My dad, he didn't want me to come here. He asked me not to. Before he died, he asked me to promise that I wouldn't come to Samoa."

Tuala continued, "Well, you see then that we were only trying to do what your father would have wanted, what Mrs. Folger asked us to do. She was very anxious that Nafanua be kept from you, and we agreed one hundred percent with that decision. I don't know much about your mother but I can tell you Leila, that she is not a good person. She has done things that are not right. When you arrived and we told you that school and this house were the only safe places for you, we were not being merely strict Samoan parents, we were hoping to shelter you from a meeting with Nafanua." He sighed and smiled resignedly, "Only one more month to go for your trip here, we almost made it."

I smiled sadly back at him. At this gentle man who was trying so hard to make sense of my chaos for me. I took a deep breath. "Uncle, I don't know what to say, what to think, what to do. I'm so confused, but what I do know is that you and Aunty Matile have been nothing but good to me since I got here and I do appreciate that." I stumbled over the words. "You didn't even know me but you were willing to host me for all this time. I'm sorry that Matile's upset. I didn't want to make trouble for you both."

He nodded wearily. "I know. You are a good girl, Leila. But you are wrong about having no family. We've told you many times before, your grandmother Folger loves you and worries about you. Like her, we only want what's best for you. I think it's time for you to go home. Back to America. We can call the airline office now and get you on the first flight out. Matile and I, we will miss you, but you belong with your grandmother. Not here."

I took a deep breath before replying. "Please don't misunderstand me, I mean no disrespect and I don't want to hurt Aunty any more than I already have – but I can't go back. Not now. All my life I've wanted a mother. My father knew that. I know he loved me, but I need to find out why he lied to me, why he kept me from that woman. Please don't make me leave now."

Another deep sigh and Uncle Tuala gave a resigned shrug of his shoulders. The gently creeping evening was beginning to fill the room. "Leila, as you wish. Of course you can stay here with us as long as you like." A smile. "We have grown to care for you. Even Matile – in her own way – would miss you should you leave now. We will let this matter rest. At least for a while." He turned to leave the room. "Now, I must tend to your aunt. This day has been very difficult on her."

And with that, our conversation was ended. Concluded, but far from satisfactory because I had a million and one questions, and no-one to ask them of. I tried calling Grandmother Folger but her secretary said she was in New York for a board meeting and I hung up before she could transfer me. I didn't really want to talk to my grandmother. She had been part of the web of deceit I had lived in for eighteen years. I was in shock.

I had woken that morning with no parents and before night fell – I had a mother.

I was still in a mild daze at school the next day. Ms. Sivani had to repeat her questions on poetry several times before she could jolt a response from me. At lunch, I told Sinalei and Simone to go on ahead without me to the canteen, I couldn't stand the thought of trivial conversation when I was plagued with doubts and questions. I took a seat at the furthest classroom block. Which is where Daniel found me.

"Hey, here you are" his smile turned to a question at the sight of my expression. "What's wrong? Are you okay? Are you still feeling sick from yesterday?"

He sat down beside me on the wood slat bench. I could tell he had come from PE class because his hair was still wet from the showers. The burnished red sparkled with moisture. He leant closer, waiting for my reply.

"No, I'm fine," I tried lying first. But he raised an eyebrow. He wasn't buying it. I threw privacy to the winds. "Ok, well actually, I'm not fine. Remember that red car outside my house yesterday?"

"How could I forget it?" Another smile that caught at my dark mood and entangled it with lightness.

"It belonged to this woman called Nafanua. She says she's my mother." There I'd said it. The 'M' word sat in the open air, daring me to defy it. Daniel's face was puzzled.

"Your mother? But I thought you said your mother died when you were a baby?"

"Exactly. That's what my dad told me, that's what everybody told me. My whole life, the single most defining feature – the fact I had no mother – turns out to be a big fat lie." My voice climbed higher and higher as the words poured out. "You know, ever since my dad died, it's been me against the whole world. I've been so alone, there hasn't been anyone I can trust, anyone I can count on who really knows me, who really cares about me. But I could handle that, because I just held tight to the memory of my father, I held on to him in here and it didn't matter that I was alone. Because I knew he loved me." My voice sank to a whisper. "I knew I was worth something." I shook my head in despair. "And now, I find out that the man who said he loved me more than anything, the father who was everything to me – well, it turns out he was a big fat liar!" I caught myself and turned away, battling for composure. Daniel took a deep breath before he spoke.

"Leila, this is a huge shock for you. And I can understand how upset you must be, but think about it. Your father really loved you, everything you've told me about him, well, let's just say, I'm envious that you have those memories. Of a dad who wanted you, cared for you and was obviously proud of you. Now, if he did conceal your mother from you, then there's got to be a reason. If there's one thing I know from my observations of adult relationships, well, they're complicated. There's always two sides to the story and when you're standing on the outside, you sure don't hold all the pieces to the puzzle you know? I'm not saying this doesn't bite, this is rough, I'm just saying, don't be quick to condemn your dad or this woman who's supposed to be your mother. Are you sure she really is who she says she is?"

I nodded with troubled eyes. "Yeah. My Aunty Matile knows her. And there was one photo of her and my dad together. It's definitely the same woman. There's no getting around it. That woman is my mother." I shook my head, remembering again the cold beauty of the woman in vivid red. "I don't get it. It's like everyone was in on it. This whopping huge conspiracy or something. Aunty Matile knew. Even my Grandmother Folger knew. My dad told everyone the truth except me. He lied to me." The words died away, mired in sadness.

Daniel's tone was gentle. "So what are you going to do? This woman, this mother of yours, where is she?"

"I guess she lives here. Matile seems to be either terrified of her or completely hates her. I don't understand. The woman said she wants to talk to me more. Says she wants us to know each other, but I don't know."

"I seem to remember talking to a girl a few weeks ago who said the exact same thing. She said she came to Samoa because she wanted to get to know her mother better. Hmm, now where did I hear that from?" Daniel's eyes were dancing. I grimaced at him.

"That was different. I thought she was dead. You can't just waltz into someone's life and tell them you're their mother then expect everything to be hunky-dory. Life doesn't work that way."

"Oh, so how does it work then? If it isn't hunky dory?"

"I ... I don't know. It's too weird. And ..." in the blazing light of the mid morning, my fears seemed silly, "she's kind of scary. She gives me a strange feeling. I can't explain it. It scares me."

I stared at the floor, thinking he would laugh at my confession. It did sound ridiculous when I spoke it out loud. His hand under my chin gently raised my face to look at him. His eyes were soft.

"Leila, that's not silly at all. All your life you've believed your mother was dead. Then some strange woman walks into your house and announces, *ta-da here I am*. It's totally understandable that you would feel strange. And even a little frightened. You've been through a lot the past year I can't imagine what this must be like for you to see her, almost like meeting a ghost."

My mind heard him, but my senses were drinking in his closeness. Sitting there side by side, we were alone at the furthest reach of the school. He was golden red in the sunlight, all heat, muscle and warmth. Always ready with that smile that tugged at my insides whether they wanted it or not. Always finding me at my most vulnerable moments. Like a programmed missile that honed in on my sadness. Something kept bringing him to me when I needed him most.

He was waiting for my response. I smiled weakly and nodded.

"I guess you're right. It was kind of eerie seeing her like that. And maybe, I should give her a chance to explain. I'll think about it." I felt better already, just saying it. Deciding that I would go ahead and contemplate the possibility of a living mother.

Sensing my light shift, Daniel smiled. Still he held his hand to my face, one finger drawing a delicate caress against the side of my cheek. Still he did not pull back. Our eyes were caught, melded as one. His smile drew me closer. I wasn't thinking any more about my new-found mother. Or about anything else. I breathed in nothing but Daniel. My gaze flickered to his lips, a heart's breadth away from mine and I wondered what they would feel like. What they would taste like.

The bell rang, jarring through our connection. Daniel dropped his hand and looked away down the hall.

"I guess we better get to class." He stood slowly, his bag over one broad shoulder. I remained seated, my thoughts struggling to pull away from the possibilities that had crammed into the moments before. I took a deep breath, *steady Leila, breathe.* I gathered my things, hoping the mundane would distract me from the other-world of delight. Daniel stood beside me waiting patiently. He reached out his hand.

"Here." I looked up at him but his expression was unreadable. He took my hand in his as I stood, his firm grip steadying me. I was up, standing as tall as I could beside his towering height, but still he didn't release my hand.

"What class do you have?" He asked casually, as if unaware of our still-clasped hands.

"Math. In block C. How about you?"

"English. Ms. Sivani. In block C as well."

"Oh." I couldn't think of anything else to say. Anything that wouldn't sound idiotic. As we began strolling down the hallway with our fingers entwined. It didn't seem possible that something as simple as holding another person's hand could have such an impact. Where minutes before I had been sinking into that darkness that I had lived in a few months ago, I now glided, as if nothing but Daniel's hand kept me anchored to the earth. Students met us further down the hall, headed in the opposite direction. I tensed, and flexed as if to pull my hand away, before prying eyes could flame with curiosity but Daniel was quicker. His grip on mine tightened. I turned to look up at him and he had a question in his eyes. As if to ask, *is this okay with you? Are you alright with this?* In answer, I kept my hand in his and walked on beside him. I could have walked with him through fire, but all too soon, we came to my classroom. Where a muffled squeal from Sinalei confirmed that yes, she had seen me walking with Daniel. Holding hands.

"Are you feeling a bit better?"

I nodded silently giving him a grateful smile. Still, he seemed unwilling to say goodbye, to let me go. "I'll see you later?"

My fingers were slipping from his grasp when he suddenly took two steps back, around the corridor corner, away from prying eyes, gently tugging me along with him. "Come here." The unexpected move had me reeling and he steadied me against him with my back to the wall. The corridor was empty and so – for all intents and purposes – we were alone.

I looked up at him questioningly, "What is it?"

"I just wanted to tell you something. Back there when you said how alone you felt? How, without your dad, you've got no-one to trust, no one to turn to?"

Again I nodded, this time unwilling to trust words as all my senses screamed at Daniel's closeness.

"Well, you're wrong. You're not alone Leila, you've got me. I don't ever want you to feel that way. You can trust me. Whenever you need me, I'm here. Just remember, you're not alone. Okay?"

His sincerity pierced me to the core. Standing there enveloped in his arms, I knew I would never feel as secure and protected as I did when I was with him. Before I could respond, he bent his head towards me and breathed a fleeting kiss against my cheek. And then, just as quickly, he moved away and was walking on down the hall, throwing another glance back at me before he quickened his pace to the next class.

It took a few moments for me to catch my breath, before I could go to class. When I entered the classroom, Maleko stood to attention with a mischievous grin. "Ahh, here she is."

He bowed with a flourish and knelt in front of me. "Oh please my lady, can I hold your hand too?"

The room erupted into laughter. I ignored them all and found a seat beside an excited Sinalei. Thankfully, the teacher walked in and started class before she could harass me with her curiosity. I couldn't evade her when we changed rooms, though, for last period.

"Ohmigosh Leila, what's going on with you and Daniel?! I didn't know that you two were … you know,close!"

"We're not. I mean, not really, not like that. We're just friends that's all. He's been really helpful with some stuff I'm going through. Friendly. That's all."

Sinalei rolled her eyes. "Whateverrrr."

Simone interrupted. "Shut up Sinalei, can't you see the girl is trying to be discreet. And what's a little hand holding? I hold hands with Daniel *alllllll* the time and with Riki and with Mark and with Leo and with Sanerivi, with everyone!" He frowned, "Wait, strike that - okay, maybe I don't hold hands with Maleko though."

All three of us burst out laughing as Simone twirled a pirouette in the corridor, bumping straight into the Principal, Mr. Raymonds.

"Ooops, sorry sir."

"Watch your step Simon, and the rest of you, get going to class before I put the whole lot of you on detention."

With that stern warning, any more talk of Daniel and I was pushed aside and the focus turned instead to a discussion on how to cope with the latest load of assignments.

SIX

I was still swept through with the delighted rush that Daniel evoked in me when I walked down the drive after school to catch my bus. So much so, that when I saw the red car at the gate, the sight didn't fill me with dread. My conversation with Daniel had prepared me for this. I was ready to see that woman again. I wouldn't call her my mother. Not yet. But I wouldn't run from her either. I steeled myself with the memory of Daniel's hand in mine and kept walking. Until I stood beside the still humming car. A cluster of boys were admiring the sleek lines, but they had even more to drop their jaws at when the driver alighted from the air-conditioned comfort. A naked, slender leg exited first, her long white skirt slit on one side to the thigh. Cut to show the patterned markings of a *malu*, the traditional Samoan tattoo given to a woman. I rolled my eyes. I'd give her this much, this woman knew how to make an entrance.

She unfurled from the car, a blinding vision in white that hugged her every sinuous curve. Gold stiletto heels should have made her unsteady on the rocky drive but she walked with confident ease towards me. Chunks of gold banded her bare arms, and again at her neck. Sunglasses obscured the cold eyes. The thick brown hair was pulled up into a generous coil. She didn't walk as much as she seemed to glide, emanating sensuality.The more daring of the boys threw her a whistle.

She didn't even flinch.

But out of a perfectly blue sky, a jagged flash of lightning whipped, distracting all eyes heavenward. Startled, the crowd of leerers jumped. I stood and watched her with impassive eyes.

"Ah Leila, how lovely to see you again." Her smile seemed genuine as she stopped in front of me, raising sunglasses to her forehead. "Seems I came just in time to catch you. Can I give you a ride somewhere?"

Aware of the still-ogling crowd whispering behind me, I shrugged. "Sure, why not. Beats waiting for the bus. Let's go."

Neither of us spoke as we walked to the car that still purred with cool ease. In the front seat, I threw my bag in the back before securing my seatbelt. The latch had barely clicked before we were accelerating away from the school. The car was blissfully cold after the heat of the day.

With eyes on the after-school traffic, the woman spoke casually, "I want to apologize for our abrupt meeting yesterday. I don't think we got off to a very good start. Perhaps we could start again?"

I too kept my eyes on the road ahead and shrugged non-comittally. "Maybe."

Encouraged, she continued. "If you're free this afternoon then, I'd like you to come visit me at my home, have some tea, give us a chance to talk. Clear things up. You must have some questions for me."

Again she dangled the lure of information in front of me. She knew that was the one promise I couldn't resist. Questions I had a-plenty. And yes, the chance to clear the mass of confusion that plagued me overcame all my apprehension about this woman.

"That would be okay. I mean, I'm free now. I'm ready to do this today." Silently, I thanked Daniel. If it hadn't been for our conversation at break, for his advice, there's no way I would have been in any state to sit and talk to this strangely frightening woman this way.

There was no more conversation for the remainder of the drive. She drove with practiced ease, while I studied our surroundings with interest. I'd been in the country now for over two months and still hadn't left Apia. School, church and the shops were the full extent of my sightseeing. Oh, and my night pool escape. And the mountainside river with Daniel. His mysterious secret place. The memory brought a little smile to my face. And another welcome boost of courage. To still the panic.

Where were we going? We whipped through town, turned at the Mormon temple and continued inland. Up winding roads. Which got greener as we went along. And the land sloped upward. The few houses were bigger, more stately, more further apart. Set back from the road, behind cement walls and lined with palms. Still we drove on. Now the road was emptier and the houses rare occurrences. We turned off the main tarseal onto another road and continued climbing upward and inward. There were no houses here, just thick, lush forest. Massive trees spread their arms above us, laced with ferns and hanging vines. Colorful birds regarded us solemnly as we drove past. I looked back and saw the coast splayed out behind us and the line of the horizon lancing the blueness. Finally, the car slowed beside an imposing set of gates. The woman pushed on a remote and the gates swung open quietly. We had arrived at my mother's house.

A long driveway curved ahead of us, embraced by trees. The woman gestured,

"Flame trees. They flower in December, and then it's just one long continuous line of crimson and orange. Stunning."

We drove slowly up the drive. Stretching away to my right was a vast expanse of garden, careful rows of greenery that marched endlessly away to the hills. It looked like fruit trees, herb bushes, and further away, vegetables, perhaps?

To the left was a rich riot of flowering forest, a cacophony of color. I recognized some favorites but many more had me puzzled. Frangipani trees of every color, hibiscus bushes, thickets of torch ginger, a multitude of bougainvillea. It danced on forever, in the distance I thought I caught the sparkle of water, a river? For someone who loved plants as much as I did it was almost paradisiacal. I couldn't hide my delight.

"It's beautiful. This is amazing. Who looks after all of this? There must be acres and acres of it!"

The woman smiled with satisfaction as she too looked out over the surroundings. "One hundred and twenty acres in fact. It goes all the way to the crest of the mountain. I have *ifilele* and *poumuli* forest in that direction, mixed with taro and bananas. But here are my flowers, and where I get all the food for the house, and the plants for my medicines. It's all organic and completely self-sustaining. There are no chemicals anywhere on my estate. The orchid collection is at the back of the house. Wait until you see that."

I turned bemused eyes on this woman who was supposed to be my mother. Less than an hour in her company and already I had the answer to one question – the origins of my plant obsession. I shook my head slowly. Someone who loved plants this much surely couldn't be that bad, could she?

I dragged my attention from the greenery and looked ahead to the house that was pulling into view. And gasped again. It was a colonial mansion straight from a southern belle movie. The car eased to a stop and I got out, mouth agape. Stately columns graced the wide verandah that encircled the white wooden two-storey structure. The ground floor seemed to have no walls as paneled accordion doors graced the full length of three sides. On this afternoon, they were all open, welcoming in the mountain air. You could clearly see the interior, the curved staircase. The chandelier that sparkled in the sunshine. The ornate bamboo furniture with its cinnamon cushions and wine red throw pillows. Traditional *elei* patterned drapes embraced each doorway. My eyes did all the talking as I walked up the stairs behind her and into the house. There was music playing somewhere unseen, a pitcher of lemon water called from a stained *ifilele* wood table, nuggets of ice dotted with slices of green. A platter of cut fruit. It all looked so inviting. Welcoming. Like the woman had been expecting company, like she had anticipated my acceptance of her invitation. Her confidence, assurance, made me grimace slightly.

She gestured to the kitchen counter sink, "Would you like to wash up before some refreshments, Leila? You do prefer the name Leila, don't you?"

I nodded silently as I scrubbed my hands free of school-day grime before joining her at the table. She passed me a plate and I helped myself to slices of papaya and mango. She continued. "So how long have you been here in Samoa?"

"Two months." The lemonade made me brave. "I came to find out about my dead mother. But nobody seemed to want to talk about you. Why do you suppose that is?" My gaze was confrontational, my tone like steel.

She was not fazed in the slightest. She took a slow bite of mango before answering. "I suppose because, as you can see, I am not dead. I am very much alive." She threw a jab of her own. "And tell me, Leila, what of your father? How is it that you are here and he is not?"

I strove to be as calm and collected as she. Even now. As thoughts of my father pierced me like coral slashing through my heart. Red and ragged. "My father is dead. For real. He died eight months ago. Brain tumor."

I wanted to see her flinch. To see her hurt. To see her shocked at least. I was disappointed. She smoothed an errant wisp of hair from her cheek and her eyes were thoughtful but distant. "I am sorry for your loss Leila. I cannot imagine how you must have felt. How you must have struggled. Do you have family watching over you? A stepmother perhaps?"

"No. My dad never remarried. It was just the two of us."

Again, she betrayed no emotion. She was polite and cool. One would think we were discussing a complete stranger to her – not a man she had loved and had children with. Coldness gripped me on this sun filled day. My father may have lied to me about my mother being dead, but I knew he had been honestly and completely in love with her. Of that I was sure. And to find that she did not seem to return the emotion seemed even more chilling then finding her alive when she should have been dead.

"So Leila, without a father and, it seems, a mother, who was taking care of you?"

I bristled. "I'm eighteen years old, Nafanua. I haven't needed anyone to take care of me for a while."

She laughed. Quietly. "I apologize Leila, let me rephrase that, I mean, did your father have no family to be your guardians?"

I nodded. "Yes, his mother, my Grandmother Folger. Before I came here, I was staying with her."

"Oh and how did she feel about your trip to Samoa? She just allowed you to fly halfway round the world by yourself?" There was sincere puzzlement in the woman's eyes.

"Well, she didn't like the idea. But she trusted my judgment," The lie came easily.

"I see. And your aunt and uncle, how has your stay with them been?"

"Fine. They're a lovely couple. I've been going to school, Samoa College, since I got here."

"Ahhh yes, my old school, once upon a time. So, what do you think of our country?"

"Well, I haven't seen very much of it really. Just school, church, home. A few trips to town. Aunty Matile really didn't want me going anywhere. Now we know why."

I was impatient with the conversation. I had come for answers and so far she had been asking all the questions. I struggled to regain control of the afternoon. "Nafanua, why did my father lie to me? Why did he tell me you were dead?"

There was stillness. Outside, a slight breeze slipped through the trees and, faraway, birds called. I studied the woman in white seated across from me at the table, waiting for her response. She took care with her words.

"I have not spoken to your father since before the hurricane. He left and took you with him without warning. Without my knowledge. Without my consent. He left. And I never saw you again. Do you know what that was like Leila? For me? For a mother? I knew that he loved you, I knew that he would be a good father to you, but do not expect me to speak well of the man who took my only daughter from me and then kept her from me for eighteen years!"

Her voice had raised a chilling octave and I felt a coldness in the room. Abruptly, the afternoon sun darkened as if storm clouds had moved overhead, and there was a distant rumble of thunder. Nafanua continued before I could find words to fill the silence.

"Leila, I do not wish to desecrate your memories of your father. I can see that you loved him very much and I am thankful that you had a good life with him. The problems that he and I had – they were between a man and a woman. A husband and a wife. He did me a great wrong by stealing you and taking you away from me. For that, I can never forgive him. But that shouldn't color what you shared with him. I look at you, a beautiful young woman, and I am just so grateful that you chose to return. I am hoping that I can now have that chance to know my daughter, I am hoping that it's not too late."

Tears glistened on her cheeks as she turned away from me to gaze outdoors where a light rain was falling.

I was speechless. I had come prepared for battle. For interrogation. I had stockpiled anger, resentment, and bitterness. I had strategized attack plans for confronting haughtiness, coldness, possessive pride, but this? This, I was not ready for. I had nothing in my armory for sadness. Pain. Loss. Grief. Hurt. Hope.

Nafanua stood and walked to a side table, returning with an album. "Here. Pictures of you. Of us. Before. They are all I have of you. Your father never wrote to me, never called. Eighteen years and these are all I have of you."

Without words, I took the album and carefully turned the pages. There I was. Sitting on her lap. Lying on a mat under the shade of a frangipani tree. Peeking from the arms of a richly beautiful Nafanua, grabbing at the red flower in her hair. A little brown baby with a shock of thick hair. Even then I had the bushy eyebrows and the sour expression. I turned puzzled eyes to the woman beside me.

"But where is my brother? How come he's not in the photos?"

For the first time, Nafanua looked unsettled. "How do you know about him? Did your father tell you?"

"No. Aunty Matile said I was a twin. I have…I had a brother. Who died when we were only a few months old. Before my dad took me away with him."

Nafanua relaxed slightly. "Yes. There were two of you." Another sad smile. "Twins. What a shock that was for me, let me tell you. They say a mother is supposed to know what she carries growing inside her, but I was completely caught by surprise that night. You were born on the beach, you know. There was a light rain, a cool sea breeze. I remember it was high tide because the water was catching on my legs when you finally came."

Her eyes took on a faraway gaze. "I didn't know then why I wanted to give birth on the beach. I had prepared a birth house in the forest, with all my favorite plants around me. There were golden *mosooi* flowers to rub on your skin with coconut oil. Everything was ready, but that night when the pains started, something called me to the ocean. Of course, your father, he wanted us to go to the hospital, ah" she shook her head impatiently at the memory. "But what does a man know of birth?"

"I went to the beach while he fetched the *taulasea*. There were dolphins there, you know. Silver ones. Waiting for me. For him." Her voice had trailed away so softly that I couldn't be sure of her last words. *Her? Him?* I hardly dared breathe, unwilling to break this spell of reminiscing, wanting to hear the story of my birth. And my brother's birth. "I should have known what they wanted. I should have suspected then that the boy was coming. But I wasn't listening, I wasn't thinking. I had felt your strength, your warmth, I knew you before you came. And that was all I was focused on. So when that boy was born, he was a shock. To all of us." Nafanua was quiet for so long that I was forced to prompt her.

"What happened to him Nafanua? What happened to my brother?"

She shrugged. "It wasn't meant to be. He was not meant to live. He was not strong enough. That happens sometimes with twins. At four months, I knew he would not live. But your father, he did not take it well. That's when things went bad between us. Again, I should have seen it coming. I should have known that he might take you away. But again I was not focusing. I had other concerns on my mind. And so, one day, I went out to a meeting with my sisters and he insisted on keeping you home with him. And when I returned, you were gone. He had it all arranged – the airline tickets, the temporary passport, everything." There was unwilling admiration in her voice. "He concealed his plans from me very well. I underestimated him. And so, he took you away."

"Did you ever try to see me? To contact me? To get me back?" There was pleading in my question. Hidden under nonchalance.

"Of course. But the might of American bureaucracy is stronger than a single Samoan woman who has lost hold of her baby. Your father was not without his connections. I could never get a visa to the States. No matter how hard I tried."

I thought of Grandmother Folger. I thought of her might, her steel resolve, her money, her willpower – and I could well believe Nafanua. A blanket of heavy sadness came to rest over me. My dad had lied to me. My dad had stolen me away from my mother. I knew I should have felt anger. But there was none.

I had questions that would probably never be answered now that he was gone, but it was impossible to summon hatred or venom when all I felt whenever I thought of him was love. Longing. Grief. I hung my head, focusing on the picture in front of me. I recognized this one – it was the photo my grandmother had sent me, but someone had cut it in half, leaving only the proudly beautiful woman and the baby. I shrugged to myself, I guess I shouldn't be surprised that Nafanua hadn't wanted to keep a reminder of the man that had kidnapped her child.

I took a deep breath. "I don't know what to say. This is so much to process at once. I can't understand why my dad did what he did. And part of me wishes he hadn't. All my life I wanted a mother. A family. That was more like me. I never quite fit in with the Folgers, but then" a half smile "my dad never quite fit in with them either, so I guess that made two of us. When he died, I had never felt so alone in my life. I came here looking for answers, I guess to be honest, I came here looking for a family. Aunty Matile and Tuala, they've been good to me, even though they didn't want me here. Now I find out I have a mother. And you're a mother that my aunt and uncle happen to hate. Aunty Matile seems to even be afraid of you." I turned curious eyes on Nafanua, "Why does Matile hate you so much?"

Nafanua shrugged non-committally. "Family issues. Such ancient history I can't even remember how it all began. Leila, I know this is a shock to you and I understand if you need time to process it." She stood again and walked out onto the verandah, pausing beside a luxuriant bird's nest fern. With her back to me, she spoke. "I would like to have a chance to get to know you. You are a grown woman and I'm sure you don't need a mother forced upon you but I would like to invite you to come and stay here with me for awhile. For as long as you like. So we may know each other – not necessarily as mother and daughter, but as friends. As family." She turned, a cautious smile on her face.

Whatever I had expected, it wasn't this. But as I sat there, I faced the hidden reality that I had secretly hoped this would happen. But then, maybe, every child with a long-dead mother dreams of a day that the impossible will happen and her mother will come back to life and want her? I know that my every waking dream was that my dad would somehow be alive somewhere. That the past eight months had all been some cruel nightmare and I was going to wake up.

I looked at this strange woman who smiled at me with my eyes and half shrugged. "Sure. I guess. I can come stay for awhile. I don't think Aunty Matile will like it, but I'll explain to her that you – that we just need a chance, to catch up."

Her smile lit the room and the air seemed to crackle with electricity. "Yes! That's great Leila, I'm sure you won't regret it. Now, shall I take you back to get your things. No, do you drive?"

"Yeah."

"Good. It's probably better if I don't go with you to your aunt's house, let's avoid confrontation there. You can take the jeep and get your things. Do you think you can remember the way back? Or text me and I can meet you at the intersection by the Mormon temple, I'll tell Netta to get your room ready." Nafanua was walking up and down the living room waving her arms excitedly, counting off a list on her fingers, "Oh, and we must have a dinner tonight to welcome you and, oh, there are a million and one things to do."

She stopped mid stride and laughed. Long, low, and musical. "Oh Leila, I am happy that you came home."

I hoped desperately that she wasn't going to hug me. I hated physical contact with strangers and it was far too soon to even consider faking affection for this woman. Thankfully, she did nothing of the kind, merely walking out a back door, throwing a summons over her shoulder. "Come on, I'll take you to the garage. I don't want you driving back in the dark so you better get going."

I followed her to the door of a huge four car garage. The estate made you think there would be a carriage or horse and cart in the garage – not the three gleaming vehicles that stood there. My mouth was agape. Clearly, this woman liked her trucks.

There was a land cruiser, a Hummer. And a Wrangler Jeep. All midnight black and silver. "Can you drive a stick-shift car?"

I nodded dumbly.

"Good." She threw me a set of keys. "Take the Wrangler. It's yours."

I was too numb to catch the glinting bunch of silver. The keys landed at my feet. "I can't. I can't accept a car from you. I'll drive it to pick up my stuff but it's not mine."

Nafanua raised a questioning eyebrow. "Why not?"

"I don't even know you. It's just ridiculous."

She put one hand on her hip and pouted. I could see it working magic on a man. "Leila, now *you're* being ridiculous. You're my daughter." She threw her arm expansively to the estate behind us. "You see all that? It's yours. All of it. Well, it will be yours one day. All your life I have given you nothing. Your father made sure of that. Now you are eighteen, surely I can give you this one thing? You would deny me this one thing? Who's being ridiculous?'

Without even waiting for a reply, she turned to walk back in the house but then came back with a business card. "My cell. Text me when you get to the intersection and I'll come get you. Don't want you to get lost on your way back. Not when I just found you."

A half smile and she went back into the house. The conversation was over. I felt like I'd been bamboozled without even realizing it. I don't know what I had been expecting when I drove up here with this woman, but here I was an hour later – her long-lost daughter, driving her Wrangler, and coming back to stay in her house with her. So we could get to know each other better. With my brain still in numb shock, I slowly drove the unfamiliar car down the sloping driveway. I hadn't driven a car since I arrived and it felt incredibly freeing. I drove with the windows down, the wind in my hair, on my face. I could have driven like that all around the island but too soon I had to pull up in front of the square house with the frangipani tree in the front yard. It was time to tell Aunty Matile and Tuala of my decision.

They didn't like it of course. Aunty Matile cried some more. Silent tears, shaking her head. Uncle Tuala only sighed, long and low, "Are you sure Leila? Are you sure this is what you want to do?"

"Yes. Uncle, please understand, I'm not trying to be ungrateful for all that you and Aunty have done for me. I don't want to hurt you. I just want to get to know this woman better. I have no father. No family really. Please just allow me this chance to know this mother a little."

He smiled sadly. "Leila, you are a grown woman, not a child. You are our guest, not our prisoner. It is not for us to decide where you stay, where you go. And while we may think you are making a mistake, this is your decision to make."

He helped me take my bag to the jeep. I was slowly getting into the driver's seat when Aunty Matile came out of the house. "Leila, you be careful, you hear me? You be careful. And when your visit with that woman is finished, you come back here and stay with us again. We are your family, you hear me? And be a good girl." She waved at me. "Be a good girl, Leila. And come back soon."

They stood and watched me drive away in the fast-approaching evening. I was sad. But tense with excitement. I was Leila Pele Folger. I had a mother called Nafanua. And I was going to stay at her house.

The rest of the evening was one of discoveries. Nafanua met me at the main road intersection and drove the rest of the way back up to the stately house in the forest. She showed me to my room on the second floor, a huge retreat with a king-size four-poster bed and French doors that opened out onto a balcony overlooking the back of the property. There was an ensuite bathroom, masses of flowers in clay jugs, abundant ferns trailing their green sweetness all throughout the house. My one bag of clothes looked rather dismal in the vast wardrobe. I didn't have much time to dwell on it though before Nafanua was calling me downstairs.

I met Netta, the housekeeper, an unsmiling woman with grey hair pulled tightly back in a bun whose scowl deepened as she stared pointedly at the dirt on my shoes where I stood on the polished beauty of the wood flooring. *Oops.* Quickly, I excused myself to take my shoes and leave them at the door. I was rewarded with a curt nod.

The rest of the house flowed seamlessly into a library, another two bedrooms and Nafanua's master suite. Every room beckoned to the outdoors though, with the opening French doors and wrap-around verandah, so coolness and light flowed endlessly. At the back of the house was a square block building almost overgrown with bougainvillea. There was excited anticipation in Nafanua's voice as she threw open the door.

"My lab. Here's where I do all my work."

I followed behind her. And stood still in awe. Again. There were plants everywhere, hanging from pots suspended from the ceiling, in baskets lining the wall. The center of the room was lined with two long benches crowded with gleaming steel equipment. A computer or two. Machines that beeped and hummed. Glass boxes that held orchids and drooping branches under artificial lighting. There were two shelves crowded with beakers and test tubes, plastic tubing, and pipes.

"Wow." I couldn't manage anything else. But Nafanua didn't seem to notice.

"Here's where I spend most of my time. Nights especially are my favorite time to work."

"What are you working on?"

"Medicines, plant grafting, seed propagation, different things. As you know, plants are where we get most of our modern medicine from. My sisters and I, we're traditional healers so we have the benefit of many hundreds of years of knowledge handed down to us by our mothers. Too often, modern science and Western medicine rip off traditional healers. They take our plants, they take our knowledge, 'invent' a cure for something and then get filthy rich off it. And maybe they throw a few cents over their shoulder for the villagers who were foolish enough to give them the information in the first place. Well, thanks to our work here in the lab, we don't need them. In the last many years, we've successfully patented several plant-based medicines and ensured that the profits come back where they should. Here. And we in turn put them back into village-based projects."

"So that's what you do then? You're a science researcher?"

She shrugged. "Among other things. I do a bit of consultancy work for different environmental organizations as needed. My sisters and I are lobbyists in the region as well as locally. But enough about me. You like plants, yes?"

I nodded, glad to find common ground. "Yes, they make more sense than people for me. I had a little collection of my own at home that my dad would help me gather samples for. Nothing as extensive as yours though. Wow." I walked around the lab, foraging thoughtfully through the specimens and labeled containers, "This is pretty amazing stuff."

"You're welcome to come in here whenever you like, look around, help yourself to everything. Later on when you're settled, I'd always appreciate an extra hand with my work. If you want to."

She made the offer openly without reservation but I wasn't ready to embrace it. A non-committal shrug, "Sure."

As if sensing the hesitation she moved on. "Come, you must be tired. Would you like to go in and shower, get ready for dinner? I decided against having you meet my sisters on your first night, thought it would be a bit much for you, so it's just us and Netta. But she is making something extra special for your welcome dinner, so I hope you're hungry."

I smiled and nodded. Food I was always ready to embrace. A cold shower and a change of clothes later and I was sitting at Nafanua's table while Netta served a delicious array of food. Sweet baked fish in honey ginger sauce. Crayfish. Octopus in coconut cream. Watercress and lettuce salad with mint. Nafanua explained. "We don't eat a lot of red meat. Everything on this table comes from our own land. The other side of the property fronts onto the ocean so we get fresh fish daily. Netta caught this octopus just this morning, didn't you Netta?"

Dessert was the grand exclamation mark after an already full paragraph. *Faausi* – papaya dumplings in a caramel sticky sweet sauce. And mango pie. Coconut milk custard. I groaned. "I will definitely need to go for a run tomorrow morning Netta, this has been so delicious and I've eaten way too much food. Thank you very much. I can't believe you made all this just for us."

The grim-faced woman softened to a smile. Which widened appreciatively as I jumped to clear the table and helped with the washing up. As I was drying the last dish, Nafanua called from the living room. "When you're done, Leila, can you come walk with me for a little bit?"

The night shadows were heavy with the scent of jasmine as we walked slowly through the garden in the silver moonlight. Nafanua paused beside a cluster of gardenia bushes and reached into her pocket, bringing out a soft *siapo* cloth bag. She held it out to me.

"I want you to have this. I made it for you during those months when I was carrying you. It was to have been a gift when you turned twelve. The age that we, that my family considers the age that a girl becomes a woman. It would bring me great joy if you accepted this gift now, even if it is late. Because I hope it isn't too late Leila, for you and I. To be family."

I didn't know what to say. Instead I reached out for the bag, and opened it. Out tumbled a bone carving that gleamed whitely in the darkness. Intricate patterns and swirls marked its smooth surface. I exclaimed with the beauty of it. "It's lovely, Nafanua. You made this? What is it made from?"

"Whale bone. Our ocean cove is where the Pacific whale comes to die. It is a place of peace and rest. When their time is near, they know they can find refuge here. And in death they know they can find reverence. We perform the sacred death rites and in exchange we take a piece of bone. It is saved for when we have a daughter and we engrave it with some of our legends. Our history. And our hopes for her future." She carefully showed me a similar carving that hung from a gold chain around her own neck. "This was made for me by my mother and I wear it always. She's long gone now but this is my link to her, to our past, and to my family."

My breath was an indrawn hush in the white moonlit night. Without knowing why, tears threatened me and I turned away in the darkness to contain them, my emotions a swirling mess. It was too much. All my life not only had I been reconciled to having no mother but I'd battled to fit the mold of requisites for being a bona fide Folger, failing miserably more often than not. And now, to have a mother, to have a legacy, links to a past, and a family – it was more than I had ever dreamed possible. I had been living in thick choking darkness ever since my dad died and this light just seemed too bright to be real.

"Leila, are you alright? If you don't wish to accept the carving, I will understand. I can hold on to it for another time. For when you're ready?"

I shook my head. "No, I'm fine. I like it. I would like to wear it. Thank you. It's just that, this ..." I waved my hands at the richness around us "all this, it's a bit much to take in all at once. I used to dream of having a mother you know. I would pester my father to marry again and once I even signed him up on an online dating service."

I smiled at the memory. "He thought that was hilarious. And he even let me help him pick some possible listings to go on a date with. And then I hated them all in person anyway and he thought that was even funnier. Nafanua, I appreciate this, I really do. I just need time to take it all in."

"Of course, I understand. We have all the time in the world. And you will find that I am a very patient woman, Leila. Now, come, it's getting late and we both need sleep."

Together, we moved back into the house, Nafanua pausing before going to her rooms.

"Oh, we won't see each other in the morning. I will be off early on a project with my sisters. But Netta will be here to prepare breakfast. You can find your way to school from here can't you? You won't get lost? And if you are here tomorrow evening, there will be a dinner with my sisters."

"Well, school finishes at 2:30 so I can get back here before 3 unless I get put on detention or something. I'll try not to be late."

Nafanua waved an airy hand carelessly. "Leila, one thing you must get clear. I don't know what it was like to live with Matile but here in this house, everyone comes and goes as they please. You have the car. Take it where you will as you need it. You are not a child. I don't expect you to check in or out. I've opened a bank account for you, here's the card. So if you need money for anything, it's there."

Before I could protest she held up her hand with finality. "Leila, remember what I said to you earlier. I have been denied the choice of being in your life for 18 years. Please allow me some choices now. It's not much. A home to stay in. Netta's finest cooking for you to eat. A car to drive. Some money for expenses. At least allow me that much. Your father's choices denied me your childhood, please allow me to do something to help you now."

I couldn't argue with her. How could I? Instead, I silently accepted the money card, resolving never to use it and went upstairs to bed. It was a night without dreams. A night without tears.

The next day at school I was bursting with excitement, eager to tell someone, anyone, about the new development in my life. Well, I amended, I would be honest, not anyone, I wanted to tell Daniel about my visit with my mother. The morning classes dragged interminably. As soon as the bell rang for break, I was up and out of my desk, so quick that Maleko whooped as I bolted past him, "Hey, Leila where's the fire, girl?" I ignored him, too impatient to even poke my tongue at him.

I walked quickly to block C where Daniel had class, and couldn't stop the foolish grin when I caught sight of his red gold perfection. I had to stop myself from breaking into a run as I moved towards him. There was an answering smile on his face as I came to a halt in front of him. Suddenly, awkwardly shy. "Hi."

He had one eyebrow arched quizzically. "Hi, why do I feel like I'm in trouble or something? You look like you're about to explode. You're not going to attack me about being racist again are you? What have I done now?"

His grin softened the words. I laughed, giddily. "No. Nothing. I mean you have done something, you did do something. Already. Yesterday. When I was upset about that whole surprise mother thing? Well, you were right. And it worked out good."

My tumble of words stopped as he started laughing, raising up his hands in mock surrender. "Hey, hey, slow down. I can't follow a hundred words a minute you know. Here, let's go find somewhere to sit down and you can tell me all about it. Slowly."

Shaking his head, he led the way down the hall and out to a bench under the palm trees swaying beside the rugby field. Once we were both seated, he looked at me sideways.

"Okay, I'm ready. Now let me have it. What's happening?"

I replayed the previous day's events, oblivious to the lunch break activity around us. When I came to a stop he didn't speak. Just regarded me with inscrutable eyes. I waited, feeling foolish.

"Umm, what? Why are you looking at me like that?"

"Like what?"

"Like I'm a certifiable lunatic or something? What is it?"

His smile assuaged my worries. "Nothing. It's just that you're so different when you're happy, excited. So alive. When you first came here, I remember, you walked like a half-dead person. You *were* a half-dead person. Or a seriously attitudinal one."

I narrowed my eyes at him warningly so he rushed to finish his sentence. "I mean – don't shoot me yet – what I meant to say was, you're beautiful. Watching you talk with all the hand motions and the emotions coming out everywhere. You're beautiful."

Whatever I had been expecting, it wasn't that. Shock had me speechless. Stunned silent. What do you say when a gloriously beautiful boy tells you that *you're* beautiful? If I'd been white, I would have blushed red. But since I was brown, I just sat and my every thought stuttered. I dropped my eyes and longed for a rock to crawl under. Somewhere to hide. So I could process what had just happened. What Daniel had just said.

In the heavy pause, someone called Daniel's name.

"Daniel! Are you coming?"

We both turned. It was Mele, looking petulant with one hand on her hip. "Everybody's waiting for you, prefects meeting remember?!"

Daniel groaned and stood quickly to gather his things. "Damn. Sorry Leila, I forgot. Manuia, the Head Girl, called a prefects meeting for lunchtime today and I kind of need to be there. That's awesome news about your mom though, can we talk about it later today? After school?"

I nodded, just thankful for the reprieve from the awkwardness. The chance to recover from being sucker punched by a compliment *you're beautiful*. That's not something I heard often. Correction, that's not something I heard ever. Double correction, my dad told me I was beautiful all the time, well, he used to. But then he was monumentally biased and not to be believed. A dark scowl plagued me as I walked slowly to join Simone and the others beside the canteen. Because I was remembering that there were other things that my dad obviously couldn't be believed on either…

The rest of the day passed uneventfully. My feet dragged as I made my way to the student parking lot under the mango tree beside the back tennis court. Not even the sight of the black Wrangler jeep could slice through my dread.

I was supposed to meet Daniel here. Daniel who had told me I was beautiful and I still hadn't figured out how to respond to that. At the jeep, I chucked my gear in the back and unzipped the canvas cover. It was another hot afternoon and I wanted to drive with the wind in my face. I didn't hear Daniel come up behind me until the long low whistle had me turning.

"Nice ride! Since when do you have a Wrangler, Ms Leila?"

He walked over to run his fingers lightly along the side of the jeep, until he stood far too close to me for breathable comfort. Unconsciously I backed up several steps.

"Oh it's not mine. It's my ..." I stumbled over the word, "mother's. Well, it belongs to Nafanua. Just letting me drive it to school since there're no buses up our way."

"Oh have you moved?" His eyes were curious.

"Just for a bit. She invited me to stay for a while, so I took her up on her offer. She lives up at Aleisa and I'm just going to hang out there while we talk, maybe till I know a bit more about her. Before I go back. Home."

A huge smile lit his face, "Hey that's great Leila, so you're going to give her a chance? Your relationship a chance? That takes courage, I like that. I'm happy for you." Then he faked a huge frown. "But can you please not park next to my green bomb next time you come to school? I mean, heck, don't make him feel bad! You'll be giving him inadequacy issues next to this beauty."

The light banter was a relief. It was as if the lunchtime conversation hadn't happened. I rushed to fill the gaps with more ease. "You want to go for a ride? I'm still not used to driving it yet, so don't expect Mario Andretti skills or anything."

"Leila, Andretti driver skills are the last thing I would expect from you, from any girl. Haven't you heard that female drivers are absolutely shocking?!"

I parried his gibe with a threat. "If you keep that up, the closest you'll be getting to my Wrangler, is when I run you over with it."

He just laughed as he lightly flexed and climbed into the passenger seat, making a big deal about adjusting the seatbelt. "Bring on the worst that you got girl, I'm all buckled up and ready for the ride."

I merely rolled my eyes at his drama and started up the engine. "Where do you want to go?"

He looked thoughtful for a moment then lightened, "I know, let's go to my place, I want you to meet my grandmother."

He gave me directions as I drove out of the school compound, studiously ignoring the curious spectators. I wasn't sure if they were gaping at the car or the ruggedly beautiful boy sitting in the front seat with me.

I was thankful for the firm grip of the steering wheel, which was the only thing steadying me. I had only limited experience with grandmothers, and they weren't positive. The thought of meeting Daniel's grandmother made me feel slightly queasy. And since when did teenagers want to take their friends to meet their grandparents? Back home, meeting grandparents was something only old, married people did. I kept quiet and shrugged. Oh well, maybe this was another of those weird cultural habits that I didn't know about yet? Maybe everyone at school had met Daniel's grandmother and vice versa? Maybe I was supposed to invite people to meet *my* grandmother? I stifled a giggle as I thought of the First XV traipsing into Grandmother Folger's white-on-white living room. Sweaty and shirtless. I had to laugh.

Which had Daniel looking at me. "What? What are you smiling about?"

"Nothing. Just thinking about my grandmother back home. I wouldn't want anyone to meet her. She's a dragon lady. What's yours like?"

"We're each other's only family. She's everything to me." He spoke simply, an obvious truth. "I was born in Tonga. I didn't know my father, and my mother died when I was a baby. She had been their only child so I became their only son. We lived in Tonga until I was about five, then we moved here. Grandfather was a welder and started his own workshop. I worked with him every day after school. He taught me everything I know. When he died two years ago, I kept the business open. So it's been pretty much just me and Mama."

His openness caught me off guard. I snuck him a sideways glance. In that moment, he looked every inch his nineteen years and then some. I couldn't imagine having to take on a business at the age of seventeen and was impressed again by his sense of responsibility. He spoke so matter of factly about death and the loss of loved ones that I felt almost ashamed of my own struggles to cope.

"So let me get this straight. You run a business, play sport, and go to school? I don't get how you manage it all? How do you do it?"

"It's a lot of work – what with school and training – but we've got three welders that work with me. So as long as I'm organized properly – I manage to stay on top of things. Grandfather was sick for a long time before he died and so I was already helping out a lot at the workshop. Then when he died, I took a year off school to run the business. I wasn't planning on going back but grandmother wouldn't let me give up on school. So we worked out an arrangement so I can still manage the shop and school. I've really had to be organized – but then Mama wouldn't let me not be focused! Usually I don't take a lunch break. That's when I do my assignments because there isn't much time for homework after school. The coach was great. I talked to him about my situation so he moved rugby training to the early mornings so I could still be on the team. I *was* going to quit but Mama wanted me to still play – besides, my chances of a scholarship are better if I keep up the rugby. I had a few offers last year for rugby scholarships at some high schools in New Zealand and one in Australia, but I wasn't prepared to leave Mama. If I can get a contract at the senior or professional level, then I can afford to close the business, take engineering as a part-time student and even take Mama with me. She doesn't know about *that* part of the plan though – she would hate the idea of moving."

I didn't know how to respond. He had clearly thought out every step of his long-term plans for at least the next five to ten years of his life. Clearly, his desire to provide for his grandmother was a key factor in those plans. And his every daily decision now, revolved around those plans. I was awestruck at his vision and commitment, which I had never encountered in a teenager before. I thought of the girls in my year at Washington Girls, planning as far as what dress they would buy for their sweet sixteen, how they would spend their graduation presents, whether they would summer in Aspen or Paris. And I thought of my own self-absorption as I had carried out my decision to sell my car and come to Samoa – no matter what Grandmother Folger said or how she tried to stop me.

Guiltily, I confessed to myself, that concern for my safety and my happiness would have been paramount on her agenda as she had tried to block my attempts to come here. Sitting there listening to Daniel share his visions and dreams for the future – his future and his grandmother's *together* – I was confronted by my own contrasting selfishness and an uncomfortable reality. *This boy is far too good for me.*

Thankfully, he distracted me from my morose thoughts. "Turn up here, my house is up this way."

Daniel lived in Moata'a village, only a few minutes' drive from school. "Some of the best rugby players in the world come from Moata'a." he announced proudly as we pulled up in front of a green brick house with a sweeping breadfruit tree in the yard. To the right was a grand old church with gleaming stained glass windows and lacy spires. On the left was a steel frame warehouse with a faded sign blowing in the wind. *'Daniel's Welding.'* The double doors were wide open and a man in blue overalls, his face obscured in a steel helmet, was welding a chain link gate. I stood mesmerized by the golden red sparks as they danced and fizzed on the concrete, and was sorry when the man noticed our arrival and abruptly extinguished the hot blue flame of the welder. Lifting his helmet, his weathered face lit in a smile, he walked to greet us.

"*Sole* Daniel! I wasn't expecting you back this early. No game today?"

"Nah, games got suspended for a few weeks while they sort out the mess over the fight the other day. Too bad, cos we were ready to take on Avele College." He turned to nudge me forward with one broad shoulder. "Sene, I want you to meet my friend, Leila. She just moved here from the States and I'm bringing her to meet Mama."

The older man raised one bushy gray eyebrow as he looked me up and down. "Ahh, I see. It's nice to meet you Leila. This is something new. Danny doesn't often bring friends home to meet his grandmother." Sene wiped grease-stained hands on his overalls before reaching forward to give me a firm handshake.

I swallowed nervously. Was he meaning that 'Mama' was so scary that nobody wanted to meet her? Great. Just great.

"Well, I'm looking forward to it. What were you working on Mr. Sene?"

Both Daniel and Sene smiled at my words.

"Just Sene will do fine. I'm fixing up a gate for a customer. Since Mr. Rugby Star here has been too busy lately to get this order finished – but then he doesn't know what he's doing half the time anyways ... he'd probably screw it up as usual."

Daniel replied with a guffaw. "Ha yeah right! Leila, I taught Sene everything he knows and I've still got tons more in reserve. He can't handle too much information at his age, can't teach a old dog new tricks, you know."

Sene waved him away with a good-natured grin."Yeah, yeah – there goes the boss – mouthing off as usual. You better get Leila inside to meet your grandmother before she changes her mind about wanting to hang around a loudmouth who can't weld half as good as he talks."

I couldn't resist jumping in. "Actually I've never been inside a welding workshop before. Do you think I could have a look around well, I guess later after I meet your grandmother of course?"

"Sure." Daniel was surprised. "If you like, we can come back out here and check out Sene's work. Only we'd better be careful, he's not too steady on the arc welder and we might get our faces burned off."

Sene's only reply was to pull his helmet back down, turn the welder on and wave it at us threateningly. Daniel laughed his golden laugh and took my hand in his.

"Come on, let's go in. Mama will probably be out back in her garden, where she always is."

Loving the feel of his hand in mine, we walked around to the back of the house. I stopped short in amazement at the sight that greeted me.

"Ohmigosh. It's beautiful."

Gold green sunlight danced on the abundant garden before us. It was a slice of rainforest heaven – but with some semblance of order to its lushness. Coral rock pathways meandered through giant ferns and low-lying *tamaligi* trees. Everywhere, stunning orchids trailed their seductive branches. Rare purple, orange, white blossoms. Where Nafanua's acreage was a vast expanse of green lushness, this was a far more compact but harmonious collection. It felt like every sprig had been handpicked, every leaf was known, every flower beloved. The earth spoke of love and closeness. Not since the nightmare reaction in Nigeria had I felt such a powerful emanation from a piece of land. This garden was speaking to me. Of serenity, happiness, and peace.

I turned accusingly to Daniel. "You never said anything about your grandmother's garden!"

His reply was a casual shrug, his face somewhat puzzled by my excitement. "Ahh it's no big deal. She loves plants. Uses them to make different medicines and stuff. People are always coming to her for help when their kids get sick and stuff."

"Your grandmother is a native healer?"

His green eyes flashed warning fire. "Hey, we don't take too kindly to being called natives you know."

I hastily tried to explain. "I didn't mean *that* kind of native. Sorry, I meant native as in she uses plants native to your land for healing. This kinda stuff is sort of what I was into back home. This is really big, Daniel. There's tons of research being done nowadays on traditional medicines because Western science is finally opening their eyes to the fact that the answers to all sorts of disease could be found in traditional knowledge and - oh, look at that ..."

I stopped short in my spiel, my eye caught by a green- and red-veined plant clinging softly to a coconut stump. Kneeling beside it, I gently touched it, hardly daring to breathe on it.

"Daniel, do you know what this is?"

His blank face and raised eyebrows were answer enough. I spoke in hushed tones.

"This is the *mamala* plant. There's a lab in the States studying this right now because initial trials show it inhibits the cells that cause HIV. Can you just imagine? This tiny plant right here, from an island in the South Pacific that most people have never heard of, could be the cure for several million people worldwide. And yet, native Samoan healers have been using this plant for centuries in their medicines. There's just so much Western science has to learn from native healers in all cultures."

Daniel's face was quizzical as he stood looking down at me. "Leila, just when I think I have you figured out, you go and add another piece of you to the mix and I have to start all over again."

"What do you mean?" I was suddenly embarrassed by my response to his grandmothers garden. Seeing myself through his eyes. Kneeling in the dirt, fussing over plants, ranting about science and medicine.

Good one Leila, now he's gonna think you're a freak.

"Well, as far back as I can remember, Mama has taken care of her plants and I gotta say I never really paid much attention to it at all. Was just real thankful for her garden when she cooked me up nasty concoctions every time I got sick. I remember this one time. It was real bad. Just about everybody in the village was sick with a real bad stomach virus ... ugh ... you did not want to be anywhere near us then! Anyways, Mama made a special drink for everyone that worked right away. I had never been so grateful for her garden as I was that night. Then, not only that, she also took some plants to grow by the side of the water spring where most of us get our drinking water. Said they would disinfect the water so we wouldn't get sick again. And it worked."

He paused to shake his head at the memory, then continued. "But like I said, I don't pay much attention to Mama's plants. Just help her when she needs it. Then I bring you here and you make me think about curing HIV and native healers and all that and well, you just make me open my eyes a bit that's all." As if sensing my disquiet, he smiled reassuringly at my hesitant stance. "I like it. Go on, tell me some more. How about this plant? Don't tell me this ugly thing has some use?" He poked with his foot at a prickly cluster of red leaves.

Before I could answer, a quiet voice spoke from behind us. "Daniel. Who is this?"

Guiltily, I jumped up, brushing the dirt from my knees, hoping I didn't look too disheveled. Daniel turned to greet the grey-haired woman who stood motionless behind us.

"Mama, this is my friend Leila that I was telling you about. She was just admiring your garden. She loves plants too."

There was an edge to the air as I moved to greet the old woman. She was a lean, imposing woman, almost as tall as I, wearing a man's grey buttoned shirt and slacks, a woven ribbed hat, and chunky boots. She shook my hand lightly, almost unwillingly, as if she couldn't wait to release it. She had searching brown eyes that regarded me with questions. With unease? I shifted my feet apprehensively. Without even speaking a word, I knew this woman didn't like me. She didn't want me here. Daniel seemed oblivious to the tension though as he continued.

"Leila's mother just gave her a car so she was trying it out, I had her give me a ride. Thought we could check out your kitchen, see what treats you cooked up this morning?" His teasing tone was hopeful and the old woman's face softened in response.

"Ahhh, Daniel, always thinking of food. Will things ever change? You're in luck. I made some coconut buns this morning. Leila, why don't you take a seat out here while Daniel helps me with some refreshments?"

The two walked into the house while I moved to sit on the wrought iron bench beside a honeysuckle bush. Through the open window, however, I could hear them in the kitchen as they moved about with plates and cutlery. There was no mistaking the old woman's statement.

"Tanielu. She is not for you." The words were spoken with finality.

"Mama, what do you mean? Leila's my friend." Daniel's answer was puzzled.

"Tanielu. I mean exactly what I say. She is not for you. You would be wise to stop this friendship before it goes any further. Before it's too late. No good can come from it."

"Mama, you speak in twists and turns. You've always trusted my judgment. Why not now?"

"Because there are things I know that you do not. Things I can sense that you cannot. I speak not to hurt you, my son. Nor to cast doubt on your judgment. I tell you with a clean heart, Tanielu. That girl is not for you."

A typical teenage boy would probably have stomped and muttered. Ranted and raved. Thrown a tantrum. Sworn and smashed things. Stormed out. Leaving a parent shaking their head at the rashness and ignorance of youth. But Daniel was no typical teenage boy. And clearly, his relationship with his grandmother did not follow 'normal' societal rules on parent-teenager interaction.

There were the sounds of glasses rattling as Daniel continued preparing the lemonade. The silence was not one of seething angry resentment, but of careful consideration. Numb with shock and anger at the exchange happening in the kitchen, I realized Daniel was thinking over his grandmother's words, thinking what to say. What to do? About me?

I clenched my fists, willing myself not to get angry. What had I done to make this old woman hate me? What did she see that I didn't? What could she sense that I couldn't? For a brief moment, I didn't care what Daniel's answer would be. I felt a rush of familiar heat and all I wanted to do was storm out of the garden and get as far away as I could from Daniel and his grandmother. It seemed that I would never have any luck with grandmothers the world over...

They came out to the garden before I could act on my impulsive thought. Daniel carefully balancing a tray of glasses, chock-a-block with ice, a glass jug of clear lemonade. Mama had a platter of coconut buns, napkins. Daniel sat beside me on the crowded seat while Mama served the afternoon tea. I was subdued, frostily polite.

"So Leila, tell me about your parents?"

"My father is American. He died last year from cancer. My mother is Samoan. I've been visiting with my aunt and uncle and only just met my mother a few days ago actually. I'm staying with her for a little while but I plan to go back to the States in a few months."

"Oh yes, and who is your mother?"

I paused, realizing I didn't actually know her surname, "Her name is Nafanua."

The shattering glass had both Daniel and I on our feet. Mama had dropped the glass of lemonade. It lay on the ground, the scatter of glass fragments like glistening teardrops on the cement.

"Mama, are you okay?" Daniel was full of concern but the old lady waved him away.

"Yes, yes, I'm fine. Don't worry. So clumsy of me, the glass just slipped right out of my hands. Perhaps I'm a little tired, a bit too much sun. If you'll excuse me, I might go in and take a little rest." Mama stood and turned to me. "Leila, it was a pleasure to meet you. I always enjoy meeting Daniel's friends."

With that, she walked back into the house, leaving Daniel and I to clean up the mess. I was shell-shocked. I just knew that the woman had dropped that glass because she heard me say my mother's name. She hated me. She had warned her grandson to stay away from me. She knew something about me, about my mother, that I didn't. My hands were shaking as I helped Daniel pick up the glass and take the dishes inside.

In the cool dimness of the kitchen, we worked together to wash the cups. My appetite had vanished, so Daniel consumed four of the coconut buns while I dried everything and put them away. I looked around. It was a comfortable kitchen. Baby pictures of a chubby little boy with cheeky green eyes smiled at me from the fridge door. A baby held by a distinguished silver-haired man in blue overalls.

"Is this you and your grandfather?"

Daniel smiled. "Yep, that's us."

"You're lucky, to have such good parents. A good home. It feels so complete here. Thank you for bringing me. I'm sorry that your grandmother didn't like me." My tone dared Daniel to contradict me.

He shrugged easily. "Hey, isn't that classic though? Your parents are never supposed to like the girl you bring home. I bet your dad despised the boys you took home."

The laughter spilled out before I could stop it. The idea of boys wanting to go home and meet my dad was ridiculous. The thought of boys wanting to go anywhere with me was even more funny. Daniel looked at me curiously but I just shook my head and declined to offer any explanations. It was quiet in the house. And too close for comfort in the kitchen. Daniel was too tall, too big – he filled the air, every breath I took tasted of him. And while I thrilled to be alone with him, I was conscious of his grandmother somewhere in the house. Probably seething at my presence. My eyes flashed,

"Hey, can we check out the workshop now?"

"Sure. What time do you have to be home though? Don't you have a super tight curfew?"

I waved my hand airily at him as we strolled out to the shop. "Nah. That's the one bonus of staying with my mother. She doesn't mind me being out late. She's a little more in tune with the 21st century."

The rest of the afternoon whiled away in fascinating fire and sparks. Sene was working on a set of wrought iron gates in the far corner, so Daniel and I donned helmet and overalls. He then proceeded to walk me through some of the welding basics. It was hot, humid work but enthralling as the blue fire alternately cut through and joined pieces of metal. Daniel left me to practice welding a straight line on a scrap piece of metal while he helped Sene to solder two frames together. It was with a jolt that I realized the sun was setting, as Daniel turned off the welder.

"Hey, welder woman, it's time to quit! You're going to burn a hole right through the floor soon."

Sene laughed as they both stood and watched me come out of my blue fire daze. I was flushed and exhilarated. "That was amazing! Thank you, I loved it. If you're taking on apprentices, then I'm the woman for the job."

Sene's reply was a rough guffaw, "Just what we need, another complete novice around here, as if I don't have enough to deal with trying to clean up Daniel's messy work."

The two men continued to joke as they put the gear away and packed up the workshop. It was a cool relief to peel off the overalls, down to my thin t-shirt and cut-off denim shorts. I bunched my wiry mane of unhelpful hair into a messy chunk at my neck, longing for a cold shower as I walked out to the Wrangler. The ocean was coming in at high tide across the road and the setting sun was throwing crimson fire haphazardly across the blue easel of sky. I paused.

"Wow, you get to see that every day... this is a great spot to live. You must go swimming every day."

Daniel avoided my eyes. "Nah. The ocean isn't my thing. Shall we go get my car?"

I didn't pursue his swift changing of the subject. I had completely forgotten about his truck. "Ohmigosh, I'm sorry, yeah, we better get your green bomb," I teased, "otherwise she might think you've run off with a sexy black Wrangler and abandoned her forever under the mango trees!"

We farewelled Sene and drove back to the school where deepening shadows were beginning to slink from their hiding places. The place was deserted, the only activity coming from across the field where the hostel students were gathering for dinner at the canteen. Daniel hopped out and walked over to the driver's side. Concern creased his face as he looked down at me.

"I'm sorry I kept you so late. I don't like you driving home by yourself. It's not safe."

"I'll be fine. I'm driving a new Wrangler, how unsafe could it possibly be?"

He was unconvinced. "I'm going to follow you though. Just to make sure you get home okay. And give me your cellphone number so I can check you get in alright."

He wouldn't take no for an answer. Night was fast falling as we drove the long route up to Aleisa and I had to admit that the reassuring gleam of his headlights behind me was a comfort, especially when I had to turn off the main road to the long drive up into the mountain isolation. We were almost to the house when my phone buzzed. It was him.

"You okay? I'm glad I followed you, your mom's place is miles away from anything."

"Yeah, I'm good. And thank you. For following me. I was kind of worried."

"No problem. I'll make sure not to keep you so late next time. Drive safe."

"Umm Daniel?"

"Yeah?"

"Thanks. For today. I had a great time. Even though your grandmother hated me."

His laugh was low and sweet, his voice sending ripples of electricity through me. "She doesn't hate you. She's probably just worried that you're a wild woman who's going to lead me astray or set fire to the workshop with your over-enthusiastic welding attempts. See ya tomorrow Leila."

He blinked his high beams twice before turning to drive away back down the road. I continued on without him, warmed by the memory of the afternoon. I had parked the Wrangler in the garage beside the other vehicles, when my phone beeped with a text message.

'Wan 2 go running 2 moro afta skol? Wan 2 c if u as good as Maleko says u r!'

'U R On. B redy 4 d-feat.' was my swift reply.

There was a loopy smile on my face as I went in to the house. Which slipped once I heard the hum of voices. My mother had company. There were five women gathered in the living room with Nafanua. Sipping tea, talking, laughing.

Everyone paused in their conversation when I came in. Their every gaze took me in from head to toe. Stale sweat from a day in Samoan humidity. Grease stains on my legs and arms. Two band aids where I had burned myself on the welder. Hair a disheveled bird's nest. Mismatched jandals. A t-shirt that used to be white. I cringed and waited for the restrained displeasure that I was so accustomed to in the Folger family. Displeasure that didn't come.

My mother stood and welcomed me with a smile.

"Leila! Here you are. How lovely. I'd like you to meet some of my sisters. I've told them all about you and they've been dying to meet you. Please, come in and let me introduce you."

I smiled weakly and gestured to my oily state. "Umm, nice to see you ladies. Nafanua, if it's okay with you, I'll just run upstairs and take a shower first? I'm ah … kind of nasty."

There was a ripple of laughter from the women. Nafanua joined in and waved me upstairs with graceful ease. "Yes, maybe it's best that you shower first. Come down when you're presentable." As I lightly tripped up the curved stairs she called out, "Leila, I hope you don't mind, I did a bit of shopping and got you a few things. They're on your bed. I hope you like them."

I groaned, imagining the outfits she would have picked out for me. The sight of my double bed overflowing with shopping bags had me coming to an abrupt halt. "What the - ?!" There must have been at least a dozen of them if not more. I took a swift peek, there were shoe boxes and glimpses of denim, neatly folded piles of cotton tees, other mysterious folds of emerald green linen and startling red. Shaking my head, unsure what to think, I took a much-needed shower. Standing under the cold sluice, I smiled as I thought back over the afternoon with Daniel. So what if his grandmother didn't like me. That was nothing I wasn't used to. My own grandmother didn't like me so it shouldn't bother me if his didn't.

It took two generous handfuls of shampoo to get the welding smoke out of my hair but still my enthusiasm for the work did not dim. My pulse raced as I thought about Daniel and I welding side by side, the flash of his eyes laughing at me from behind the protection of the steel helmet. I relived my flush of happiness at his closeness, his protective shielding of me as the flames spit and hissed. Thinking of him brought another pang of delicious excitement, but also a knife stab of uncomfortable dread. Because – while I was completely entranced with this beautiful boy who could sense my saddest of moods and replace them with soaring lightness, who could make me alternately smile and grimace at his teasing – I wasn't sure how he felt about me. And that was enough to bring me back down to earth with a crash.

I put Daniel out of my mind while I foraged through Nafanua's purchases. Only one day in her house and she had read me well. Yes, there were some rather elegant and slinky outfits that I pulled a face at and shoved aside. But mostly there were items I could see myself wearing. The beloved denim shorts and jeans. Relaxed fit. The white cotton tees and singlets. There was a bag of lingerie too. More of my Bendon favorites. Nothing too racy. But the shoes were not standard Leila issue. Gold wired sandals, black stilettos, red platforms, even a pair of gladiator-style wrap shoes that would reach above the knee. Ha, I threw them all in the closet with a snort. But I didn't want to keep Nafanua and her friends waiting too long. Quickly, I dressed in the new clothes, denim and cotton, dragged a brush through my hair – I didn't want Nafanua to be ashamed of me. Not so soon anyway. I walked back down the stairs, bits and pieces of conversation drifting up.

"She's beautiful, Nafanua – she looks so much like you, incredible!"

"How much have you told her?"

"Yes, what does she know? What can she do?"

Nafanua put the talk to a stop, catching sight of me on the stairs. "Ah Leila, please come and meet everyone. These are my sisters."

I met a bewildering array of women – all stunning, with long hair and dark liquid eyes, the sultry pout to their perfect lips, all with the same ageless look Nafanua wore with such ease. The kind where you take unobtrusive glances every so often trying to search out unblemished skin, unwrinkled foreheads and try to put a finger on an age. They each wore vibrant colors, so together the room seemed like a bouquet of tropical flowers.

Fouina in green, seemed the youngest of the group. A slight woman with russet brown hair and pale skin who hung back and greeted me shyly. Manuia had no such hesitancy. Tall, with a majestic luscious figure that she displayed with fiery confidence in a shimmering purple dress – it left little to the imagination. She greeted me with loud exclamations and a perfume-laden embrace. "Oka! Nafanua, what a stunning daughter you have here. Leila, you eclipse your mother in every way, totally eclipse her, *a ea* girls?!"

They all laughed at her teasing as I turned to meet the third stranger. Fotu was tall and slender with sandy blond hair and piercing blue eyes that made a striking contrast with her golden tanned skin. Her fuchsia ruffled outfit flounced as she embraced me warmly. Then there was Mina, her red silk kimono-style dress emphasizing her Asian-Samoan features. The final sister did not move to greet me. Sitting languidly in a straight-backed armchair, she merely stared at me with a half smile on her lips.

Sarona. Midnight black hair that fell in straight lines down her back. Together with heavily black-lined eyes, she had an almost Egyptian air about her. There was something else too. Something hostile. Her red smile didn't reach her eyes. "We meet again Leila Pele Folger."

Puzzled, I shook my head, "No, I'm sorry I don't think we've met."

Another cold smile and an airy wave of her hand. "Oh, yes we have. Only you wouldn't remember. I was there with your mother when you were born. Now that was a night to remember, wasn't it Nafanua?"

My mother looked disconcerted and her eyes flashed a warning at Sarona as she drew me to sit beside her on the long sofa. "Enough of that, so Leila, tell us all about yourself. There's so much we want to know about you."

With introductions out of the way, the women settled back around the table laid with platters of finger foods. I sat and listened to their chatter, answering their questions – school, hobbies, likes, dislikes, my plans for the future. They carefully avoided any trespassing into the zones that would include my dad so, after a while, I relaxed. As evening wore on, the group went back to their conversation and I nibbled on dinner and listened. Listening to them was answering some of my questions about my mother – chiefly – what did she do?

As far as I could gather, Nafanua worked as an environmental consultant for a few of the regional organizations that had their headquarters here in Apia – like SPREP and UNESCO. But most of her time was spent in her garden and her lab. There she worked with traditional remedies to make medicines and other concoctions that she then offered to Western research companies to bid on.

"We own the patents for several plant-based drugs. That's how we're able to fund our other ventures that are very dear to us." explained Nafanua.

Sarona interrupted before I could speak. "Oh yes, thanks to your mother's plant work, the sisterhood is filthy rich, isn't it girls? Only the rest of us don't get much say over what happens to all that filth, since your mother is the leader of our foundation. And the rest of us have to grovel to big sister, the holder of the purse strings."

"Sarona!" Nafanua's voice was low and venomous.

There was an awkward silence as the bitterness in Sarona's comment settled into the room, curling up in nooks and crannies, squirming into every empty space. Nafanua and Sarona locked eyes and an invisible wire of tension strained to break between them.

I rushed to redirect the conversation. "So what kind of ventures do you fund?" I asked.

There was eagerness as the other women seized on the conversation shift. They explained that while Mina worked closely with Nafanua in the lab, the rest of them ran two main operations. The first was an animal rescue hospital. Fouina was a qualified vet and worked with two other volunteer vets from New Zealand to carry out village education programs on animal welfare, and provide free animal medical care. Her eyes lit up as she described how their program worked and the progress they had made in several areas with raising animal care awareness. Fotu also helped out but was really a dancer. "She's the best dancer on the island." Fouina added eagerly. "Everyone brings their daughters to Fotu hoping she will choose to instruct them. But she only ever teaches a couple of girls each year."

The second was a Women's Refuge that provided legal and financial assistance to women and children trying to escape abusive homes. Manuia was the patron. Sarona was a lawyer with her own practice and provided the legal counsel for the refuge clients. Manuia's face darkened as she spoke of the frustration of assisting battered women who then refused to prosecute their abusive partners and then – after their injuries had healed – insisted on returning home to their abuse.

Sarona chose the moment to comment sardonically, "Well Manuia, what do you expect, they're just ordinary women. Pathetic. Weak. And taught no better than to lie down and take it. With a smile."

Nafanua concluded, "Well, there you have it Leila, that about sums it up for us. You'll see a lot of my sisters – they each have their own homes spread out over the estate but we come together every day. We're just a regular family. We work together, play together, and, of course, sometimes we fight together. But then, that's what makes families so special isn't it?"

The others raised their glasses in agreement, even Sarona. "Hear, hear!"

Nafanua continued with a warm smile, "It's a joy for us all to welcome you to our family, to our sisterhood, Leila."

I smiled weakly at the women. I didn't want to tell them that – no – I had no clue what made families so special. Because I'd never really had one. Just a father-daughter tag team taking on the world. And now here I had not only a mother but also five vibrant women offering me familial ties, offering me sisterhood.

The rest of the evening passed by in a blur. Nafanua and the others were in good spirits and kept opening yet another bottle of wine. I fingered the bone carving Nafanua had given me the night before and tried to understand why I could not shake the slight feeling of unease. I had found my mother. And a family that embraced me. I should have been over the moon. Instead, I kept replaying my recurring nightmare in my mind. Why and how would I have dreamed of Nafanua well before I met her? And her story about my dad and their reasons for separating, for lying to me? It didn't make sense. I could not reconcile her portrayal with the man I knew. The father I had loved more than anything. I knew that I was not ready to trust this eerily beautiful woman and her sisters.

Not yet.

SEVEN

The next day, Daniel was waiting for me at break. Unfolding himself gracefully from the corridor bench, strolling towards me, "I thought I better feed you today so you can handle our run this afternoon. I don't want you collapsing with exhaustion. I know you by now – you're so stubborn that even if I totally wipe you out on the track, you won't give up. You'll just run yourself silly trying to catch me."

I laughed, playfully aiming a punch at his shoulder. He nimbly edged away in the nick of time, well practiced at evasion from the rugby field, then looped one lanky arm over my shoulders, pulling me close for a kiss on the cheek so light that I could have imagined it. I went hot and cold at his touch.

Unwilling for him to sense the effect he had on me, I made sure I walked several feet away from him as we bought his lunch and found a spot under the tamarind trees. I watched him consume two sandwiches and a muffin while I ate my food prepared from home. He looked speculatively into my lunchbox.

"Hmm, I never knew a girl who brought a lunch to school. You don't have a Barbie lunchbox somewhere do you? What you got in here anyway?"

"Oh, Nafanua is an organic, green person. Everything comes from her own land. In here I've got taro crab cakes, spicy Thai green papaya salad, some of that *faausi* stuff, and some cut fruit. Want some?"

Daniel looked vaguely horrified. "Nah, I prefer my food drowning in chemicals thank you very much. And preferably with lots of blood."

"Daniel, what's a *telesā*?"

I cringed as I asked the dreaded question, waiting to gauge his reaction. But there was none. He only shrugged, still digging through the lunchbox, sniffing things and making 'yuck' faces. There was no embarrassment or horror. Clearly, whatever *telesā* meant, it didn't have anything to do with prostitute which had been my secret worry.

"It's a legend. A myth. Eww, Leila, do you really eat this crap?" He had taken a tentative bite of a crab cake and spat it out in his hand emphatically. I grinned up at him. He had a fleck of green on the side of his lip. Daringly, I reached out and wiped it away. He sat motionless while I touched him, regarding me with lazy eyes. I couldn't tear my eyes away. The scar that cut through one eyebrow, a chipped tooth, the way the wind played in his hair.

"What? What is it?" he demanded, but I shook my head, pulling my hand away and rushing to speak about something, anything – except for the electric wire that pulled me to him no matter how hard I tried to remain distant.

"So tell me about these legends, anyways?" I asked lightly.

"Well, apparently there are these insanely beautiful women who watch over certain areas, like a particular river, or pool or forest. They have some kind of strange powers and can put curses on people who mess up their areas. Or don't show them enough respect."

I felt coldness in the sunlight. His words cutting through the lightness of the day. *Telesā*. Beautiful women. Aunty Matile's fear, tears, *telesā telesā telesā*. I shook them away. Ridiculous. It was ridiculous. Foolish legends and myths. I shook myself away from the dread and pushed further.

"But what are they? What do they do?"

"Hmm, I don't know a lot about it."

"I mean – are they ghosts? Spirits? Demons? What?"

Daniel laughed at my serious tone. "Hey, it's just a legend remember? And I'm not big on legends."

"Please? Just tell me as much as you know then."

"Alright, well they're not spirits or ghosts. They're like real people, like us but they've got supernatural powers I think. They put curses on people when they get annoyed with them. Oh, and they hate pretty girls who flaunt their beauty."

"What do you mean?"

"When I was little, our neighbor was this old lady, Silulu. She used to sit in the front of her house and whenever a young woman walked past with her hair down, or with a flower in her ear, Silulu would yell out to her to "go home! Put your hair up! Get that flower off! Or *telesā* will punish you!" I think it was just a way to make sure girls stayed out of trouble, you know? A way to keep girls humble. But I never took much notice of those tales and I don't think any of the girls I grew up with did either. It was just old stories."

"What else?"

Daniel furrowed his brow in concentration and thought for a moment. "They prey on handsome men that are foolish enough to trespass on their territory. They particularly prefer men with light hair and green or blue eyes ... *palagi*-looking ones." He fluttered his laughing eyes at me. "If one catches their eye, they entrance him using their special powers, have their way with him and then kill him. Or if they take pity on him, they let him go free, wandering off in a daze."

I gave him a suspicious look. "You just made that up!"

He protested, laughing, "No I didn't. Honest! That was a big part of the legends. When I was little, Mama used to take me to certain forest areas to gather her plants and she would always cover my hair and wrap my face with a *lavalava*. Because she said *telesā* liked to steal fair-skinned little boys. So they would grow up and be their slaves." He laughed and shook his head at the memory, "The things Mama would do to get me to stay close to her and not run off! Freaking me out with wild stories. But hey, you gotta admit that if *telesā* existed, I would be in real big trouble."

I had to smile. "Oh really? And why is that?"

He pretended to preen and pose, "Well, just look at me. My green eyes, my fair coloring, my super hot physique – not to mention my legendary debate skills – they all add up to the perfect prize for a *telesā*." He was straight faced but his eyes danced.

I looked down my nose at him disdainfully "Oh really? I've got news for you. If I was a *telesā*, I wouldn't take a second look at ya." I shook my head emphatically. "Uh uh, nah. Not a glance your way at all. Sorry."

"You don't say? Hmm, so what would I have to do before you would put me on your lure and kill list huh?" He jumped to his feet, scattering sandwich wrappers everywhere. "How about if I took off my shirt, hmm? Would you consider me then?" Swiftly, he unbuttoned his shirt and took it off. Thankfully he had a white singlet on underneath, but still...

"No – Daniel – stop it. People are looking!" Laughing, I tried to give him back his shirt.

"No my feelings are hurt. I need to know what lengths I have to go to so I can be considered by the insanely beautiful *telesā* woman. Ahhhh I know, how about if I do this?" Triumphantly, he tugged his singlet over his tousled head and, as if the sight of his amazing body in all its muscular glory wasn't enough, he jumped on the bench and struck a body-building pose.

There were loud cheers and catcalls at his performance from the crowd of students by the canteen.

"Woohoo! Go Danny-boy – take it *aallll* off! Yeah!"

"Show her what you got, Danny!"

The loudest jeers came from his team mates. I groaned in disbelief and shut my eyes, shaking my head at his goofiness. I hissed at him.

"Daniel – get down before you fall over and hurt yourself ... you ... big show off."

"No, not until you tell me what it'll take for you to hunt me down. I know. This has got to work."

To my horror, he started undoing the ties on his *lavalava*.

"What the heck are you doing? Stop it. Stop it! Ohmigosh." I was left speechless as he whipped off the *lavalava*, baring his muscular thighs - in their drawstring rugby shorts. Whew, what a relief...

It seemed now as if the entire school was enjoying the spectacle of their Head Boy doing a strip in the middle of the lunch area. Still laughing helplessly, I grabbed his hand and pulled him down to sit beside me again, trying to ignore the fascinated crowd.

"Okay, okay, so you win – you are disgustingly handsome – not to mention a huge show off – and any *telesā* would be absolutely *desperate* to have her way with you!"

"Ahhh, but what about *this* beautiful *telesā*?" His tone was light but his eyes were serious. I caught my breath and tried to still my accelerating pulse. Where a moment ago we had just been two people playing, now we had strayed into far more treacherous territory. His lips were far too close to my ear for me to keep an unruffled composure and his now-naked chest gleaming in the afternoon sun, light playing on every muscular curve and ripple, certainly didn't help. The spectators, the school yard, the heat of the day – everything faded to a distant blur and it was just Daniel and I in a taut shell of questions. Daniel's voice dropped to a whisper, "Would you?"

"Would I what?"

"Choose me?"

Our gaze met, caught, and held like coconut fiber rope that braided stronger with each shared breath. I nodded, hardly daring to speak. "Yes. I would."

Who knows what would have happened next. If the bell hadn't gone. Reminding us both where we were. I stood up and started packing away my things while Daniel put his shirt back on.

There was a disappointed jeer from the canteen crowd. "Awwwww Danny, is the show over?"

He smiled at them all and stood to take a bow at them before wrapping his *lavalava* around his hips.

I shook my head at him ruefully. "I can't believe you just did that. I mean – I thought you were supposed to be all grown up and mature and responsible ... not this ... impetuous cheeky jock."

He shrugged. "I like to make you laugh. To see you smile. You don't do that enough."

My pulse leapt at the softening of his eyes as he gazed at me thoughtfully. My heart rejoiced at the emotion I saw reflected there. Only a few short months ago – I had not believed such happiness was possible. Yet here I was, in a sea of shocking orange and yellow, with the brilliant tropical sun blazing overhead, a light breeze caressing my face – and beside me, the most amazing boy professing his concern for my happiness. I wished I could freeze frame this moment and keep it forever. I studied every contour of his profile, every strand of hair, every mark on his skin – wanting to commit him to memory. Just in case. We parted, but not before Daniel reminded me not to chicken out of our race that afternoon.

Sunset tinged the horizon as we finished our run. My lungs were filled to bursting, adrenaline pumping, muscles aching from the exertion. It had been so long since I had trained that my body was positively singing its delight at the return to the track. I mentally kicked myself for staying away from what my body knew and loved, knowing full well it would make me pay for it tomorrow. But for now, I would just exult in the sheer thrill that sprinting always gave. Daniel shook his head at me as we walked slowly to cool down, his tone accusing.

"You chose ten laps for us on purpose, so you could get me tired before the sprint at the end. You didn't tell me how fit you were."

I smiled in answer. "You never asked. Besides, if I had told you, then maybe you would have been too scared to run with me today. I think I saw you struggling to keep up there for a few laps."

"Oh whatever, I was holding back. You know, didn't want to hurt your feelings by leaving you in the dust and all."

"Really? Well, next time don't worry about my feelings. I've run enough races that I can handle competition. That is – if you think you're man enough to risk losing a race to a girl."

"Actually, I *was* a bit stretched on that last lap there. I was surprised. Next time we better come and race in the middle of the night when nobody's watching. It just wouldn't do for the competition to hear the SamCo team captain got beat in a race by a girl." he laughed at the idea, shaking his head. "You should go for the athletics team when we have the inter school competition. There aren't many girls fit enough to run long distance in Samoa."

I checked to see if he was making fun of me, but his eyes held only admiration as he turned to look at me. "How long have you been running?"

I shrugged non-committally. "A while. My dad was a running buff."

He would try to do two marathons a year. He used to joke that he started running when he was a teenager so he could get as far away as possible from his mom. She didn't like that joke. And she hated him running. Thought it was dangerous. Was always cutting out news articles of people getting hit by cars when they were out running. Anyways, he started taking me with him to the track when I was a kid and it just grew from there. When he was on assignment, he would be away for weeks at a time. It would be just me and Margaret. That's the housekeeper," I added in answer to his questioning look. "I didn't have much else to do besides school work, so I would run every day by myself. Just me and my iPod and the road. Grandmother hated that too. But when Dad was home, we would drive to different cities every weekend to go in fun runs. Everything from 5k to half marathons. Just for fun – not racing hard out. Those weekends were the best." I lit up at the memory. "We would stay in a motel, order our favorite takeout, catch a movie. If it was on the coast, we'd go to the beach. The next day, we'd do the run, Dad would take lots of photos of the before and after. Then we'd explore the place a bit. He'd make me go to a museum or a gallery ... always trying to force feed me some culture and refinement. Then we'd head back home and it would be back to reality." I sobered at the reminder. Of reality. My reality.

"And what was reality like?" Daniel prompted.

"Ah nothing much. Just school and boring stuff like that." I waved away his question, unwilling to delve any deeper into memories I worked hard to suppress, jumping instead to change the topic. "So you think I'd have a chance on the athletics team?"

He shook his head once at my question before answering, as if to tell me that he was well aware I was wriggling out of a sensitive subject. "Definitely. Not many people run in this country. Especially not long distance. We're rugby fanatics. And netball players. If you wanted to try it here, I doubt you'd have much competition. From anyone in our school, or any other school for that matter."

"I haven't run much in the past few months. Since...well, since my dad. But it did feel good to get out there on the field today. I need to start training again. I'm sure my ... mother ..." I stumbled over the unfamiliar word, "Nafanua wouldn't mind me running but once I get back to Faatoia, it might be a problem. Aunty Matile doesn't like me out of her sight. School and home. That's my world."

He laughed. "Hey, that's the world for most girls in Samoa. School, home – oh, and church. That about sums it up. None of this excessive freedom that you American teenagers are so glutted on."

"Excessive freedom?" My exclamation was a high-pitched shriek. "I couldn't even go to the store in this country without getting permission from Matile. And you'd think night time was only for evil spirits and demons the way she reacted the other evening when I told her I was going for a walk." My voice took on an artificial severity. "*A good Samoan daughter does not roam around at night. She stays at home with her family, safe in their protection.*" Aaargh, you'd think I wanted to hit a nightclub or a rave or meet some drug-dealer friends or something. I mean, she'd just die if she knew I was here with you – and ooh look, the sun is going down and I'm not safe in the family's protection." I gesticulated wildly at the silken evening sky.

Daniel stopped at the bench where we had left our bags and, without warning, flexed bronzed arms to casually pull his shirt up over his head. I halted mid step, dumbfounded at the sight of his contoured back, muscles glistening with sweat, the play of fading red-gold light on his tattooed shoulder. I was following close enough behind that I bumped into him and I shied away instantly as if I had been burned, unwilling for him to think I was touching him *on purpose*. As usual, the glorious perfection of his toned body sent my pulse racing and a familiar wave of heat shuddering through me. Not wanting to get hit with a heat attack, I itched to get as far as possible from him. Taking several steps away from his breathtaking nearness, I averted my eyes as he rifled through his bag, searching – for another shirt I hoped. No such luck.

"Aha, here it is." He turned triumphantly to me with a water bottle in his hand. "Want a drink?" He held out the bottle, reaching towards me with one magnificent arm, the other on his hips where ragged shorts clung to his rock-hard frame. Deepening shadows played on his torso, a light breeze set the coconut palm behind him dancing. Jade green eyes smiling in the jade green evening. At me. Us alone, on a green field embraced by scarlet hibiscus bushes. The heat within me surged stronger and I was almost frantic in my reaction. Didn't this boy have a clue what impact he had on me? Against my will, the words tore from me.

"Why do you people keep doing that!?"

"Doing what?" His eyes conveyed genuine puzzlement.

"That. Taking your clothes off all the time. Without even a warning for goodness sake!" My words tumbled over themselves in my frustration as I waved my hands wildly. "It's … it's indecent! Y'all get hot – you take off your clothes. You get wet – you take off your clothes. You get dirty – you take off your clothes. Just like that, in front of everyone." My voice went one octave higher as Daniel raised a perfect eyebrow at my descent into hysteria.

" I don't know." He shrugged, baffled at my attack. "We just do. It's hot here. It's no big deal. Heck, before the missionaries came around, you women would be shirtless too and we'd think nothing of it." His eyes glinted mischievously at the thought.

The thought of *both* of us without shirts had me gasping for air. He was definitely not being helpful. Roughly I snatched the water bottle from his grasp and moved to sit on the grassy rise as far away from him as was politely possible. I drank deeply, the cold water a welcome relief. Neither of us spoke as he pulled another bottle from the bag for himself.

I was focusing so hard on calming the heat wave within, that I barely noticed when he sat down beside me. "You can look now. I have a shirt on. Now that I know you Americans are so easily offended by our Samoan indecency. I'll be more careful next time not to take my clothes off." I gave him a sideways glance. His tone was teasing but his expression was dead serious. Thankfully, a singlet now covered most of his upper body.

Ashamed of my outburst, I stared downwards and muttered into the ground. "I'm sorry. I didn't mean to be so rude. It's just different here and it takes getting used to. I shouldn't be bringing my cultural hang ups and imposing them on you. Please forget I mentioned it. Of course you can take your clothes off whenever you want to. It's fine. I want you to…I mean …" I stumbled to a halt, aghast at how my words sounded.

Daniel's hoot of laughter was so riotous that it disturbed a scatter of myna birds from the coconut tree beside us. "Aah, so you *want* me to take my clothes off whenever I want to ay? You *want* me to get naked!"

"No. Oh you know what I mean. Stop twisting my words." My mortification lent added sharpness to my tone, but Daniel wasn't fazed. He nudged me in the ribs with his elbow.

"Come on, it's funny. You know it is!"

I fought an answering grin, unsuccessfully. "Okay so you're right. It was funny." I relaxed in the sultry twilight." And I'm still sorry for getting on your case about the naked thing. You gotta remember, you're talking to a girl who's been in an all-girls school all her life. No brothers. No close cousins. I haven't had much contact with boys." Especially not one as flawless as you, I added silently in my mind.

Daniel stopped laughing and turned serious."So did you have a boyfriend back home?"

I went silent, wanting desperately to say yes. So then I wouldn't look so pitiful. The shift in the mood unnerved me. "Umm, not really."

There was laughter in his voice. "*Not really*? What does that mean?"

"It means no. I guess." Great. I was aiming for mysterious allure and instead was ending up with extreme idiocy. Taking a deep breath, I struggled to save some measure of cool calmness.

"It means not lately." There, that sounded better than the truth. The truth being *are you out of your freakin mind* of course no boy is gonna pay attention to a overgrown sour-faced hostile brown girl. Not in a universe peopled by perky cheerful blondes and beautiful blasé brunettes. I hoped he couldn't read minds. Or detect lies. Or put two and two together and come up with the painful truth of four. I hastened to deflect the focus from me and my boyfriend-less state. "How about you? You gone out with anyone lately?"

"Nobody."

"Oh. Why not?" I deliberately kept my tone light. Friendly. Just two friends. Hanging out. Going for a run. Talking about girls. I could do this. He shrugged his broad shoulders and took another gulp of water before answering.

"Nope. It doesn't really fit my plans to have a girlfriend right now." He spoke with such finality that I was left fumbling for a reaction as a cold fist plunged straight into my heart. I thought of the light kisses, butterflies in the sunlight, his hand warm and firm in my mine. The way my breath caught at the sight of him.

"Oh. Okay. Of course. I get it." A sophisticated woman would have left it at that. (And then swept him away with her sensuous languor so he would have no choice but to have a girlfriend.) But I couldn't leave it at sophisticated. No matter how hard I tried. I was too direct for that. "Actually, no. I don't get it. What are your plans?"

It was his turn to squirm under the microscope.

"Umm, just stuff. You know. Plans."

"Yeah, like what?"

"Like I don't want to be welding gates for the rest of my life. Don't get me wrong, I enjoy my work and I'm lucky to have it. My grandfather taught me all he knew and I loved working with him. But I don't want the welding shop to be me and Mama's future. I don't want rugby to be our future either." His brow furrowed as he spoke carefully, as if anxious to convey the right thoughts, "I like rugby. I'm good at it. It can open lots of doors for me if I train right. But really what I want to do is Civil Engineering, specifically Fluid Mechanics." He halted and looked at me with some trepidation, as if unsure of my reaction.

"Wow, you've certainly put a lot of thought into your plans. What's Fluid Mechanics?"

"That's the branch of engineering that focuses on everything to do with water. Stuff like dams, and hydraulic systems, and pipelines, and stuff like that ..." his words trailed away as he smiled sheepishly, as if embarrassed by his disclosure. "Water. It's fascinating to me. All the stuff you can do with it, you know? I mean, here we are on an island surrounded by the stuff, and every rainy season we're deluged with it – but we don't hardly do anything with it. Leila – the possibilities are endless. Hydro-power is only barely being tapped here. And there's just so much pollution of the present water catchments that we're basically shooting ourselves in the foot."

He halted and took a sip of water, his face flushed with excitement. I smiled, wanting him to continue but instead he waved a hand at the flushed evening sky spread out before us.

"Isn't it amazing? I keep taking for granted how blessed we are to live here. Look at that, I said I wouldn't keep you out late and here it is night coming in."

I turned and for several minutes we sat in companionable silence on the green hill in the green evening, watching as night softly crept out of her hiding shadows. The quiet school block slumbered behind us, far away we could hear the sounds of people strolling home on the main road. I was surprised to realize how quickly the field had emptied and now it appeared only Daniel and I were left.

The sunset's riot of color had dimmed and the expanse of sky was now a velvet grey blanket upon which night was scattering handfuls of shimmering silver stars. For some reason, Daniel's choice of words had me vaguely uneasy. Without looking at his profile beside me, I asked quietly. "Are you religious?"

He shrugged. "I believe in God." He turned his head to consider me. "How about you?"

"I never really thought about it until recently. We never had much time for religion when I was growing up. My grandmother went to church. But I always thought it was more of a social status thing, ya know? Like, she went because that's what rich people did on a Sunday morning. When Dad was home, we just did lots of outdoors stuff on our weekends. Now I'm here, and I realize that going for a two-mile hike or spending the day at the beach is a bit sacrilegious."

His quiet laugh in the evening shadows drew me to turn and face him. His liquid emerald eyes considered me thoughtfully. "And now? What do you think of God now?"

"I guess, I don't know. When my dad died, I realized that this can't be it. This can't be all that we are. Just here one day, and then gone the next. We're not just chunks of flesh and bone running along like … like auto bots that get switched off. People are more than that. There's a spirit, there has to be, and we were somewhere before we got here and there's somewhere else that we go after. There has to be. He's still alive, existing, real – somewhere. Call it heaven maybe." I turned pleading eyes towards him. "Right?"

I caught the outline of his smile in the growing darkness and he nudged my shoulder with his. "Yes he is. I totally believe that, Leila. Not just that, but nothing can take away the love he had for you. That you have for him. I think, in that way, he'll always be with you."

Others had tried to comfort me with similar words in the past months since my dad's death, but my grieving heart had not been ready to listen. Tonight was different. Hearing it from Daniel, now, a seed of warmth, of hope, was planted. He continued, "And you're luckier than most. You have lots of good memories of your dad, your time together. Nothing can ever take that away from you."

I nodded slowly. "You're right." And remembering what little he had told me about growing up without his father made me eager to change the subject. And ask a question that had been itching at me ever since the day we had first met. "Tell me about your tattoo. When did you get it done?"

If he was surprised at the shift in the conversation, he didn't let it show. "Three years ago. When I turned sixteen. Kinda my present to myself."

"Why?"

"Why what?" He was puzzled.

"Why did you do it? I mean, it must have taken ages, it's so beautifully intricate … and I can't even imagine how much it must have hurt. Why did you do it?" As someone who had to psyche herself up for a booster shot, the thought of willingly subjecting one's self to hours of needles seemed like insanity.

He didn't answer for several minutes and I wondered if I had offended him. "Sorry if it's personal. You don't have to answer me. I didn't mean to pry."

He smiled at my apology. "No, that's not it. It's not some deep state secret or anything. I'm just trying to see if I can explain it in my head to myself and have it make sense before I put it into words." He took a deep breath before proceeding. "My mom was Tongan and Samoan. But my father was *palagi*. I never knew him. Don't even know his name. Don't know what he looked like. Don't want to know. He abandoned my mother when she was pregnant. Up and left her. Never looked back. Never thought about what that would be like for her. Only eighteen years old. No husband. Pregnant. Not long after she gave birth to me, she drowned. They never found her body. Everyone says she killed herself. Apparently she was an amazing swimmer. Spent all her time in the sea, knew all the currents and tides and fishing spots like the back of her hand so no-one could figure out how it was that she drowned." A gentle smile and a shrug. "So I grew up being half and half. You know what that's like. For all intents and purposes, I'm Samoan. With a bit of Tongan. I speak it. I live it. But I'm stuck with these eyes and this damn coloring," he pulled at his hair wryly, "and 'real' Samoans love to remind me that I'm not really Samoan. That I had a *palagi* father who couldn't even stick around to see me. That I had a mother who was naïve enough to fall for his lies. With not enough good girl morals to keep herself 'pure'and chaste."

His tone was light-hearted, but the cut of his words betrayed the depth of his emotions. I almost wished that I hadn't asked about his tattoo. He took a deep breath and continued. "So you're wondering what the heck does that have to do with my tattoo! I decided when I was sixteen that I wanted to make a statement to myself about who I am. Yes, I'm *afakasi* and don't know my father. I can't escape that. But I'm tired of being ashamed of that. I decided to stop making excuses for what I am. I designed the pattern myself. See? It incorporates symbols from all of my cultures and it's got a lot about the people in my life who mean something to me."

He leaned his arm closer to me, pointing out different shapes. I had to peer closely to make out the symbols in the dim light. "These fish and waves – those represent my mother. Mama said she loved the sea. It was her home. What gave her joy. Those leaf patterns are for Mama of course. And the flowers. Here's fire, my grandfather and our welding. And this koru shape – that's for New Zealand. Apparently that's where my father was from. This line is the horizon and a canoe on the waters, you know, for *papalagi*."

"No, I don't know. All I know is that's what people say to me in town when I can't understand them. What's it mean?"

Daniel's smile was soft, his eyes alight with understanding.

"*Papalagi* – that's what Samoans use for white people. A long time ago when the first white people came in their boats, Samoans thought they had literally exploded through the sky, so they called them 'sky bursters.'"

"Oh, I get it now." Pleased to finally have the word make sense to me, I went back to studying his tattoo. "It's beautiful. I like it. I wouldn't ever get one done myself, I'm way too chicken. But this is beautiful."

"Thanks. I'm getting myself prepped to get a *sogaimiti* done later this year."

I turned questioning eyes at him. "What's that?"

"You know, the full body tattoo that the men get? Have you seen any? It's not as common as it used to be, but there's still quite a few around."

I blanched as I realized what he was talking about. I had seen pictures of the detailed tattoo that covered a man's body from waist to past the knee, and I had heard horror stories about people who died from it. "Daniel, are you crazy? Why would you do that? What does your grandmother think about it. Is this her idea?"

Daniel shook his head. "No, she hates it. Whenever I talk about it she reacts pretty much the same way you are now. It's the one thing we argue about, well, besides you... She's still determined to change my mind. But, I'm sure. It's what I want."

Almost stupidly, I asked again, "But why?"

"Traditionally, a *sogaimiti* marked the passage of a boy to manhood. And it was the mark of a warrior, one who was brave enough to defend the village, his family. My grandfather had one – a Tongan one, and I would like to honor him and my culture by having one done as well." He spoke simply and I could see there was no swaying him.

"May I?" I gestured to his arm, dying to do what I had longed to since the first time I saw him.

"Sure." He shrugged.

Hardly daring to breathe, I reached with a trembling hand and traced the pattern of his tattoo, beginning at the tip of his shoulder and moving down his forearm, dancing over the swirls, the bold geometric designs. Leaning closer, I peered intently at the patterns, seeking their hidden stories. I wished I dared to put my lips on his skin. It felt so ... smooth. I was surprised.

"I thought it would feel bumpy – you know – scratchy. Like raised patterns on your skin."

"No. When a tattoo is well done, there's none of that. The patterns blend with your skin." His short tone confused me. Was he angry at my invasion of his space? I dropped my hand quickly.

"Sorry. I was just curious."

"Don't be. Sorry I mean. It's not you. It's ..." For once he seemed to be struggling with words, oddly ill at ease.

"What's wrong?" I wanted to smile at his discomfort. It was nice to see *him* be the one out of sorts for a change. I peered at him closer. "You're squirming! What is it? Come on, tell me."

He ruffled his hair – a gesture I recognized now as a sign of when he was ill at ease. He took a deep breath, bracing himself. When his words came, they stumbled over each other in a rush to be spoken. "I can't handle it when you touch me like that. I don't like it – I mean – I like it but I can't handle it. This. I can't handle this."

There was an awkward silence as I struggled to process the punch to the solar plexus that his words had dealt me. "Oh. I see." But I didn't. He liked me touching him but he didn't? What did he really mean? What was he really trying to say? Was he trying to tell me nicely that he *didn't* feel anything physical for me? Like those inane teenage romances, was he trying to tell me that he liked me but he 'just wanted us to be friends'? I wanted to scream with frustration. Arrgh. Why couldn't people just say what they felt and be done with it? Come to think of it – why didn't I?

He watched me intently, trying to gauge my reaction to his statement. "Do you *really?* Do you get what I'm trying to say?" His question was earnest. I decided to go with total honesty.

"No. I don't. I don't get it, Daniel. You like it – but you don't? Why don't you just come out and be straight with me? Don't I deserve that after everything we've been through?"

He bit his lip, still seeming unsure. "Leila, there's a reason I don't have a girlfriend. Why I don't even play around with anyone. I won't risk doing what my dad did *to anyone*. My mom killed herself because of what he did. Getting her pregnant. Leaving her. I promised myself I would never treat any girl, any woman that way. But now, with you, the past few weeks … it's like I can't stop myself from wanting to see you. To be with you. I tell myself, it'll be okay, we can be friends, we can hang out. I like hanging out with you. It's all I look forward to every day. But when you're so close to me like this and you touch me like that, I keep thinking of things that I shouldn't. That I promised myself I never would."

"Things?" I whispered the question so softly that he had to lean closer to catch it.

"Yeah things. Like … this." He leaned close, so close I hardly dared to breathe. I kept still, so still. His breath was hot against my skin as, hesitantly, his lips met my cheek, lingered and then danced to my mouth.

When his lips touched mine, they were feather soft and gentle. His hands came up to cradle my face as we kissed, caressing my throat delicately as if he feared I would shatter in his embrace. He tasted like he smelled. Sweet pineapple and a salty edge of coconut. All my senses drank him in deeply.

He was the exhilaration of the rushing falls against my naked skin on a steaming tropical night, the burn of volcanic rock, baked hot in the noon-day sun. He was the caress of a jasmine fragranced breeze as I danced barefoot in a moonlit night. He was all this and more. I drank him in deeply, my hands moving of their own accord to clutch fistfuls of his tousled hair.

"Oww!" His shocked exclamation interrupted our embrace, as he pushed himself away from me, leaving me bewildered. "Aargh that hurts!?" His face was puzzled and disbelieving as he looked from me to his hands, and then reaching to feel his lips.

What was happening? Flushes of heat swept through me. Again and again. No, something was wrong. The kiss was over but flames were lapping at my feet, burning my insides. I felt hot. So hot. Too hot. The air burned in my chest like a furnace. Burning, burning – like that boy's face. Flesh scorched and peeling. No, I shook my head in protest.

"No this can't be happening. Not again. Not now. Not to you. Please!" I lurched to my feet, looking wildly for an escape. I had to get away from here. Away from Daniel – before I hurt him. I would die rather than hurt Daniel.

"Lei –Leila, what's happening? Leila!?"

He put his strong arms around me to keep me captive, stop me from fleeing – only to drop them instantly, wincing with pain.

"Leila?" The fear in his voice was reflected in my eyes. He was afraid of me. The boy I wanted near me with every fiber of my being – was *afraid* of me. That awful realization only served to heighten the raging fire within. Burning pain like hot knives stabbed at me from all sides, I couldn't stop it. *Please, make it go away. Make it stop.*

"Daniel! Daniel, get away from me. Get a-way – from – *ME!*"

With all my might, I shoved Daniel away from me and fell to my knees as the pain overwhelmed me. I screamed and, with my scream, the fire tore loose and I could contain it no longer. It was an amazing feeling of release to let it go, like the steam in a pressure cooker blowing its top. Flames burst from my entire body, dancing tendrils of red and gold, a fiery sunset lancing the night sky. There was a rushing, crackling in my ears, like I was trapped in the midst of a blazing forest. Yet, incredibly there was no more pain. I was hot – but deliciously so. Like an arctic dweller who glories in the welcome return of the sun. A sunbather reveling luxuriously in sun-baked sand.

I stood, raising my arms, gazing in wondrous awe at the liquid fire that swirled and rippled all over them. My clothes had vanished – incinerated in one explosive heartbeat – but a minor detail like nakedness meant nothing to me now. I was on fire. And it didn't hurt! I was living, breathing molten fire – contained no more in a pitifully weak body of flesh and blood. Skin was replaced by flowing red and gold, like lava. I felt my cheeks, my hair. I breathed and the fire pulsed brighter. I twirled on tiptoe and my flames danced with me. I flicked my fingers – and a tiny fireball flew out, landing, fizzling harmlessly in the evening air. A rush of pure joy ripped through me as I gloried in the full realization of my fiery power. I was virtually indestructible. No-one and nothing could hurt me now. It was the most exhilarating feeling I had ever experienced.

"Woohoo! Yes!" my exultant scream ripped through the darkening evening, scattering a flock of feisty myna birds in the mango tree beside us. I laughed again and experimented, flicking my hands to watch a bigger, basketball-sized circle of fire shoot from my fingers and land on a fallen coconut frond. It burst into flame and I was awash with glee. It was beautiful. It lit up the night and *I* had created it! I wanted to dance around the flames.

"Leila? Is that you?" the voice was hesitant behind me. I turned, vaguely irritated with the interruption.

Daniel, beautiful Daniel, stared at me in shock, shielding his eyes from the heated sparks that emanated from my new body.

"Yes it's me! Daniel, I'm on fire and it doesn't hurt a bit and its glorious. See?"

I concentrated for the briefest of moments, unsure if my idea would work. I held my breath, letting the steamy furnace build until I could hold it no longer and then blew a huge whooshing breath into the air. A line of fire spewed out of my mouth like fireworks, spinning and spiraling through the sky until it landed several meters away, setting the dry grass alight. I laughed delightedly.

"See? Its magical." More, I wanted more. More fire, more flames. More fuel. More heat. More power.

Turning to the expanse of grass behind me, I threw balls of fire one after another like an endless flame thrower. The entire field lit up the night. I had never realized how many different colors danced in a fire. At the heart was a scatter of red rubies mingled with sapphire green, twisting upwards into ropes of gold flecked with black diamonds. The smoke was a blanket of grey velvet, plumed with feather-white pearl tendrils. It was mesmerizing. Who could resist it? I walked into the beckoning flames, savoring its embrace. I worshipped the fire and it danced and breathed to my command. Dimly, I heard a voice calling.

"Leila! Leila! Don't do this, wait. Think about what you're doing. Leila!"

Daniel was bent double, racked with coughing as smoke choked him. Foolish boy. Why did he not turn and run? Why was he trying to follow me? I motioned for him to go back. The path to the road was clear. He could be out of the fire's range and breathe easy.

"Go away Daniel! Don't worry about me, I'm fine. Get out of here."

I strained to hear his reply over the crackling hungry flames all around me.

"No – Leila – the hostel, don't do it. The hostel!" He pointed behind me, his hoarse scream piercing me with coldness as I followed the direction of his gaze.

My glorious blaze was fast consuming the field and heading straight towards the school dorms. Only a thin ribbon of tarsealed road separated it from the bushes that skirted the shabby array of buildings. The dining hall, the study, the bedrooms. Rooms where people slept, studied, laughed, lived, and breathed.

It was like a deluge of ice shocking me out of my fiery mania. No what had I been thinking? What was I doing? People were going to get hurt. I could have hurt Daniel, standing there choking in clouds of smoke he could already be in great danger. Waves of panic swept over me. Where moments before the inferno had been my soul mate, my friend – now it seemed like an uncontrollable beast, hungrily devouring everything in its path. What had I done? What had I created?

"No … please … no, stop. How to stop it? How can I stop it?" I burst into useless tears. Tears that fizzed and hissed in a heartbeat of heat. No amount of crying would help us now. I wrung my hands. No way out of it. It was hopeless. In a few short moments I would be a mass murderer. A killer. In my mind's eye, I could see it now. People on fire, running in circles, frantically beating at the hungry flames. The smell of flesh scorching, peeling off ashy bone. Screams. Pleas for help. Help that wouldn't come. I sank to my knees, drained of strength. Unwilling to watch the carnage but unable to take my eyes away. I was drowning in a sea of fiery despair. Suffocating in a red night of terror.

A clear, calm voice spoke with authority and assurance. The voice of one accustomed to being obeyed.

"Leila. Call it back. You can do it. Call it back. Call it back NOW."

I looked up, eyes glistening with molten tears. Daniel stood as close to me as he dared. The edges of his clothes singed and charred.

"I can't." Abject despair in my voice. "I don't know how."

"Yes, you can. You have the power. You know you do. You spoke to it before. It listens to you. Call it back now – before it's too late. Please."

It was the *please* that did it. That snapped me out of the depths. Daniel wanted me to call the fire. He believed that I could. And I wanted Daniel to believe in me. Slowly, I raised myself from the ground, closed my eyes and willed for that fiery beast to come home. To listen to me its mistress. To return and feed instead on my molten core. I trembled at the very thought of that massive blaze finding its way back inside me. How could I possibly summon it all when it had grown so exponentially as it fed? But this was my fault. I had to find the strength from somewhere. I opened my eyes and shuddered at the majesty of the sight before me.

Directly ahead of me was a massive wall of fire. The fire had stopped advancing across the field and now it stood waiting. The beast waited for my command. It had halted its onslaught and turned its head. Now, it asked – what would you have me do? Opening my arms, every ounce of my being quivering with fear, I summoned it home. I burned. Inside and out. I burned. There was indescribable pain and the knife edge of pleasure. It was ecstasy and hell all at once. Then, as swiftly as it had begun, it stopped. I was empty. A dried husk scorched beyond belief. Withered and dead. The steaming wet darkness claimed me. As I fell, I cried his name.

"Daniel" *Please don't leave me.*

It was dark for only a few moments. I heard sirens blaring in the distance, people shouting. I was cold. So cold. Shivering. My eyes flew open, panicked – was the fire still going? Why else would there be sirens? I lay on the dry scratchy grass, the expanse of southern sky staring down at me accusingly. I had defiled the night with hungry flames. It was peaceful no longer. Dogs barked frenziedly up and down the main road, excited by the sounds of panic. Shivering to my very core, I shifted awkwardly, aware that I was wrapped in Daniel's school shirt. He was kneeling beside me, eyes full of panicked worry.

"Leila – Leila, come on, we have to get out of here before the fire trucks show up. Come on, can you stand?" He whispered urgently in my ear, his hands already raising me to my feet, hurrying me along the graveled drive back to the car. Numbly I complied, too dazed to argue or question. Just grateful that he had not abandoned me to face the consequences of my actions alone.

I managed to choke out a question. "The fire? The dorm?"

"It's fine. The most of it is out, only the grass is still kinda burning low. Don't worry, the fire truck can deal with the rest."

I was in no state to explain or to justify this night. Within minutes, we were in the car, reversing and then speeding out the front school gate.

"Where are we going? Where are you taking me?"

"The hospital. You could be hurt. We need to get you some help."

"No. I'm fine. Honest. Please just take me home. There's nothing wrong with me."

We both knew that wasn't really true but instead of arguing, Daniel just sighed and nodded. "Fine."

I sat back in the seat, watching as one and then two fire trucks sped past us, catching glimpses of the worried faces of the fire fighters. Anxious what awaited them at the scene of the fire. Waves of shame railed me. Battering at my frail composure, taking breath-sized chunks out of me. As I thought of those men hastening to stop what I had created, putting their lives at risk for the safety of others, I started to cry. Huge gulping sobs wracked me. And when I remembered the intensity of my fierce joy as the flames had lapped higher – I cringed within and sobbed harder.

How could I have done that? What had come over me? How could I have so quickly become a creature so unfeeling, uncaring of those around me? Of Daniel even – for heaven's sake. He had stood there, daring the heat, trying to save me from myself, trying to save those people – while I? I had wanted more. I felt sick to my stomach. Daniel didn't speak as he concentrated on the road, every so often taking quick looks over his shoulder and in the rear-view mirror. I imagined the revulsion he must be enduring just having me in the same space as him and I sobbed more.

We drove like that for about twenty minutes. Me crying and him focused on the road. Until we came to a halt midway up the long drive to my mother's house. He didn't speak for several minutes after quitting the engine.

"Leila, are you alright?" He spoke carefully. Was he afraid I would burst into flame again? Was he dreading our every moment together, wondering which breath would be his last before I incinerated him as easily as I had the night? I cried so hard I could barely make out my words.

"D-D-D-Daniel, I'm so-so-so-sorry. I d-d-d don't know wh-wh-what hap-hap-happened. P-p-please f-f-forgive me."

He didn't answer. Just considered me with those flint green eyes of his, a troubled look on his face. The distance between us in the confines of the front seat, gaped screamingly – a vast chasm of unspoken fear and uncertainty. He took his eyes away from me and stared out the window while replying.

"I have never seen anything so beautiful – and so terrible in my life." His voice was a hushed whisper I had to strain to hear. "Leila, you were on fire. You were burning but not only that, it's like you were possessed by it. I thought you weren't going to stop, that you were going to burn down the whole school." He took a deep breath to steady himself then turned to gaze at me earnestly. "That wasn't you. It wasn't. That wasn't the Leila I know. It wasn't you."

He was trying to convince himself as much as me that tonight had been an aberration. Some maniacal misfit had taken my place. Some psychotic split personality perhaps. He sought some rational explanation for what did not make sense.

I remembered the countless times my Dad had sat me on his lap to gently explain, yet again, that our tempers were something we needed to control, we needed to master. That we must not let our emotions rule us. No matter how powerful they were. I thought of the martial arts training with the finest instructor he could find – always emphasizing the need for inner control, inner peace, mind over the body. I remembered as a young child, the tantrums at my grandmother's house when my dad went away on assignment, scratching, kicking, biting people. Smashing her fine china. Being forbidden to return until I had learned how to behave. And finally, I thought of the deep sense of satisfaction when I had punched the face of that blonde girl at school, the complete shock in her blue eyes as my fist connected with her nose – breaking it in two places and requiring plastic surgery to restore it to its former artificial glory. Refusing to apologize, the only thing separating me from expulsion and possible assault charges, the donation of a brand-new science lab and a ridiculously large cash settlement for the blonde to assuage her pain. Her return to school two months later, triumphant with new breast implants as well as a new nose but never again daring to call me the daughter of a island whore. Unwillingly I faced my truth. No, my fiery temper was nothing new. My joy in anger and violence had always been there.

"Leila?" Daniel waited for me to answer.

I was unwilling to meet his gaze. If he looked into my eyes now, he would see what I already knew. That the monster he had seen tonight was me. The real me. Revealed in all its ugliness. The monster who reveled in administering pain to others, in destroying beauty, and wielding unlimited power. I felt a cold, steel resolve dry my tears.

I must not let him see me again. He must never be threatened by such a monster again. I could not and would not bear it if tonight happened again. I forced coldness into my words.

"Daniel you don't really know much about me at all. What you saw tonight? That was me. The real me. I have to go." I opened the car door roughly, pausing once to look back at him in the darkness. "I'm sorry about tonight. I don't know what's going on with me but please, can you not say anything to anyone about it? Please?"

"Of course. But Leila, wait! We need to talk about this. We can't just leave it like this. Come back."

Swiftly, he got out of the car and came over to stop me with one hand on mine. "Don't go. Please. I don't want you to go."

I gazed up at him, the concern and pleading in his eyes and I almost faltered, leaning into his strength for one fragile moment. But it was enough. For me to see the slight redness on the side of his face, the splatter burns on his arms and bare chest. My indrawn breath was one of pain as I reached out to gently trace the evidence of my fiery outburst. Shaking my head, I spoke with finality.

"I hurt you tonight Daniel. And I'm sorry. I never want to do that again. Let me go. Nafanua will be worried and I don't know how to explain this to her. I'm tired. I don't want to be with you any more. I shouldn't have kissed you tonight. It wasn't what I wanted. This – you and me – it's not going to work. I don't want it to. I just want us to be friends, that's all. Just let me go, okay?"

His face shut down at my words. He nodded stiffly and released me, backing away slowly. "Oh, of course. I'm sorry. About tonight. About earlier. About all of it. I'll see you tomorrow."

His impassive face belied his disinterest. Where once I had burned – now ice gripped me. This was it. Daniel would never want me again. Hold me. Kiss me. Love me.

"Good night Daniel." Without waiting for a reply, I turned and walked up the drive, too numb for tears. His reply was to gun the motor and drive back the way we had come.

The house was dark and I welcomed the shadows as I opened the front door.

"What happened tonight, Leila?" my mother's voice startled me from the living room. She stood, with arms on her hips and repeated her question."Leila, what happened to you tonight?" There was no anger in her voice. No recrimination or accusations. Rather, there was a sense of subdued excitement as she walked forward, turning on the light to better appraise my appearance. The tense excitement in the air was so thick it almost crackled. Her eyes were gleaming, red lips stretched wide in a hungry smile. She sniffed at the smoky air around me. Like a Doberman on the hunt. I had never been so afraid of anyone then as I was of her at that moment.

I backed away several paces, until my back was against the front door. "Umm, nothing?"

"Oh don't be ridiculous, you foolish child. Look at the state you're in." She waved a hand impatiently. "I'm not angry. I want to know – I need to know – what happened to you tonight? Tell me everything."

"I went out with Daniel. We went to the school field to train together. And then, something happened." I stopped short, unwilling to put into words the horror of the night.

She grabbed my arm, red nails digging into already tender flesh. Her face was alight with a terrible joy that threatened to explode. I wondered how my father had loved this woman with her frightening beauty and steel-like edge.

Abruptly, she loosed her grip to take a deep breath. Her voice softened as she changed her tactic. "Leila I can tell that something…wonderful has happened to you. I need you to trust me enough to tell me what that something was. I can help you, but you must trust me and tell me. What happened tonight?"

How I longed to believe her. To trust her words. I needed to find some sanity in this night of madness. I started to shake, waves of coldness rushing over me in a delayed reaction of shock. Nafanua held me close in her arms, patting my hair and soothing me softly as I shook.

"There, there … it'll be alright. Hush … hush … we will take care of you. Don't be afraid … Come sit, you're like ice."

She guided me to the sofa, still keeping me close. I tried to speak but the shivering wouldn't allow it.

"It's alright, my daughter. It's alright. I am here." Nafanua continued to rock and soothe me for several minutes until the shaking subsided. She brushed strands of hair out of my face, pulling some of it close to breathe the smoke that soaked me.

"Oh my daughter you have much to tell me!" She was triumphant, rigid with excitement again. I was so relieved to have a mother to confide in that I ignored the warning instinct that whispered unease within.

"I don't know what happened ... I ... I was with Daniel and then I was so hot I was burning and then I exploded – I literally exploded into flames. My whole body was on fire but it didn't hurt. I still don't understand it ... I can't believe it – but it was real. Nafanua – it was real – I swear it." I pleaded with her to believe me. I needed her to believe me. To make sense of it for me.

Rather than the incredulous reaction I expected, Nafanua jolted to her feet, her whole body exultant. "Yes! I knew it. I knew it." she seemed to forget I was there as she paced back and forth, muttering to herself. "I told them, I knew it, I felt it. She's the one. She has to be."

I felt very tired. Very dirty and very unclothed as I sat and watched her jittery high. Nafanua stopped mid mutter and refocused on me.

"Leila, you are descended from a very powerful line of spirit women called *telesā*. What happened to you tonight was – magical – you could call it. We – I – like to call it a – a – spiritual manifestation of the earth goddess. Pele, the goddess of fire, of earth has chosen you to be her conduit. This is a sacred gift, Leila. Not something to be taken lightly – but then not something that should frighten you or inspire dread. As my daughter, it was always a possibility that one, if not more, of the earth's forces or powers would be gifted in you, lying dormant until you reached maturity, but we could never be certain."

I couldn't have been more confused than if she spoke a stream of gobbledegook. Spirits? Goddesses? Earth powers and forces? What the heck was this woman on about? Was she insane? Was this why my father had warned me away from coming to this place? Because he knew his wife, the mother of his only daughter, was mentally unwell? And he didn't think I could handle it? Nafanua's explanation continued.

"What you're telling me about what happened tonight – I have been watching and hoping it would be so. Only I wasn't sure. There are those who doubt the gift of Pele still lives within us. They believe that it's been far too long and the bloodline has been too diluted. It doesn't help that more and more people turn away from our gifts every year. They are so eager to embrace the knowledge and medicine of the Western world that they trample the gifts of the earth mother under their feet." Nafanua's face darkened, her eyes flashing black fire in the night. I hugged Daniel's thin shirt closer to me and shivered. I wished suddenly that he were here. That he hadn't driven off without a backward glance. Or that I was with him in the comfort of his grandmother's kitchen. Instead of sitting here, alone in an empty house with nothing but a madwoman for company.

"I see that you doubt my words, that you think me crazy." Nafanua laughed. It only served to heighten my growing alarm. I tensed as she sat down next to me, taking my hands in hers.

"Leila, I know that you are scared right now. Confused. Something happened to you tonight, something terrible but beautiful in all its splendid immensity. It made you feel limitless. Untouchable. It took you far beyond yourself. Am I right?" she looked at me searchingly.

I nodded slowly. "Yes."

She continued, "Tonight you felt terror but you also felt great joy unlike anything else, didn't you?" She cast a slow sideways glance at my shocked face.

She *knew*. This woman knew what I had felt tonight. Maybe she *was* crazy, but what a relief to find someone who could understand my experience. I let out a huge pent-up breath.

"Oh Mother," it was the first time I had called her that, but if she noticed my inadvertent slip up, she made no sign of it "it was terrifying, truly it was. The fire, it burned so strong and fast that the whole school field was in flames but it was the most beautiful thing I had ever seen. I wanted it to grow, to cover as far as I could see. It's like me and the fire were one. It was consuming me, but I loved it. I could throw fire balls and spit fireworks and sparks…and I nearly burned down the school dorm and I could have killed people. I'm a horrible person!" My excited rave turned into chagrin as I remembered how close I had come to causing tragedy.

"No, don't be foolish. Of course you're not." She spoke sharply, as one confronted with a nonsensical child. "The gift of Pele is awe inspiring. You must *never* be ashamed of the joy it gives you. You must embrace your birthright. You would be ungrateful if you did anything different. And Pele does not tolerate ingratitude kindly. So, you set fire to a field. So what. And a school dorm? It's good for people to be confronted with the powers that they so easily forget. I would not give it a moment's thought. Clearly, you did not kill anyone, so let us move on." She leapt to her feet again, pacing with nervous excitement. "Oh my precious daughter, there is so much to be done now. You don't realize how long we as a people, have waited your arrival. Have longed for the power that you will give us. The simple fact alone that Pele has chosen once again, one of her daughters to speak and act for her. There will be much rejoicing amongst us. But there's so much for you to learn, so much we must teach you. You have been denied years of essential training because of that man's stubbornness."

Through my tears, a cold fist clenched at my insides as I heard her mention 'that man,' my father. The father who had lied to me and gone to extreme lengths to keep me from ever even knowing my own mother. I had been angry at his deceit, but as Nafanua ranted on about 'spirit sisters' and sisterhood meetings and other meaningless jargon, I knew with a clear certainty that it had been a mistake to trust her. So what if Dad had lied to me. He had been trying to protect me. I was sure of it. From a scene exactly like this one. I looked at her wild exultant eyes, her gleeful smile as she spoke of the volcano goddess and I felt an overwhelming pull of love and appreciation for my Dad. I sent him a prayer of thanks. *Thank you for sparing me a mother like this. Thank you.* But now he was gone. And thanks to my choices in the last few months, here I was in my crazy mother's house.

The unease that Nafanua invoked in me was now heightened with the realization that not only was she not surprised by my fiery explosion, but it was as if she had even been expecting it. Waiting for it. My mistrust grew. She had sought me out. Professed to love me. Wanted to get to know me. Pleaded with me to come and stay in her Aleisa colonial-style mansion. Given me extravagant gifts. Unlimited freedom. I shivered.

I thought I wanted someone to make sense of my fire but now, seeing it in a new light of cold calculation made me wish that she had run screaming from the room at my story and made plans for my admission to a psych ward. It was all too much for me. I closed my eyes wearily, waves of exhaustion shrouding me in their drowning pull.

Abruptly Nafanua stopped in her fervor as if remembering I was there. "But of course you must be exhausted. You need to shower, sleep, take a breath. Give it time for everything to sink in. And then tomorrow, when you're rested, we will talk again. I will tell you everything. And all of this uncertainty and doubt, it will be gone."

Gratefully, I clutched at this escape clause, no matter how temporary it might be. "Okay, yes. I need to sleep. This has all been too crazy for me. Can we talk about it tomorrow, please?"

Nafanua embraced me fiercely and whispered in my ear. "Of course. I'm so proud of you Leila. So excited for us. The future is limitless for us now!"

She stood at the foot of the stairs and watched me as I went up to my room. In the quiet confines of my room I shivered, hugging my arms to my body, trying hard to instill some measure of sanity to this night. *Get a grip Leila. Get a grip. Breathe. You can do this.*

I had confronted two realities on this cataclysmic night. I had gone running with Daniel and he had kissed me. Or rather we had kissed each other. And it had been amazing. Far more head spinning than anything a lame teen movie could ever depict. For those brief moments, I had been sure that Daniel felt as powerfully for me as I did for him. My brain shied away from what had come next, but I forced myself to confront it.

Then I had burst into flames. My whole body had been on fire, and it hadn't hurt and that had been amazing too. In fact, it had been more exhilarating than the kiss that had provoked it. I halted the train of thought with a jarring crash. Wait up. Had his kiss provoked the fire? Or rather my swirl of heat and adrenaline and hormones and all sorts of crazy chemicals going haywire at a first kiss – had those ignited the flames? What did that mean? I thought back to the previous occasions when the heat attacks had threatened to overwhelm me. The day of the fight at Leififi when the boy had tried to hurt me. I had been scared – no, then I had gotten angry, and the fire had burned and actually manifested outwardly.

And then tonight, the kiss. I had been awash with sheer pleasure and excitement. And the fire had exploded. As I tracked the timeline, I realized the fire had been simmering ever since I arrived in Samoa.

And it had grown. It exploded when I was threatened, when I got angry and when – I blushed in the darkness – I was physically aroused.

A horrible possibility began to dawn, did that mean that any hope for a relationship with *anyone, forever* was doomed? I thought of Daniel. The sunlight of his smile. His golden laugh and the way it warmed me. The strong, sure way he held my hand in his, the peace and contentment it gave me to be with him. At our rock pool. In his grandmother's garden. At the workshop with fireworks skipping about our feet as he guided my trembling hands with the welder. The way a simple half grin from him could soothe my heated temper and avert one of my mini meltdowns. I thought of the joy of finding someone who could know your soul in all its misery and still want to be with you. I was certain a bond like that didn't happen very often in one lifetime. And now, would I have to give it all up? Because it was too dangerous to be with him?

Bone tired, I fell asleep with that final thought. Curled in a crumpled heap on the floor. In the house of a madwoman who was my mother.

I awoke with a start, cramped muscles aching from their night on the floor. Disoriented for a few moments, I could only shake my head blearily, wondering why I was asleep next to my bed. Then the thirst hit me. And all I could think of was the raging drive to find water. Now.

Stumbling to my feet, I made my ragged way to the bathroom sink, turning on the faucet and taking huge gulps of water. Too thirsty to worry about the nasty bugs probably squirming their way into my system right now. It seemed I would never get enough water. I felt a headache beginning to pound its way through my brain and a wave of dizziness had me gripping the sink tightly for support.

Looking at my reflection in the mirror, I was horrified with what I saw. Yes my eyes were bleary tired. And my cheeks were smudged with black soot. And words could not describe the state of my hair. And yet, even under all that, a stranger looked back at me. I looked different. I gazed at the stranger in the mirror, and she stared back at me. She was beautiful. High cheekbones, sensuous lips, even the lush eyebrows had shape and definition. The stranger looked familiar.

She looked like my fiercely beautiful mother and her sisters.

No, I had to be imagining things. People don't just wake up in the morning after a hell-ish night and look like something else. Shaking my head in denial, I stripped off Daniel's shirt and stepped into the shower, hungry for the rousing jet of cold water. Unwilling to emerge to face my reality, that's where I stayed for at least half an hour, taking the longest shower of my life. Wishing that the spray could erase the night before. Wash away the weird genetic discrepancy or whatever it was, that would cause a person to erupt into flame. Set my world on fire. And almost fry the boy I loved to a crisp. A night where my unnaturally strange mother would become even more unnatural. And claim me as hers. As one of her 'spirit sisters'. Whatever the heck that was.

I felt bile rise in my throat as I was reminded of Nafanua's exultant response to my story the previous night. Panic pulsed in my chest. I gripped the walls for support. *Stay calm Leila. Get a grip. Breathe.* I knew I had to think very carefully and not run screaming from my mother's house. Because I had the awful suspicion she wouldn't let me get very far. More than ever before, I needed to be in control of my emotions. I needed to be the consummate actress. I needed to be as calm and unruffled as … as Grandmother Folger in any crisis.

I smiled weakly to myself as I thought of my grandmother. And caught a sob midway in my throat as a wave of homesickness assailed me. It surely was a time for firsts. Because this was the first time I had ever longed to be in Grandmother Folger's house. Safe in the civilized world of decorum and etiquette. More than anything, I wanted to call my grandmother. And ask her to come rescue me from my life.

And as the tears escaped, I admitted to myself and the four walls of my shower, that if I called her, she would come. And she would do anything and everything to keep me safe. That realization alone gave me strength. To make some decisions. I was leaving. This house. I was going to get as far away from Nafanua as possible. Once I had distance between us, I was sure that I could figure things out.

I dressed and shoved my few belongings into a backpack. Thank goodness I was a light traveler. Taking a deep breath and steeling my resolve, I ran lightly down the stairs, hoping I could slip undetected out the back door. Raised voices from the kitchen stopped me. Nafanua and Sarona? Arguing.

Nafanua's voice was menacing. "I am the Covenant Keeper, Sarona. And I say that this child is the solution we have been waiting and hoping for. She can right the imbalance once and for all."

Sarona interrupted her, "Until a few days ago, you hadn't even met her. What do you really know about her? Nothing. Your feisty husband made sure of that. I will tell you the only thing we do know with certainty – she's not a child. She's already eighteen years old. Far too old to be trained, to be pliable. She cannot be trusted or controlled. You know I'm right. It would have been different if we'd found her when she was ten or even twelve. As it is, she's nothing but a threat to us. And she needs to be dealt with."

Nafanua, almost pleading. "It's not too late. I know it. This girl is strong willed. But she trusts me. I can train her. I can mold her."

Sarona spoke with cold finality. "No Nafanua, if she does have Pele's gifts then she's a nightmare in the making and you would do well to put an end to this now. Before it's too late."

A dry voice from behind me, had me jump. "Good morning, Leila. Don't you think you should join your mother in the kitchen?"

Damnit! It was Netta. Her lips pursed in disapproval at my eavesdropping. I gave her a weak smile. "Yeah, actually I was just going to slip out, I've got somewhere to go."

Hearing our voices, Nafanua opened the door to the kitchen, "Leila? Is that you? Come in, we've been waiting for you to get up."

I threw a glance over my shoulder at the front door, which now seemed an eternity away. There would be no easy way to get out of this. I squared my shoulders and walked into the sun-filled room. The two women sat at the kitchen table. Sarona with an enigmatic smile on her face as she took in my backpack, my hastily dressed state. Nafanua smiled,

"Ah, good morning daughter. Did you have a good rest? Are you feeling better?"

Sarona spoke before I could answer as she stood and walked over to pause a foot away from me. "Of course she's better. Can't you see Nafanua, she's dressed to impress and packed ready to leave. Ready to run back to Aunty and Uncle."

Again the mere presence of this woman had me on edge, only today, it was worse. I felt a prickling at the back of my neck, and against my will, my whole body tensed as if for flight. A flush of heat, unbidden, started to build within me at the smile that didn't reach her midnight black eyes. I struggled for calm, to halt the heat before it built to raging fire. Sarona tilted her head to one side and considered me thoughtfully.

"Why, Nafanua do you feel that?"

"What?" My mother looked as puzzled as I.

Sarona raised her eyes and hands to the ceiling. On her face a half look of … awe?

"That. The temperature in here has just risen several notches. And the heat is coming from her." She turned cold eyes upon me. Angry eyes that flashed dangerously. "Nafanua, you just may be correct about this daughter of yours."

Half closing her eyes, she breathed deeply and from nowhere, a light breeze danced through the room. It should have been a welcome cooling relief in the tropical heat yet, for reasons I could not fathom, it set my teeth on edge and only accelerated the rise of heat within.

What was she doing to set my instincts on hyper drive like this? I felt myself begin to smolder. And I welcomed it. I smiled. And Sarona's face darkened in anger. Her smile was replaced with steel loathing and she flicked one wrist rigidly. Impossibly, the breeze became a swirling current of wind that tugged at my hair and pulled at my clothing. A vase toppled to the floor, smashing in a thousand pieces at our feet. What was this woman doing to the air? Panic rose in me. And with it came fire. Would I stop it? Did I want to? My every sense screamed that I was in danger and all I wanted to do was allow the flames to erupt, because with them came fearlessness. I was afraid of this woman. And I didn't want to be. A delicious warmth begin to smolder from somewhere deep inside. The air in my chest and lungs was hot. Steaming hot. I could feel the edges of my skin start to blister. There was alarm in Nafanua's eyes.

"Leila. Leila stop it. I said stop it." There was an edge of panic in her voice as she shook her head at me. She grabbed Sarona's arm. "Stop it, you're scaring her. Provoking her. This is not the way we want to deal with this."

Sarona smiled and shrugged her shoulders. "What? Alright, alright. I've stopped. Now get your brat under control. Remember, you need all of our consent to allow her entry to our covenant. And I don't like what I see."

As if I was but a pesky dog yapping at her heels, a dog she was tired of, Sarona turned and stalked out of the room. A wave of hate ripped through me, so strong that it had me reeling. I took a deep breath and fought for control.

But there was none to be had. Fire exploded from me. But unlike the night before, this time it was only my hands that erupted into flame. And it hurt. So badly I screamed. Flailing and stumbling, I fell to my knees, shaking my hands trying to get the fire away. Which only sent jets of flame ricocheting through the room.

"Leila!" Nafanua ducked for cover as a flame bolt narrowly missed her face and hit a cupboard behind her. I was terrified. The fire seemed to have a life of its own, I was not in control at all as sparks leapt at will from my fingers, no matter how hard I tried to stop them. Glasses shattered, a toaster exploded, a rope of fire snaked its way along the bench top.

Dimly I was aware of Netta and Sarona running in, coming to a halt in shock just as a fire flash sprayed the wall above the doorway. I curled into a ball, trying vainly to curb the fire with my body by clenching my fists tightly against me.

"Help me please. It hurts. I can't stop it. I don't know how. I don't know what to do!"

Half the kitchen was in flames now and I could hear Nafanua coughing on the smoke. "Sarona, we have to get her out of here! Get her out into the open."

Crouched in the doorway, Sarona shouted back. "Oh and just how do you propose that we do that?"

I was paralyzed with confusion. I couldn't understand it. Last night, yes there had been a moment of pain when the fire first exploded, but that was it. This? This was like a thousand daggers stabbing the flesh in my hands again and again. And every time a new flash emitted, it ripped through the skin like a razorblade. And no matter how hard I tried, I couldn't do anything to stop it. No, this was vastly different from the night before. I knew Nafanua was right. I needed to get out of the house before I burned the place down. Before I hurt one of them.

I rolled over onto my knees then stood, staggered and half fell out the back screen door onto the verandah. A few more steps and I was out onto the expanse of green, leaving behind a kitchen billowing with smoke. Still the fire burned my hands and still I tried to subdue it, beating them uselessly against the grass. Would the agony ever end? "Leila stop panicking. Be calm." It was Nafanua. She had followed me out onto the lawn, leaving Sarona and Netta to deal with the mess I had made inside. She hung back a cautious distance and ordered again. "Stop it! You're doing this to yourself. Take deep breaths and calm down."

I shook my head. "I can't. I can't stop it. I don't know how! It hurts. It hurts. Please make it go away."

I turned away from her and resorted again to my attempts to stifle the flames, throwing sparks everywhere. Then it happened. From nowhere, from the silk of a blue sky, it started to rain. Hard and heavy, it came in a deluge, so thick and strong I could barely make out the outline of the house. Or of Nafanua.

The coolness distracted me from the torture of my hands, giving me the chance I needed to breathe, *calm down Leila. Stop panicking. You made it go away last night. You can do it again. Tell it to stop. Tell it to go away! Breathe Leila. You can do this. Calm down.* I breathed and, as I breathed, the fire dimmed, hissed, and fizzed. And died. Leaving me a bedraggled heap on the ground. I lifted my charred, blistered palms to the heavens and welcomed the soothing relief offered by the rain.

The fire was over. And, as quickly as it had begun, the rain ended. Leaving me wet and cold on the grass. Shivering with delayed shock, I picked myself up and walked back up the stairs where Nafanua stood.

"Are you alright?"

I nodded. But still she reached for my hands, examining the damage. "These don't look good. You're going to need some of my aloe ointment and probably a draught of *ti-moana* juice, a sedative, for the pain. Come in the house."

I followed her back inside, dreading the damage I would find there. Yet, it wasn't as bad as I had expected. Clearly, Sarona and Netta had managed to subdue the flames quickly. Netta was sweeping up broken glass in a kitchen with blackened walls while Sarona was nowhere to be seen.

"She left. In a huff." Explained Netta in answer to Nafanua's querying eye.

"That's probably for the best. Come into the living room, Leila, while I gather my medicines for your hands."

A few minutes later my hands were bandaged and I was wrapped in a towel. A long sip of Nafanua's ti-moana liquid and already the razor edge of pain was numbing. Nafanua sat across from me and studied me carefully, waiting.

"How are you feeling now?"

"Better. Much better. Thank you." I took a deep breath. "I'm sorry. About ruining your kitchen. About almost hurting you and Sarona and Netta. I don't know what happened. Well, I do know but I can't explain it. It doesn't make any sense."

Nafanua waved my apology away with her hand. "Ah, a kitchen is easily repaired. And me and my sisters, we are stronger than we look. You can't hurt us, don't worry. It's alright."

I interrupted her in a rush of words. "No it's not alright. Last night I almost burned the school down. I could have killed Daniel. Today, Sarona gets on my nerves a little – and so I react by setting the place on fire? This is not alright." I paused, struggling for calm so I could recite the words I had practiced all morning in the shower. "Nafanua, I need to go home. To America. I appreciate all that you've done for me in these few days, but I really think it's better if I move back to Aunty Matile's. And then I'm going to see what's the earliest flight I can arrange to leave, to go back to D.C. I'm sure you understand that I just want to go home. This fire thing, whatever it is, it all started when I got here and I know, if I just go back to D.C., back to my old life, then it will go away."

Nafanua turned quizzical eyes on me, one eyebrow arched. "You don't get it do you?"

"Get what?"

"The last thing you should be doing right now, is going home. Is going anywhere. Last night was only the beginning. Your *telesā* fire is only just starting to manifest, which means that you have a way to go yet before you achieve full strength. In the meantime, you're probably the most dangerous, most volatile person on the entire planet right now. You have no idea what you're dealing with. You have no clue what's building up inside you right now or what metabolic changes are taking place in your system, changes that are precipitous and unstable. What just happened in that kitchen today? That was only a preview to what could happen tomorrow. You're unstable matter, you could blow up if someone is unlucky enough to bump into you on the street. You could set the whole town alight, Leila, do you understand that? Do you know how dangerous you are to people around you?"

"No, no." I didn't want to hear this. I didn't want to open my mind to the terrifying possibilities she was telling me about. "No. This is just a weird aberration or something. This isn't really happening. I'm going home to D.C. and I know that everything will go back to normal. It has to."

Nafanua regarded me with pity in her eyes. "Leila, this is a part of you. This is who you are. I'm sorry, your powers are not going to go away, no matter how much you may want them to."

I was hostile. "How the hell do you know that?"

Nafanua did not speak. She stood and walked the few steps out the open front doors and down the verandah steps. I followed her, confused as to her intentions. Almost lazily, she beckoned with her right hand and out of a blank blue sky, thunder clapped loud enough to make me jump. Another hand flicked gracefully and white light jagged, crackled and hissed as lightning seared the ground beside her. I gripped the verandah rails for support, my mind struggling to accept what I was seeing. Nafanua spun in a soft circle and the lightning burned out a path around her. When the circle was complete she stopped and stepped out of the smoke, brushing a stray piece of cindered grass off her skirt. She looked straight at me.

"I know because I am *telesā*. And you are my daughter. I am *matagi*. Storm. Air. Wind. Lightning. You are *fanua*. Earth. Blessed with earth's fire. And your gift is not going to go away, no matter what you do or where you live. It's part of who you are and the sooner you accept that, the sooner you can get the help you need to make sure that you don't hurt anyone. Unless you want to that is." She half smiled and walked slowly towards me. I slid to sit on the wooden step.

The morning sunlight danced over the garden and a blue kingfisher sat on the wood railing and regarded me with dark eyes. It was supposed to be another day in paradise. Yesterday I had kissed a beautiful boy that a girl like me could only dream about. Today, here I was, watching the woman who was my mother call down lightning from the sky and burn circles of fire in the grass.

Nafanua sat beside me on the step and together we looked at the bees moving ponderously through the gardenia bushes. And the kingfisher looked at us both. I took a deep breath. And then another. And tried to still the thoughts that were drowning in confusion in my brain. Nafanua spoke again. "Leila, there's something else that you should know. Look at me." I looked. "How old do you think I am?"

I shrugged and half smiled at the ordinariness of the query. "My dad always warned me about tricky questions like these ... *there's never a right answer, Leila – to 'do you think I'm fat?' And 'how old do you think I am?' So don't answer 'em.*" I turned away from the memories and focused on the woman beside me. "I don't know. You tell me. How old are you?"

"I'm 116 years old."

The day faded hazily around me as I looked into Nafanua's eyes. I was wishing for insanity but all I saw there was truth. I shook my head dumbly as Nafanua continued.

"All *telesā* have a gift with plants. We are healers. We know what plants will cure diseases, soothe discomforts, heal all sicknesses and prolong life. It's not that difficult or that big of a secret. If more people adhered to a truly natural and organic diet and lifestyle – then more people would live healthier and longer lives." She shrugged. "We *telesā* are not immortal or invincible, we just know what to do to ensure we live long lives. The mixture I've been giving you to drink every night is a standard elixir blend that we all take daily. Now that your powers are awakening, your body is changing. Your genetic code is unleashing certain anomalies that make it possible for you to channel fire, to tap in to the earth's strength. Please believe me when I tell you that this – this is only the beginning for you. *Telesā fanua* can move the earth beneath our feet, summon volcanoes, channel earth's fire and make it do their bidding. You will need a great deal of training to help you control these gifts. You will need me to help you, to teach you. You cannot do this alone. Imagine what havoc you will wreak when you make the earth heave and roar. Think of the people you could endanger. Do you want to risk that? Is that what your father would have wanted you to do?"

I paled. That was a low blow. Mention of my dad ripped me like a serrated knife. I wanted to curl into a ball and cry till my father scooped me into his strong arms. I wanted him to take me away from here. Away from my living nightmare. But that wasn't going to happen. I gritted my teeth and prayed again for calm strength. Again the image of Grandmother Folger and her steel resolve was my focal point.

"When we first met, you said nothing to me about this stuff. Now it all makes sense what Aunty Matile was freaking out about, she kept going on and on about *telesā* and spirits. I had no idea what she was talking about. Why weren't you open with me when we met? When I first moved in here?"

She smiled pityingly. "Honestly, would you have wanted to listen? Would you still have come to stay with me if I started spouting off to you about spirits and powers and all this? I don't think so! Besides, we *telesā* have ... I suppose you'd call them – rules – for this kind of thing. My sisters and I, we are *feagaiga sa.*"

"A what?"

"*Feagaiga sa* – the closest English word would be covenant. It's a sacred promise that we enter into. One that binds us to each other, stronger than blood. It enables our gifts, our powers to be multiplied many times over and renders them void against each other, making it impossible for any of us to attack the other. We are bound to protect each sister in the covenant against any harm. We are covenant to many things, including secrecy. We cannot share *telesā* knowledge with anyone. Yes, people know of us, they hint of us in their quiet little chats, revere us in their legends and frighten children with stories of our punishments, but ordinary people do not, cannot really know us and what we can do. So, I could not tell you anything, until now. Now that you have come into the light of who you are. One of us. My daughter. My sister."

My mind was busy at work, searching for the answers that would help me carve a way out of this choking mess. "Wait, so let me see if I get this. We have these power things. Mine is catching on fire and blowing things up. Yours is like Storm from the X-Men?"

She arched an eyebrow at me, "Excuse me? Storm who?"

I shook my head impatiently, already moving on to the next thought. "Oh never mind, she's just some comic book character. You know, a fictional person in a book, nothing like this boring reality staring at us in the face right here. You and your sisters, you can all do things with lightning and rain and wind, right?"

A nod.

"All those women I met the first night I was here, the ones that are always in and out of this place, those are your covenant sisters?"

Another nod.

"But me, my fire thing, I'm different? So where are the *telesā* that can do what I do? Where do they hang out? Where's their *feagaiga sa*?" I stumbled over the unfamiliar words.

Nafanua frowned and took a thoughtful moment before replying. "There aren't any. That we know of. In fact, most *telesā* think *telesā fanua* are only a myth, a scary tale dreamed up by our mothers to fascinate and frighten. None of us have ever met one before. I am the eldest of my sisters and even I have never known one. As a young child, my mother would tell me of her grandmother, Sau'imaiafi. She herself had never met her but they would speak of her with awe. With fear. It was she that raised these islands up from the ocean. She led her people from their original homeland and they travelled many miles, many months across the sea in search of new land to settle. After many days they arrived at a small cluster of islands – far too small to support them. The people were weary of travelling, hungry for taro and green things, tired of eating fish. They cried to her for help. Sau'imaiafi spoke to the earth, she summoned a volcano, the earth rose up out of the ocean in a magnificent eruption, and the islands of Samoa were formed. Can you imagine it? Mountains of lava and red fire moving to this one woman's command, running over the ocean, forming valleys, rivers, rich fertile earth. Is it any wonder then that Polynesians call the earth fire goddess, Pele – the creator and destroyer of worlds?"

I paled. If Nafanua was trying to impress me with the 'awesomeness' of this fire power, then she was succeeding. It was so 'awesome' that I wanted to vomit.

"So did you know that this was going to happen to me? When you had me?"

She was shaking her head but I rushed on, my voice building to a crescendo as the rage rose within me. "How about when you came to Auntie's house, when we first met? Did you know then that this was going to happen? All these weeks, I've been having these heat attacks and freaking out, not knowing what was going on with me. Why didn't you come tell me? You should have warned me. Prepared me. Given me some formula or something to take so this wouldn't happen." I turned on her. "All my life I've never belonged anywhere, always been the outsider and now? Now I'm really a freak! Why didn't you stop this? You should have asked me if I wanted this. It isn't right. This isn't fair. I never asked for this. You had no right to do this to me!"

Nafanua tried to calm me, "It's not like that. Your gift is part of who you are. It's written in your genetic code. It's not something you can take a miracle cure for. Or wish away. Nobody put a spell or voodoo curse on you, you're my daughter and so you're blessed with special powers. Powers that many others would give their souls to have."

"No. I don't want them." My shoulders slumped defeatedly as I stared at my bandaged hands. "I don't want to set things on fire. I don't want to hurt people. Please, can't you just give me some medicine to make it go away? I don't want to be different, gifted, or special. I just want to be regular. Belong somewhere for the first time in my life."

Nafanua moved to stand beside me, gently taking my hands in hers, raising my face to look in my eyes. "If that's what you want then stay with me. I can teach you how to control this. I can make sure you don't hurt anyone. I'm your best chance at regular."

Did I really have any other options? Was there really anyone else I could turn to for help? Shoulders slumped resignedly, I followed Nafanua back into the house. I wasn't going anywhere.

It seemed ridiculous that something as mundane as school on Monday should even still be happening. The universe – for me – had imploded. Nothing was as it had seemed and all that I had believed to be 'real' and 'important' now seemed meaningless. Insignificant. Of what import was Ms. Sivani's English class, now that I knew such things as *telesā* existed? Spirit women who lived impossibly endless lives. Who could summon storms. And burst into flame when they kissed. Or burn a boy's face off when they got mad? I was no longer the same person. I was an earth fire spirit. And my mother was really a hundred and sixteen years old. And she could call down rain from the heavens. And throw lightning with nonchalant ease.

I spent Saturday in a numb trance, following my mother around as she continued to explain what we were. The floodgates were opened and she was on a giddy high as she recounted for me the history of 'our sisters.' Our kind. It was like cramming for a lifetime worth of exams in a day as she tried to 'catch me up' on the sisterhood.

The sisterhood.

The word scraped at my insides like fingernails against a chalkboard. There was an electric thrill to the air as we walked through her garden, wisps of lightning kept dancing in the overhead sky as she spoke. I listened politely with one half of my brain filing everything away neatly. The other half I kept protected. The half where I was screaming. Soundlessly.Wishing she was just a certifiable lunatic spouting rubbish.

"Leila, all of us have a special affinity with our mother the earth. She speaks to us and we cannot help but listen. To her pain, her cries for help. This gift manifests very early. A toddler will delight in her mother's garden, flowers. She will cry when the earth is scarred. Burned. Defiled. She will grow to love plants. All life. Things will grow to her command, thrive to her nurturing." She paused beside a gardenia. "Our very presence will bring joy to a gardenia and vice versa. Where did you think your gift with plants came from?"

I shrugged. For as long as I could remember, plants had made more sense to me than people. But I had always just assumed that was because I was a miserable people person. Even now, my mind shied away from my link to my garden back home. Or the time I had gotten ill when Dad and I had visited a mass burial site in Nigeria.

Standing on the plain with wind whipping through my hair, a wave of nausea swept over me, so powerful it brought me to my knees. Leila?! What is it? Are you okay? Dad's anxious hands helping to lift me. My vision blurring a hazy red. Everywhere there is blood. Dark, thick, wet blood that stains the soil. Soaks it. It cries out to me. Speaks to me. A child huddled beside her mother. Screams. Bodies being hacked to pieces. Gunshots. Raucous laughter. Dirt. Shoveled earth. Covering but never forgetting. I stumble away from the site to throw up again and again beside the rental car. My dad holds my hand and worriedly gets me a drink of water. I am crying. Mumbling incoherently. "Dad, can't you feel it? Can't you see it? There's blood everywhere. This earth can't even breathe, it's so smothered with it. Please, Dad, take me away from here, please."

She continued, oblivious to my discomfort. "We are protectors. Guardians of this land. That is why we have these powers. Anciently, *telesā* were guardians for specific areas of land and the people of that area would pay her homage. It was her responsibility to watch over that space and its life, make sure that the balance of our mother earth was not disrupted. Things are different now. Man tramples haphazardly over earth and so we *telesā* have had to band together more. Unite in sisterhood. I am the leader - the Covenant Keeper - that holds our sisterhood together. You have met all my sisters. The six of us make up our covenant.

Now, there are three different gifts, each attuned to one piece of our mother. First, there is *telesā matagi*. We are woven to the atmosphere's currents, and patterns. We can speak to the wind, storms, the rain." She turned and waved her hand gently. One gesture is all that it took and a gust of wind rushed past me, almost ripping my hair out of its clips in its ferocity. Another flick of her wrist, a half smile and a light sprinkle of rain misted down out of nowhere, soaking the plants beside us. I stood still, fighting the urge to run screaming for the house. My dad would have been impressed with my self-control as I shrugged my shoulders and continued walking beside this woman who could summon rain and send wind to rip out your hair.

"The most powerful of us with this gift can manipulate the air currents so we can fly." I was relieved when she didn't give me a demonstration of that one. I didn't think that my overloading brain could handle the sight of my mother flying. "But it takes many years of nurturing one's gift and building your bond with air before you can enjoy that kind of ease with it. I have it, but Sarona, for example, she is younger and not as experienced, so her mastery still needs improvement. She can be impatient and headstrong at times that one. I am trying to be forgiving of her impetuosity. Before you came, I had thought it necessary to indulge her as she was the most obvious choice for my successor." She had a thoughtful look on her face as she regarded me in the afternoon light. "Everything will be different now that you are here. We can move forward unimpeded now." Her step quickened and a flash of lightning, far more vicious and vivid than the others crackled through the sky, setting my teeth on edge and making me jump.

"The second gift is water. Well, ocean. *Telesā vasa loloa.* They are woven with the sea and, to some extent, rivers and streams. They speak to water and can summon tidal waves and whirlpools. It's somewhat different from the other gifts because they usually have a close affinity to the animals of the sea. The most powerful of them can speak to sea animals. The legends tell of them living as one with dolphins and whales. They are amazing swimmers. I knew one sister whose gift spoke very early in her life. She was only eight years old when she summoned a wave to upset a fishing boat – some fishermen were hunting a pod of dolphins she had befriended and the two men were killed." She pursed her lips, disapprovingly. "It can be very dangerous when a gift speaks to one so young, children have little self-control and are very impetuous. I had worried about you so far away and what would happen if your gift spoke to you before I could find you." She shook her head at unspoken thoughts and remembering the raging inferno I had caused at the school, I couldn't argue with any of them.

She drew me to sit beside her in the garden chairs under the frangipani tree and took both my hands in hers. "That brings me to the final gift. Yours. Earth. *Telesā fanua afi*. Earth fire. It is potentially the most powerful and the most rare. We have not seen anyone with this gift for several hundred years and so we don't really know much about it and how it works. Polynesian mythology speaks of the volcano goddess Pele, as the creator and the destroyer of lands. Your gift comes from the earth's core. There is incredible heat, pressure, and movement there. You will be attuned to the earth's movements, currents. You will control fire. Summon volcanoes. Call earthquakes. *Mafui'e*. And in many ways, Pele can call on the gifts of her sisters. Your earthquakes can move the waters. Call on the earth to bring forth life. But understand me clearly my daughter – Earth does not give her gift without a price. Yours is the power that is most difficult to control. Once unleashed, *fanua afi* does not often willingly recede. Your gift is intertwined with your emotions. Anger. Fear." She took a deep breath before rushing on. "And physical desire. The fire will not allow you to love. At least not without dire consequences for your lover. Do you understand me, Leila? I would not recommend that you attempt to test your fire's limits. It is not so with us air and water *telesā* but still, we do not have attachments. We will take a lover but we will not love. This is imperative. It is the first rule of the *telesā*. Men cannot be trusted. They can never understand our gifts. Or be aligned with them. They will only seek to control us for their pleasure and their own agendas. We must never allow ourselves to be emotionally beholden to any man. The other night when you were …" she paused delicately, "with Daniel, your powers ran wild because you did not have the necessary training and other controls to handle such physical contact. But now, together, we can work very hard to ensure that such a thing does not happen again. I will teach you. The first key to control is to master your emotions. As you have found out for yourself, extremes of feeling are enough to spark your powers. So, you need to work on self-control – don't get angry, don't get upset, don't get excited. You have to strive for inner peace and calm. And there are other things you must do."

I looked at her questioningly. "What things?"

Nafanua led us back inside to the kitchen where she poured me a glassful of green liquid from a pitcher in the fridge. "Here, drink."

I sniffed at it suspiciously. "What is it?"

She rolled her eyes at my mistrust. "It's a blend of too many plants for me to explain right now. Suffice it to say that all *telesā* drink it. It refines our awareness of our gifts and our control of them. Go on, the sooner you start taking a glass every day, the easier it will be for you."

Steeling myself for something disgusting, I drank and was pleasantly surprised by the slight hint of mint and whiff of papaya. "Hmm, not bad I guess."

She smiled at me. "Well I have been blending medicines and treatments for a very long time, so I think I can make it taste halfway decent."

I ignored her effort to make light of this whole nightmare. "What else do I have to do to master this thing?"

Nafanua took a deep breath and grimaced slightly. "I'm afraid that the other control is not so easily undertaken. You will have to prepare – mentally and physically – before we can give you the other vital tool for *telesā* self-mastery. You are not ready, it will take time."

I pressed her. "What is it? Tell me."

In answer, Nafanua slipped off her seat and with one swift movement, hitched up the side of her skirt to the mid thigh, revealing the band of black patterns tattooed on her skin. It began at the knees and ended at the height of her thighs. "A *malu*. The traditional tattoo given to women."

I stared at her aghast. "That? I have to get a tattoo like that? No way. I can't. I'm not doing that. No. I won't do it."

Nafanua raised her hands appeasingly. "Hush my daughter. Don't worry. It's not something that you have to consider right now. There will be plenty of time for it later. And we *telesā* have herbs that mean it is not that painful. And it will be quick. We won't speak of it again until you are ready, until you have reached a certain point in your training. The *malu* is the final step in the journey towards becoming a *telesā*. It is essential to your mastery of these gifts. The inks are made with certain plants that will give you the infusion you need to be in complete control of your fire. We prepare the inks and administer the *malu* ourselves. Now come, we have much more to talk about and there are things I want to show you in my lab."

I was happy to have her change the subject as I slowly followed her to the backyard lab. A tattoo was the last thing on earth I would ever do. No way in hell was I going to get one of those. For a brief, unwilling moment, an image flashed in my mind, of Daniel with his tattooed chiseled arm. The look in his eyes as he explained the different markings. The edge of excitement as he told me about his plans to get a full-body *pe'a*. The feel of his skin under my fingers as I delicately traced the black patterns. His kiss. No. I resolutely slammed a wall on that image. *Stop it Leila.* It was too dangerous to think about Daniel. No. I wouldn't go there. I had almost killed him and I could never allow myself to get close to him again. That was the only thing I knew for certain.

The rest of the weekend passed in a blur. Daniel called. Again and again. But I switched the phone to silent and just watched the ring tone dance on the receiver. And each time I ignored his call, another piece of me withered. He tried calling the house phone. But Netta politely told him I was unavailable. And each time she did, I cut a little deeper.

Monday, I told Nafanua I didn't want to go to school. Tuesday, Wednesday, Thursday, the same. Instead, I slept. And slept some more. Simone texted me. Sinalei called. But I sent them vague replies, telling them only that I was busy with family stuff. Nafanua spent most of her days at work. She had endless meetings with some environmental agents visiting from Europe. Something to do with logging rights. And a volcanologist expedition on the other island of Savaii. I slept. I didn't want to feel. Didn't want to think. Didn't want to remember. If 'inner peace and calm' was the key to control then I figured the best way to achieve that was not to feel anything at all. Sleep was the answer.

Friday morning, a green truck pulled up out front. Daniel. I watched him walk to the door from my window. I felt nothing. A bland dullness. I was disengaging. He couldn't be part of my new life, so the quicker I cut him out of my consciousness, the better. Netta told him I was sick but I could hear him arguing with her, insisting that he needed to see me. I wanted to do nothing but lie in my curtained darkness and sleep, but sympathizing with timid Netta's attempts to obstruct a six-foot tall rugby player, made me drag myself out of bed and go downstairs.

He stood in the living room, his face flushed and defiant, shoulders rigid, fists clenched. I stopped short at the sight of him. I was wrong. A week had not lessened the impact of his beauty on me. It pierced my numb soul and cut through my dead stupor.

"Daniel ..."

He took two steps toward me, halting when I instinctively shifted back. His eyes were pained.

"Leila what's going on? Are you okay? You haven't been to school, you haven't been answering my calls. I've been worried about you."

I would have sobbed. The old Leila would have cried. With happiness that he cared about me. And ran into his arms. But this was not the old Leila. This Leila was a *telesā*. Who could fry the love of her life to a crisp. And make the earth open up to swallow his green truck. No, I was not the same Leila, and the sooner Daniel realized it, the better.

"Daniel, you shouldn't be here. I'm fine, really I am. You don't need to worry about me. I've been a bit sick, but it's no big deal and I should be back at school next week. You should go. I'm sure you have lots of stuff to do at the workshop."

I tried to smile. Casually. But he wasn't going to make this easy for me. Shaking his head, he took the remaining steps that separated us. I backed up again until I felt the wall behind me. He had me cornered. He put a hand on each shoulder, trying to look me in the eyes while I stared away.

"Leila don't do this. What happened the other night, we need to talk about it. I need to know if you're alright. I need to know what's going on. Don't shut me out like this."

With fingers on my chin, he gently raised my face to his, his emerald-chipped eyes unwilling to let me hide. I felt the heat of his skin on mine. I remembered what it felt like to drown in his kiss and it gave me the cold strength I needed. I leaned both hands against his chest and pushed him away firmly. My voice was hard and clipped.

"Daniel, this is ridiculous. What makes you think you can come in here and make me talk to you when I don't want to? I'm not like one of your puppy dog rugby players ready to run and ruck whenever you tell them to. I have nothing to say to you. I want you to leave."

I turned to go back up the stairs before the tears came. His hand caught me softly. "Nothing Leila? Do you really have nothing to say to me?"

I took a deep breath before rushing on. "Actually I do have something I want to say." I faced him full on, composing my features in the blandest expression possible. "You're a really nice guy, but, I'm sorry, I don't think we should hang out any more. We both have stuff going on, and it would be better if we just stopped this before someone got hurt. I mean, you told me so yourself, you've got plans and I don't want to get in the way of that. And me, now's not really a good time for me. I need to be spending time with my mother so she can help me with my … my problem. That's the most important thing right now."

The air was heavy and full when I stopped.

"That's all you're going to say about the other night? About what happened? That's it?" His voice was low and edged.

"Yes. That's it. We both know that I've got a problem and I need help to fix it. I'm really glad that you helped me the other night and I would really appreciate it if you could keep it secret. I'm working on doing something about it."

He looked exasperated. "Leila, I'm not talking about you bursting into flames. I'm talking about you and me. Us. Our friendship. We kissed. I'm talking about what's going on between you and me. Don't tell me to just forget about us."

"That's exactly what I'm saying. There is no us. We aren't an 'us'. It's impossible. And it's the last thing I want right now so would you please just leave? Before I ask Netta to call the police or something?!" My voice rose to a semi-hysterical shriek as I felt the now-familiar prickle of heat creeping up my spine. The fire was coming and I didn't want him to be anywhere near me. "Just get out okay? Go away!"

Without waiting for a reply, I pushed past him and ran out into the garden. He watched me go, with defeat in his stance. I ran blindly over the grass and into the forest trees, pushing through branches, ignoring their scratching, cutting grab. I ran and, as I did, the fire came. Pulsing like the adrenaline through my veins. Trampling through my insides, ripping through my pitiful defenses. With Daniel's shocked, pained expression in my mind, I collapsed to my knees and let the fire out. I prayed that I was far enough away from the house that Daniel wouldn't hear my anguished scream of pain. Or see the pillar of fiery smoke that seared the sky.

I had been dreading the return of the fire, hoping and praying every day that I wouldn't explode. And yet, as I stood there in green forest and burned, I felt better than I had all week. Nothing seemed to matter much any more. Maybe because when you're standing in the middle of an inferno, things like a broken heart seemed kind of trivial. Or maybe it was because when I was on fire, I technically didn't have a heart anymore. I felt free. Unchained. Released. Unstoppable.

That day in the forest after Daniel left was very liberating. I was alone in a forest that for miles around had no-one in it. There was no-one to hurt. To burn up. No-one to hear me. No-one to see me. No-one with a heart to break.

It was with wondrous awe that I stood and let the flames ripple over me. Then I started running, and what a rush that was. I could train for years and never run as fast or as powerfully as I could when I was on fire. My power seemed to give added speed to my feet, they literally skimmed above the ground. I don't know how long I ran like that, running like lightning through green trees, making sure to take all my fire with me. I was beginning to be aware of the flames. Where they ended, where every spark and cinder landed. Aware enough that I mentally collected them as I ran, unwilling for any errant spark to set the forest ablaze.

I only stopped my wild rush when I came to a pool. Not as beautiful as our pool. Me and Daniel's pool. But similar enough to make me to pause and catch my hot breath. *Daniel, where are you now? What are you feeling now? What do you think of me now?* But no, I must not allow myself to think of him. He did not belong to my world now. I must remove any piece of him from my thoughts. Scourging them, burning them like a cauterized wound. I gave myself over to more experimenting, playing with my powers. Kneeling, I dipped my hand into the water. It felt cool. Could I change that, I wondered?

Eyes glinting, I stilled my hand and focused, breathing deeply. The water started to churn and steam rose to fill the clearing. I laughed. Coldly. Ha. I barely had to even exert myself at all to do this. This was baby stuff! The pool began to boil, bubbling up and over its rocky circle. I laughed some more. Until fish floated with the bubbles. Dead. And baby crayfish. Dead. Abruptly, I jerked my hand away. Death, is that all I would be capable of causing with this power? Would any good come from it?

Tears flowed. But they were useless and I was tired of wasting my time on them. I ran on through the forest. And as I ran, I danced. Delighting in the fiery patterns my hands drew in the air. If nothing else, I was beautiful. In the fire, I was beautiful. And I would need no-one.

Not even a boy called Daniel with laughing, green eyes.

EIGHT

When night fell, I crept back home, tired and spent. I had run for miles. But at least I was too exhausted to cry myself to sleep. My mother did not bother to even ask me about Daniel's visit. Netta had probably briefed her. She merely mixed me an extra dose of the medicine I needed. Which I drank without hope. I didn't believe it could really do anything for me any more. And if I didn't have Daniel, I didn't care what happened now.

She regarded me quietly over breakfast the next morning. My black-circled eyes. The lank unbrushed hair. She wrinkled her nose at me. "Leila, this has to stop. This infatuation for a boy has got you completely in disarray. I've given you time to sort yourself out, but I think this moping has gone on long enough."

I stared at her dully. She forged on. "You must realize that these emotions you are experiencing, they are but childish things. Once your power fully matures, you won't be plagued with such trivialities. You will understand better our world and your place in it. It may be difficult to accept now, but trust me when I tell you that in a few short months, your feelings for that boy, they will be but a brief memory. You must embrace who you are and unchain yourself from all transient things. Men – all men, are unnecessary. Amusing, yes. And some even likeable. But they cannot even begin to comprehend what we are and what we are capable of. You must start practicing to be less easily swayed by them."

Her eyes contained nothing but kindness. She truly did believe what she was saying. And the jagged pieces of my heart longed to believe her. I didn't want to love Daniel. I didn't want to hurt like this. I didn't want to feel like this. Like I could never laugh again. My dad had died and left me incomplete. Daniel had not only filled that void – he had carved a whole new world in mine. One where joy lived. And contentment. Completeness. How could I forget that?

I sat at the breakfast table and cried. Instead of hugs and empty platitudes, my mother took me outside. "Come, I think it's time we began your training."

So that was how my first day of learning to be a *telesā* started. We stood under a blue sky and she made me kneel. "Place your hands on the earth. Shut your eyes. I want you to tell me what you feel. What you can hear. What you can see."

Because I was past feeling, I didn't feel ridiculous. Instead, I listened. And beneath my fingers, I felt it. I heard it. A humming. Like breathing. Like a heartbeat. Like a being.

My eyes flew open and I jumped back. "What is that?!"

Her voice was triumphant. "It's *fanua*. Earth. She hears you. She speaks to you. She has waited a long time for you. And she rejoices at your return, your awakening to your gifts. Now, let us see if we can tame this fire of yours."

I hated to admit it, but Nafanua was a good teacher. But then I supposed I shouldn't have been surprised. She had been teaching *telesā* for decades. She was patient but firm. I had to start by calling the fire into the palm of my hand – without exploding. It was frustratingly difficult. The rush of heat that came in answer to my thoughts didn't want to be tamed. It didn't want to only speak through a single fingertip. It wanted to rage and burn and tear up the air, combusting every molecule of oxygen it could find. Nafanua asked for a single flame from my hands and I could only set my whole body alight, destroying yet another set of clothes.

"No, Leila not like that. Turn it off and try again!"

"I can't." I whined, feeling like a mistreated toddler. "It's impossible!"

"No, it's not. You must speak to it softly, but with strength. You must learn to summon your gift with strength and not with anger or temper. Otherwise, the fire will always control you. Now, call it again."

I stopped wearing clothes to our lessons. What was the point? I came in a *lavalava* and let it go when the surge of flames came. A week of practicing and still I had come no closer to any kind of control. If anything, the fire seemed to get angrier as the week progressed, as I got more frustrated with myself. And my teacher.

The one thing I was happy about was that my lessons went a long way to distracting my mind from its torment over Daniel. Because, no matter how hard I tried, I couldn't vanquish my feelings for him. At day's end, tired and sweaty, with burn circles on the lawn, I would tramp heavily upstairs for a shower and bed. Tired but not tired enough to sleep without dreaming. Of auburn-edged hair and dancing eyes. A light-filled smile. A scar-flecked eyebrow. Sweat trickling down a tattooed bicep. I cried a lot. Silently. Unwilling for Nafanua to detect that I was still not over my 'childish things' so unbecoming of a *telesā*.

The lessons were hard but I poured my soul into them. I desperately wanted them to work. Because then if I could control the fire, I was one step closer to getting rid of it entirely. If I could tell it what to do – then surely I could tell it to go away and never come back?

The week drew into two and then three. I could call the fire now, as easily as flipping a light switch. I didn't need to get angry or emotional for the burn to start. Now, I reached out with my mind and felt for the raw ingredients that needed to mingle and combine for fire to live. It was scientific. For all Nafanua's spouting on about earth and nature, summoning fire was like a chemical reaction ignited by my thoughts.

There was my favorite – oxygen molecules. They were delightful little things that rushed into my lungs with every breath. Adhering to red blood cells, best friends. All they needed was a spark to burst into happy celebration. The party would start in my blood then bubble out like champagne in a victory dance. It would then draw on more O_2 in the air around me and everyone would join in, ejecting CO_2 as we partied on. My fire was all about energy. Energy that started with me then multiplied as it mingled with the energy all around me. In the air. Even the earth beneath my feet. I couldn't even begin to comprehend the energy store in the ground that could theoretically fuel my fire.

It was still unpredictable though. If I didn't get enough sleep. Or even if I didn't eat regularly. Then I couldn't guarantee that flashes of fire wouldn't rip from my hands, my eyes, at the most unexpected of moments. I couldn't go anywhere. Nafanua made sure no-one but her and Netta were ever at the house.

My days were fire lessons with Nafanua. The nights were on the internet, poring over chemical equations and science websites. I still couldn't 'see' the sense of me. I was the catalyst that set the equation in motion. And where the spark came from confounded me. But the rest of it – the fire I could breathe. And throw. The fire I could wrap around trees and ripple along the grass. It all made sense, chemically. Nafanua thought I was wasting my time on fripperies.

"Why seek a Western explanation for it? You will not find it in their limited understanding of life and creation. Your fire is from earth. From Pele. From the mother of us all. You are *telesā*. What more do you need to know?"

But still I persisted. I had never been fond of mysteries. And I didn't like being one. I even began exploring Nafanua's gift. If lightning was a giant spark of electricity – that meant it was energy. Jumping between clouds. But energy nevertheless. So, theoretically, it was energy that I could harness. Capture for myself and convert to fire?

I asked Nafanua to hit me with bolts of her gift when I was aflame. She was unwilling. But interested too in the results. We made a strange sight there on the lawn that day. Like two gunslingers in a western movie showdown. I made the first move. Taking off my *lavalava* to stand naked in the sunlight for a brief moment before exploding into my jeweled conflagration. I had grown to love that feeling, the pleasure outruling the pain as heat surged through me.

Then Nafanua made her move. A flick of her wrist and the giant zigzag spark leapt from the sky. A thirty-million volt charge of pure electricity – enough to light a small town for several months. I focused. On widening my chemical reaction. Converting energy into fire. All energy. I was afraid but determined. I told myself that if my experiment failed and I was fried to a black crisp – then at least that solved my problem of being in love with a boy I could never have.

The lightning strike knocked me back about fifty meters. Smashing me into trees and winding me. But though I ached everywhere from the impact, the actual lightning hadn't hurt. I was jubilant.

The days melted into a pattern. Every morning we would practice. After lunch Nafanua would leave for work, usually returning late in the evening. The afternoons I would spend carrying out my own little experiments. Seeking the limits of my fire. Making little volcanoes in the back yard. That had Netta pursing her lips in disapproval as she tried to do her gardening.

I would always remember the first time I summoned the fire and it came gently. Without setting my whole being alight. Without pain. When it was but a light ripple of flame that swayed in the palm of my hand, dancing over my fingertips. I was in awe. I had dropped my *lavalava* before I called the fire, sure that it would again erupt everywhere. Yet here it was, just a little light in my hands. I stood there naked in the afternoon sunlight and cried, cupping the flame in my fingers. Sinking to my knees in the grass, I wept tears of relief. Of gratitude. *Yes, thank you!* I could control the fire. I could make it do what I wanted. I didn't have to be a killer. This was the first indication that I could walk among regular people again. Without setting them all ablaze at the slightest mild annoyance.

That night was a happy one at Nafanua's house as she joined in my elation.

"Netta, see what my daughter can do. Finally, she is becoming what she was destined to be, a daughter of the earth. Leila, tonight we will go out. We will celebrate!"

We laughed together and I felt a little of the cloud of despair rise. Just a smidgeon. I hardly dared to engage that whisper of hope. If I could control the flames, then maybe, just maybe I could go back to school? I could see Daniel? Not go too near him, no, I wouldn't risk that, but at least see him? Hear his voice without the need of any voicemail recorder?

When Nafanua brought me an outfit to wear for our celebration, I put it on eagerly. I hadn't left this place for three weeks now. The thought of going somewhere, anywhere, was dizzying. The dress she brought me was like nothing I had ever worn before, but I doubted jeans and a t-shirt would pass muster for our outing. Netta came to help me with my hair at Nafanua's bidding. I tried to refuse – I wasn't a child who needed help with her hair! But, as always, Netta spoke few words and did exactly what she pleased. Expertly, she worked her way through the tangled mass that was my neglected hair, coiling it up into a graceful swirl. A fuchsia bloom completed the ensemble. A glance in the mirror had me gasping. That wasn't me. It couldn't be. I hadn't looked at my reflection since that nightmarish first morning.

A stranger regarded me with shock in her eyes. She was tall, almost willowy. The black sheathe dress hugged smooth curves. Slit to the thigh on one side, revealing legs that seemed to go on forever. The pink *elei*-patterned border at the bust was the only color. Which made my neck seem even more graceful as it met the elegant coil of hair, adorned with the hot pink flower. Before I could react, Netta added a brush of rich lipstick to my mouth, a dab of blush. That wasn't me, it couldn't be? Once unruly brows had now tamed themselves into curved arches. The deep-set eyes were still there, but now they glowed with a seeming endless allure, hidden depths of fire. There was a strange glow to the woman in the mirror. And I wasn't sure that I liked it.

Nafanua walked in before I could pursue that unease. She smiled at me. "Leila, you are stunning. No-one could resist you tonight."

I tried not to show how pleased I was at her compliment. Pleased enough that I even allowed her to convince me that I needed to wear the nightmare black stiletto heels with the wrap ties that went all the way up to my knees. I teetered all the way down the stairs, regretting my decision when I tripped and almost fell while I was getting into the car … *dammnit!*

Nafanua drove us in her car, regaling me all the way to town with talk of her day. Apparently she was having a few clashes with the science team here to study Samoa's volcanic activity, the lead researcher in particular was proving difficult. I hid a smile in the darkness, obviously it wasn't often that a man refused Nafanua and it was driving her nuts.

"He's just so stubborn, Leila. You wouldn't believe it. I mean, I helped to fund this project and so I should have full access to his results, but no, he keeps fobbing me off with excuses, about professional integrity and how results can't be released until the survey is complete, and he won't make any assumptions without gathering all the data. All I want is for him to give me the courtesy of access to results I am helping to pay for. Typical male, he probably thinks he doesn't need to update me on his progress because I'm a woman. Argh. I want you to spend time with him tonight, talk to him, put him at ease and forge a connection, do you hear me, Leila?"

There was a Coldplay song on the radio and I was only half listening to Nafanua's tirade when her last sentence had me jerk upright.

"Now, I'm counting on you tonight Leila, to get through to this man. Maybe you'll have more success with him seeing as how he's American, so you two will have things in common to talk about."

I interrupted, "Nafanua, excuse me? What do you mean? Did I miss something?"

"Please pay attention Leila, this is important. I told you, we're having dinner with Dr. Williams and some of his team. And I want you to connect with this man, you know, befriend him. You look stunning tonight and I'm sure that no man in his right mind could resist you. Use any means necessary, I want you to get an invite onto the site and full access to the research, do you understand? "

Before I could protest, the car slowed to a halt in front of Aggie's Hotel on the waterfront. The lacy white banister verandahs were ghostly loops in the evening and a full moon played on the black water rolling in softly against the seawall. I was still struggling for the right words, the right response while Nafanua hurried me inside ahead of her. She paused to smooth my hair, catch a stray strand of hair and then gave me a vivid smile. "You look amazing Leila, there's no way he will be able to resist you. Do whatever you need to. I want that research data."

I was in a daze of shock. My mother wanted me to 'forge a connection' with some man I had never met? Just so that she could get access to some volcano research? I half stumbled behind her as we walked to the restaurant *fale* where the main buffet and show was already taking place. A throng of people moved slowly down the line of tables, choosing from the delectable assortment of cuisine. Others sat at scattered dining tables lit with flickering coconut candles. Far off to the right of the restaurant was a massive swimming pool that gleamed silver-black in the moonlight and reflected its ring of palm trees and hibiscus bushes. A band was playing island music on a stage, a beautiful accompaniment to the hum of dinner conversation.

I was having a tricky time with my heels and so had to walk with careful precision, following Nafanua as she moved through the restaurant, eyes searching for someone.

"Ah, there you all are!" she spoke with smooth velvet confidence as she walked up to a table where four men were seated. One of them, a large paunchy man with sweat beads on his forehead, couldn't seem to stop staring at her, his jaw dropping as she leaned to give each of them a requisite greeting kiss. Beside him, a balding man wearing a Nirvana t-shirt barely looked up from his plate piled high with food. The other was an older man, possibly in his sixties, with silver graying hair and a tired demeanor. Dr. Williams. My eyes were taken first though by the third man. Young, maybe in his early twenties, blond crew-cut, blue-eyed, a white button shirt and khaki slacks, a gold stud in one ear.

"Gentlemen, I'd like you to meet my daughter, Leila. She's just moved back here from the States." Nafanua drew me to the blond-haired man with the piercing blue eyes. The one who looked like he belonged on a beach with a surfboard instead of in a science research team. He stood as I stepped to the table, hand outstretched to greet me. He spoke before Nafanua could complete the introductions.

"Leila, this is a treat for us. Not one, but two captivating ladies to dine with tonight. I'm Jason. Won't you sit and join us?"

His handshake was firm and warm, and it lingered just the slightest bit longer than necessary. As I sat in the chair beside him, I could feel the admiration in his eyes as he watched me place my clutch purse on the table. I didn't need a playbook to read this one. He liked me, I could tell. I wanted to laugh. Nafanua wanted me to bedazzle Dr. Williams? Well, I would throw a spanner in the works and instead, turn on the charm for this young one, Jason. It would send her mental with fury if I 'connected' with the lowly assistant. Ha, he was probably the gofer. Or the one who did the dusting or something. I straightened in my seat with a thrill of fun. I was going to enjoy this. And it would serve her right for expecting me to prostitute myself with a stranger just so she could get information on a stupid volcano.

Nafanua had taken the seat beside the grey-haired man and was telling him her drinks order. I heard her asking for lemon water for me. I took a deep breath. I had nil experience with being alluring, but hey, there was a first time for everything right?

Languidly, I reached back and unclipped my hair from its coil, shook my head lightly and ran my fingers through the brown waves. I gave Jason a sideways glance from behind a curtain of hair. His eyes were appreciative.

"Oh I just hate having to get all dressed up for these things, don't you? I much prefer my shorts and t-shirt but Nafanua will insist on me wearing this thing." I pouted petulantly and let my hands run down the length of my body-hugging dress. I leaned forward with my elbows on the table, my chin clasped in my hands, with an imploring look in my eyes. "What do you think Jason? Isn't it just so unkind of her to make me dress up?"

The man laughed. It was a warm, golden sound. He regarded me somewhat sardonically, as if he knew something I didn't. "Leila, I'm in complete agreement with your mother. You are sinfully stunning in that dress and a treat for the eyes. However, I must add, that from where I'm sitting, I'm convinced that, had you worn shorts and a t-shirt tonight, you would still have been the most enchanting woman here," he nodded to Nafanua, "present company excluded of course Nafanua!"

Nafanua laughed back at him and raised her glass. "Thank you, Jason."

I flushed. This wasn't how I had planned the evening to go. Nafanua was still smug and self-satisfied. She should be getting mad by now. I gritted my teeth. *Right, time to step it up a notch.* I placed a hand on Jason's arm, dancing my fingers along his wrist.

"Jason, I'm starving, can you come with me to get some food?" I tried to simper. It was probably a hideous failure on a thug brown girl like me but hey, I was trying! Jason seemed to like it though. Without hesitation, he stood and took my hand to walk to the buffet table, only releasing it to pass me a plate. We meandered along the length of the tables, choosing our dinner. I kept trying to remember to *be a bimbo, be a bimbo* … I smiled foolishly. And laughed at everything he said. Even if it wasn't funny. I pretended to be horrified by the sea slugs, the palolo sea worms and even the crab. "Oooh Jason, that looks soooo yucky!" And the *piece de resistance* … I asked him for a taste of his lemon cheesecake, then stood with my mouth open so he could slip me a morsel on a spoon. Just like a dumb movie chick, I closed my eyes in pretend ecstasy, "Mmmm, oh Jason, that's so delicious!" Inwardly I cringed, as I thought what a fool I must sound like. A fleeting thought of Daniel had me cringing even more. He would be thoroughly appalled by such an idiot if he could see me now, but then, he wasn't with me, was he? And I was mad at my mother and was on a mission.

After dinner, Jason asked me if I wanted to go see the swimming pool in the moonlight. By then I was getting tired of being alluring and forever enthused. *Gosh, how did real bimbo chicks do it? Stay so chirpy for so long?* It was exhausting. And my feet were killing me in the black stilettos. I didn't even try to slink as we went to the pool. I gritted my teeth and basically stomped my nightmare shoes on the cement paving. Once out of sight of Nafanua, I relaxed. Time for the charade to go to rest. With a groan, I slumped to sit in one of the pool chairs, muttering darkly under my breath as I struggled to take off my shoes.

"Damnit, stupid things, who invented such idiotic contraptions ..."

Jason surprised me with a roar of laughter. He knelt down beside me. "Here, let me help."

I was in full thug girl mode now. "No. I got it." I pushed his hand away but he was insistent.

"I can help, here, you just have to unclasp this bit here."

I shoved his hand away again and stood in full-frontal assault attack. "I said – I got it ... aaaayyiii!"

I took two angry steps away from the overly helpful blonde, tripped over my own heels and fell. With a gigantic splash, right into the pool. I resurfaced to the sounds of more uproarious laughter. Which only had me madder.

"Dammnit! I told you to leave it alone. I told you I could fix it myself."

He looked down at me in the pool and shook his head. "Leila, you can't even walk properly in those silly shoes let alone undo them by yourself. It's a bit ditzy for a woman to wear shoes she can't control. "

That comment was the most insulting of all. I didn't care if I had been behaving 'a bit ditzy' all night, he needed to pay for that remark. I smiled up at him sweetly and put out my hand. "Oh Jason, you're so right, could you please help me out of here?"

He leaned down to take my hand in his – whereupon I pulled with a mighty heave. And smartass Jason was in the pool too. And it was my turn to do the laughing as he spluttered and splashed his way up. I pulled myself to sit on the poolside, wringing out water from chunkfuls of my hair, still watching him with cautious eyes. In case he got any ideas about retribution.

The surfer dude swam over and climbed out to sit beside me, taking off his wet shirt to toss it to the side. "Thank you Leila. I'm not sure that I deserved that, but I'm a gentleman even if you're not a lady. So why don't we call a truce?" He held out his hand. I stared at it suspiciously. Then shrugged and shook hands. Heck why not. I wasn't planning on ever seeing this guy again. Funnily enough, it seemed that with both of us wet and all splashed out, the pretences were removed.

"So tell me, Leila, why are you wearing such crazy shoes – which, by the way, are incredibly sexy – if you don't like them and ah...find them tricky to walk in?"

I half grinned and wrinkled my nose as I considered how to answer him. I decided to go for the whole truth and nothing but the truth. "Well, if you must know, I was on a mission tonight."

"A mission?"

"Yeah."

"What sort of mission? To see how gracefully you could fall into a swimming pool fully clothed? And wearing stilettos?"

"No you idiot. A mission to make my mother mad."

It was clear that wasn't an answer Jason had been anticipating. The smile was replaced with puzzlement. "What do you mean?"

Now that I had started to confess, I felt awful at the awfulness of it all. I hung my head, ashamed. It had been childish. And pathetic even to play up the whole simpleton routine.

He nudged me. "Go on, what do you mean?"

"Nafanua wanted me to dazzle the head scientist, You know, the old guy, Dr. Williams? She's been going nuts because he won't give her full access to all his data on the volcanic activity in the region and she said she wanted me to be nice and friendly because he was from America like me. And she basically asked me to lure him and fawn over him, get him to like me. I got so mad at her in the car for asking me to do such a despicable thing. I mean, you have to understand, she's not really my mother. I mean, she is, but she isn't. I only just met her a few weeks ago. Before that she was dead to me. And there's a lot of stuff about her that doesn't add up, doesn't make sense. So we've been trying to get to know each other and then she has to go and do something stupid like bring me here all dressed up and tell me to be nice to some stuffy old scientist. Like I'm some sort of prostitute or something! What kind of mother does that to her daughter?" I halted abruptly, uncomfortably aware that I had probably said waaay more than I should have.

Jason's expression was unreadable. "Yes, what kind of mother does that?"

I rushed on, "So when I got here and saw you, I decided to try and dazzle you instead. You know, because you're just a lowly assistant or the digging boy or something, not the real scientist she wanted. I thought that way she would get raging mad and I could punish her that way?"

My words died away as I waited to see how Jason would take my confession. He smiled at some hidden joke. "I see. So that explains your dazzling behavior tonight ay?"

I bit my lip, "Sorry, I'm not really that much of a ditzy blonde bimbo oops!" I stopped short as I involuntarily glanced at his hair, "I'm sorry again, you're blonde and I didn't mean any disrespect. And I hope you're not offended that I said you're only a lowly assistant. I'm sure you're a very good assistant, very helpful to those guys over there ..." I was babbling and Jason stopped me with a single finger to my lips.

"Hey, shush. Listen to me now. Let me see if I can get this straight. Which bits are true? Is your name really Leila Folger?" I nodded, "and you haven't really been coming on to me tonight – that was just an act?"

I nodded again and mouthed a silent sorry. He shushed me again, "And you're not really a stiletto-wearing, slinky-outfit kind of woman after all? That was an act too?" I was too ashamed to even nod this time. I just hung my head, staring into the pool.

"Leila Folger, it appears that you have a lot to apologize for. You have misled me, you have mistakenly bedazzled me with artificial dazzle, and to top it all off you have gotten me all soaking wet with a dunk in the pool." He spoke severely, but his eyes laughed at me. "I think you owe this blonde bimbo lowly assistant big time, Leila the fake bimbo!"

Our eyes met and together we both burst out laughing. Sitting beside a shimmering pool under a moonlit sky. I realized that when you had no agendas, no love feelings for a guy, you actually could be relaxed with him. Like the pressure to perform was off. Like you could just be yourself and not worry if they still liked you or not.

"Jason, I apologize. How can I make it up to you?"

"Hmm,let me think. You could promise never to wear those shoes in my presence again. They're deadly objects. Aha!" His eyes lit up. "I know, you can come visit the research site tomorrow with me. See what an assistant does. When he's assisting. And digging."

I smiled warmly. "I'd like that." I said it without thinking, but when I paused, I realized I meant it. This Jason person was funny. And I could certainly use all the friends I could find these days. The thought of visiting the volcano was intriguing. I had been putting it off because I was afraid of what my fire would do when confronted with its birthmother, but what the heck. Today, I had mastered fire in the palm of my hand. Surely I could handle a little visit to a volcano?

"It's a date then. I'll pick you up in the morning." He helped me take off the silly shoes and then slowly we strolled, wet and laughing back into the main fale. Where Nafanua was patiently waiting, sipping cocktails with the others. She bestowed a radiant smile on me and raised one perfect eyebrow at my disheveled state but said nothing. There was only impeccable politeness as we farewelled the men.

In the car, I waited for her anger. Her rage. But it didn't come. Instead, she was exultant. "Leila, you are a genius. I admit I wasn't sure if you could do it, but you were perfect!"

"What do you mean?" I was confused.

"Why, you did it. You had Dr. Williams completely enthralled, It looks like the two of you had a wonderful time tonight." A cold fist of realization clenched around my heart.

"Wait, what do you mean? I barely even spoke to Dr. Williams the whole night. I was with the assistant, with Jason."

Nafanua laughed again. And it was coldly musical in the speeding darkness. "Yes, Dr. Jason Williams! Well done Leila, it appears you will make a brilliant *telesā* after all."

"No, aaargh." I stifled my exclamation of shock and sat rigid with amazement as I replayed my night with the blonde. Why did these dumb screw-ups always happen to me? What an idiot I was. And he had totally let me play the fool. My eyes narrowed in the darkness as Nafanua continued prattling on triumphantly. What was the man's agenda anyway? I had confessed and instead of getting mad – at my mother, at me – he had played along. Actually, if I was being honest, truthful - he had been quite pleasant about the whole thing. But why? I reserved my cold anger for Nafanua. The strange Jason I could excuse.

At the house, I stomped up the stairs without responding to Nafanua's good night. But I couldn't contain myself when she asked, "Why Leila, what's the matter? Didn't you enjoy yourself tonight?"

"No … yes … oh, that's not the point." I took a deep breath before continuing, "Nafanua, you haven't had much practice being a mother, so maybe I should cut you some slack here. Let me spell it out for you plain and simple. No mother in her right mind asks her daughter to … to … prostitute herself the way you expected me to tonight!"

Nafanua arched an eyebrow but I rushed on. "What you did, what you expected me to do … telling me to play up to the scientist so he would give you what you wanted, that's just sick. Deceitful, cheap, and sick. I can't believe you asked me to do that."

Nafanua spread her arms questioningly. "But you had a great time with him. I saw you. You two were laughing and talking and he seemed quite taken with you. Are you saying you didn't enjoy yourself tonight? Are you saying that befriending Dr. Williams was a chore for you?"

I gritted my teeth, "That's just it, I didn't know he was Dr. Williams. He introduced himself as Jason. I thought the old guy was the scientist."

Nafanua was puzzled even further. "So why were you so quick to ooze all over Jason then … oh, I get it." She frowned and folded her arms, looking up at me from the foot of the stairs with awareness. "You were trying to defy me. You thought you would antagonize me by focusing on the young, obviously junior, member of the group. I get it."

Like two fighters sizing each other up in the ring, we stared at each other. My fists were clenched and I was ready to snap and snarl. But Nafanua laughed. Loud and long. So much that she sat weakly on the bottom step.

"Oh Leila, you're funny." She turned to wave me to a seat beside her. "Come down here, sit with me. This is classic." Cautiously, I took the several steps to sit beside her. "You're right, I don't have much experience with being a mother, with teenage daughters, with beautiful young women who know their own minds and aren't afraid to speak them. I forget that you are new to all this. You still have much to learn about *telesā*, and I must be patient as you go forward on this journey. Will you accept my apology?"

Mutely, I nodded. She didn't try to hug me or touch me – which I was grateful for. The touchy-feely stuff was still far too uncomfortable.

"Now, apart from that, did you enjoy your first night out in Samoa?"

I nodded. "I guess. I've been stuck here training for so long now that it was good to get out and be around regular people. I didn't even think about my fire stuff."

Nafanua frowned. "Yes, you did well tonight, but still you must never let your guard down. Never forget what you really are. You don't want to be caught unawares and have your fire unleash. Always be watchful." She repeated the mantra that I must have heard a thousand times over the last few weeks. "A *telesā* must always be in control of her emotions. Only then can she hope to truly be one with her gifts."

"I know, I know. I'll keep that in mind."

"So am I forgiven?"

I shrugged. "I guess so."

We said goodnight and I went up to bed, grateful to finally be able to peel off the sheathe dress. Unlike other nights, sleep came quickly.

NINE

I was ignoring all sounds of morning when the raucous car horn woke me.

"What the heck?" I stumbled to the window to see who could be defiling my Saturday sleep in. There was a red monster truck in the driveway. And standing beside it with one hand on the car horn was a blonde-haired, blue-eyed demon. Jason.

Behind me, Netta spoke dryly. "The Professor says he's here to pick you up. I believe you have an appointment with a volcano?"

I groaned. The last thing I wanted to do was spend my day with a man who had witnessed my miserable attempts to be an "alluring temptress" the night before. And who had known what the joke was before I did.

"Tell him that I'm sick, please Netta. I don't feel good at all. Thank him and tell him maybe another day." *Or another lifetime*, I thought as I stomped back to my bed in search of sleep. Which still was denied. As Jason honked on the horn again. I hid my head under the pillows and waited for Netta to send him on his way.

Another "ahem." Netta again. "He said he's not going anywhere until you get down there. He said you owe him. Big time. He said, and I quote – tell her I will come up to her room and drag her artificial bimbo self out of bed, with or without stiletto heels." Her tone sharpened,

"Leila, you better go down there and talk to him yourself because I'm not climbing these stairs again to pass on any more messages." She sniffed at me derisively before trudging away back down the stairs.

"Damnit!"

There was no escaping this one. Not while the car honking kept going, one long continuous blare as I hastily dressed. What did one wear to visit a volcano? I rifled through my wardrobe, settling on long denim jeans to protect my legs and a cotton tee. I had a harder time finding my sneakers. It had been so long since I had needed to wear closed-in shoes, they felt awkward to pull on. I washed up but didn't bother with much else, twisting my thick hair into a ragged bunch. Downstairs, I raided the refrigerator for a water bottle and two of Netta's muffins. She looked at me sourly as I waved goodbye. Nafanua was reading the newspaper in the living room.

"I'm going out. With Jason."

She shrugged indifferently but there was a smirk on her face. Which had me fuming. And less willing to be amiable.

On the veranda I stood still to yell at the horn honker, "Do you mind shutting that thing off now! What the heck is wrong with you? People are trying to sleep round here!"

Jason paused mid-honk to smile. Wavy hair ruffling in the breeze, a shade unshaven and rumpled in khaki shorts and a red tee. "Why, good morning, Leila Folger! Aren't you just bedazzling this fine morning."

I poked my tongue at him and stomped down the stairs. "Oh just shut up. An old man like you shouldn't be up this early. I mean, wow, at your age, I'm surprised you're even still allowed to drive." I pulled up in front of him, my arms folded in front of my chest, my stare accusing. "Dr Jason *Williams*, I believe?"

He had the grace to look abashed, pulling his white cap back and rifling through his hair. "Nafanua busted me ay?"

"Yes. Yes she did. And I have to say, that I'm surprised you have the nerve to still show up here on my doorstep. What do you have to say for yourself?"

He gaped. "Excuse me? Aren't you the one who should be groveling in supplication? You're the one who was out to deceive me and mislead me with your alluring bimbo slinkiness! Don't you feel bad? What if I had believed your act last night huh? What if I had fallen deeply and desperately in love with you? You would have had the blood of my lovesickness on your hands Leila Folger."

I hid a grin. This man was interesting. Funny. Likeable. Like Maleko and someone else all rolled into one. Someone like … my dad. The realization hit me. That was it. The teasing jibes and the light banter – that was totally like me and my dad on a regular day. He was looking at me with his head tilted to one side, gauging my reaction. I grumpily pushed past him to the other side of the truck. "Oh just shut up. And stop calling me by my full name for goodness sake. It's just Leila. You make me sound like my grandmother."

I climbed in the passenger seat and slammed the door with so much force that the side mirror rattled. He didn't react to the manhandling of his truck, merely got in and started up the engine. But there was a dancing grin on his face.

"Oh, I'm just trying to make sure you remember that I'm a full-blown genuine *bona fide* mantle geochemist … DOCTOR Jason Williams. In case you mistake me again for a lowly pitiful assistant who's only good at wiping the volcanic dust off people's boots."

I groaned and rolled my eyes heavenward. I could see this was going to be a very long day.

Jason took me first to a grassy airfield at Fagalii. Where there was a helicopter waiting. My very first chopper ride was a stomach-heaving event. Thankfully, the magnificent view of the island distracted me enough from the antics of the pilot, who seemed to think he was a gunner pilot in World War II. We flew low over Apia, splayed out like a collection of child's toys, then over the blue ocean cloth towards the big island, Savaii. Jason had to shout over the chopping blades as he pointed downwards.

"We're based back in Apia but we spend most of our time onsite. We've got a camp up ahead on Mt Matavanu, the site of Samoa's last volcanic eruption. See there!"

One could clearly see the spread of black that stretched for miles down to the ocean. It was awe inspiring. It wasn't difficult to imagine the surging, rolling flood of red lava consuming the land as it spilled over the top of Matavanu. I shivered, remembering my quick Google of local eruptions. What a terrifying experience it must have been for the villagers, fleeing before the wave of fire that would not stop. The volcano itself was misleadingly dull looking. I tensed as the chopper descended to a flat space beside a collection of brown canvas tents that billowed in the upwind. As the blades whirred to a halt, Jason helped me out. He mock bowed. "Your highness, welcome to Matavanu, this lowly assistant grovels before you. Our tent is yours."

I studiously ignored him, far too enthralled to react to his teasing. We were a short distance from the peak. It loomed before us, a craggy black chute like a vast chimney. I knelt and touched the black earth. It was solid lava rock, broken here and there by tufts of green as grass struggled to find space in the blackness. My breath was a hushed indrawn breath. I felt her. I heard her. She was real. A rush of sweet heat burned through me like none I had yet felt. It was like sinking into a pool of hot chocolate and then being slowly drizzled with black cherry sauce. Warm, sinuous, fragrant with delicious sweet promise. I closed my eyes in contentment and wanted to melt with happiness. There was no denying it. Somewhere deep beneath my feet on this decades-sleeping giant, someone or something was happy to find me. To feel me. To know that I was here. Call her Pele. Matavanu, whatever – something or someone lived. She called to me. Through layers of rock and sediment. Through subterranean water and metal, from where rivers of red fire slept. I could have knelt there all day.

But from a faraway distance I heard the puzzled worry in Jason's voice. "Leila, hey? Are you okay? Leila?"

I shook myself out of my trance, pulling myself unwillingly away from the heat that was calling to me. Opening my eyes, I had to shade them against the sun. Jason was kneeling beside me, a hand on my shoulders where he had been shaking me. He looked anxious. I rushed to calm him with a smile.

"Hey, yeah I'm fine. Sorry about that. Was just a bit dizzy from the flight up here. And cos I didn't get enough sleep last night. Was supposed to sleep in this morning you know, until a know-it-all Professor interrupted my beauty sleep."

His face creased into a relieved smile. We both stood. "Whew, you had me worried there for a moment. First time I bring a guest up here to the site and she gets all spacey on me."

I waved a hand at him. "Oh, it must be the ditzy bimbo in me. You should be able to relate to that."

We were back to the casual banter. It was light, fun, and so easy. I looked around. "Where is everybody? You know, the rest of the team?"

"They're further up taking readings. Soil, temperature, water – all that stuff. We do it every day so we can track what's going on. Trying to figure out the patterns so we can decide what Matavanu's plans are. You know she's been dormant for almost a hundred years so she shouldn't really be doing anything at all, but – as your mother probably told you – there is something fishy going on with Matavanu."

I was intrigued. Just as Nafanua had been. I strove to keep my tone light and casual. "Oh? Like what?

Before Jason could answer, there was an excited shout from further up the mountain. We both looked up at the same time. It was the three men from the previous night. Scrambling and half slipping down the loose dirt slope. With them were another two. Both about Jason's age, both with brown lanky hair and the same surfer physiques. One wore glasses. Catching sight of Jason, the group increased their speed and I braced myself, doubtful they could make it down without slipping and smashing into us. All five of them looked very excited about something. I glanced worriedly at Jason – maybe my coming here was breaking a science camp rule or something and they were rushing down here to yell at us? But Jason looked as puzzled as I felt.

"What's going on?"

The young guy with glasses was the first to reach us and the first to catch his breath. He pushed his glasses further up on his nose before launching into an explanation, words tumbling over each other like bubbles in a soda fountain.

" Jason, you have got to check out these figures! It's crazy, I've never seen anything like it."

The grey-haired tired-looking man interrupted, his hands fluttering and gesturing wildly. No longer did he look worn and wasted. Now he was jittery and jumpy. "The data Jason, the data. It's incredible. We should all be burning up in a lava river right now according to the data – nothing makes sense!"

Jason held up both his hands for calm. "What are you talking about? Slow it down, slow it down. Marcus" he motioned to the paunchy man, "Marcus, what the heck is going on? What's got Blaine all excited?"

Privately, I thought he had made a poor choice for spokesperson. Marcus looked like he was battling a heart attack he was so out of breath from his frantic run down the mountain behind the others. But Jason waited for him to suck enough oxygen from the humid air.

"Jase, its true. We were finishing up the usual tests, about to pack it up and come back down when out of nowhere, all the machines just spiked. The readings were so high, they set off the alarms, near gave us all a stroke I can tell you."

Jason lost all the boyish teasing and his whole stance changed. His brow furrowed, his eyes darkened and his shoulders tensed. In that moment, he looked like the lead scientist of a geothermal expedition. "Well what are we doing standing around here? We need to evacuate immediately, and get a warning out to the Disaster Management office, you're saying Matavanu is going to blow?"

All of the men chimed in, "No, no, that's just it, Jason. The machines spiked but then they all went back to normal, well, they're still above normal, but at least not at danger levels."

Jason shook his head. "So it was a mistake then? There must be something wrong with the equipment?"

The guy with glasses rebuffed that idea. "No, I checked everything. It's all working fine. And there's no way every single machine could have malfunctioned at the exact same moment, you know they're not all linked."

As one, everyone moved to the main tent that contained a motley collection of chemistry gear, canvas folding chairs, a couple of camp beds, accumulated piles of dirty clothes and beer cans. I wrinkled my nose – apparently even scientists were messy. The men seemed to have forgotten I was even there, which suited me just fine. I found a chair to perch on and continued listening. Apparently, a few minutes before, all their equipment had registered heat and seismic energy levels so high that they could only have been possible had we been in the middle of a full-blown eruption. Only there wasn't one. And just as quickly as they had spiked, the gear had stilled back to normal. Well, not quite normal. All the readings were now several notches up from what they had been, but still nowhere near eruption levels. I was thankful the men were too involved to notice me, because all of a sudden it hit me. I realized what had made their machines go crazy. The timing was right. It all made sense. They were monitoring geothermal activity in Matavanu. And I had just set foot on Matavanu for the first time. I had spoken to her and she had answered. Even the memory of that spine-tingling meeting had my temperature rising several notches and brought a smile to my face. The earth goddess had chosen me. I don't know why or how. I still wasn't sure that I wanted it to. But I could no longer deny it – the earth goddess had chosen me. And deep within me, I was answering.

My visit to the volcano came to a rushed end that day. Jason still wasn't convinced that Matavanu was trustworthy and, as he shortly informed me, there was no way he wanted an extra person to be responsible for if the volcano did decide to blow. He sent the team back up to the peak to monitor their machinery for the duration of the night, until they could be sure that the spike was not the forerunner of something far more dangerous. He hurried me back on to the helicopter and was rather distracted for the remainder of the trip back home. When the truck pulled up at the house, he turned to me with serious eyes.

"Leila, I would appreciate it if you didn't mention this morning to anyone. At least not yet. We aren't sure what's going on up there and I would hate to panic anyone unnecessarily. Please?"

There was no more teasing as I gave him an answering smile of reassurance. "Of course Jason. I won't say a word to anyone. Not even to Nafanua. Well, especially not Nafanua. It will drive her nuts." We laughed together. "Seriously though Jason, you will tell me if anything does happen? It was fascinating being up there today and if things quiet down enough, I would love to take another trip to Matavanu, that is, if you don't mind dragging me along again?"

Blue eyes were warm in their response. "Definitely. You didn't get to see much today, that wasn't really what I had in mind for your first meeting with a volcano. Tell you what, next Saturday, if she hasn't blown up in my face by then, I'll take you up again. And this time, we'll go down to the funnel okay?"

I was ecstatic as we said goodbye to each other. Jason didn't realize it, but today had been of earth-moving significance for me. Today I had met my earth spirit. Today, Matavanu had spoken to me far more than Jason and his horde of instruments could ever understand.

Nafanua was waiting for me when I walked inside, a vague air of apprehension tinged the room.

"Well, how did it go? Did anything happen?"

I smiled at her nervousness. I laughed. "Oh Nafanua, it was amazing! Matavanu spoke to me. She really talked to me. I don't quite know how to explain it, but she's alive, she's real. And she knew me. As soon as I set foot on that volcano, I could feel her. There was this incredible rush of ... joy, exhilaration. Like nothing I've ever felt before. And then all Jason's equipment went nuts and had them freaking out, it was hilarious. And I hated to scare them like that, but it was amazing nevertheless." I took a breath. "Nafanua, for the first time today, I felt like this *telesā* thing really could be a gift and not a curse. Like, maybe it's not so bad to be this after all." I turned to her with pleading, confused eyes. "Does that make sense? Is that wrong of me to actually, maybe like this? I thought all I wanted was to be able to get rid of this thing, but today, I don't know, maybe it is possible to be *telesā* and still be me? Maybe *telesā* IS me?"

Nafanua looked exultant. She took a few steps forward and carefully held my hands in hers. "Leila, hearing you say this, gives me great joy. I haven't wanted to force this on you. I know how confusing and frightening this has been for you, and I have wanted nothing but for you to be happy. To be at peace with this gift. Because, Leila, it is a gift. Once you have full control of Fanua, then you have no more need to fear it. To worry that you will hurt people. Your gift can be glorious Leila, it can do great things – if you just let it." She paused and then carried on. "If you are ready, Leila, then our sisterhood would gladly welcome you. We are *Matagi* but we can carry out the final steps necessary for you to be truly *telesā*. If you are ready ..." her voice trailed away as my gaze dropped down to her *malu*. The tattoo markings seemed to ask me their own question. *Are you ready? Are you truly ready Leila?*

I thought again of how it felt to be at one with Matavanu. Of that day I had stood naked in the sunlight with a single flame burning in the palm of my hand. Knowing that I had summoned it, knowing that I could make it bend and weave, burn and rage – and then still and smolder. Maybe this was the path for me? This power, this fire wasn't going anywhere. And if I wanted to be its mistress then I needed to complete the training necessary to make sure it would always do my bidding.

Because how else could I be totally sure that I wouldn't accidentally hurt people one day? I took a huge breath and clasped Nafanua's hands tightly in mine.

"I'm ready Nafanua. I want to get a *malu.*"

For the first time since I was a child, my mother hugged me. And for the first time since arriving in Samoa, I felt like I truly belonged.

A *malu* is a tattoo given to women in Samoa. It is applied using hand instruments. Mini chisels and adzes with razor sharp edges made from animal bone are used to repeatedly tap and cut the skin open while hands pull the skin taut and tight. When the skin is pierced and blood flows, the adze is dipped in the pigment ink. And the adze taps again, cutting into the skin, leaving its markings. While the tattooist does their work, women sit there beside the recipient. They sing songs of her ancestors. They tell stories of the women who walked before her. The lives they led. The battles they fought. The children they bore. The men they loved. They trace her lineage back to Nafanua the war goddess. Back to *Tangaloa-lagi*, god of the earth. They distract her from the pain of the instruments. The biting gnawing pain as the adze cuts and cuts again. They wipe the sweat from her brow and if there are tears, they will wipe those away too. When she cannot continue a moment more, they will pause with her, give her cold water to drink. Help her walk down to the beach to bathe in the ocean, supporting her with strong arms as she flinches against the bite of the salt. The cut of the whipping wind and the grate of the sand. And then back to the biting adze. When the pain builds in waves, threatening to overwhelm her, they will hold her hands in theirs, holding her firmly to the earth, holding her captive to consciousness. Keeping her firmly anchored to this mind-numbing agony. They will not let her escape it. But they will her the strength to endure.

Endure. Endure. Endure. We are with you. Endure.

My *malu* took three days to complete. My mother ground the pigment herself from bark and roots she had grown with her own hands. My ink was made for *Fanua Afi*. To it she added the red burn of chilli pepper – to make fire burn strong. And the root of red ginger flowers – because fire is beautiful. There was black rock from the lava field of Matavanu – to give fire the enduring strength of the earth from whence it sprang. And a sprig of mint and lemon leaf – because fire is a cleanser. She stirred in the rich roasted koko bean – because fire is sweet heat and passion. And finally, she added vanilla bean. Her personal gift to me. Because fire can be comfort and warmth. Fragrant and uplifting.

My mother watched while the *telesā* held me down, pulled my skin taut, and cut me. I heard her voice sing to me through a haze of endless pain. And tell me the stories of ancient *telesā*. At night, when the moon called to a silken sea, she helped carry me to the ocean so I could bathe the open wounds in the salt water. And she cut fresh banana leaf fronds for me to lie on, their coolness soothing the cuts that burned with chilli pepper and lemon leaf. And when the *malu* was complete, my mother fed me with *vaisalo* and succulent baked crab. Salty *limu* seaweed and raw fish in coconut cream. Slices of papaya soaked in lemon. Food for healing. Food for strengthening.

By day five, my *malu* was just a dull ache. And the *telesā matagi* planned the celebratory feast for the displaying of my tattoo. The house was filled with the aroma of Netta's cooking. The excitement of women planning a festive occasion. My mother helped me dress. In a brief piece of unpatterned *siapo* cloth, soft and gentle against the healing skin. A shift that ended where the *malu* began, at the thigh, so as to better display its beauty. They rubbed my skin with *mosooi* coconut oil and put a red hibiscus in my hair. The celebration was outdoors. Feather-edged mats spread out underneath the trees, awaiting the first time I would expose my *malu* to the sun. My mother led the way. I sat next to her at the feast. It was just us *telesā*. Six *matagi* and now one *fanua afi*.

The sun was a glorious blaze of gold and the gardenia was in full bloom. I sat there and looked at these women, my sisters. My *malu* spoke to theirs, adding to the story of our ancestry.

I was *telesā*.

TEN

My buzz lasted about twenty-four hours. Until Nafanua informed me that she thought I was ready to go back to school on Monday.

"Leila, you're ready to rejoin society, honestly, you're making far too big a deal about this. You've made great progress with controlling your fire and there is no way you are going to set anyone on fire. Not unless you want to of course." she laughed lightly. Her voice took a serious edge. "Leila, no daughter of mine is going to be an uneducated simpleton. *Telesā* need the knowledge of the Western world if they want to be able to use it for their purposes. You're going back to school tomorrow. And that's final."

It was a surprisingly typical teenager-mother conversation. One that ended with me stomping up to my bedroom to throw my pillow across the room in silent fury. But that was about the full extent of my tantrum. Because even though I was dreading the thought of school after being away for over a month, I was aflame with nervous excitement at the idea of seeing Daniel again. My mind danced slowly over the memory of his face, his smile, his laughing eyes. What would he think when he saw me? Would I be strong enough to stay away from him? Instinctively, my hands went to my *malu*, as I longed for it to give me strength, for control. I prayed silently to whatever gods were listening for help, for the strength I would need to keep Daniel safe. From me.

Nafanua didn't leave me alone to sulk for long. There was a sharp rap on the door before she walked in. I sat upright at the sight of her unusual outfit. I had never seen her wear pants before, or all black. She seemed hesitant, unsure of herself.

"Leila, umm, I was wondering if you wanted to join us –my sisters and I – tonight. We've got some work to do that will involve us using our powers, and I thought you might be interested to see just what it is that we do. And, we could kind of use your help. Please?"

I was puzzled but intrigued. It only took a moment for me to decide. "Sure, where are we going? What do you need?"

"Oh, you'll see when we get there. Wear something dark that covers your legs, they might get scratched. We leave in ten minutes, the others will be arriving any minute now." As she turned to go downstairs, we both heard the roar of more than one truck making its way up the long driveway.

I peered from the bedroom window as Nafanua went out to greet the women. Tonight none of them wore the usual tropical colors. All were dressed like Nafanua, in black – long pants and figure hugging tops. It would have been funny, kind of like a gaggle of women playing at being night assassins or something, with their black outfits and hair slicked back, standing beside their monster trucks. Yes it would have been funny, if I didn't know what they all were. *Telesa.* Every one of them capable of a lightning strike. Calling a cyclone. Summoning a whirlwind. I stifled a slight edge of unease as I quickly changed into a similar outfit and tripped down the stairs. The disquiet dissolved though as I joined the women in the kitchen. They were chattering, laughing, helping themselves to a platter of Netta's banana fritters and greeted me with open, smiling faces and warmth. Everyone except for Sarona. But I was used to her thinly veiled antagonism so it was no problem to ignore her.

"Hi Leila – so you're joining us tonight? How fun!"

"Nafanua must be thrilled to finally have you on the team ay?"

"Ready for a great night out Leila?"

Sarona merely regarded me with confronting eyes then turned to ask with bored impatience. "Well, are we going to get moving or what?"

Nafanua only smiled as she called everyone to attention. "Alright ladies, shall we make a start? Leila has school tomorrow and can't be up too late." Everyone laughed as I grimaced at the reminder. I resolutely put the next day's torment at the back of my mind, following everyone outside and joining Nafanua in the front seat of the Land cruiser.

"So, when do I get to find out where we're going?"

Nafanua smiled, there was a buzz of excitement in the air as we drove out the driveway and down the Aleisa road with three other Land cruisers following behind us. "Patience, patience! Youth can never wait for anything." A laugh. "Just wait until you're a hundred, then maybe you'll have learned a bit of patience."

I winced at the reminder of the longevity thing. Until my dad died, I had never thought much about death, but I did know that there was no way I wanted to be a hundred years old. My mind skipped, as it so often did, to Daniel. Where would he be when I was a hundred? Long gone probably. I scowled in the darkness. Who wanted to live that long if the people you loved weren't with you?

Nafanua interrupted my dark thoughts. "Well, it's not much further so I suppose I better brief you a bit. Her tone had turned serious. "You remember I told you that *telesā* are guardians, protectors of the land? Our mission has gotten more and more difficult with time. More of our people are embracing new ways of living and turning their backs on what gives them life. I'm sure I don't have to tell you about how man is polluting the earth – the water, the air, the very ground we walk on."

Her eyes were trained on the road ahead but I could hear the edge of anger. "We do our best, but at times, it feels like we are fighting a losing battle, like what we really need is to do something cataclysmic, something that will force our society to sit up and take notice. To finally comprehend the gravity of what they are doing, how they are living. Anyway, every now and again, we are called upon to do something a little more drastic to set things right. We're here."

The truck passed a fenced compound filled with the dark shapes of warehouses and storage tanks. A soft drink bottling company. Security lighting scattered shadows intermittently and there were two guards at the front gate. The men looked up as our car drove past and then turned back to their card game as we continued on down the road. Not until we were out of their line of sight did Nafanua pull over in a cluster of trees by the roadside. The other cars didn't follow though and I looked questioningly at Nafanua.

"Where are the others?"

"They'll distract the guards. Come on, we don't have much time."

"Wait, distract them from what? Wait up!" I hurried to join Nafanua as she moved to stand beside the perimeter gate. "What are we doing here?"

She didn't answer as she busied herself with a pair of wire cutters, snipping expertly through the chain link and pushing open an entry for us. "Shh, come on. Follow me."

I had to run to keep up with her, still trying to get answers. "Nafanua what's going on? Would you please tell me what we're doing?"

She pulled me to a halt beside her, whispering over her shoulder. "Look, there. See that tank? The one connected to that pipeline?"

I peered around her in the dimness. "Yeah so?"

"So that's what we're here for. That tank is filled with a chemical solvent that the company has been using to clean their bottles."

I struggled to keep the impatience out of my voice as Nafanua started running again, darting through tanks and past to where the pipeline began its journey somewhere in the darkness. "So? That still doesn't tell me why the heck we're here. Nafanua?"

"Keep your voice down. Just follow me."

She continued on. The pipeline snaked its way along the ground, through the bushes and the ground started to get boggy. And there was an unmistakable stench in the air. One of rot. Putridness. Death.

"Ugh! What is that?"

We came out in a clearing and I stood still in horror. The pipeline was spewing its contents into a mangrove swamp that skirted the ocean. Green waste was slowly but surely pumping out into the sludgy water, but that wasn't where the smell was coming from. The rot was emanating from the water where dead fish floated. Dead dogs. I covered my nose and struggled not to vomit as I thought I caught sight of a few dead pigs too. "What's this?"

Nafanua spoke sharply. "This is their waste disposal."

"This can't be right. I don't get it. How can they just be pumping this stuff here? It's so close to them and they're happy to just leave it out in the open? This is dangerous. Look at all the dead animals. It's disgusting. It's criminal! What about if a kid comes here? And it's all going into the sea and probably the tide is just taking it right back down there where the village is that we passed on the way. This is horrible." Nafanua nodded grimly. "Yes it is. We just got word today about it. They were pumping the waste into trucks that took the mess up to the Tafaigata landfill site but the company decided that was too expensive an option, so they just put in this pipeline last month. Decided to offload the waste here into the mangrove and just count on the tide to move it away from here."

"We have to report them. We can't let them get away with us. Have you called the police? The Ministry of Environment or something?"

Nafanua gave me a sardonic look. Like I was a simpleton. "You're joking right? You really think the police care about stuff like this? You're not that naïve are you?"

Gingerly, she walked along the outskirts of the swamp, making her careful way closer towards the effluent pipe. Battling nausea, I followed her, whispering frantically."Nafanua! Wait. So what are we doing here? What are you going to do?"

She stopped and looked back at me with an impassive face. "What are you going to do, Leila?"

I stopped short behind her. "What do you mean?"

She gestured expansively to the mess in front of us. "Well, we can take out the tank with a well placed lightning strike but that's an unpredictable method for dealing with the situation."

I was confused. "What are you talking about?"

"We're air element controllers, remember? We can summon lightning and that will set things on fire, but we can't control what that fire will do or where it will go. That's where you come in."

"Wait – you want me to, what, set this place on fire?!" I was incredulous.

"You said it yourself, it's criminal what they're doing – to the land, the ocean, not to mention the people who live here. And you can do something about it. The question is, will you?"

I shook my head. "But that's wrong. That's illegal! You're asking me to sabotage this company's tank? And destroy stuff? You're nuts!"

She raised an eyebrow at my outburst. "No Leila, what's nuts is to stand here and do nothing when it's in your power, literally in your hands, to be able to right this wrong. Now that you have seen this, how can you walk away from it when you know very well that all it would take is a thought and you could safely clean this site up? Can you do that? Could you sleep well tonight if you turned your back on this mess? If you walked away from it?" She turned to point away in the distance. "Just beyond those trees, is a village. With families, children, elderly. Shall I bring you back here tomorrow so you can see where the children go swimming every morning, just a few hundred meters up the coast from here? Shall I take you upriver so you can see where the village boys go to trap freshwater shrimp? From this very water? Can you look at those people and feel peace knowing that you allowed this – desecration – to continue?"

I tried to find words that would negate her logic. "But, that's not fair, Nafanua, that's not right. This pollution isn't ours to fix, it's not our responsibility. It wouldn't be right."

"Exactly. It's not fair. It's not right. That a few rich and powerful people should be able to do whatever they want so they can make more money and hurt countless others in the process. You're right Leila. This isn't fair. So you can walk away from here or you can step up and help take responsibility. This is what we *telesā* do. I won't force you to do anything you don't want to Leila. But know this. We came here tonight to fix this. And we will use our gifts, our powers, to make this right, the best way we know how. You can wait in the car until we're finished."

The conversation was over. She turned her back on me and quickly walked back to where the tank was situated. Numbly, I followed. Two other dark shapes slipped from the shadows to join her – Sarona and Fouina.

"The guards are taken care of. Let's do this."

I didn't have time to wonder what 'taking care of the guards' meant because Nafanua held one clenched fist to the sky and summoned the first lightning strike. It hit the tank and, as it did, the women turned to run, pulling me with them.

"Come on. Run!"

The explosion behind us was deafening and a wave of heat and air half threw us several feet through the air. I hit the ground with a *whoosh* of impact, all the wind knocked from me. The others, more practiced than I, rolled to their feet, impatiently pulling at my arms to drag me further out of reach of the burning inferno behind us.

"Get up. Move!"

Still in shock, I allowed myself to be rushed along until they found a spot they deemed safe. They halted and we stood to look back at the flames as they danced higher. Sarona was exultant.

"Yes! Beautiful. That should take care of them."

She and Fouina laughed together but Nafanua's brow furrowed in concern, her gaze trained on the blaze. "Damnit."

The others turned. "What? What is it?"

She pointed to where the seething flames were now rippling along the ground. Towards the factory buildings. "It's spreading. Leila, you've got to do something."

Fouina protested. "Do what? I thought we wanted to burn the whole place down?"

Nafanua sent her a look loaded with meaning and pulled at my hand. "Leila, the fire's moving in the wrong direction. We need it to follow the pipe and burn the dump site so it can be cleansed. Quickly, you need to channel it back and then monitor it at the dump site. Come on."

I shook her hand away. "No. I told you I wanted nothing to do with this."

The other two women laughed. Sarona arched an eyebrow. "Well Nafanua, teenagers ay? Just can't make them do what you want. Let's go back to the trucks Fouina. I'm tired of this."

Sarona and Fouina walked quickly back the way they had come, leaving me alone with Nafanua and a quickly escalating fiery situation. She appealed to me again.

"Leila, people could get hurt if you don't help me channel this in the right direction. I need your help. Please?"

I knew she was right. If the blaze reached the factory it would be unstoppable. And remembering the poisonous accumulation at the mangrove swamp, I made my decision. I took several steps closer to the fiery chaos and took a moment to calm my ragged breathing. Yes, I had practiced controlling fire, but that was always in the privacy and peace of Nafanua's garden. Tonight was different.

Breathe Leila, focus, you can do this. O_2 party in the molecules, come on. Breathe. Talk to me ... With my thoughts I reached down through my feet to the ground, nudging, seeking for the energy that always lay dormant there. Awakened it. Called it to a party in my fingers and, just like that, my hands burst into flame. *Yes!*

I focused all my concentration on the runaway flames. And even though I hadn't started the fire – it listened. The fiery energy in my own hands called to it and it answered. I beckoned fiercely and pulled it back like a beast on a leash. Clenching my fists I gestured back towards the pipeline, back towards the dumpsite and the flames followed eagerly. Like a puppet master, I manipulated the fire, standing firm against its heat as it rushed past me while Nafanua stumbled in her haste to get away from it. I felt the flame as it found the pipeline, as it ran along its length, devouring everything in its path, as it arrived at the swamp site.

I chased after it, coming to a halt swamp side. Now this was the tricky part, I wanted it to burn – but only until all the chemical waste was extinguished. No further. I stood guard on the land watching. Whenever the flames leapt out to a gnarled tree, I flicked my fingers and called it back in place. When one rushing ball of fire barreled across the ground, I stamped my foot irritated and forced it back.

"No! Get back."

Beads of sweat trickled down my forehead as I struggled to stay focused, in command. This wasn't as easy as it looked and I could feel my strength sapping with every minute that I exerted control over the inferno. Starting a fire was one thing, but then telling it to stop was a whole different exercise. When fire is having a party, it doesn't want to quit. I waited a few minutes until the flames began to falter and the chemical fuel in the water was all consumed. The fire flickered, whimpered and slowly died, leaving only wisps of black smoke curling skyward. I walked right around the edges of the swamp pool to make sure there were no stray cinders smoldering anywhere that could catch light in the first breath of wind. Nothing. To be sure, I stood motionless, closed my eyes and reached out with that part of me that spoke to earth, that knew fire intimately. Nothing. The fire was no more. I heaved a huge sigh. And felt very, very tired. What a night.

I made my way back to where I had left Nafanua. The rest of the *telesā* had now joined her and everyone stood in a tense huddle, speaking in angry whispers that broke off abruptly as I came into sight. "It's all burned out. Now can we get out of here?"

The women looked at each other and unspoken accusations knifed the air. Nafanua spoke first.

"Yes, let's move. The authorities will arrive shortly and we do not need to be flustered with their inquisitions." She paused to smile at me. "Well done, Leila. That was excellent work. You made sure the factory was protected. Thank you for your help tonight."

Sarona spoke with a cynical edge. "Yes, Leila. You saved the factory. The one that makes chemical by-products that kill the environment and cause birth defects in children. Thank you so much."

Anger powered my response. "I don't know what you were trying to do, but a lightning strike of that size could have set the whole place alight. What are we? Arsonists? Criminals? You were prepared to burn the whole place down? What the hell was that?! Someone could have been hurt, killed even. At least what I did got rid of the chemical pollution problem. Go on, go back and take a look for yourself. It's all gone now. The place is clean."

Thunder shuddered the sky as Sarona snarled. "You foolish child. Are you that idiotic to think that your pathetic little bonfire is going to stop these people? Give them one week or two, and they will have the place running again, the tank and pipeline rebuilt and spewing its guts out in the mangrove again. What are you going to do then? Come back every fortnight to burn their rubbish for them?" She laughed shortly. "Maybe you should go work for them. Hire out your services as a rubbish disposal system."

I tried not to show how deep her words cut me as their truth serrated me raw. Anger and frustration had my temperature rising, my hands itching with the familiar prickling heat. I don't know what would have happened if Nafanua had not interrupted.

"That's enough. We came to clean up the chemical dump and disable the system and the job is done, thanks to Leila. We achieve nothing by arguing here. Now, everyone MOVE before we are caught."

Approaching sirens emphasized her words and all of us moved as one back to the vehicles. Nafanua gunned the engine and with a spin of tires we were hurtling along a side road and away from the factory site. I stared out the window as Nafanua navigated potholes and speed bumps with skilled ease and my mind was a turbulent swirl of questions. I had just participated in destroying someone else's property. I had watched as my mother and her sisters had tried to burn it to the ground. And then I had used the fire to burn a pipeline, consume a chemical dumpsite and now here we were running away from police and fire teams. *What have I just done? What are these women? What have I gotten myself into?* I thought of my dad and sincerely hoped that he couldn't see anything of the night's events from heaven.

Back at the house, Nafanua asked me to go upstairs while she spoke with her sisters. I caught fragments of strained conversation. Sarona's voice was the loudest. "She could have ruined everything tonight Nafanua. She's not one of us, when are you going to accept that?"

Nafanua's reply was harsh and brooked no argument. "Silence. She's young and new to her gift. She needs her sisters to be patient – all of them. We must give her time."

I was exhausted. My every pore cried for sleep. But it was a long time coming. I lay in bed staring at the ceiling but all I could see was flames. As a factory tank burned. What had I become?

School looked exactly the same as when I had left it. I parked under the mango tree by the tennis courts, remembering the day Daniel had first kissed me on the forehead underneath its rippling shade. *Focus Leila. Get with it. You're not here for Daniel. He's not for you. He's not for you.* It was my mantra. Maybe if I said it enough, my heart would believe it?

I was concentrating so hard on my shaky resolve that I almost missed it when Maleko called out to me. "Whoa hey Leila, is that you? Wait up!"

I half turned as the exuberant boy ran up behind me. Taking one long look and then coming to an abrupt halt with a look of uncomfortable awe on his face. He whistled long and low. "Damn girl what did you do?"

Confused, I shook my head. "What do you mean?"

He looked searchingly at me again before a smile I had never seen directed at me before lit up his eyes. Appreciative eyes. That raked meup and down. "Leila, you are lookin good! Your long break must have done something to you. Where have you been?"

I shrugged and kept walking. "Sorry gotta run Maleko, the bell's gonna go and I have to check in with Mr. Raymond before I can go to class. We'll talk later?"

Maleko was acting very un-Maleko–like, and I wanted to get away from him as quickly as possible. I left him standing there, still gazing after me with that admiring look in his eyes. "I'll be waiting Leila!"

Shaking my head, I rushed to catch the Principal with the note from Nafanua justifying my long absence. Again Mr. Raymond didn't seem to be too concerned with disappearing and reappearing students. More tired sighs and harrumphs. A reminder to keep out of trouble, stay off hard labor, don't skip class. It was all over in less than five minutes and I was safe to get to my first period. Geography. *Daniel, where are you?*

Mrs. Jasmine had begun her droning lecture on the weather conditions in the Australian outback when I slipped into the classroom, finding a seat beside Sinalei. I felt him before I saw him, sensed his presence at the other side of the row. I tried to resist looking at him but within minutes I had turned. Our eyes met and caught each other captive. My breath was an indrawn hope. His eyes were unreadable. He didn't smile. He didn't frown. He just looked at me. What were my eyes saying I wondered? Were they telling him how much I loved him? How much I longed to reach out and entwine my fingers with his?

After class, we met halfway in the hall, an invisible barrier between us.

"Leila."

"Daniel."

He spoke with supreme politeness. "How are you?"

"Fine. Thanks."

"So you're back."

"Yeah. Back to school."

"For how long?"

"Huh?"

"How long? How long are you back for? Don't you head back home to the States soon?"

"No." I swallowed and nervously pushed my hair off the side of my face. "Plans have changed. I'm sticking around for a while. Probably a long while."

No, I wanted to scream, *I can't ever go back home. I'm a freak remember? I'll lose my temper one day and blow up my school or something, and a team of mad scientists from the X files will swoop down and lock me away forever. No, I'm stuck here forever.*

Those are all the things I wanted to say. But didn't.

"Danny, you'll be late for practice. I'm waiting for you." It was Mele. Slipping her hand into his, fingers curling into the empty spaces that had once belonged to mine. I was stunned. Daniel didn't pull away from her. He didn't let go of her hand. He smiled at her. A half smile that had once quickened my heart rate and set my world alight.

I felt sick. Empty. Mele was pulling on Daniel's hand and he was turning to follow her. "Good to see you're well, Leila. See you round."

They walked away while I tried to pick up the shattered pieces of my heart that lay like a million glass fragments on the ground all around me. Catching the cruel sunlight, blinding me, burning me raw. *No*, I whispered to myself, *no burning, Leila, no burning*. I wanted to run back to the jeep, I wanted nothing more than to leave school immediately and get as far away as possible from the reality that confronted me. Daniel and Mele. Mele and Daniel.

I walked in the opposite direction, wanting to get as far away as possible from the encounter. But there was no privacy to be found. Simone caught me. And his eyes lit up with sincere pleasure. "Leila! I wasn't sure whether or not to believe it. Maleko said you were back. Where have you been? And why didn't you answer any of my texts? We thought maybe you'd gone back to the States early ..." his voice died away as the same look of surprised awe as Maleko's crossed his face. Trust Simone to be direct though. He put one hand on his hip and his tone demanded truth. "Leila, what in hell have you done to yourself girl?!"

I was nonplussed, my hurt at seeing Daniel and Mele momentarily forgotten, brushed to the back of my mind. "Why do people keep asking me that? Whaddya mean? I haven't done anything. I'm still me. Same hairstyle, same face, same me."

Simone shook his head. "Nope. That's crap. Leila, you were okay-looking before, but now, you are something else entirely. I can't quite put my finger on it, but you're different. Something about you is different. What did you do?"

In reply I just rolled my eyes and then pulled him over to sit with me in a corner of the classroom. I knew Simone well enough to know that he wouldn't let the issue go and the only way to distract him would be to really give him something to look at. I inched up my uniform skirt and showed him my tattoo. "You're right. There is something different. I got a *malu* done. That's one of the reasons I was out of school for so long."

His squeal of excitement had heads turning our way. "OHMIGOSH girlfriend, no way! No freakin way!"

We talked and it felt great to be catching up with teenagers in the 'real world.' Where things like lightning strikers and fire summoners had no sway. Where I could feel, for a brief while, like a regular person.

School. Although everything seemed the same, some things were different. The school was caught up with preparing for its annual culture night. Every student was assigned to one of four 'houses' – Vaea, Stevenson, Williams, and Calliope. Each house had to present an assortment of traditional skits and dances. Everyone was busy with learning songs that accompanied the skits that were all based on early myths, and periods were shortened every day so that there was time for the practices. Ms. Sivani assigned me to be in Williams House. I was glad because that was the same as Simone. But when we got to the sweeping tamarind tree where the practice was being held, I wasn't glad anymore. Because a familiar figure caught my eye. Daniel stood at the front of the seated group of about eighty students. He held a guitar loosely in his hand. My heart sank even further when I saw Mele in the group. Laughing delightedly with her friends. I groaned. Simone gave me a sideways glance.

"Problem, Leila?" the usual teasing tone was missing. So I was more honest than I usually was with him.

"I don't want to be in the same House as those two. I hate seeing them together. I hate it." I spoke vehemently, fists clenched.

Simone's eyebrow raised in question. "But Leila, you're the one who dumped him. Everyone knows you didn't want him."

My reply was agonized, "No. I did not dump him. And I do … I do …" My words trailed and I took a huge breath to steady my emotions. Because although I did want Daniel more than breath, more than fire wanted oxygen, I couldn't. I couldn't want him. I couldn't be near him. And if that meant seeing him with Mele, than that was as it should be. I turned a smile on Simone. "Oh, never mind. You're right. Me and Daniel were a passing moment. And it's just silly for me to get bothered if he's moved on with Mele."

Simone now raised both eyebrows questioningly. "Moved on with Mele? Where did you get that from ? She wishes."

Simone was interrupted by the lead teacher calling everyone to sit. Practice needed to start and our conversation was forgotten. A senior student led the singing practice. Samoan group singing is like nothing else in the world. Everyone follows the commands of the *faipese*, the conductor, who is a complete comedian. Ours was a slight sixth former who walked with a limp. He used his whole body to lead the songs, calling for the group to clap out intricate beats in time with the music, dancing, and pirouetting as we sang. It was an exhilarating experience to be part of the music. Everyone swayed in unison, clapped and laughed together at the right moments. I had never felt so caught in oneness. Even though I didn't know the words, it made no difference.

After the singing, the girls took to the field in the sun to dance. I sat back with the rest of the boys, excused for today. The dance was exquisite to watch as their hands moved through the air, telling a story. It wasn't difficult to pick out who the lead dancer was. Mele's grace was unmistakable as she danced in the front line. I sighed, even an idiot like me could see what a natural dancer she was. No wonder Daniel was with her now. I looked over where he stood with the other prefects in the shade. He was looking at me. Again our eyes caught, again sadness and longing wracked me. Resolutely, I turned my eyes back to the dance. *Focus, Leila, focus.*

When the dance ended, the boys moved on to the field, taking their shirts off as they went. Lined up in rows, sun glinted on brown skin and muscle. And, at their lead, was Daniel. The familiar tattoo that I had once felt under my fingers, rippled as he led the boys in a slap dance. I was awestruck. No European dance routine could compare to the majestic sight of forty bronzed Polynesian 'warriors' pouring fire and passion into their war dance.

Beside my ear, Simone laughed. "Mmmm, beautiful aren't they? Love to get me a piece of that…"

The dance ended with a roar as the lines charged forward and the boys flourished in a final challenging stance before returning to the shade, sweaty and laughing. Everyone except Daniel. He walked to pick up the guitar leaning against the tree, returning to sit on a wooden chair in front of us. *What was this?* Simone leaned over to answer my unspoken question.

"The house item ends with a duet number. Daniel's singing about the legend of Sina and the dolphin warrior." Knowing I had no clue what that was about, he continued, "According to legend, Sina was the daughter of a high chief from the coastal village of Nu'umanu. Her beauty and gift for dancing the *siva* was legendary and many warriors came from faraway islands to try for her hand in marriage. But she fell in love with a Tongan warrior named Vaea, which angered her father big time. There was a war, lots of killing, and Sina was taken captive by her own people and out to sea on a canoe to get her away from Vaea. He swam out to sea to try to be with her and turned into a silver dolphin that swam alongside the boat. And she was heartbroken and leapt into the ocean to be with him, changing into sea foam, forever dancing on the waves. Legend tells that every full moon, Sina and Vaea are changed back into human form for one night only and he sings to her on a golden shore in the moonlight while she dances."

"That's so sad – and so beautiful." I exclaimed.

Simone rolled his eyes. "I guess so, but so unrealistic, like most legends. Because you just know what they're **really** getting up to one night a month on a moonlit beach – singing and dancing, my ass!"

I punched him lightly on the shoulder, "Simone! Keep the legend clean thank you very much." Our banter was cut short, however, as the teachers called for silence so that Daniel could begin. Simone whispered in my ear.

"He's going to sing for our House item while one girl dances."

I knew the answer but I couldn't stop the question. "Who?"

Simone shrugged. "They haven't picked a girl yet, but of course it will be Mele. She's always the *taupou,* the lead dancer every year."

The whispered conversation stilled as Daniel began to play. A sliver of hurt spliced through me. He had never mentioned to me that he played the guitar. But then all thought fled as he began to sing. The words were Samoan, the melody unknown, but the song heartbreakingly familiar. The whole field hushed as he sang. Of heartache. He had loved. And lost. And the world had emptied of color and meaning. When the song ended, the silence ached with sadness, bittersweet. Then applause rang out, prompting a half smile from Daniel as he stood to walk back to the side.

Everyone clapped, except for me. I was stunned. "Simone, I didn't know he could sing like that."

Simone threw me a sly glance, "Yeah he's a dream isn't he? Too bad you won't get to see what it feels like to have him sing you a love song ay? Seeing as how you kicked him to the curb."

I pretended to ignore him as we walked back across the field towards the classroom. But Simone was not fazed as he continued, "Yeah, Daniel's the best musician in the school, he writes a lot of his own songs. But this year is the first time we're going to use one of them for a solo like that. Usually the *taupou* dances while the whole house sings, but Ms. Sivani has us going for a more modern, artistic feel this year. Gotta admit, it should look really impressive when Daniel sings to the *taupou*" he gave me one of his devious grins, "Mele will love it when he sings to her, a dream come true for her."

A grimace was my only answer. The thought of Daniel singing while Mele did her super duper graceful number in front of him had the heat surging and all I wanted was fire to burn the picture away, not good. I gave myself a mental shake as I gathered my things and headed to the jeep. Simone was staying for netball practice and didn't need a lift, but I did promise to pick him up in the morning.

"I will never forgive you if you don't give me a ride in your Wrangler, Leila, absolutely refuse to be your friend ever again." was his stern threat as he farewelled me. I laughed. And then stopped. There were four boys standing beside my car. My pulse quickened and my steps slowed. Daniel? But it wasn't him. Instead, it was Maleko's eager grin that welcomed me. He and Sam – the hulking ex-prisoner – were waiting for me with another two boys from the rugby team.

"Leila, there you are. We're checking out your sweet car. Can we get a ride to Pesega field? We've got a late game there this afternoon."

Without waiting for an answer, they piled in, Maleko shoving for the front passenger seat. Rolling my eyes, and muttering, *bloody nuisance boys,* I hopped in the driver's side. "Well I guess I can't say no now can I? It's not like I can physically eject you rugby beasts out of my car."

Maleko's raucous whoop had heads turning as we reversed and started out the drive. Not for the first time, I was thankful that Nafanua didn't care what I did because a car full of boys wasn't something I wanted to explain. The ride to Pesega was loud and rambunctious. They wanted the stereo on full blast. I conceded to midway. They wanted to see how fast we could go on the smooth new road at Vaimoso. I refused. They called out to St Mary's schoolgirls crossing the road, inviting them to *come take a ride in our jeep baby!* I told them to shut up or else get out. I was relieved when we finally got to Pesega, which was crowded with different schools, spectators for the afternoon games. Everyone piled out, calling out their thanks before taking off. Everyone except for Maleko. Unusually subdued, he waited till they were out of sight before turning to me with a hesitant grin.

"So Leila, you wanna come watch the game?"

"No thanks. The last game I went to I got caught in the middle of a brawl, remember? Rugby is not really my thing."

He laughed quietly but he was still not ready to get out. "Oh yeah, that's right, the one where you came to watch Daniel."

I didn't bother to try and deny it. A shrug. He rushed on. "So what's up with you two anyways? Anything going on?"

I tried to hide my surprise, reminding myself that boys weren't known for confiding in each other. "Nothing. Nothing's going on. I guess we're friends. You know, regular, just regular."

"You know, me and Mele aren't going out anymore." He announced it triumphantly, like telling me I had just won the lottery, pausing to see how excited my reaction would be. I gave him puzzled eyes.

"Umm no, I didn't know. I'm ah … sorry to hear it." I had no clue where this conversation was heading. So his next question knocked the wind out of me.

"Yeah. So I was thinking that if you and Daniel aren't a thing and me and Mele aren't a thing, then that means you and me could hang out sometime. You know, like go out. Together. You and me."

I stumbled for a reply. One that wouldn't offend. "Oh. I didn't think. I didn't realize. I'm not sure that's such a good idea. You know, because you and Daniel are good friends, wouldn't that be weird?"

He waved his hand airily. "Nah, you guys are through. Why would it be weird?"

I tried again, groping blindly through a blank repertoire of 'ways a girl turns down a boy she doesn't want to go out with.' Seeing as how I'd never had to do it before, I wasn't confident of much success at finding a ready solution.

"Oh I don't know Maleko, we don't really know each other at all."

It was the wrong thing to say. Right there in the afternoon sunlight with people milling about only a few feet away, he leaned towards me, sliding one arm smoothly behind me on the seat. He spoke softly, inviting me to move my head closer to his so I could catch his reply. "Leila, that's why we should spend some time together. I can't wait to get to know you better. I just know that you and me, we could make beautiful music together, ay?"

It was so much like a bad teenage movie that I wanted to laugh. But in that split second, something happened that drove away all thoughts of laughter. A battered green truck pulled up beside us. Daniel's truck. He turned and looked directly at us. At me. At Maleko with his arm around me, the way his mouth was inches away from my ear. Time froze. But for no-one else but me.

Daniel smiled, a cold tight smile at the both of us, getting out of the truck, slowly getting his bag of rugby gear from the back. Maleko jolted to his feet, rocking the jeep slightly.

"Hey Danny, Leila's Wrangler beat you here ay? You better retire the green bomb."

Daniel's reply was ice cutting through the hot afternoon. "I didn't realize Leila was providing a taxi service to rugby games now or else I would have hitched a ride too."

I stared at my schoolbag on the front seat, cringing at his tone but Maleko seemed indifferent to the tension. He straightened up but left his arm on the back of my seat. A grin. "What do you think, is Coach going to let me play wing today?"

"Oh I don't know, you were kinda slow at practice yesterday man." Daniel came up to the window, keeping up the banter with Maleko while all the while his eyes were on me. Unsmiling. "I think a game against Avele College needs someone with a bit more speed and power, you know?"

Maleko hopped out of the car, reaching for his bag. "Whatever man! Coach knows I'm ready for it. Today's the day, I'm sure of it."

I sat still in the front, a smile plastered on my face. Daniel paused "So, Leila, you coming to watch the game today? I guess you want to check out Maleko's moves on the field?" His eyes dared me to contradict him. Maleko answered for the both of us.

"Nah, she said she doesn't want to get beat up again. I think you ruined all rugby games for her." He was joking but I saw Daniel's shoulders stiffen, the cut in his eyes before he hid it behind the coldness. When he spoke it was with exact politeness. "Of course. I understand. Your first rugby game was not something you would want to remember. It didn't turn out the way it was supposed to, the way I wanted it to."

I tried to repair an already broken situation. "No, it didn't, but I didn't care. It didn't matter. I mean, I liked that day. Oh whatever!"

Now both boys were staring at me confused. "Huh?"

I rolled my eyes and got out of the Wrangler. "Maleko's wrong. He doesn't know anything about what I want. I'm staying to watch the game. Of course I am."

And with that, I stalked away from both of them, unwilling to listen to any more. I walked to the field, joining the pack of other onlookers as the boys got their gear on. I wanted to be alone with my thoughts but a voice cut through my swirl of emotions.

"Leila."

It was the last person in the universe I wanted to talk to. Mele and a cluster of other girls from school.

"Mele."

"Coming to watch the boys play?"

"Yeah, just for a bit anyways."

She looked at me appraisingly. "We thought you'd gone back to the States. What happened to you?"

"Oh, I've been sick. Much better now."

Her dark eyes appraised me thoughtfully. "Yes, you do look different." We stood in silence and watched the boys warm up, running the length of the field. My eyes trying not to linger on Daniel's perfect form.

"So when will you be moving back home?"

I tried to make my tone as artificially casual as hers. "Probably not for a long while. I'm staying with my mother now and so this is pretty much home for me."

Mele smiled at me. Sweetly. "Oh. That's too bad."

Before I could react to her venom, the referee blew a whistle and the game began. Mele and her coven moved away further down the sidelines, leaving me to watch the game alone.

The roughness of the play wasn't as shocking to me as it had been the first time. I was following the game with mild interest when suddenly, there was a scuffle on the field, a scrum that refused to break and scatter. But at its heart were only orange and yellow uniforms. Two. Daniel and Maleko. One had the other in a chokehold, the other reaching up to throw a juddering punch at the other's jaw. The ref was frantically blowing the whistle, the rest of the team were trying to break them up, dodging blows as they pulled the two apart. It took three of the forward pack to restrain Daniel, Maleko was shaking loose from the hold of two others, wiping blood off his chin, as he cursed at an enraged Daniel.

"Break it up, break it up right now!" the coach was furious. "Just what the hell do you two think you're doing? Are you crazy? You're going to cost us the game, get off the field both of you, now!"

It took all my restraint to not run on to the field to Daniel's side. His three companions escorted him towards the sidelines, and my eyes anxiously searched for any sign of injury. Apart from a trickle of blood from a cut lip though, he seemed to be okay and I breathed a sigh of relief. As if sensing my gaze, he chose then to look up, and our eyes met. His expression was unreadable, but his whole body stiffened and seemed to scream accusingly at me before he turned away, shaking off the hand of his teammate and stalking towards his green truck. I stood, frozen, and watched as Mele ran lightly after him. "Daniel, Daniel, wait up. Are you okay? Daniel!"

I wanted so badly to be her at that moment. More than anything. To be a regular girl. Able to run after the boy she loved. I couldn't bear to see any more. I turned and ran back to the Wrangler, and drove away without a backward glance. I needed to get as far away from Mele as possible. Because all I could think about was how easy it would be to incinerate her with a single thought.

That night at dinner, I was quiet and Nafanua sensed my mood. Over Netta's pineapple pie (which wasn't half as nice as Aunty Matile's, I thought wistfully) she probed. "So, how was school today? Any problems?"

"No. It was fine."

"Ah, so none of the things you were worried about happened? You didn't blow up, set anybody on fire, burn the school down to the ground?" Her face was serious but her eyes sparked with mischief.

My retort was sour. "No. None of that happened. Just a regular day. Like a regular girl."

My own answer gave me a mild boost of lightness. Because it was true. I *had* had a regular day. Not once did I want to blow up. I had thought about fire – but only because I wanted to stop thinking about Daniel and Mele walking away from me. Together. My quick flush of happiness evaporated just as quickly with that memory. Nafanua picked it up immediately.

"So why are you down? What else happened? What 'regular girl' stuff has you moping? Was it that boy?"

"No." I refused to discuss Daniel with Nafanua. I didn't want her anywhere near the mere mention of his name. I leapt to another topic, sure it would distract the both of us. "Everyone at school is getting ready for Culture night. You know, the dancing and the singing stuff. Our house is doing this dance and I don't know how to *siva* and I feel kinda like an idiot. A clumsy idiot."

She smiled. With unrestrained pleasure, pushing her chair away from the table. "Leila, you could never be a clumsy idiot. Even if you wanted to. You are my daughter. You are *telesā*. We are not clumsy. Foolish child." The smile softened the words. "Come." She went into the living room, choosing music at the stereo.

Confused, I followed. "What? What are you doing? And what do you mean, what does dancing have to do with *telesā*?"

Nafanua flicked her hands impatiently. "Leila, where do you think our people first derived the *siva* from? The gift of dance was a gift from the gods. Pele is the goddess of dance and you – you foolish child – are a daughter of Pele. Hello!" Hands on her hips, she regarded me with frank bemusement. "Now come over here. All you need is one lesson and you will be dancing circles around the rest of those girls."

I shook my head at her excitement. "Nafanua, I hate to burst your bubble, but I don't think it's going to happen. I'm not from here, I mean, I didn't grow up here, I haven't been dancing the *siva* all my life like the other girls. I have no clue how to do any of it and I think it's a bit late to expect any Pele-sparks to be rubbing off on me now."

She waved away my protests, pulling me by the hand to the centre of the room. "Shush. Now listen, listen to the music."

I wanted to argue but she wouldn't let me. "Shush! Listen."

We stood there in the deepening twilight and listened. The song skipped and fluttered through the air, tugging at me. "Now watch." Nafanua began to dance, like the way the girls at school had danced today, the same but different. Her entire body moved in one fluid movement, her hands told a story and it was impossible not to be in awe of her. She pulled me to stand beside her, "Come here, do what I do."

It took an hour but it was an hour well spent. By the end of the impromptu lesson, I was thrilled with the new discovery. Not only did I know how to dance the Samoan *siva*, I loved it. The beauty of it reminded me of my fire when it pulsed all around me, the worshipful thrill was the same. Again I had to admit, my mother was right. I was *telesā*.

And *telesā* knew how to *siva*.

I went to bed tired but happy. Tomorrow I would join in the dance practice. I was a clumsy idiot no longer.

ELEVEN

At school the next day, Simone and Sinalei were both waiting for me when I drove in. Excited.

"So tell us ... tell us!"

"Tell you what?"

"About yesterday. We heard about Maleko and Daniel fighting, what's going on?"

"Nothing. Absolutely nothing."

They refused to accept that. But I was adamant that I knew nothing and had no information to offer. Yes, I'd given Maleko a lift to the rugby game, but that was only because he wouldn't take no for an answer. Yes, I had seen a fight break out on the field but I had no clue what it had been about. There, that was it. Frustrated with my lack of gossip enthusiasm, they soon let me be, which was a relief.

When the bell rang for lunch, I was headed towards the canteen when a tall shape detached itself from the crowd of boys beside the rugby field. Maleko. I groaned. *No*, he was the last person I wanted to see right now. He had a black eye and a cut lip – they screamed at me accusingly. If that's what he looked like, I didn't want to see Daniel.

"Hi Leila! How was Biology?"

"Good."

I kept walking but he persistently kept pace with me. "So about yesterday ..."

I interrupted him. "Yes, about yesterday. What the hell was that Maleko? I mean, what were you thinking? I've been here for months now, and we're friends. What was that yesterday?"

He seemed startled by my outburst. Now that I had allowed myself to get angry, I could feel the slow burning wave of heat building inside me, and I knew I needed to calm down. Before it got out of control. I needed to get away from this jerk. Fast. "Look, just forget it okay, I don't know what that was about yesterday, and I don't want to know. You're a funny guy, fun to be around, but I'm not interested in going out with you. Not the slightest little bit. So stay away from me with all your sleazy lines and your touchy-feeliness, you hear me?"

I stalked away before he could reply. Before the fire could sweep up and outwards, overwhelming my control. I walked into the sunlit courtyard, breathing deeply the way Nafanua had trained me. Not fleeing from the heat that spoke to me, but gentling it. *Breathe. Assure it, all is well. You are not needed right now. Sleep, slumber on.* It was my first real test at self-control since I had been back at school, and I was pleased with the results. Another deep breath and the fire simmered and died.

My buzz faded when I saw Daniel at the far end of the driveway. With Mele walking beside him. I couldn't see his face so I didn't know what damage Maleko had inflicted on him. I hoped fervently that there would be none. Too ashamed to see for myself, to see the hate that must be burning in him, I turned back and slipped upstairs. It would be another lunch period spent in the library. Oh well, I was so far behind that I needed all the study time I could get.

After lunch, we moved to house practice. Again we gathered under the trees and again, we went through the songs first. A few of the words were starting to be familiar to me and the actions were no longer foreign. There was a delicious breeze blowing across the field and it was good to be outdoors. I carefully nudged a thought pattern to the ground below us and felt an answering warmth in return. All was well. It was time for the girls' dance. This time I joined them, Simone making room for me at the end of the front row. The music started and the first movements caught me and swept me along with them. I didn't know all the routine, but it didn't matter, the music caught my hands, my breath, my body – and every part of me danced to its call. I thought I would be nervous, hesitant. But there was nothing but joy. In the music and in the answer that my hands danced. Everything else faded away. The heat of the afternoon. The sweaty crowd of students gathered underneath a wilting tree. Even all thoughts of Daniel and Mele. Nothing else existed but the music and the dance as my hands spoke to its call. When the song ended, I was flushed with happiness but embarrassed with the silence. People were looking at me funny as I went back to sit beside Simone. He turned sardonical eyes on me.

"So what the hell was that !?" He prodded my shoulder with one lithe finger, his liquid-lined eyes demanding an explanation.

I couldn't stop the laugh. "What? I was dancing, you know, doing the *siva* like everybody else up there."

He shook his head firmly. "No, you weren't like everyone else up there and you know it, you self-satisfied evil thing. Stop gloating! It doesn't make sense. Yesterday you can't dance a beat and today you're all of a sudden Miss Samoa graceful and dance diva? What's going on?"

I hastened to chase away the suspicion in his eyes. "Okay, okay, I confess, my mom gave me some lessons. I told her I was sick and tired of being the odd one out during practice, the brown *palagi* girl who couldn't *siva* and so she helped me out." Sudden anxiety gripped me. "Was I okay? Did it look alright?"

Simone waved his hand airily. "Girl, you were more than alright. You were freakin fantastic. I'm jealous. *I'm* supposed to be the only feminine graceful one in this relationship!" He scowled, and then a cheeky grin lit up his face. "Ohmigosh, you should have seen Mele's face when she realized Daniel was staring at you the whole time. It was wicked!" A huge sigh of pleasure. "If looks could kill you would have been riddled with holes by now. I don't know how your mom did it, but she sure turned you into a *taupou*."

I tried to hide how pleased I was to hear that Daniel had been studying me as I watched the boys do their slap dance, memorizing all over again the way sunlight danced on Daniel's shoulders, over the perfect symmetry of his chest. Unfortunately, the slap dance was over far too soon and the boys returned to their section in the shade. Someone handed Daniel his guitar for the solo, and I was so focused on waiting to hear his singing again that I missed it when the lead teacher, Mrs. Lematua, called my name. Simone poked me in the ribs and hissed. "Leila, she wants you."

I was dumb with surprise. "Huh?"

Mrs. Lematua sighed with sweaty frustration. "Leila Folger I said, can you get up here please."

Slowly, I got up and walked to the front, unsure what I was being disciplined about. "Umm … yes?"

"We want you to do the *siva* while Daniel sings his song. We're trying out different girls for the *taupou* this year. Go on, it's hot and we don't have all day."

Heat choked me as understanding sunk in. She wanted me to dance. All by myself. In front of everyone. In front of Daniel. I felt nauseous. This was not what I had planned. Yes, I wanted to know how to *siva* and yes I wanted to not look like an idiot up there, but I didn't want to be humiliated like this in front of the school. And especially not in front of a lethally glaring Mele, a gleefully leering Simone, and especially not in front of a boy I was in love with. Who was determined to be cold and distant. I tried to squirm out of it.

"Mrs. Lematua, I don't think that's a good idea, I mean, I'm new to this *siva* stuff and I really think someone else would be much better for this. I …"

Mrs. Lematua silenced me with one upraised hand. "Miss Folger, I know you're relatively new here but I'm surprised that you haven't learned already that when a teacher tells you to do something, you do it. Without arguing. We want to try different girls out for the *taupou* and it's your turn. So get up there." Without waiting for a reply, she turned to Daniel. "Daniel, the song please."

I was terrified, and, in my terror, I turned to the one thing that could give me strength. Pele. As the first strains of Daniel's song began to lilt through the air, I shut my eyes and felt for that now-familiar heat. In the ground beneath my bare feet. I called her softly. Gently. Asking for help. I thought of fire. The way it danced. Sparkled. The way it moved me. I let the song in Daniel's voice dance over me, let it tug gently at my hands, my feet. I felt a sweet warmth that did not come from the blazing sun but from the earth below and I welcomed it, allowed it to take over ever so slightly. It was deliciously dangerous. Playing with fire. Communing with Pele *without* allowing her to make me explode into flames. I let her power inspire and move my hands, my body, my entire dance was hers.

There was silence when the music ended. I bowed the way Nafanua had showed me and walked slowly back to the shade. I could feel Daniel's eyes on me as I found my way back to Simone.

Mrs. Lematua seemed disconcerted. "Okay, thank you Leila, thank you. Umm, well that's it for practice today people. We'll see you all back here tomorrow. Leila and Daniel can you stay behind for a moment please?"

Simone dug his fingers into my ribs, startling me. "Ha! See, you rocked, ohmigosh, I bet they're going to tell you that you're the *taupou* and Mele is going to KILL you!" Laughter gleamed in his eyes, wicked and delighted. I pushed him away.

"Oh whatever, doubt it. Besides, who said I want to be the *taupou* anyway?"

My sniff of disdain didn't fool him one bit. "Oh please, Leila, I can cut the connection between you and Daniel with a bush knife, I don't know who broke up with who but there's something going on there. I'll be waiting at the classroom. You promised to give me a ride today remember?" And with that he dashed off.

Mrs. Lematua was waiting for me with the other three house teachers. And Daniel. She got straight to the point. "Leila, we've chosen you to be the *taupou* this year. We know you're new and this is your first culture night, so we will expect you to put in a lot of practice and work closely with Daniel to get this item perfect."

She didn't wait for a reply but I tried anyway. "But, Miss, I …"

She turned impatiently. "What?"

All four teachers were staring at me. So was Daniel. The look in his eyes unreadable. Was he disgusted with this new development? Was he mad? Was he hating me even more? I couldn't tell. I swallowed nervously before replying. "I don't think I can do the *taupou* for the House performance. I don't know enough and I wouldn't do a good job. Please choose someone else?"

The other female teacher jumped in before Mrs. Lematua could answer. "Leila, you're a natural dancer, I don't think I've ever seen such grace before. You need to trust us on this one. Besides, we're doing something new this year and so we want someone new. Someone different from the usual. This performance is meant to be more than the usual *taupou siva*, it has to be a performance of the song, the story contained in the song." Her brow furrowed. "That's right, you can't speak Samoan, can you?"

I shook my head. She looked thoughtful for only a moment. "Ah, not a problem." She turned to the brooding young man beside her. "Daniel, you'll need to go over the lyrics with Leila, translate them for her, explain the legend associated with it and make sure she understands what she has to re-enact with her dance, alright?"

Daniel shrugged. What else could a Head Prefect of the school do? The teachers all looked relieved. Cheerful. "Right, that's settled then. We'll expect to see your practice tomorrow." With that they walked away to the staffroom, leaving Daniel and I alone under the tamarind tree. I was suddenly cold. The last time Daniel and I had stood alone under a tamarind tree, he had kissed me. And I had burst into flames. The memory had me steeling my resolve. *Be distant Leila, be cool, be aloof.* My tone was casual and collected.

"So Daniel, what time works for you? I'm sure we can get through this in half an hour tops. How's interval tomorrow?"

He shrugged and shook his head. "No. I've got a makeup test to do with Michaels."

"Oh, so what works then?"

"I can try for today, after final form period. But you better make it short because I've got work to do at the workshop. I'll stop by your classroom."

And with that brusque retort, he turned and walked back to the school block, leaving me alone with the breeze rifling through the tamarind trees.

The room had emptied by the time Daniel walked in. I was sitting at a desk, trying to concentrate on Math but so nervous that nothing was getting through. He paused in the doorway before greeting me and, for a moment, I was taken back to that day, only a few months before, when I had first seen him, when he had first walked into my life with sunlight catching on the red and gold glint of his hair, his smile."Hey."

"Hi."

He pulled up a chair opposite me, his broad frame making the desk between us seem very small. I managed a weak smile and prepared to take notes while he explained the dance to me but he didn't seem to be in a rush to get to our assignment.

"So, how have you been?"

"Good. And you?"

"Same." He took some papers out of his bag. "I wrote down the lyrics to the song for you." He paused. "You're different. You look different."

Instinctively my hand went up to smooth back my hair, fidget with my blouse collar. Was there something on my face? "What do you mean? How different?"

A shrug. "I don't know. Just different." He looked away from me, down at the ground and then his eyes widened in surprise. "Is that a *malu?*"

Edgily, I straightened and pulled at my skirt, trying to force it further down to cover more of my legs. "Um, yeah."

Daniel stared at me. There was shock in his voice. "You got a *malu* done? When? Why? I thought you said you would never get a tattoo?!"

"Yeah, I know. I kind of changed my mind…" He couldn't seem to take his eyes off my legs and I shifted uneasily in my seat.

"Who was the tattooist?"

"My mother and her sisters."

Now there was disbelief. "What?! You're kidding, right?"

"No. Nafanua prepared the inks and then her sisters worked on the designs. They did it in sections over three days."

He shook his head. " I've never heard of women giving the *malu*. And I'm not trying to be my sexist self here, okay? It's tradition here that all the tattooists in Samoa are men. As far as I know, anyway."

I had to smile at his speedy attempt to head off any attacks from my usually over-defensive self. He leaned in closer, eyes still trained on my legs. "I don't think I've ever seen a *malu* like yours before. Those patterns are unusual." There was soft concern in his eyes. "You said they did it over three days? How did you handle the pain?"

"It wasn't as bad as I thought it would be."

He looked up with a half-smile. "Really? I'm glad. I know you hated the thought of a tattoo. That day when we were talking about my tattoo, when..." He stopped short, words colliding into the memory of what other things had happened on that day.

Both of us looked away. Anywhere and everywhere except for at each other. Remembering the night we had kissed was a sweetly torturous thing. It was now or never. I knew I may never get the chance again. "Daniel, I wanted to thank you."

"For what?"

"For not telling anyone about me, about that fire thing." I looked nervously over my shoulder to make sure there was no one in earshot. "I really appreciate it."

He shrugged. "It wasn't my place to tell anyone. Besides, you asked me not to."

"A lot of other people would have loved to spread that kind of news around."

He interrupted shortly with a frown. "I'm not like other people. I wouldn't break that confidence. I wouldn't do that."

"I know that. I never thought you would. But, I just wanted you to know that I appreciate it."

"Sure. So, how's that going with you then? Has it happened again?"

I exhaled and gave him a wry smile. If he only knew. "A little bit. Nafanua's been helping me to deal with it. You know, control it."

"I've been worried about you." He spoke the words without any emotion. Their simplicity caught me unawares.

"Oh."

"I must have called you and texted you a hundred times. Nothing." Now there was a ragged tightness in his voice. "And I've driven up your road to your mom's place every other day, hoping to catch you. Nothing."

There was nothing to say. I stared at the desk, at the cuts and scratches of juvenile grafitti. He continued. "And then finally after a month, you show up back at school, acting like there's nothing wrong. Like we don't even know each other. And all of a sudden you're best buddies with Maleko?" There was disbelief in his voice. I looked up sharply.

"No Daniel, I had nothing to do with that. Honest. I got back to school and he's acting all weird and I have no idea why or where it's coming from. And then that day, they all basically forced themselves into my car. I wasn't even planning to go to the game."

He had a tired grin. "Yeah, well I guess Maleko can be pretty insistent when he puts his mind on something."

"I'm sorry. About that fight or whatever that was during the game. I'm not sure what that was about but I'm sorry anyway."

He shook his head lightly. "Nah, it was nothing. Me and Maleko go ways back. We've been butting heads for years. He was just mouthing off in the scrum and we both lost it a little. Coach has really twisted our ears for it, I can tell you. But him and me – we're fine."

"I'm glad. Maybe I shouldn't have yelled at him then "

"What do you mean?"

"Well, I was really mad at him for the whole sleazing onto me thing so I kind of yelled at him the next day and basically told him to keep a mile away from me – or I would make him regret living."

Daniel laughed at that. "And how's that warning working for you two?"

"Put it this way, he's barely said Boo in class since then. Actually

Ms. Sivani was asking him today if he was sick or something since he's been so subdued."

We laughed together. And it felt good. Like before. But then the laughter ended and we were left with uncomfortable silence again. Filled with unspoken questions. Daniel cleared his throat. "Leila, does it hurt? The fire? Does it hurt you?"

"What? Oh, that. It's kind of hard to describe. Yeah it hurts, especially when it first erupts, but it's kind of a good hurt? Does that even make sense?"

"Not really. Where does it come from? Why is it happening?"

I took a deep breath. Heavy in my mind was Nafanua's warning about keeping *telesā* secrets from men. Any men. These were the questions I had been dreading. The ones I had been rehearsing answers for over the past few weeks. Answers that still didn't even make sense to me.

"I'm not sure. I know it sounds unreal, but apparently it's got something to do with me being able to tap into the earth's core heat and fire. Like volcanoes and stuff. Nafanua's an ... expert on it and she's been helping me to understand it a bit better and control it. That's why I'm able to be back at school – because I kind of have a better handle on it now. There's still a lot we don't know though, I'm still afraid of what it, I mean what I can do if I let my guard down for even a moment." I stole a glance at him. "I haven't been able to stop thinking about that night when it first happened, what I did, what I almost did, how I nearly hurt you and all those people. I hate myself for that. Can you ever forgive me?"

He leaned forward and reached across the desk to take my hand in his. "There's nothing to forgive. It's not like you planned that to happen. It came out of nowhere, and besides, you stopped it, you called it back, you saved those people."

"Aha yeah right, from a fire that I started. And I only did it because ..." I trailed off, unwilling to say the words, afraid of what he would think of me. I pulled my hand away from his and resolutely clenched my fists in my lap.

"Because what?"

"I only called the fire back because you asked me to. Because you told me to. If you hadn't been there, things would have been very different. If you hadn't stopped me, that hostel would have burned to the ground and all those people would likely be dead. And I would have been celebrating the entire time, loving every destructive minute of it." His eyes flashed. "Leila that's not true. Don't say that. I know it's not true."

I stood abruptly, the chair grating loudly on the cement floor. "And just how do you know that Daniel? How well do you really know me anyway? You don't know where I've come from, what kind of family or mother I descend from, you don't know all the things that I've done. You don't know what I'm capable of. Your grandmother was right on the very first day. I'm no good for you. I have to go. This was a bad idea." I shook my head as I hurriedly packed up my books. The room suddenly felt stifling. Hot. I needed to get away from there, away from Daniel before I lost control. He stood as I started to back away from the desk.

"Leila, wait – don't go – please."

Sadness choked me as I looked at him. The concern. The pleading in his face. "I'm sorry Daniel, I have to." I reached over and took the paper of lyrics. "I'll read over this tonight and if I have any questions about it, I'll ask Nafanua to help me. Hey, it's not like we really need to work on it together – you'll play and sing your song and all I need to do is dance. We don't need to meet and practice together to get that right. I'll see you tomorrow."

Daniel didn't try to say anymore. He only stood and stared after me as I hurried out, breaking into a run when I caught sight of my car in the parking area. I was impatient to get home. I had emotions running riot and I wanted to erase them with flames.

By evening I was calm. I had spent the afternoon throwing fire balls at the rock wall of an abandoned quarry I had found on one of my many breathless runs through Nafanua's vast property. The quarry dated back to twenty years ago and was the perfect spot for practicing my aim. And for letting off steam. I had come back to the house more at peace with myself, ready for the delicious dinner Netta had prepared for us, ready to settle down to doing some homework. I was submersed in Calculus when Netta called from downstairs. "Leila, you have a visitor."

Puzzled, I came halfway down the stairs then stopped with a grin when I saw who was waiting for me in Nafanua's living room. Rumpled blonde hair, blue eyes, sun-burned face...

"Jason. Hey! What are you doing here?"

Nafanua gently chided me. "Leila, is that any way to greet a guest?" I hadn't seen her sitting there at her writing desk and winced.

Jason smiled with open ease. "Sorry for dropping in like this, but I didn't get your cell number and I was in the neighborhood so I thought I'd stop by. Hope I'm not intruding?" All three of us knew how ridiculous that was as we stood in a house that stood alone amidst acres of forest. Nafanua arched an eyebrow and a knowing smile danced at the edge of her lips.

"Nonsense Professor, we are always delighted to see you. Leila was studying but I'm sure she would like to take a break. I was just going out to the lab. Please stay and visit for a while."

I narrowed my eyes at her but I wasn't annoyed. Quite the opposite. Calculus was not my forte and hanging out with Jason ranked light years higher on my list of things to do. We both waited as she exited. He spoke first. "So, I wanted to tell you that Matavanu has calmed down a bit and you can come visit anytime." I saw uncertainty flash on his face for the first time "that is if you're still interested in a volcano?"

I grinned. "Of course I am. I barely got a chance to see anything the other day, you rushed me out of there so fast. What's been happening up there?"

"Not much. That day was pretty much the bad temper highlight of our whole study so far. You sure picked the wrong day to visit."

I hid a knowing smile, I knew why Matavanu had heated up and the secret warmed me.

We went through to the kitchen. Math always made me ravenous and I knew Netta had coconut cookies hidden in the cupboard somewhere.

"Aha! Bingo, hungry?"

"Definitely. Are those homemade?" He took a bite. "Mmmm these are delicious, we don't get much decent food up at the camp, pretty much living on canned tuna and crackers for the last few months."

I took pity on him and brought out the rest of the dinner Netta had made earlier. Fresh river shrimps baked in coconut cream with a touch of curry, green bananas, roasted pumpkin and eggplant with sprigs of mint, a chilled bowl of fruit salad.

Jason protested, laughing with hands upraised. "Whoa, how much food do you think I need? Wow." He surveyed the dishes spread out on the table. "You ladies eat like this every night?"

I was busy expertly zapping a plate generously heaped with dinner in the microwave as he pulled up a seat at the bench top."Oh yeah, Netta does the cooking and I think she forgets we're not a household crawling with twenty million extended family. You should see what she made last night – baked ginger fish ... hmm ... some of that should be still in here too, let me see."

Within minutes I had Jason set up with enough food to feed a small army and he was digging in with great enthusiasm. I sat and watched, nibbling on coconut cookies, laughing as he attacked the shrimps, licking his fingers. "You should come over every night, we always have tons of leftovers and its terribly wasteful all the food that sits around in this house." Inwardly, I winced as I realized how the invitation sounded and I hurried to qualify it. "In fact there's probably enough food here for your whole team, where are the others anyway? And what are you doing here on Upolu?"

"They're all back at the camp. I came over this morning to do our grocery shopping and uplift some gear that came on the boat for us, then I went surfing and kinda missed the ferry back."

His cheeky grin had me guessing that the missed boat had been deliberate."Surfing? Where do you do that?"

"Oh there's some good spots out on the south coast, my favorite is just past Salani Surf Resort, caught some sweet barrels today. Do you surf?"

"Who me? No. Never tried it. Back home we lived in Maryland so not much surfing opps there. And then here, I've never been to the beach here."

He looked horrified. "What!? That's just sinful. How could you be on an island and *not* get to the beach yet?"

I laughed at his shock. "Well, I've only been in Samoa for a few months you know and I've been kinda busy with a new school and stuff.

Besides, when I first moved here I stayed with my aunt and uncle and they were intensely strict. They didn't want me going anywhere."

He frowned. "That must have been rough."

I shook my head. "No, it was okay, they were just worried about me. They were really sweet actually." As I rushed to defend them, a pang of sadness cut me as I realized that I missed them. I resolved to go visit them this weekend and smiled as I thought about Aunty Matile's grouchy face and how she would struggle not to smile if I gave her a hug.

Jason helped himself to some more shrimps. "These are really good. I don't know how you can have such a hot body when you're eating all this stuff every day." He continued on talking about his afternoon but I was momentarily disconcerted by his reference to my figure. Nobody had ever commented on my looks in such blunt terms and I wasn't sure whether to be pleased or annoyed. But as he rattled on about food, surfing, and more surfing, I shook off the moment as I realized he hadn't been making a play for me. I was fast realizing this man had nothing to hide, he was straight forward and up front. He said what he thought and didn't stop to analyze it first. There were no secret agendas.

"So you wanna try it?"

"Try what?"

He looked exasperated. "Leila don't be ditzy. Have you been paying attention to anything I've been saying? Surfing, do you wanna try it?" I had to smile at his eager expression.

"Okay, I'd love to." I couldn't resist the dig. "But are you sure you're qualified to be my teacher? I mean, you being such a bimbo and all and not to mention you're kinda old to be standing up on a board in the middle of the ocean aren't you?"

He narrowed his eyes and got up to clear away his empty plate. "Little girl, you are soooo going to regret that." He spread his arms out expansively. "I'll have you know that you're looking at the two time surf champion of Rosewood Beach Surf Club. Standing right here in your kitchen eating leftovers!"

I was impressed. "Wow, okay that's impressive. What's the Rosewood Beach Surf Club?"

He grinned the cheeky grin that seemed to be his trademark.

It always seemed to tug an answering smile from me whether I wanted it to or not. "Actually, the club is made up of a grand total of six of my buddies – all at the science faculty – that surf in our spare time. So the term 'champion' is kinda relative but I'm still a surf champ and I have the two beer can trophies to prove it!" He struck a surfing pose on a dining table chair and had me laughing. Again.

"Okay, okay, I'm convinced, I shall take surf lessons from a master and be extremely humbled with the opportunity and I shall pay you with Netta's dinner leftovers. Anytime you're in town, you will have to come by and get fed."

With that settled, Jason proceeded to clean up his mess before plonking himself down on the sofa."So what homework were you slaving over before I got here?"

I rolled my eyes. "Calculus. A mild nightmare for me, especially since the Math teacher is quite horrible."

"Want me to give you a hand? I'm not too bad at Math. I had to do a little bit here and there – you know, while I was finishing my advanced science program and being the youngest person ever to graduate with a PhD in geophysics from my university." He sighed with exaggerated modesty and adopted a bored expression.

I had to laugh. "Okay, you've convinced me. Let me go grab my stuff from upstairs. I'll be right back."

The next hour flew by as Jason went through the Calculus problems with me. He was a good teacher who managed to make the most complex equations simple. It was going on 10:30 when we finished. Jason stretched out wide, "All done! I guess I better get going. I didn't mean to bother you so late."

I had a pang of disappointment at the thought of him leaving. The time had gone by so fast and without a single reminder that I was a *telesā* walking on the edge of fire at every moment. I didn't want the evening to end. Suddenly, the house seemed constricting. If Jason hadn't been there, I would have gone for a flame-driven run through the forest but instead, the thought of swimming in a moonlit ocean sounded just as appealing. I stopped him on the way to the front door."I know, why don't we go now?"

He was confused. "Go where?"

"Surfing. Let's go now. Can we do that?"

He shrugged. "Well yeah, we can, but it's late. What will your mom say?"

I was up and lightly running up the stairs before the words were even all out of his mouth. I threw back a flippant reply over my shoulder. "Oh, she doesn't care what I do. I'll text her. We could have wild sex upstairs and it wouldn't bother her. Let me just grab my stuff." It was too late to take back the thoughtless words or to check even how he had taken them but with a rush of excitement, I didn't care. I was thrilled to be getting out. The spur of the moment mood reminded me of my dad and I deciding what road trip to take on a long weekend. I couldn't wait to get out into the night.

I wriggled into the two-piece suit Nafanua had bought me that I had never even bothered to try on and threw a cotton tee and shorts over it. A towel and jandals and I was ready, fingers sending a quick text to Nafanua. *Goin surfin w/Jason.* I was back downstairs when the reply beeped through. *Hav fun.* I was triumphant as I showed it to Jason. "See! What did I tell you. She's not bugged. Come on, let's go. Bye Neafanua!" I yelled out to the quiet house.

Still somewhat bemused, Jason followed me to the red truck. A board glistened in the back cab. "So your mom just lets you go wherever? Whenever? I don't know much about Samoa but I'm pretty sure that's kinda unusual for a Samoan parent?"

I smiled at him in the dark interior of the truck as we drove down the long flame tree-lined drive. "Nafanua's not a regular Samoan mother. And I'm not a regular Samoan daughter. Remember we didn't even know each other until a little while ago. Besides, I'm eighteen and used to doing my own thing. Even when my dad was alive, I was on my own a lot while he travelled for work." I didn't want to dwell on the sadness of the past, not on this most thrilling of moonlit nights. "So how long does it take to get to Siumu?"

"About half an hour." Jason was still unwilling to let my mother-daughter relationship go. "So how come you two didn't know each other anyway?"

Quickly, I briefed him on the bare necessities of information about Nafanua and I, leaving out, of course, the bits about *telesā* and the small detail of my propensity to burst into flame when I got mad. Or when a boy kissed me. The drive to Siumu was fun. I pestered Jason for details about his volcano work and about his background. He was one of six children in his family and I was intrigued by his stories about what life was like when you were never alone. Always squabbling. Sharing a room. A car. Sharing clothes. Sharing a mom and a dad. It sounded heavenly and I sighed the sigh of an only child when they compare the cheerful madness of a crowded household with their own solitary upbringing.

It was 11:30 when we got to the beach, bumping down a rough sandy track through breathing forest. We came out to sand painted white in the moonlight and an ocean shimmering with black diamonds. Jason tugged his shirt over his head before lifting the surfboard out of the truck. His toned physique didn't fit my stereotypical image of a scientist and I tried not to let my surprised eyes linger on the rugged arms with their tan line, or the way the contours of his chest looked in the moonlight.

Suddenly I was self-conscious. Up to this point I had seen him just as a funny, easy-to-be-with boy, kind of the way I imagined an older brother would be. But, as I watched him walk easily down to the water's edge and into the gentle swells, I saw him for what he really was. A twenty-five-year-old man, Professor of Tectonic Science, leader of a team expedition, and disturbingly striking to look at in the ocean light.

I gritted my teeth. *Ugh.* This feeling was not one I wanted. I liked being relaxed and laid back with Jason. I wanted him to stay locked in the 'big-brother' zone. *Relax Leila – so he's kinda cute and sporting a rather hot body, so what. He can be your super-hot, older man, best buddy.* Determinedly, I pulled off my t-shirt and ran to join him in the water. It was surprisingly cool, "Yikes! It's cold."

Jason laughed as he began swimming through the deeper water. "No it's not. Don't be a wuss. Okay, get over here and let's get you started with your first lesson."

An hour later I had learned several things I didn't know before. Surfing was really hard. Standing up on a board that is determined to slip away from under you is kind of scary. And falling down in water starts to hurt when you get to the twentieth time. Oh, and having a surf tutor who insists on laughing at you every time you fall over is *really* annoying.

"Would you quit it?"

"Quit what?" Artificial innocence.

"That! Laughing. Teasing me. I'm sure I would do heaps better if you weren't making fun of me the whole time. " I was getting more sour by the minute. "You know, if a student totally sucks then they usually hold the teacher responsible."

He paused beside me in the black water and regarded me speculatively, as if gauging the magnitude of my mood. I scowled while he grinned hugely and nudged my shoulder. "Come on Leila, don't be so grumpy, everybody falls off on their first try and I can't help laughing. You should see yourself up there. You get this psycho serious look on your face and then it changes to complete panic just before you fall off. And when you come up out of the water, you're so mad. It's really cute. Come on, relax, why do you have to be so intense about everything? Can't you just have fun with it?"

I fought to stay mad and failed. "Cute huh?"

Jason smiled and his brilliant blue eyes demanded a response. "Yeah. In a freakishly psycho sort of way."

I relented and let an answering smile break free. "Okay, let's do it again."

The lesson continued and after another ten minutes and three more faulty, wavering tries, I was able to stay standing up long enough for the board to actually move along with a small wave for a few feet. I let out a shout. "Yes! Woohoo!"

Right before the damn thing slipped out from under me and I was down, only, this time as I went under the water, something hard slammed the side of my head. I tried to say 'ouch,' only to suck in a huge gulp of seawater. Flailing and spluttering, there was an instant of panic before Jason's hands gripped my arms and pulled me up. Through my coughing, I could hear the worry in his voice, "Hey, are you okay? Leila?"

I wiped the salt out of my eyes and looked at him ruefully. "Yeah, but my head doesn't feel so good. I think the board may have hit me when I went down." I gingerly reached up to feel my temple. "Ow."

Jason still had a firm hold on me and, without hesitation, he started towing me back in to shore, pulling the board. "Come on, let's get you up to the beach, I think that's enough surfing for one night."

We sank onto the sand and my wobbly legs were feeling the effects of an hour of trying to balance on the board. Jason sat beside me and together we caught our breath. He turned to peer closely at my forehead. "Let me see, hmm, yeah you have a bump there but it doesn't look too bad. It didn't break the skin or anything. You'll be fine."

Our shoulders were touching, his fingers were gentle on my head and I could taste the closeness of him in the slight breeze. Droplets of ocean beaded his chest, catching fire in the moonlight. He glistened with silver wetness and I had to force my gaze somewhere else. "Oh, so you're a doctor now are you?"

He laughed his ever-present laugh and dusted sand from his hands. "Well hello, I do have a PhD, which basically qualifies me to have a super intelligent opinion on everything. Seriously though, are you feeling okay?"

I hastened to reassure him. "Yeah, I'm fine. But I'm tired; I had no idea surfing was so much work, well, trying to surf anyway!"

"Hey you didn't do too badly. Next time I bet you'll only fall down fifty times instead of a hundred."

I slugged him lightly on the shoulder as we slowly made our way back to the truck. I was tired but it was a good tiredness. Every muscle ached but, for the last two hours, I had been more relaxed and free than I had felt in a long time. I struggled to keep my eyes open on the drive home and was startled awake when the truck growled to a stop outside the big white house. Lights still gleamed in the living room. Jason walked me up to the door.

"Thanks, I had a good time."

"Even with a tormenting, teasing teacher?"

I gave him an answering grin, pausing in the doorway. "Yeah. I don't know if I would nominate you as instructor of the year, but I guess you'll do."

"So do you want another lesson tomorrow night?"

I smiled, "Don't you have to go back to Matavanu tomorrow?"

A shrug, "Yeah, but I can come back on the last boat. And you can feed me some more of Netta's amazing leftovers and then have your second lesson."

"Okay, I'd like that. Let's do it."

He ran lightly down the steps to the car, pausing to turn back once more. "Hey, don't forget to put some ice on that bump, just in case." And with that final reminder, he was in the truck and taking off down the drive.

The weekend turned out to be one of the best I'd had since moving to Samoa. In the morning, Nafanua and the sisterhood took me with them to a massive forest fire that was raging out of control on the other side of the island. Every fire-fighting team on the island was there, struggling to contain the blaze that had consumed over a hundred acres of forest. We drove to a section of the fire where there were no witnesses and took a two-pronged approach to the battle. Nafanua and Sarona summoned rain while Manuia and the others used wind to try and redirect the movement of the flames. There was no way I could control such a huge mass of energy but slowly and steadily I worked alongside the others to channel and subdue various sections of the fire. It took most of the day before the fire was under control and we could slip away and leave the rest to the firefighters. I was exhausted but exultant. It had felt amazing to use my gift to help. For good. As we celebrated back at the house with chilled lemonade and sandwiches, I looked around at the other *telesā* and felt happy to be one with them. Today was a good day to be a *telesā*.

That night, Jason took me for another surf lesson and, this time, I was almost able to understand the thrill of it as I spent more time standing up then falling down. We didn't get back to the house until two in the morning and both of us were buzzed with my progress.

"That was awesome, Leila. Pretty soon you're going to be able to tackle the serious surf with me."

I gave him a huge smile, even as I disagreed with him, "No way, I think I'll be needing quite a few more lessons, thank you very much."

He paused on the verandah and replied, "No problem. I'll give you as many lessons as you like." He gave me a brief hug before running lightly back down to the truck. I hated to see him go. He was like a piece of 'home' – the America that used to be when my dad was alive in it. And no matter how much time I spent with the sisterhood, I could never shake the slight edge of unease that I felt with them. On the outside they smiled and told me I was one of them, one of their 'sisters' but I couldn't deny that deep inside, I was still afraid of them.

I called out to him, "Hey Jase, you wanna hang out tomorrow?" He smiled back, "Sure. Hey, how about I give you a tour, a drive round the island? I bet there are lots of places in your Samoa that you've never even heard of."

"I can't argue with that, seeing as how I've been like, nowhere. You're on."

And just like that, a glorious Sunday out with Jason was guaranteed. We visited three different waterfalls, stopped for lunch at a gorgeous little restaurant at a place called Taufua Beach Fales at Lalomanu, and then went snorkeling at a marine reserve close to town, Palolo Deep. I spent a whole day without remembering once that I was an (often unwilling) member of a *telesā* Covenant. That I couldn't be with a boy called Daniel, who I loved as much as I needed air. It was a perfect day, which ended with Jason's invitation to Matavanu. Monday was a public holiday and so it was an invitation I accepted eagerly.

I was still smiling when I went in the house and Nafanua remarked, "Well, I guess I don't need to ask how your day went. Looks like you had a lot of fun."

I nodded, "Yeah, and tomorrow Jason's taking me back to Matavanu. He's promised me that this time he'll take me down into the cone for a closer look, so it should be awesome."

Nafanua looked concerned. "Leila, you will be careful? Pele is unpredictable at best and in that close proximity, your control could be sorely tested. Especially if you and Jason engage in physical intimacy."

I blanched at her matter-of-fact reference to the possibility of 'physical intimacy'. "Excuse me? You've got it all wrong. Me and Jase aren't like that. We're friends. There's nothing like that going on."

She looked taken aback. "And why not?"

"What do you mean?"

" He's a very attractive man. And he does seem to be quite entranced with you."

No adult had ever discussed my 'lovelife' with me before. (Which wasn't surprising since I'd never had the remotest possibility of having one.) Embarassment squirmed inside me like red hot millipedes and I rushed to escape it. "Because, like I said, we're just friends. Besides, he's old."

Nafanua had to laugh at that one. "Leila, you're talking to a woman who's over one hundred years old. A twenty-five-year-old man is nothing but a child."

I grimaced at the unwanted reminder of her *telesā*-induced longevity. "Okay, if you put it like that. Look, the point is that I don't like him that way and he doesn't like me that way and we're cool just the way we are. So there's no big deal here. Now, I'm going to bed."

She did not reply until I was almost to the door of my bedroom. "Whatever you say, Leila. Just remember to be careful around Matavanu."

TWELVE

It was an overcast day the next morning and rain was threatening as Jason and I took to the sky in the chopper. The rest of the team were in town for the long weekend so it would be just the two of us at the camp. I remembered Nafanua's warning and did an internal 'sweep' to check on my heat levels before we got off the helicopter. Rain was lashing at us as the pilot took off again, leaving me and Jason to make a wild dash for the tents some distance away.

"Whew! What a day to visit. I hope the wind doesn't pick up or else the chopper won't be able to come back for us." Jason looked worriedly out at the boiling sky but I was more interested in our excursion.

The rain had stopped by the time we started ascent. The hike to the peak was a demanding one. The terrain was steep and the loose soil kept sliding in places. But the climb was well worth it. Standing at the brim of Matavanu was like looking down over a massive steaming cauldron of fiery energy that had been covered in a flimsy sheet of grey rock. Here and there were cracks in the ground through which seams of red peered. Behind us, the horizon beckoned in the distance and a tugging wind had my hair blowing in every direction. It was breathtaking.

I turned to Jason, "Can we get any closer?"

"We could, but it's kind of a tricky descent." He was hesitant.

"Please Jason? I'll be careful, just a bit closer?" He gave in to my pleading tone.

"Okay, but stay close behind me and just try to step only where I do okay?"

I nodded eagerly and together we started inching our way down a rough track. The heat hit us in waves and Jason's shirt was soaked in sweat, his face red, as he turned back to check on my progress.

"You alright? Just a bit further, see that flat section there?" He pointed to a piece of rock about fifty feet away. I nodded. "That's about as close as it's safe to get. We usually set up the instruments there. Any further than that the ground gets kind of thin."

We continued towards the section, with Jason reaching back to steady me as we gingerly stepped over cracks and fragmented chunks. Once there, a rush of heat enveloped us. I watched while Jason knelt to check the readings on the little steel box attached to a metal prod.

When it happened, it happened fast. I felt a rush of heat that came not from the volcano we were standing on, but from deep inside my chest. It caught me off guard, and my first instinct was one of pleasure. Welcoming a friend. Before I could wrap it securely in cotton wool control like I usually did, there was an answering surge of heat from beneath my feet. The seam beside us glowed red, and Jason jumped back. "Whoa! Watch it, Leila!"

The words were barely out of his mouth before the crack split wider and bubbled over with red. I shouted a warning, but Jason had already seen it. He turned and half grabbed me in his arms, trying to rush me up the cone slope. "Go! Go! Leila, we have to get out of here."

We took three, four steps, and there was a groaning hissing sound. The ground beneath us, that had seemed dead a moment before, was now a mass of rivulets that steamed and glowed. The earth was shaking. Jason shouted. "Leila, get out of here!" He pushed me with an almighty shove and I fell forward on the side of the rocky face, scraping my arms and face on the ground. I turned back in time to see the ground split open, and Jason and I were separated by a mini river of lava. He staggered for balance on his piece of rocky island that now seemed to be moving underneath him.

I screamed. "Jason!"

He turned wild eyes towards me, "Leila, I said get out of here. Go on, now." – before he fell backwards. The side of his head cracked against rock, and he was still. I screamed again and stood. My heart was pounding, and air was fighting to find its place in my chest. I was shaking and, as I shook, the earth shook again. Jason wasn't moving. Blood seeped from his forehead, and red lava was oozing closer towards his shoes.

In the panic, I heard Nafanua's voice. *Control, Leila. Control. The fire will not listen to panic and fear. Reassure it. Comfort it. Speak to the earth and tell her to be calm. Tell her everything is alright. You are alright.* I struggled to calm the ragged breathing, the pounding chest. *Think Leila, think.* There was about six feet of boiling mud and lava separating me from Jason. He wasn't moving, and lava had reached the edge of his shoe. The acrid smell of burning rubber stung the air. What was I going to do? What could I do? I had never 'spoken' to lava before. Never moved earth before. I was afraid and, when I was afraid, fire threatened. No. We needed no more fire right now. I needed control. Calm. I needed to be calm. I took a deep breath and focused. On lava. And earth. Fire. I needed a pathway through the lava if I was going to get to Jason. I focused on what I wanted, visualizing a chasm opening in the lava river, the way Nafanua had taught me. It was like she was right there with me, I heard her voice in my mind, *remember Leila, you are the mistress of earth. She will listen to you. But you need to be clear about what you want her to do. Visualize what needs to happen and it will.*

Hoping against hope that it would work, I held my trembling hands out over the bubbling fire rock and gestured widely for it to part. And like Moses and the Red Sea, it did. Just like that. I caught my breath excitedly, *yes.* But this wasn't the time to be high-fiving myself and my amazingness. I ran over hot earth to kneel beside Jason and shook his shoulder, "Jason, wake up. We have to get out of here. Jason!"

He groaned in response and brought one hand up to his head. "Ow, damn that hurts." He looked in my eyes and then around to the lava that bubbled, wincing with the effort, and alarm lit up his eyes. "Leila, I told you to get out of here, what the hell?" He tried to sit up and sank back down again with a groan, closing his eyes. His head was bleeding from a wicked-looking gash but he made another effort to sit up.

I slid an arm under his and helped him to stand. "Easy now, hold onto me, I've got you. Can you hear me? Are you okay?" He had his hand over his eyes because of the heat, and his shirt was soaked with sweat. He half stood and then keeled over again, coughing and spluttering, gasping for air. It wasn't until then that I realized the heat in the air was making it almost impossible for him to breathe, whereas I, of course, hadn't even noticed it.

Damnit. I don't think he's going to be much help. I braced myself and took another deep breath. I was going to try something I had never done before, ask for earth's energy and power *without* exploding into flames, I closed my eyes again and visualized the stored energy of earth flowing through me, giving me strength but appealing to the reactor that was my inner core *not* to light up. Unsure if it was working, I knelt again, firmly grasped Jason and half lifted him onto my shoulders, like a sack of potatoes. My knees buckled under his weight but I gritted my teeth and got tough with Matavanu. *Listen to me! I need strength, I need power – give it up NOW!* Her reply was immediate.

Another furnace of steam and lava blew to my right but, at the same time, a rush of exhilaration swept through me. Matavanu was mad, but she was going to do as she was told. I straightened and now Jason felt like a featherweight. With nimble feet I lightly ran across the divide in the lava and started up the side of the cone. I could hear Jason's gasping breaths but still he hung limply as I cautiously made my way over loose rock and shifting soil while, behind us, Matavanu continued with her grumbling and complaining. It should have been impossible to carry a six foot blonde surfer up a steep hillside, but I reached the level outer rim barely winded. My heart was racing though, with worry for the man who was silent and unresponsive. At the rim, I carefully lay him down on the tufted grass, peering into his face for some indication of his condition. The gash was an ugly reminder of what had just happened but the blood was drying and, as I anxiously shook his shoulder, he stirred and his eyes opened.

"Oh Jason, thank goodness. I was so afraid, are you okay?"

Before he could answer, I heard a loud rumble from the volcano crater behind us, reminding me that Matavanu and I had not finished our conversation. *No!* I spun away from Jason and ran back to stand at the crater edge, looking down at a spectacle that had my heart quickening and excitement leaping in the pit of my stomach. The pit of lava had widened still further and red and gold was pumping out of the depths like sinuous silk. Smoke was billowing skyward and further cracks were seaming all over the once-dead crater floor. Matavanu was waking up. I was entranced. I could feel the joy in every fiber of my body as the long-sleeping volcano lazily stretched and unfolded. Suddenly, nothing else mattered. As Matavanu awoke, I realized I had been only half alive until this moment. Everything else dissolved into meaninglessness. Everything. Daniel, *telesā*, Nafanua, Jason, my life before this – it was nothing. The words of a favorite song spoke to my heart.

Suddenly the world seems such a perfect place. Suddenly it moves with such a perfect grace. Suddenly my life doesn't seem such a waste. It all revolves around you ...

Without thought, I reached out – with my hands, my heart, with all my might, mind, and strength. The fire began at my fingertips and danced along my wrists, to elbow, to shoulder. I could see Matavanu in my mind's eye, opening, reaching out to me, welcoming me, and then together we could run wild over this place, out over green forest, down to the white sands and blue ocean. Even that could not stop us. We could rage and boil, over the water, building new earth. More fire. We could burn and never stop.

My thoughts came to an abrupt halt. Burn and never stop? No. That's not what I wanted. I remembered the fire at Samoa College field. I remembered Daniel refusing to run from the inferno, asking me to call the fire back. I remembered the dead fish floating in a bubbling pool. The boy with a scarred face. No. That's not what I wanted. Clear and piercing, I heard Nafanua's voice in my mind. *You are in control. You are telesa.* Matavanu was dominating this conversation and I needed to get back in control. No. There would be no volcanoes erupting today, thank you very much!

Shaking my head with a rueful grimace, I focused and clearly visualized what I wanted Matavanu to do. *We will be still. We will sleep.* She didn't want to obey. She had been locked up for a generation after all and wanted time out – to dance, to run, to play. I shook my head with a smile. *No Matavanu. Not today.* For added emphasis, I summoned a swirling fire ball and sent it hurtling down to the lava-filled cone, before mentally reaching out to the rocks and earth on each side of the sloped shaft. Gently, they responded and a wall of earth slid down into the cone. In less time than it took to utter the words, the river of red was a blanket of earth and only seams of orange glowed, like the mutterings of a resentful child. Already, the air about me was retaining its mountain coolness and a slight breeze danced through my hair as I smiled a huge smile of relief. Happiness. And turned back – to see Jason sitting in an upright position, and staring at me with shock and horror in his eyes.

Oh shit ...

Cringing under his gaze, I threw one more glance over my shoulder to ensure that Matavanu really was asleep before I squared my shoulders and strode to meet Jason. Wishing deep inside that I only had a fiery volcano to deal with.

"Hey, are you okay? That was a pretty bad bang on your head there." my attempts at casual died away as Jason only met my approach with an incredulous gaze. I knelt down beside him where he sat on the grass, holding one hand to his head. "Jase, say something, please? So I'll know that bang on your head didn't mess up your brain. Jason?"

"What was that?"

I tried for defensive offensive. "What? Nothing! What's the matter with you, we just narrowly escaped with our lives – you should be on top of the world right now."

He only shook his head at me. "Leila, what's going on? What was that?"

I looked in his blue eyes – eyes that had danced with mine after I had pulled him into a swimming pool. Eyes that had laughed with me when I fell off a surfboard for the hundredth time. Eyes that had shown only concern for me when the ground split open and he had tried to push me to safety. I sighed. I couldn't lie to him. I took a deep breath before rushing into an explanation, hoping he wouldn't think I was crazy.

"Umm, that was me. I guess. I can kind of do stuff, with fire. And volcanoes and stuff."

I waited for the horror and the disgust, but all I saw was quiet puzzlement in his eyes. "Go on, what stuff? What do you mean?"

I shook my head, "No, I need to get you back to the camp first, then I promise I'll tell you everything. You're hurt and this is not exactly the most comfortable place to be. Come on."

He didn't fight me as I carefully helped him stand and together we slowly made our way back down to the campsite. It was eerily quiet and normal, considering what had almost just happened. I sent a silent prayer of thanks that it had been only me and Jason on Matavanu today.

I don't know how I could have handled hiding my secret from the entire science team. Jason seemed to grow stronger with every step and, by the time we reached the shade of the tent, he was walking completely unaided. I rifled through their first aid cabinet for a bandage for his head, first cleaning the wound with some bottled water and savlon. He insisted I pay the same attention to the cuts and scrapes on my hands and knees. Once we were both cleaned up, we sat for a quiet minute and had a cold drink from the cooler before he once again turned expectant eyes on me. "Well?"

Another deep breath and it all came tumbling out. About me and Nafanua. And *telesā*. And burning things even when I didn't want to. And my training and how I was starting to get some measure of control over these new-found powers but they still alternately terrified me and entranced me. I told him how I had felt when I first came to Matavanu, and how she wanted to break and run free. It actually felt good to be able to talk about it, to release all the secrets, the caged fears and worries. I even admitted that I was afraid of Nafanua and her sisters – but I knew that I needed her and her teaching or else there was no telling what this power would do.

And when I was done, he responded like a good scientist would. He asked question after question. He wanted to know first of all, if I was alright. Was I burnt anywhere? Did the fire ever burn me? Once he was sure I was telling him the truth, that I really was okay, then he moved on to more technical queries. How long had this been happening? What elements would trigger the fire? What would control it? He got a notebook and started writing as I talked. I told him about the first time – about fear and anger. I hung my head in shame as I described the way fire had hissed and spat, burning the boy's face. His face darkened and my heart sank and I hoped that he would still want be friends with me, now that he knew I could hurt people.

I paused and Jason leapt into the gap. "I can't believe that little shit did that to you. I'm sorry to say this, Leila, but he deserved what he got. Hopefully he won't go around picking on women any more."

Relieved, I continued with a summary of the last month. I skipped over the parts about Daniel, telling Jason only that I had first exploded into flames after I had gone running. He stopped me.

"Wait, so let me get this straight, you went for a run and then exploded? Hmm … so overheating is another trigger. That's not good.

Go on." He scribbled some more and looked up expectantly. "What else?"

I felt deceitful for leaving out essential pieces but forged on. Jason wanted to know specifics about me and Matavanu. "Tell me step by step, what happened today? How did it start?"

He was shaking his head as I tried to explain how Matavanu felt, that she was speaking to me. Another interruption. "Leila, that's not possible. A volcano speaking to you? Are you sure? Can you describe what made you think that? As detailed as possible please. What did it feel like?"

I couldn't stop the smile as I recalled the feeling. Of welcome. Of homecoming. Of knowing. "It was like something had been missing inside me, something essential. And then I felt a heat and it was like an emptiness, was filled. And she was happy. Matavanu was happy that I was here. Like she had been waiting for me. And Jason, she's tired of sleeping. She's tired of being caged up. She's due to erupt. You know that, don't you?" I was anxious, hoping he would believe me.

He sighed and put the pen down, putting his hands to his forehead, wincing slightly as he touched the bandage. "Yeah, I know. Well, we suspected as much. All the measurements lead to that conclusion. We didn't think it was imminent though. And we still don't have enough info to figure out just how big the eruption is going to be. We're trying to gauge it, trying to get all the data together before we start informing the necessary authorities. There will need to be an evacuation organized but I'm just not sure how extensive it should be." He looked at me with a question on his face. "Leila, what you did today, moving the earth and closing that rift back up – how did you do that?"

I shook my head, looking at my hands. "Jason, I have no idea. I mean, Nafanua has told me that *earth telesā* like me can generate earthquakes, but she never said anything about *how*. I suspect, because she doesn't know. We've mainly just focused on techniques to control the fire bursts – they've been the more worrisome, more dangerous thing. Today, I kind of used the same method for controlling fire that Nafanua taught me. Focus, visualize what you want the fire – or in this case – the earth, to do and then feel it happen. And it listened. I gotta admit I was a little surprised that it worked. Matavanu didn't want to listen. She liked being out. I had to tell her twice."

Jason grimaced at my explanation. "Hmm, yeah okay, so we're back to talking about Matavanu like it's alive."

"But she is, Jason. She speaks to me, and, even though she fought me a little, she listens to me! You saw what I did today, why is it so hard to believe?" I was getting a little annoyed. "Look, I'll show you. You were knocked out so you missed this part." I stood and stripped off my now-dirty cotton t-shirt. His eyes widened in confusion.

"Leila, what are you doing?"

"Oh, turn around. Just look somewhere else for a minute. Go on. Turn around!" My eyes were blazing and Jason raised both hands in supplication.

"Fine, fine. Whatever! I'm turning around." He swung around on his stool, still muttering under his breath about the wackiness of women. I unhooked my bra and dropped it on the ground beside my top, quickly unzipped my jeans and wriggled out of them. I looked around for a covering of some kind, saw a towel bunched up on a camp bed and hastily wrapped it around me before walking a few feet out of the tent.

"You can look now."

Jason turned and lifted an eyebrow at my new attire. "Hmm okay, so what am I supposed to be looking at? I've seen you in a towel before Leila and while it is gorgeous on you, it's not really blowing my mind with scientific mystery or anything."

I gritted my teeth "Oh just shut up, Jason. I want to be able to save my clothes for after."

"For after what?"

"This." I raised my arms to the sky and before his jaw even had time to gape, nakedness was transformed into an incendiary inferno. Because Matavanu was so close, because she was so volatile right now, the explosion was a little more dramatic than I had intended. A wave of heat flashed through the surrounding air, igniting several small bushes behind me. It had Jason jumping to his feet and staggering backwards, a hand shielding his face from the jeweled conflagration.

"What the … ?" he shouted. "Leila!" he looked around wildly, grabbed a sleeping bag and made as if to run towards me. I held up a warning hand.

304 Lani Wendt Young

"No, Jason, don't come near me. I'm okay. It's me in here. I'm okay."

I turned slightly and beckoned to the wayward flames in the low brush and grass around me, gathering them back to me, containing the fire to only the spot where I stood. Jason's tortured voice called to me. "Leila? You're on fire. This can't be happening. You're on fire and you're telling me you're okay. This is *not* happening. This is *not* real!"

I sighed. Clearly, this was going to be harder than I thought. I rolled my eyes. Scientists sure were slow to process when confronted with unexplained 'unscientific' phenomena! I held my hands out and spoke slowly and clearly. "Jason, it's me. This is what I was telling you about. *Fanua afi*. Earth fire. This is my power. I can tap into the earth's stored, potential energy and convert it to heat and light. That's not all, I can sense out subterranean lava and magma rivers, trapped heat and manipulate it. I haven't figured out all the hows, the whys and whats of this, but this is me. In a nutshell. I can self-ignite. And not get burned."

Jason took several faltering steps out of the tent, still shaking his head, still with that slight panicked look in his eyes. "Leila, I … I don't know what to think. What to say right now. This, you – it makes no scientific sense. It's impossible. You're impossible."

I laughed nervously with not a little sadness. "Impossible, that's another word for saying I'm a freak right? A weirdo?" I half joked, "hey, do you think I'm even human?" I didn't wait for his reply. I turned and walked away from him, towards the edge of the sloping mountainside. I stood and looked out over the broad expanse of ocean and sky. At the slowly sinking sun. At blue painted with crimson orange swirls and focused on calm. Peace. Stilling the fire. Slowly, from the tips of my fingers to my shoulders. I picked up the towel and once the flames were all out I wrapped it around myself in one quick motion. And then turned back to face Jason.

"So there you have it. My big bad secret. I'm sorry about what happened today. Nafanua warned me what might happen if I came up here with you again. I should have listened to her." My shoulders slumped defeatedly as I thought back to the light-hearted joy of the past three days with Jason and wondered if there would be any others. Now that he had seen what I really was.

Jason walked up to me and took me in a big, strong hug. Then he backed away and reassured me, "Hey, you're not a freak. You make no scientific sense but you're still Leila. The girl who can't surf for shit and who will never, ever walk down a catwalk wearing stilettos! But you're not a freak, okay?"

As usual, I had to laugh. Jason always seemed to have that effect on me. He continued, "You and I have got a lot of talking to do, but I think it can wait until later. Get dressed and let's get the heck out of here. The further away we are from this volcano, the better I'll feel."

Within the hour, we were packed and on the helicopter back to Upolu. It had started to rain again by the time we landed. Lightning lit up the evening sky as we drove away from the Fagalii airstrip. It made me think of Nafanua and I wondered if she and her sisters had anything to do with this storm.

We continued up the Aleisa road and drove through the tall gates to the house. We had just run through the sleeting rain up to the shelter of the patio when the sight of six women walking towards us from the poumuli forest caught us both. It was Nafanua and the other storm sisters. Dressed in black and completely uncaring of the storm that raged about them. It was beautiful in a starkly eerie kind of way. The black sky was lit with streaks of lightning and wind whipped their long hair as the women seemed to glide over the grass. Without knowing why, I moved closer to Jason, seeking some kind of security in standing behind his shoulder as the women came closer. Nafanua was unsmiling as she greeted us,

"Leila, Jason – you're back. How was your trip?"

I gulped and hoped desperately that Jason wouldn't say anything about the craziness of our day. I shouldn't have worried. He smiled that easy smile of his as he replied, "Oh it was fine. I'm sorry to bring Leila back so late, I had a lot of survey measurements to do and Leila was very patient waiting for me. Then the chopper was delayed picking us up as well. The storm, you know."

Nafanua nodded. "Yes. The air is angry tonight." Her face darkened as she looked skyward. I felt a chill at her expression. But then, as if remembering her manners, Nafanua refocused back on us, waving her hand at the women behind her. "Jason, I don't think you have met my sisters." She was gracious and courteous as she went through the introductions. "We hope you'll excuse us, but we have some family matters to see to and must be going. Actually ..." she paused, and seemed to be considering Jason speculatively, "Leila, you will be alone tonight at the house. Netta has gone home already but she's made plenty of dinner and you must both be famished. Jason, please, stay and have some refreshment, keep Leila company if you are able." She turned to her sisters, "Come we have a long drive ahead of us." She threw me a casual farewell over her shoulder as they got into her Land Cruiser. Jason and I stood and watched them drive away. I wondered if they were on another mission and wondered why I had not been included. Jason interrupted my thoughts. He had a somewhat embarrassed look on his face.

"Umm, do you think she really meant that? Is this really okay with Nafanua? And with you?"

"What? Is what okay?" I had no clue what he was referring to. He had to raise his voice as thunder crashed and rolled through the mountains around us.

"This, me being here while they're gone. You know ..." he spoke delicately, "unchaperoned. Isn't this going against Samoan etiquette? I hate to leave you here by yourself, but if it's not okay, then I'll get going."

I rolled my eyes at him and pulled at his sleeve as I headed for the doorway. "Don't be ridiculous. How many times do I have to tell you that Nafanua is *not* like most Samoan mothers. she's totally fine with you hanging out here. Besides," I grinned at him over my shoulder, "she knows that I can set you on fire if you try any funny business with me."

He followed me into the living room, tiptoeing around the mats with his wet, muddy feet. "Yes, well there's lots of different ways to set people on fire, isn't there? And not all of them are bad."

I had to laugh at his cheek. "You idiot. It's exactly comments like that that will get your butt set alight and kicked out the door, boy! Watch it."Our joint laughter banished away the slight edge of awkwardness at being left alone with an entire house to ourselves. As an entire night stretched out ahead of us.

I fetched Jason a towel and some dry clothes (thank goodness for *lavalava*, one size fit all), showing him to the guest bedroom before going upstairs to shower and change myself. I rifled through my treasure trove of clothes from Nafanua, for some unknown reason rejecting the usual white tee and instead pulling on an aqua cotton embroidered top with my denim shorts. I towel dried my hair as I came down the stairs. "Jase? Are you done?"

I had just turned into the living room, when there was a particularly vivid slash of lightning and then all the lights in the house went off. I was left standing in complete darkness while a storm raged outside. Before I could rope it in, a knife edge of panic cut through me and my serial killer paranoia kicked in. I was in a colonial mansion miles away from anything and anyone, stranded in the middle of the tropical bush in a powercut. Images of blade-wielding attackers creeping up on me had my heart pounding and it was a struggle to keep the fear out of my voice as I called out again for Jason. "Jase!? Where are you? Jason!" A wild thought came to me unbidden. *Oh no, what if he left? What if he went home? What if he couldn't handle all the unchaperoned stuff and he's gone and left me here all by myself?*

"Leila."

His voice startled me and I jumped and screamed. "Hey, hey, calm down it's only me." I reached out with faltering hands towards the voice and he took hold of me. "I'm here. Don't worry, it's just me."

I clung to him gratefully. "Ohmigosh, you scared the hell out of me! I hate the constant power cuts in this country. I thought you'd gone and left me here. I gotta admit, I am *so* glad that you're here. Imagine how freaked out I'd be if I was home alone on a night like this."

I was close enough to him to feel his breath against my skin as he laughed, low and long. "What? What are you laughing about?"

He shrugged in the darkness, with his arms still lightly clasped around my waist. "Nothing. I was just thinking that a girl who can set herself on fire and blow up stuff, well she kind of doesn't need to be scared of the dark, you know?"

I put two hands against his chest and pushed myself away from him with a rueful laugh. "Okay, okay, so you've got a point. I forgot about that stuff. You gotta remember that it's all new to me and I still haven't got my head around it. It still doesn't seem real, you know?" I peered into the darkness at the outline of his face, trying to 'see' him and gauge his reaction. There was no teasing in his reply.

"I think you're doing just fine. I don't know how I would be coping if this stuff was happening to me." Then his voice changed to anticipation. "Hey, maybe you could make us a light? So we can figure out where the lanterns are in this house."

"Sure." I stepped away from him and cupped my hands in front of me, focusing my energy, my thoughts. It was a simple thing and the flame that lit in my hands was a beautiful shimmering warmth. I smiled as I looked up at Jason, "See? Let there be light!" the words caught in my throat as the flamelight danced on the man standing in front of me. "Oh."

Jason was barefoot and shirtless. The red and black *lavalava* I had given him clung to his hips, the t-shirt was flung over his shoulder. Lightning ripped through the outdoors again, and the white flash highlighted every cut of his chest and tapering stomach with its faint blush of blonde hair. I had never thought of him as being beautiful before – that was a word I had reserved for Daniel. But standing there in a shadowy kitchen with only a piece of cloth wrapped around his waist, Jason was all gold, tanned skin, muscle and sinew. Words fled as I realized that only a moment ago, I had been encircled in those arms, pressed against that skin. I flushed and the air suddenly seemed a constricting hot thing. It seemed I couldn't take my eyes away from the sight of him and I was struggling for composure. *Get a grip, Leila! Snap out of it.* Jason had been distracted by my lit hands but now he turned his excited eyes to mine, "Leila, this fire thing, it's amazing, so useful …" His words trailed away as our gaze locked.

For what seemed an eternity, we just stood there, our bodies separated by cupped hands of flame while a storm raged and thundered outside. I couldn't read the look in his eyes. I was used to the mischief, the teasing glint, the concern, even the serious intensity – but here, now, in his eyes, there was something different. He leaned closer toward me and reached with one hand to lightly brush my cheek. He whispered in the electric night. "You're beautiful." And now his eyes spoke what I could understand – he wanted to kiss me. And before I could stop it, the mere thought of his lips on mine provoked a surge of heat that rushed through me like a blast from a furnace, a blast that fired the flames in my hands, sending them shooting upwards to light up the whole room, sending Jason jumping backwards in alarm.

"Whoa! Watch it!"

As quickly as I had lost control, I reined it in, shutting off the flames with a mental switch, leaving the house in darkness again. "I'm sorry,

I'm sorry, I'm so sorry, Jase!" I moved to stand beside him, wanting to see for myself if he was alright, but unwilling to get too close to him. "Are you alright? Did you get burned? Jason?"

I breathed a sigh of relief to hear his familiar teasing laugh. "I'm fine, but damn Leila – I thought you were kidding when you threatened to burn me up before! You could have taken my whole face off there."

I wrung my hands nervously. " I'm sorry, I didn't mean it, it was an accident, honestly. I usually have much better control only I wasn't thinking, I mean I wasn't expecting this, you caught me off guard."

"You weren't expecting what exactly?"

I moved away from him and carefully summoned the flames again so I could make my way to the kitchen where I started looking for the lanterns that I knew Netta kept stored. I faked intense concentration on getting the lamps lit while I left his question unanswered. Only when the room was flickering with light did I turn to look at him again.

"There, got it. Thank goodness for Netta's efficiency. Now, are you hungry? Nafanua said there was dinner around here somewhere." I let my own hand-held flame die as I moved to get plates and food from the oven, avoiding his eyes, avoiding him. Until he came up behind me and quietly asked, "Leila, do you want me to leave? I'm sorry if I made you uncomfortable. I didn't mean to. I can go."

I turned agitatedly. "No! Don't leave. I'm fine, it's okay. I want you to stay. I like having you here." I paused, unsure how to continue. I wanted to tell him that he was the only friend I had at the moment. Well, the only friend who I could talk to about what I was going through. The only person who could come to this place filled with strange mystical happenings and make me feel normal. He was a reminder of what life was like before. Back home in D.C. He was my friend. A smart, funny and caring friend. *Or at least that's the lie I was telling myself.* I snuck a glance at him. A "friend" who also happened to be sending my heart rate into a death spin as he stood in my kitchen with barely any clothes on. I smiled at his serious face and resolutely took a deep breath. "Jason, please don't go. It's a bit lonely – and scary – here when all the others are out. Stay, okay? I promise I won't light any more fires."

I looked up at him as he smiled that familiar roguish grin. "Okay, I'll stick around. But only if you tell me what that was a minute ago. If you weren't trying to maim me deliberately, then where did that come from?"

I shook my head unwilling to come clean. But another look at his open smile reminded me that this person was the only friend I had on hand. And he deserved the truth. "Jason, you remember when you asked me about triggers for my powers? I wasn't completely honest with you. It's kinda embarrassing. A major trigger is, umm, you know ..." I floundered.

"No, I don't know. What?"

"Well, when I'm with someone and I get kinda ... into them ... kinda ... aaargh!" I rolled my eyes and threw my hands up to the ceiling with embarrassed frustration.

"Just what are you trying to say, Miss Leila?" He was laughing now at my discomfort. Standing there with folded arms, with his head cocked to one side. "Go on, say it!"

"Say what?"

"You were trying to say that one of the triggers for your powers is physical attraction, ahem ... sexual desire, to be precise. Which is why you nearly blew up the kitchen a few minutes ago, because you are just so insanely hot for me and you couldn't handle it."

"I am not! I did not. Of course I can handle it."

He interrupted, "Ahhh, so you admit that you're hot for me!?"

I rushed on frantic and flustered, "Don't be ridiculous, of course I'm not hot for you."

"Oh? You're not huh? So what happened back there then?"

"Nothing. I was just nervous, it was dark and I hate the dark and there's a storm outside and it's making me tense and so all of that just made me flame, that's all."

He shook his head eyes dancing with mirth. "So, it had nothing whatsoever to do with me."

"No. Not at all. And you're very conceited to think that it did."

His eyes widened and he started walking towards me. "Oh so I'm conceited am I? I see, so in my delusional conceit, I only *imagined* that your pulse was racing, your heart was pounding, and you were totally contemplating what it would be like to kiss me?"

My eyes were horror-filled as he exactly summarized what had happened. I shook my head in nervous denial and took several steps back, halted by the bench top behind me.

"No, I mean yes, you were totally imagining all that. I don't know where you could have gotten all of that from! It's just ..."

He had me cornered now and shushed me with one finger lightly to my lips, "*Ridiculous,* I know, you told me. That's your favorite word. So what you're saying is that, my being this close to you has no effect on you whatsoever?"

I swallowed and shook my head defiantly. "No. It doesn't. There's nothing like that between us."

"I see." He was still smiling as he carefully brushed my still-wet hair away from the side of my face, bent his head and whispered against the nape of my neck. "And this? No effect whatsoever?"

His lips brushed a delicate trail of fire on my skin, igniting sinuous ripples of longing that coursed through me. His hands on my waist, gently but firmly pulled me closer, melding my body to the hard length of his. Of their own accord, my hands moved up his bare chest, tracing indents and contours of muscle, playing on the warmth of sun-kissed gold skin. His mouth lingered at my ear, his voice a hoarse whisper, "Are you feeling anything now Leila?"

I clenched my fists and gritted my teeth, willing my breathing to slow. I thought of Daniel and what had happened on that terror-filled night and that gave me the strength I needed to neatly sidestep Jason and push past him.

"Jason, quit it. Stop messing around. I'm trying to tell you something, something important."

The pleading edge to my voice put a stop to his teasing. He looked at me with gentle compassion. "I'm sorry, Leila. It's just too easy to rile you up and I enjoy it too much. See?" he raised his hands and took several steps backwards, "I'm backing off. And I'm ready to be serious. Honestly. Now, what is it that you want to tell me?"

I sighed resignedly. "I wanted to tell you that yes, you are ... hot ... a little bit. And it doesn't help that you know it. So just tone it down a bit okay? But nothing can happen between us, nothing. If you start kissing me and I start blowing up every time you're around, then that means we can't be friends anymore. And I couldn't handle that Jase, I couldn't. I've lost too many people already. First my dad and then I lost the right to be with Daniel. I can't open up to my friends at school because this stuff is just too weird. I don't trust Nafanua and her sisters but I have no-one else to turn to. I have to stay here with them because they're the only ones who have any clue about what's going on with me, who have any clues about how to help me make sure I don't wipe out the whole island by accident. You can't know how happy I was today to be able to share my secret with you. And to have you be okay with it. I've felt so alone Jase. You're the only friend I've got and I couldn't stand to lose you too. I just couldn't. Please don't. Don't do this – the killer smile, the telling me I'm beautiful, the naked chest thing, the breathing on my neck and making me want to kiss you – just don't. I can't handle it, I can't."

My voice had risen several hysterical octaves and I ended my tirade with a muffled sob. There was no teasing in Jason's eyes as he closed the distance between us and enfolded me in a huge hug. Instinctively, I stiffened, but there was nothing but friendship in his embrace. "Hey, I get it. It's okay. Everything will be okay, you'll see. I'm not going anywhere, you're not going to lose me. We're friends, and I'm going to do everything possible that I can to help you get through this." A soft laugh. "And I promise, no more naked chest and neck breathing – just friends."

I looked up at him with a watery smile. "You promise?"

He grinned back. "Promise." He released me and quickly pulled the t-shirt over his head before taking me in his arms again. "See? Minus one naked chest." A frown. "But I'm afraid I can't do anything about my killer smile. You'll just have to work really hard on your self-control to resist that."

We laughed together. I didn't want to move away from his embrace. It felt so good to be held in his arms – safe, warm, secure.

We stood there like that for a long moment. Just listening to the angry storm. While lamplight flickered and danced in the wind. A huge weariness settled over me. It had been a long and exhausting day. One in which I had – among other things – awoken a volcano and then told her to go back to sleep. I stifled a yawn and Jason raised my head from his shoulder. "Hey, I think you need to get some sleep. It's late."

I protested but another yawn caught me midway. "Yeah, sorry, I'm wasted. I think I'll just lie down and have a nap." I half stumbled to the living room sofa with Jason steadying me. "Will you stick around?" I turned anxious eyes on him as I lay down on the soft cushions. He looked down at me with his golden smile. "I'll be fine. Don't worry about me. I'm going to be right here." He motioned towards the other sofa. "I can sleep over there. At least until Nafanua gets back. I'll stay, I promise."

I smiled a thank you and was already drifting into hazy sleep, but not before I felt him place a feather light kiss on my forehead. I imagined I heard him whisper, "But I can't promise that I won't think you're beautiful. And I definitely can't promise that I won't fall in love with you, Leila Folger."

Outside, the raging wind intensified even more. A tall *poumuli* tree gave up its fight and crashed to the ground somewhere in the forest, the sound drowned out by the rolling thunder. There was indeed anger in the air.

The village cowered in the storm. The wood frames of the Samoan houses swayed in the wind and the woven blinds were no match for the sleeting rain. Families were running to take shelter in their neighbor's more substantial cement brick homes. Everyone was too busy hiding from the storm to notice the women emerge from the forest. Dressed only in tapa cloth, with their skin smeared with the paint of the mulberry. Their long hair blowing wildly in the wind, tangled nets of fury. Heedless of the rain, they walked through the empty village and down to the beach where the mutilated carcasses lay. Whales. A mother and her child. The stench of rotting flesh hung heavily in the air already. There was blood caked on the sand. Chunks of white flesh that had been hacked off lay discarded on the rocks. The women stopped. Sank to their knees. A wailing, keening grief. A chanted prayer to the heavens. And then rage. The leader summoned a lightning strike. It lit up the sky with a terrible beauty and then set the remains alight. The whales burned. The smell of roasting flesh was a sickening thing. The leader turned. There was cold finality in her voice.

"This village must be punished."

They say lightning never strikes in the same place twice.

That's a lie.

The storm raged. Screams filled the night.

Terror.

Agony.

THIRTEEN

I awoke disoriented from a night filled with confusing, fear-filled dreams. *Where was I*? The rain had stopped and sunlight was pouring in every window. It was mid morning, at least. I sat up and memories of yesterday came flooding back. Jason … I looked around and saw his red truck still parked out front. So he must be around here somewhere which meant Nafanua still wasn't back? I stood and stretched. Where was he? There was a whole lot of ruckus coming from the kitchen. Someone was singing. And making a lot of noise with pots and dishes. I walked over and peered curiously around the doorway, my jaw dropping at the sight of Jason cooking at the stove. The entire kitchen looking like a tornado had swept through it. Netta's spotless kitchen. I groaned. "Oh no, she's gonna kill me. Jason, what are you doing?"

He turned and his grin tugged at my annoyance. "Leila! You're up. What does it look like I'm doing? I'm making us some breakfast. Should be ready soon. Give me a couple more minutes."

I gave his enthusiasm a weak smile, resigning myself to the fact that I would be doing some serious cleaning up later and went upstairs to wash the sleep from my eyes. I checked my watch – it was 11am and still no Nafanua. Where were they?

"Leila, food's ready. Come down here."

Back downstairs, I sat at the dining table gingerly while Jason served me a plate of – scrambled eggs. Toast. And papaya. With lime and a frangipani from Nafanua's garden. I arched an eyebrow in surprise. "Umm ... this looks ... nice."

"Well, what else were you expecting?" Jason was defensive.

"Nothing. No, it looks lovely and " I took a bite "... and it tastes delicious too."

"Well, what is it?"

"It's just that, the kitchen – it's completely trashed! Like you were cooking up a seven-course banquet or something, not just scrambled eggs and toast. What happened in here Jase?"

He grinned sheepishly. "I kinda had a few failures before I got to the scrambled eggs. I wanted you to have something nice, you know, you're always feeding me these fancy dishes so I tried to fix us some pancakes using an old family recipe. Only it's so old I couldn't remember it properly. That ended up in the trash." He pointed to the still-smoldering trashcan in the corner. "So then I thought we could have banana muffins. I texted my sister back home for the recipe and her texts back were taking forever so I got impatient and got creative with a few of the ingredients and then when I tasted them, ugh. Nasty. So they ended up on the back lawn feeding the birds." He nodded his head to a fluster of birds bickering over scraps out the back.

"Jason you texted your sister in America for a muffin recipe for breakfast? You goofball. You do realize that I don't cook any of the stuff you eat when you come over to visit, right? That I can't cook to save my life? You could have just opened a box of cereal and we would have been fine or made us eggs and toast in the first place."

He shook his head laughing ruefully. "Yeah, I realized that after I trashed the place. I wanted to zip down to McDonald's to get us a Big Breakfast from there but it was after 10 so I gave up on that idea. Sorry about the mess, don't worry, I'm totally going to clean it up when we're done. Honest. I may not be a great chef but I do know how to do dishes. With four big sisters ruling the kitchen, I was always stuck with clean-up duty."

He was right. I had to admit he did have some skills when it came to swift cleaning and dishwashing and before long, Netta's kitchen was back to its pristine state.

"Leila, do you think you'll be okay here by yourself? I need to get back home to my laptop." He hesitated, a thoughtful look in his eyes. "Last night, after you went to sleep, I did some thinking. About all of this. You know, your fire problem. I'd like to help you, if you let me. I have some contacts back home, good friends of mine who I could ask to help us out. These are people I can trust to safeguard your secret and to help me figure out what's causing this to happen to you. A couple of doctors I went to school with, a physicist, a few lab guys. We could take some blood, get it back home to a lab. They could run some tests for me, try a few things, see if there's any way possible that we can stop this from happening. That is what you want, right?" He peered closely at me. "I kind of got the impression yesterday that you would like to be rid of this anomaly."

His words settled over me like a numbing haze. Some of them filled me with apprehension – tests, labs, doctors. I thought wildly for a moment of X-file labs and drugged test subjects. But another look at Jason's concerned eyes reassured me. This was Jason we were talking about. I trusted him. With my life. If anyone could be trusted to do this, it would be him. I shrugged and gave him a half smile.

"Sure. I do. I've started believing Nafanua when she tells me that there's no cure, that I'm stuck like this forever. But you're right. They've never questioned it. This stuff, whatever it is. It could totally be curable." I started to get excited by the possibilities. "That would be awesome Jason. To be normal again, I can't even dare to imagine it. To get my life back, to be just me again. And not some freakish fire girl who can fry people when I'm not concentrating hard enough. Yes. I want to try it. Please. How soon can we start and what do we do first?" I was ready to check myself into a lab that very minute, mentally psyching myself up for the needles and zap tests.

Jason laughed at my enthusiasm. "Hey, hey, hang on. Let's take it one step at a time. I'm going to make a few calls, send a couple of emails. To people I trust. We'll have to get some DNA samples off you but that will come later. Right now, I want you to write down everything you can about this fire thing. Like how it all started, early warning signs, date it as best you can remember. Oh, and also write down whatever Nafanua has told you about these powers. If what you're telling me is true, they've been living with this stuff for a long time and will know more about it than we ever can. It's important to get as much as possible down on paper" I grimaced at the thought of pages and pages of writing and he hastily amended. "Or voice record it on your iPod. If that's easier for you. The more info we can put together, then the better chance my boys back home will have at addressing the problem." He paused at the doorway to look back at me.

I hated to see him go. Some of my hesitation must have shown on my face because he paused mid-way out the door.

"Hey, it'll be fine. Everything's going to be okay. I'm on this. And I hate to sound like my usual conceited self, but I am kind of good at what I do."

Our eyes smiled at each other. I wrinkled my nose at him, "Whatever! You better get your arrogant butt out that door before I turn into a flamethrower."

I followed him out onto the porch and into the golden sun. "Jason?"

He turned at the car door. "Yeah?"

"Thanks. For last night. For listening to me and for being my friend. And nothing else."

He shook his head with a sardonic smile. "You're welcome. I was pretty good, wasn't I?" He climbed into the driver's seat and then threw out a parting shot. "Leila, you do realize what that means we get this fire problem thing all fixed? It means you won't have excuses left for why you can't give in to your insanely overwhelming attraction to me."

He laughed at the expression on my face and accelerated down the drive before I could get in the last word. All I could do was stand and watch him drive away. And smile.

The house seemed uncomfortably empty without him and it was a relief when Nafanua's black land cruiser turned into the driveway. Relieved to have company again, I ran lightly down the stairs to greet her. She looked exhausted and she smiled appreciatively at the ice-cold lemonade and sandwiches I had made. I was eager to hear about their 'mission.'

"I was starting to worry about you – you've been ages. Where didyou go? How was it?" I waited expectantly but Nafanua only shrugged.

"Fine, it was fine. Nothing major Leila."

"But you've been gone all night. And half the day, where were you? I could have helped, you know, like the other times …" My voice trailed away at the closed look on my mother's face.

"It was nothing that concerned you. Nothing that you could have helped with."

And with that abrupt statement, the conversation about her whereabouts was shut down.

Nafanua disappeared into her room for the remainder of the day, leaving me to occupy myself. An email update to Grandmother Folger – which said absolutely nothing about what was really happening in my life. Homework. Texts to Jason who seemed really buzzed about his initial contacts with his doctor friends back home. And then evening. I rustled up some dinner and then sat down to watch the news. And stared in horror, my food forgotten.

The television screamed at me accusingly. *Four killed, village burned in freak lightning storm.* The cameras showed grey smoke still rising from the blackened remains of houses and trees. My breath caught in my throat. Lightning had ripped through the village of Satumea on the southern coast, burning 25 houses to the ground. There were four men dead and 12 others had been admitted to hospital with second-degree burns. The village was too far from town for the Fire Services to get there in time and the people had stood helplessly and watched their homes, their lives, go up in smoke. In spite of the lashing rain and storm. There was disbelief. Fear. According to three of the villagers interviewed by the news reporter, the fire and the deaths were the result of a curse. They were being punished.

The day before, two whales had stranded on their beach. A mother whale and her newborn calf. In spite of instructions from the Ministry of Natural Resources and Environment asking the village to help with saving the whales, in spite of ancient taboos regarding the sacredness of the giant mammal, several men had taken to the whales with axes and bush knives. Carving out chunks of blubber and then abandoning their attack in frustration, the men had left the creatures desecrated on the beach. One old woman shook her head as she spoke to the camera, "This fire from heaven is a punishment for us. The four men who died were the ones who killed the whales. They have brought this curse on us all." She turned to stare straight into the camera. "It was *telesā* who did this to us."

The interview cut to more shots of the carnage. The words kept playing through my mind, hammering a chant that wanted to break free. *Fire from heaven ... a punishment ... a curse ... telesā, four dead, a village burned to the ground ... telesā.* I thought of Nafanua and her sisters. The way their hair would blow wildly in the wind when they called down lightning. How trees would bow to their ushering. And forests would quake at their onslaught. I remembered how they looked as they walked towards me and Jason out of their storm. The coldness in Nafanua's eyes. The suppressed rage. *There is anger in the air tonight.*

Suddenly, there wasn't enough air in the room. Not enough space. I stumbled to my feet and bolted for the door, tripping down the verandah stairs in my haste. Air, space, earth - is what I needed. I sank to my knees beside the gardenias and threw up. Retching again and again in the sweet fragranced air as my brain screamed in denial. *No.* There was a voice from behind me. Filled with concern, worry.

"Leila, are you alright? What's wrong?" Nafanua was by my side, helping me to my feet. I shook her hands off mine and backed away.

"Get away from me. Don't you touch me!"

"Leila, what is it? What's wrong?"

"Tell me you didn't do it, Nafanua. Those men, that village. Tell me you had nothing to do with it. Tell me!" My demand was jagged in the afternoon sun.

She regarded me with those dark, calm eyes. Shrugged. "I won't lie to you. Not about this. You are being foolish. Yes. We killed those men. Yes. We burned that village. But they brought it upon themselves. If you had been there, if you had seen what they did to those creatures – those beautiful, noble creatures ..." her voice died away and there was a tinge of sadness in her eyes that lit with fire as she continued. "They butchered them, Leila, a mother and her child. Defenseless. They did not even need their meat, no, they did it just because they could. It gave them pleasure. It was horrible, if you could only have seen it."

I rushed in to interrupt her, raising my voice against her soothing calmness. "But I wasn't there, was I, Nafanua? No. You didn't take me with you on this particular mission. And why not? Because you knew I wouldn't agree. You knew I would fight you on this one. You knew it was wrong. You hid this from me. All those other 'missions' we've gone on – they were all just a lie. That whole business about how we have these gifts so we can help, so we can make things right, so we can heal and nurture. That was all lies! You're murderers. Killers."

Warning fire flashed in her eyes, sparked in her voice. "Silence. You know nothing. That wasn't murder – it was justice. We are *telesā*. That is what we do. We administer punishment when men forget how to honor the earth that gives them life. Without our warnings, where do you think men would be? Look around you, foolish little girl, this earth is dying. Every day she is raped by man's greed and lust. She is bleeding as they cut her open. Choking on man's poison. If there were more like us, then earth would be better protected. Man would give her the respect she deserved. Leila, we are the protectors, the guardians, earths' weapons. *Fanua* doesn't give us her gifts so we can waste them on moping, crying, and wishing we could be 'just regular girls like everyone else.' We are *telesā* and this is what we do. The sooner you understand that, the sooner you can start paying Fanua the honor she deserves. You cannot fight against this, you are one of us. The sooner you embrace that, the better."

I shook my head, swallowing the panic, the fear, and anger, grabbing firmly to calmness before I spoke. "No, Nafanua. I'm not like you. I will never be like you."

I turned and walked back towards the house. Cold certainty giving me the courage I needed to turn my back on the woman who could call down fire from heaven when people defied her. Her voice whipped me. "Where are you going?"

I threw my reply over my shoulder. "Away from you. I came here because I wanted to know my mother." A joyless smile. "I know all I need to. I'm going back to live with Matile and Tuala. If they'll have me. And only until I can get on the first plane out of here."

I was at the door when she spoke again. Exasperated, as if berating a three-year-old having a tantrum. "How many times do I need to tell you, foolish child? There is nowhere else for you but here with your sisters. With us. We are the only ones who can help you control your fire. We are the only ones who can guide you. You are a danger to everyone else. Besides, I tolerate Matile and her pathetic abhorrence of *telesā*. My tolerance will wear very thin if she stands in the way of my only daughter becoming the *telesā* she is destined to be."

My whole body stiffened and I turned, careful rage emphasizing every word. "What are you saying? Are you threatening me? Aunty Matile?"

Nafanua's smile did not reach her eyes. "I'm saying, that you are safer with us. With your sisters. I'm saying people you care about are safer as long as you are with us. Because you forget Leila, that with one careless thought, you can do far worse than kill four axe-happy men and burn a little village. Hah. You can lay waste to this entire island and more, if you but lose your temper. Or get a little too excited by someone's silly teenage kiss. You are not a prisoner here, Leila. Go and come as you like. But remember, we are the only ones who can give you the instruction you need. We are the only ones who can keep the world safe - from you."

A flush of celebratory pride made me rash, rush to utter words I would regret a thousand times over in the days to come. "That's where you're wrong, Nafanua. You're not the only ones with answers about my powers, my genetic aberration. Jason's going to help me. He's going to find the answers with Western science, and I'm going to be that 'pathetic regular girl' you so despise. You'll see, I don't need you. Or your murderous *telesā* insanity."

She recoiled as if my words had drawn blood, leaving her white faced with eyes flashing. "Jason? You revealed your powers to Jason? You shared your gifts with a man? A *palagi* man?!" Shock and horror painted welts in the setting sun. "Leila, it is forbidden. How could you? Do you realize what you have done? What will happen now?"

I threw my reply at her with impetuous abandon. "Yes I do. Jason is going to do everything possible to help me cure this. To be rid of it. He's going to get the best scientific minds working on the problem and I'm going to be okay. You thought you could control me and make me do whatever you wanted, just because I was afraid of what these powers could do, but you were wrong. I don't need you. I don't need to become a *telesā* like you, I have a choice here. And I choose to be cured of this. I **will** be normal. And if that means I'm less like you, all the better. My father was right to take me away from you. I hate you and everything you stand for, Nafanua."

I turned and took two steps towards the verandah stairs before Nafanua screamed my name and lightning ripped the sky, striking the ground so close to me that my hair singed. I caught a ragged breath at the suddenness of it and spun around. For a moment we stood there, rigid in the green and blue day, hostility rippling like waves of fire in the deepening twilight. Nafanua spoke and her words dripped with the poison of the stonefish.

"How dare you walk away from me? You are nothing. A child. I am Nafanua, the greatest *telesā* who has walked this land in over two hundred years. You will not defy me. You cannot walk away from your destiny, from a legacy of over a thousand combined years of *telesā* guardianship."

My reply was swift. A single thought and a ripple of heat and flames burst from my core, extinguishing a weak girl made of flesh and bone, replacing her with one of lava and fire.

"And just how will you stop me, Nafanua? You and I both know that your lightning is no match for my volcano. I may be just a child, but foolish children can have deadly temper tantrums. Like this!" The outrage that had started burning when I first saw the footage of Satumea village flared and I gathered a fireball and threw it with all my pent-up anger – straight at Nafanua's black land cruiser. I was regretting my actions, even before the car exploded in an incendiary mass of flames, sparks, and billowing black smoke.

KABOOM!

Damnit! I gritted my teeth as I stared at the inferno. I didn't want to be this person. Someone who blew up cars when they got mad. No. I forgot Nafanua for a moment as I focused on containing the flames, subduing them. There was nothing I could do to save the car but at least I could prevent the fire from running wild through the garden. I sighed at the sight of the twisted remains of steel and wire and spoke over my shoulder to Nafanua.

"I'm sorry. About the car. I shouldn't have done that. I won't let you threaten me or the people I care about, Nafanua, but I really shouldn't have blown up your car. That's not who I am." I appealed to her. "Can't you get it, Nafanua? *Telesā* like you, is not who I am."

Nafanua's voice was pleading as she took several steps closer.

"Leila, you have never been an ordinary woman. You have a gift and it's been given to you for a purpose. *Fanua* needs you and the fire you hold. Can't you feel her suffering? Surely you can see it? Hear her cries for help? Join us. You can help us, you can make sure that man listens, that he changes. The earth is sick, dying, and you can do something about it. Are you going to walk away from that?"

I shook my head in angry bewilderment. "I have no idea what you're talking about Nafanua. I'm just a messed-up teenager trying to find her way through life. Truly, I'm so tired of it all. The lies, the secrecy, the powers. I don't want it. Can't you get it?"

She came up and stood as close to me as she dared, shading her eyes against the spitting flames. "Leila, listen to me. My sisters and I, we have a plan. A plan that can change everything. That can fix everything once and for all and restore the natural order, the natural balance of things. But we need you. Join us. Embrace who you really are and you could be earth's last chance. Our plans just include our islands of Samoa, but there is no reason why we could not look further afield."

My eyes narrowed. "Plans? What plans? What are you talking about?"

There was excitement in her reply. "There is a reason why Pele is called the creator and destroyer of lands. If you unleash her, tap into the core, she could do away with all this, all of man's attempts to civilize her, to control and abuse her. And then, with Pele's creative power, the land could start anew, afresh."

Horror dawned with understanding. "You're insane. You're talking about triggering a major volcanic eruption, aren't you? One that would wipe out everything? And the people? What about them? The children? The families? Homes, villages, everything? You would just have them all wiped out – for what – so you could go back to the 'old ways'?"

Nafanua waved her hand impatiently. "No, we wouldn't erase everyone and everything. Just the main town and the industrial zones. The commercial leaders and main government sector, freeing up a power vacuum. Those in the rural areas will be more likely to turn to their traditional leadership then. Which would of course involve a return to their spiritual healers and *fanua* worship. It would bring about a greater closeness with their earth mother. And we *telesā* would be honored as the intermediaries with that earth."

As swiftly as I had summoned it, I switched off my flames. Standing there naked in the afternoon, I shook my head at the woman who – I realized with dreadful certainty now – was a complete stranger to me.

"So this was your plan all along? This is why you came and got me from Aunty Matile's home? This is why you wanted your daughter back? Why you've been teaching me how to use my powers, getting me to buy into all this *telesā* sister crap? Nafanua, I don't know you. And you really don't know anything about me. What makes you think that, for a single moment, I would even consider the possibility of doing what you're asking? Hear me now, I will never use this 'gift' this 'curse' – whatever it is – I will never take part in your insane plan."

I turned and walked up the steps of the verandah, daring her with my back to strike me. To cut me down. Anything. I didn't care. "I'm leaving. There's nothing left for me here."

There was no response. In the house, I quickly dressed, packed my things, and, within minutes, was heading out to the car. Nafanua was sitting on the verandah sipping tea as I threw my bags in the back of the jeep. She spoke, "We are not done here, Leila."

I did not answer, simply climbed into the driver's seat and gunned the engine. Over the roar, I thought I heard her say, "Don't say that I didn't warn you, daughter."

I did not look back as I drove off down the driveway, my eyes on the road but my thoughts on the future.

What is a *telesā* without her sisters? Where does she belong?

Terminator ran up eagerly as I alighted from the Wrangler. I knelt to hug his scruffy self, a huge grin of relief on my face. At least someone was happy to see me. At the door, I took a huge breath before knocking. *What would Matile say? Would there be a place for me here?* I wouldn't blame them if they told me to get lost.

It was Uncle Tuala who opened the door and his smile chased away all my doubts. He turned to hastily call over his shoulder, "Matile, look who's here?!" He took my bag from me and beckoned me in eagerly as Matile came from the kitchen, wiping her floury hands on a tea towel. Another smile of greeting. This one somewhat tearful.

"Ah Leila. Come in. I knew you would come back" she corrected herself, "well, I hoped you would come back." A frown of concern. "Are you alright? Your ... mother, she is alright?"

I smiled weakly, the warmth of their greeting was making me emotional. "Yes, Nafanua is fine." I took a deep breath before plunging in, "I was hoping I could stay with you. Just for a little while. It's no longer possible for me to stay at Nafanua's. We've had a disagreement and I'm going to go back to the States. Not right away though. I'm waiting for a few things to get settled first. So I wondered if I could stay here until I go back. Please?"

I needn't have worried. Both of them rushed to assuage any misgivings I may have had about my reception. My room was exactly as I had left it and Matile set to work in the kitchen preparing a huge meal for dinner. As she bustled about, Uncle Tuala regarded me with pensive eyes.

"So. What really happened with you and your mother? Are you alright? Did she hurt you?"

I shook my head, grateful for his concern. "No. There's nothing she could do to hurt me. I'm fine. Honestly. We just disagree about what path I should take. She has plans for me that I don't agree with and so I thought it best to move out. If it's alright with you and Matile, I'd like to finish up the last three weeks of the school term and then go back home to the US."

"Of course. You know you're always welcome here. But Leila, are you sure that you're alright? Is there anything else that we should know?"

For a moment, I thought about telling him everything. About pouring out the whole story of who Nafanua really was, what she had done and what I really was. But one look at his worried face and I knew that I couldn't. Not when I kept seeing the image in my mind of Nafanua's lightning rage and hearing her threaten to harm the people I cared about. No, I could not tell Tuala and Matile what had happened. I shook my head again and plastered a smile on my face. "No Uncle, that's it. I rushed into the whole idea of having a mother and it didn't quite turn out to be the happy family that I thought it would be. I'm disappointed but I'm okay. I'll finish up with school and then head back home."

Tuala patted me awkwardly on the shoulder. "I'm sorry that it didn't work out for you. I know how important it was for you to know your mother." He smiled. "But we are certainly happy to have you back with us. Matile has missed having you to cook for! Now come, let's go eat."

FOURTEEN

It was almost as if I had never left. And so it was all too easy for me to push my deadlock with Nafanua into the darkest closets of my mind. Matile shook her head sadly at my tattoo as she muttered about the sacrilege of desecrating one's body, the holy temple of the spirit. But she was thrilled to find that I was the *taupou* for Culture Night. She was a woman with a mission as she worked to make me the "most amazing, most authentic, most beautiful *taupou* in the history of the school." (her words, not mine)

A piece of *siapo* was acquired, which she reverently cut and sewed into a strapless shift, one that ended mid-thigh. Again, I despaired of ever understanding this culture where mini-skirts were frowned upon but a *taupou* with a *malu* was supposed to not only wear the shortest skirt possible but also hitch it up even further during her dance and slap at her tattoo to better accentuate its beauty. (Never mind that her butt would be peeking out the back at the same time.)

There were coconut wood bracelets that would sit like arm cuffs, shell anklets that would help announce my arrival, a ruffle of fuchsia-dyed feathers that would belt at my waist, and a glorious jutting necklace made of boar tusks. (Mental note to self, don't trip over and accidentally stab self in the eye on pointy pig tusks). Pride of place, however, belonged to the *tuiga* – the elaborately ornate headdress I would balance precariously and try not to topple as I gracefully dipped my head during the dance. Matile explained that, in olden times, light-colored hair was prized as it bespoke of the progeny of the gods (who were supposedly fair-skinned and bringers of light). Women with light-colored hair were made to donate their locks via regular haircuts and the pieces were woven together to make *tuiga*. I had never dressed up for a school ball like other girls, nor had a mother to help me get ready for such an event, so it was a novel experience. One that was beginning to be a little tiresome though, as every day that week I came home from school to find Matile waiting for me to try on the outfit "just one more time" to check if another alteration and additional enhancement worked or not. But then it seemed as if everyone at school was just as hyped up for Culture Night as my aunt.

Simone was aflutter with designs for his *puletasi*. He was dancing with the other girls and deviously planning 101 ways to make sure that his requisite uniform would still manage to outshine the others. A slit up to the thigh, a handful of sequins artfully sewn on the green *elei* fabric "to catch the light," and, of course, a full self-applied manicure and pedicure the day of the event. He was envious of my upcoming role, but preened with satisfaction that my performance would make Mele choke with envy. He even came over to the house twice after school to check that my costume would be suitably impressive and he and Matile hit it off surprisingly well, like fashion cohorts and schemers.

I was beginning to get frustrated with all the time and effort that was getting sucked up into this *taupou* thing. It kept getting in the way of my meetings with Jason as he made good on his promise to help me. I did not want to have to explain Jason to Matile and so I arranged to meet him after school while she and Tuala were at work. Three times now he had picked me up in the red truck. Simone's eyebrows had danced suggestively the first time he had seen my tanned, blonde visitor, but I had waved away his teasing by explaining that Jason was a scientist working on a project with my mother and he had to be content with that.

"Jason, I'd like you to meet my friend Simone. He's been my life saver here. Simone, this is Professor Williams. He's leading a research team that's monitoring the volcano Matavanu over in Savaii. I'm giving him a hand with some of their work."

If Jason thought it odd that my best friend was wearing more makeup than I ever have – he didn't show it. "Hi Simone, it's nice to meet you.

You'll have to come with Leila sometime when we take the chopper out to Matavanu. That is, if you're interested in volcanoes."

Simone batted his eyelashes and gave Jason an alluring smile. "Oh yes, I've always been very interested in hot things."

I rolled my eyes at him but Jason laughed. "Well Leila, shall we get going? Simone, do you need a lift somewhere?"

Simone was regretful. "Awww, no, I've got a netball game. You two go ahead. See you tomorrow, Leila. And don't forget, we have costume alterations to work on in the afternoon. Your Aunty is expecting us at the house tomorrow for your final fitting."

I grimaced at him as Jason took my schoolbag from me and easily hefted it into the truck before opening the passenger door for me. He waited for me to get in before shutting the door. I smiled my thanks and, over his shoulder, I saw a familiar figure standing at the end of the main drive to the school. Staring right at us with an unreadable expression. Daniel. Before I could even begin thinking of what to do, he turned. And walked away.

Beside me in the truck, Jason asked, "Ready?"

I nodded silently. Jason started the engine and we drove away. I looked back but couldn't see Daniel.

The first day, Jason took me to the hospital lab where I had blood work done – samples that he then had sent to his friend's lab in Los Angeles. The second time, we went back to the rental house he was sharing with his team. It was empty though as they were all on camp at the Savaii base. In a ramshackle shed in the backyard, he had carefully hooked me up to a complicated string of wires and I had tried, equally carefully, to erupt into flame without incinerating all his equipment. It had not gone so well. Poor Jason had done lots of shouting as I charred a very expensive pressure gauge and set fire to an entire set of volcanic lava thermometers.

"Leila! You're doing it again. Watch it!"

"I'm sorry Jason, but it's a bit tricky to set my whole body on fire while at the same time, keeping two little spots turned off so your gadgets can take readings. I've only been doing this for a month now, you know. I'm not a fire genius."

It had been a frustrating afternoon. One that Jason spent muttering darkly while I muttered equally darkly. Not until the third visit did he finally get some decent measurements. Measurements that had him shaking his head and looking at me in disbelief. A look that didn't escape me, even as I quickly wriggled back into my clothes from behind the makeshift screen he had erected to give me a bit of privacy.

"What? What is it? You look freaked out. Tell me." I demanded.

He didn't answer. Just furrowed his brow in concentration as he walked back to the main house, with me following behind.

"Jase. Talk to me. Please?"

Jason sighed. Turned and looked back at me in the overgrown yard. "Leila, I'm sorry. I'm not trying to freak you out. I just … I just didn't expect readings like this." His shoulders slumped and he sat down tiredly on a rickety garden bench. He looked worried. Really worried.

"What do you mean? You knew I exploded into flames, you knew I would be hot. What's the surprise then?"

He gave a wry smile. "Yes, I knew you were hot. Just not this hot. You're registering at over 1200 degrees Celsius."

I shook my head impatiently. "So? So what does that mean?"

"You're not just catching on fire, Leila. You're not just something burning. Wood burns at about 500 degrees Celsius. That's hot. But you? You're raging at temperatures of molten lava flow. Temps that a volcano reaches when it blows. It's nuts. This is nuts. I don't know how this can be happening."

I gave him a sad smile. "You and me both." I walked over and sat down beside him on the bench. "But I believe in you and I know that you can figure this out. And figure out a way to make it go away. You're the smartest, brilliantest volcano professor I know. Right?" I peered at him hopefully.

He rolled his eyes at me and flashed the golden easy smile that I loved. "I'm the only volcano professor that you know, you dork."

"No, I know Blaine. And he's super smart. And if you're thinking about quitting on me, then I'll have to bewitch him with my bimbo act so *he* can help me," I teased, but there was a note of desperation underneath the lightheartedness.

332 Lani Wendt Young

I was rewarded with another smile and his faked look of aggrieved shock. "Blaine?! You would take Blaine's brain over mine? No way. You take that back, right now." He started tickling me mercilessly, which had me squirming and jumping off the bench, grabbing his hands trying to get him to stop his attack.

"Stop it. Stop it! I give up, I give up. Okay, okay Blaine's nothing compared to you and I would never ever even think about replacing you with him, o great scientist researcher. Spare me! Stop it."

Breathless with laughter, we both tumbled off the seat onto the grass and I landed half on top of his broad chest. The laughter faded as our eyes met. I could feel the rise and fall of his breathing, the warmth of his body under the length of mine. His lips were a heartbeat and for one taut moment, I considered what would happen if I leaned forward and met his mouth with mine. Tasted him. My pulse accelerated and instantly I pushed myself up and away from him so that we were lying side by side underneath a fading blue sky. No longer touching, but still connected. By invisible electric wires of something I couldn't understand. I battled a swirl of inner confusion. I didn't know what I was feeling with Jason. But I knew I liked feeling it. I liked being here with him. For a few quiet minutes we lay there in the grass side by side. Comfortable. And then I spoke.

"You're not, are you Jase?"

"What?"

"Thinking of quitting on me? Am I a lost cause?"

He turned and propped himself up on one elbow so he could gaze down at me. There was no more teasing in his eyes. "Leila, I would never quit on you. We're going to figure this thing out. I promise. I'm not going anywhere."

He leaned forward and I tensed against an embrace that didn't come. Instead, he gently blew a loose strand of my hair away from my cheek before leaving a quick kiss on my temple. Then he was up and offering me his hand. "Come on. We better get you home before your aunty Matile sends out the sniffer dogs."

Together, we walked back to the truck. I was relieved nothing had happened. I thought back to Daniel's stony gaze at school and my insides twisted. I couldn't have the boy I loved. But I could have Jason. As long as he stayed a friend. Gently, I slipped my fingers from his and went to my side of the truck. "Thanks for everything, Jason. For today. For trying to help me. I really appreciate it."

"Hey, I'm a mad scientist remember? We love studying incendiary mysteries." A shrug. "I just wish we were back home where I would have access to all sorts of far more advanced gear. Hey, that's an idea. I don't know why I didn't think of it before." He looked excited. "We've got another week or so before we wrap up the Matavanu project. Before we head back to collate our results. Why don't you come with us?"

I was taken aback by the unexpected turn of the conversation. "Go with you? Back to the States?"

"Yeah. That would be perfect." He slammed his door shut and walked quickly over to where I stood on the opposite side, grabbing both my hands in his. "Think about it. You could fly back with me to L.A and I could get you booked into a lab where we could run every kind of test under the sun. We could totally get to the bottom of this." His excitement was palpable, it came at me in waves.

I shook my head. "I don't know."

"But Leila, why not? What's keeping you here? You've left Nafanua and the others. They can't stop you. And to be honest, I would be more comfortable if you were a thousand miles away from them. I think they have a few screws missing upstairs, if you know what I mean – no offence. I know she's your mother and everything. But, honestly, why do you need to stay in Samoa? What would keep you here?"

I stared at him, my mind a-swirl with questions and possibilities. Jason was right. Why did I need to stay here? I hadn't been very truthful with him about my reasons for leaving Nafanua's house. I had only told him the bare minimum, making it sound more like a typical mother-daughter spat. The nightmares of *telesā* wielding lightning to raze a village to the ground, were mine alone to bear.

As he waited for my answer, I considered all the arguments. I had cut myself off from the sisterhood and their supposed offers of help with training and controlling my powers. I wasn't as worried as I had been about exploding 'accidentally' and killing people. Heck, hadn't I just proven that I had a handle on this fire stuff by getting through Jason's preliminary tests without setting him on fire? Yes, I could leave. If I really wanted to. What was keeping me in Samoa? I thought of Matile and Tuala with fondness. They were the closest thing to family that I had ever come to since my dad. But I knew they were worried for me. They knew, or at least suspected what Nafanua could do when she got angry and they would feel a lot better if I was far away from here. No, if I told them I was leaving today – tomorrow, next week – they would be relieved. I thought of Grandmother Folger and almost laughed out loud. Ha. She would pay anything to get me to leave this place and return home to 'civilization.' I looked at Jason and his still-waiting, expectant face. Grandmother would even be enthused I had made friends with such an intellectual overachiever. If she knew about Jason she would be hoping against hope that some of him would rub off on me, inspire me to get my butt in gear and go to college. I had told Nafanua that I was leaving the country, so why was I still here? I pulled my hands away from him and looked away, out over the fast setting sun.

At burnished red draped over lush green. Daniel. His name was a stab, '*a steel knife in my windpipe* ' The very thought of him took my breath away. The very possibility of leaving here, of never seeing him again was like standing on the quivering edge of an endless precipice. Not wanting to fall but flailing against empty air for a safe hold. Reaching, trying to cling to that which would give me balance. Give me hope. Give me life.

Daniel. I was here for Daniel. And the realization tore at my insides, mangled my very core. Because, very simply, Daniel was my reason for living. Even though I couldn't be with him, I could not, would not, live without him. I could not explain why this was so. I did not know where the absolute certainty came from. But it was there. I just knew it. Like I knew I was Leila. And the sooner I was rid of these flames then I could try again to be with him. That is, if he still wanted me.

Jason was still waiting for my response. I shook away my thoughts and managed a weak smile at his expectant face. "I'm sorry Jase. I was – umm – thinking." I took a deep breath and let the words rush out over each other. "You're right. I can go with you. It's the best chance, the only chance I've got for getting this stuff sorted out, right? I can spend a bit of time in LA while you run your tests and then I'll pop back to D.C. to visit my grandmother who is hating the very idea of my being here in Samoa anyway. And then …" my voice died away as I considered my future. Did I really have any options? Did I really have choices? "And then I'll probably come back here."

"You mean when we've figured out a cure for you?"

"Yes." My heavy heart lightened to a skip and jump as I thought about the possibility of being rid of my fire. Of being able to hold Daniel, kiss him, love him. "Yes, definitely. If we can put a lid on this thing then I will come back."

"Aha." Jason studied me with an unreadable expression, like there was something else he wanted to ask me. Then he pushed it aside and smiled lightly. "It's a date then. I'll talk it over with the team so we can confirm our travel dates and then I'll let you know. Are we agreed?"

I nodded. "Yep. Agreed. Now you've got to take me home or else my life won't be worth living when Matile gets her hands on me."

That night after dinner and dishes, after I'd said goodnight to Matile and Tuala and gone to my room, I dialed Daniel's number. The sound of his voice cut through me. Both raw and delicious at the same time.

"Hello?"

I held my breath and was silent, not trusting myself to speak in case I melted into tears. A heavy pause.

"Hello? Leila? Is that you? Are you there?"

I wanted to speak to him. Tell him of the love that choked me. The pain I drowned in without him. But I couldn't. Instead, I pressed END and cried myself to sleep.

Friday was a busy bustle at school as everyone worked to decorate the hall with red ginger flowers and woven coconut fronds on all the posts. The teachers hoped to stage all the performances on the field under the stars, so everyone was hoping for a clear night. Matile wanted me to do one more fitting after school, which had me chafing and muttering curses under my breath.

Prayers were answered and the night was clear. A half moon graced us with her presence and a panoramic southern hemisphere sky guaranteed that nature herself would be the stage for our culture performances. Our house performance would be last. It was a great night, one I knew I would always remember. For its ease, its beauty, the relaxed natural way people greeted me, spoke to me, the way Simone and I sat and clapped for the house performances, the way he critically analyzed each one, reassuring me that, of course, nobody was as perfect as I would be. I had never had a night like this one. I was at one with other teenagers and it felt great. Our turn was announced. I could see Matile and Tuala in the audience as they sat proudly with anticipation, and a thrill of nervous adrenaline rushed through me. Simone moved to the side of the hall with the others as they lined up for the *ma'ulu'ulu* dance. The conductor led us in song and the words rippled and swelled, filling the field and the night sky. Then Simone and the other girls took to the field for their dance. I hid a smile as moonlight caught on Simone's sequins, gracefully ensuring he did stand out. I stood in the shadows and watched as Daniel led the boys in the war dance. My breath caught in my throat as my eyes feasted on his lithe form, the strength in every sinew and rippling muscle as he leapt and danced, invoking the gods of war, of strength and power to take them to victory. So I was caught off guard when Mele spoke beside me.

"He's beautiful, isn't he?" The ice of her tone was accusatory.

"Who? What are you talking about?" my words sounded lame even to me.

She laughed without mirth. "Oh don't pretend. You think I don't know that you're crazy about him? That you're sick with longing for him? The whole school knows how pathetic you are over him."

I looked at this angry, spiteful girl and saw her for what she was. I sighed. "What do you want Mele?"

Her features contorted, "I want you to stay away from Daniel. I want you to go back to where you came from. You don't belong here. You're not one of us. You can't have Daniel, he doesn't want anything to do with you."

I smiled sadly. "I think Daniel's old enough to decide what he wants. I'm pretty sure he can handle making his own decisions. And I know that he can speak for himself as well. Why don't you just leave me alone? I've spent a lifetime in places where I don't belong – and now I'm home." As I said the words, I realized that I meant them. It was true. I was home. Samoa was home. I had a huge smile of self-realization as I continued. "And Mele, nobody – especially not a jealous little girl like you – is going to drive me away from where I belong. Sorry."

"I'll make you sorry. Don't you speak to me like that!" Mele's reaction was swift. A vicious slap to my face. I'd felt worse, but she was wearing a ring and the metal caught cuttingly on the side of my mouth. I tasted blood on my lips. Heat flared threateningly, but it was a small matter to subdue it. This girl wasn't worth a fire storm. I simply wiped the bead of blood from my lip. "Well, I hope you feel better now, because I won't give you the opportunity to draw blood again. Now excuse me, I have a performance to get ready for." I couldn't resist the petty gibe. "You know, the one where Daniel sings about how much he's in love with me?"

Dark eyes flashed dangerously and she raised her arm to hit me again, an arm that I grabbed in a vise-like grip, allowing ever so slightly, the flush of fire to heat up through my fingers. Skin heated uncomfortably, and Mele's eyes widened in fear and pain. "Ow! What are you doing?" She struggled to pull away but was no match for my strength. I leaned forward to speak with steel softness in her ear.

"Don't ever try to hit me again, do you hear me? No more threats, no more attitude. Stay out of my way, because, trust me, you have no idea what you're dealing with."

She pulled away, wincing as I released my grip, rubbing at the red welt on her arm. I could hear the announcement of our *taupou* presentation, so I quickly turned away from her, struggling to calm the rush of nerves as I took a deep breath, reaching up to check my *tuiga* was still on straight.

"It's perfect." Simone was by my side. "You look stunning. Now, don't fall over and don't forget to bow to all three sides of the audience, and try not to drop the danceknife, and don't rush your moves, and remember to feel the words as Daniel sings them, and you've got to hitch up your skirt and display that *malu* of yours, you've got to really work it and …"

I raised my hands in laughing protest. "Simone! Quit it, you're making me a wreck with all those reminders. You're not helping."

He paused and put one defiant hand on his hip, "Fine then! No more words of wisdom from this supermodel. You go, girl."

I peered from the tent out to the audience and breathed deeply again. Daniel walked out to take his position first. The stage had been set to represent a forest clearing with a pool in its center, ringed by burning flares, a cluster of rocks was where he would sit. He wore a brief piece of *siapo* tied at the hips. His burnished chest was bare save for the single bone carving that hung around his neck. His whole body gleamed with glistening coconut oil and his tattoos spoke their story clearly in the moonlight. He was the noble warrior of every myth and legend and there was a hushed breath of awe before the audience rippled with applause, the more feisty among them whistling and catcalling. *Woohoo! Go Danny! Work it, baby, work it!*

The appreciative noise died away as Daniel took his seat and picked up his guitar. The incomplete night waited for his voice. Daniel sang. And everyone was swept along in the story of his music. Even though I had heard it many times before, Daniel's singing never failed to entrance me. If *telesā's* gift was dance, his was song. It had a similar effect on one. It tugged on memories of a past you never knew you had, on a history you did not fully understand, on the power of an earth that you knew you would never completely comprehend. I was silenced by its beauty and Simone had to nudge me when the time drew near for me to enter.

"Leila get ready, you're up."

I took a deep breath and moved to position. Daniel's solo came to a lingering, breathtaking finish and then the entire House started singing, blending their voices with his in an orchestra of worshipful harmony that called to the *taupou* to enter. This was it. *Here goes nothing, wherever you are Dad, it would sure be good if you sent some positive wishes my way.*

I began the slow, graceful run of a *taupou* as she answers the call of the crowd. I was terror ridden, right up until I bowed to the audience, three times, as directed, and then allowed my hands to begin telling their story. Then, the fear was replaced by the fire. The joyous welcome of *Fanua* as she joined me in rejoicing in the dance. I wanted to laugh with the joy of it. I didn't know why I had ever been afraid of this in the first place. I was *telesā* after all, and we were the creators of the *siva*.

I was only dimly aware of the applause from the crowd as I danced, of my aunty and uncle beaming proudly in the front row. My heart, breath, and soul were completely focused on the *siva* as it told its own story, as it listened to Daniel's words and replied. He sang with the House from behind me, but every fiber of my being was aware of his presence as his voice enveloped me. Delighted me with its expression of love, and then moved me to painful anguish as it spoke of loss and heartache. Too soon, the song ended, my dance came to its bittersweet finish. I bowed again and walked back to stand beside Daniel just like we had practiced, only this time, our hands found each other and the glances we gave each other were filled with meaning. We stood like that for a moment, with the rest of the house standing behind us in all their finery, united in our exultation of a successful performance. And this time, the crowd roared, people leapt to their feet to clap and cheer. Daniel and I were surrounded by a triumphant crowd of students and our clasped hands slipped apart.

I clung to the memory of his look, the feel of his hand in mine for the remainder of the night. As Simone and Sinalei congratulated me wildly. As Mrs. Lematua told everyone we were the best culture group she had ever worked with (Simone whispered narkily, "yeah, usually she's in the losing house every year.") As the judges announced that we were the year's winners. As everyone cheered again and threw their flower leis in the air in triumph. And then groaned as the Principal requested the winning house to stay behind and clean up. Aunty Matile came to help me change out of my costume, carefully removing the *tuiga* and reverently packing the various items of jewelry into a voluminous bag. Uncle Tuala gruffly congratulated me with an awkward half hug and then both of them thanked Simone for all his help "teaching our Leila how to *siva* like a true Samoan girl." Simone merely preened and accepted their compliments like the Queen that he was and I rolled my eyes at him from a safe distance.

"Aunty, is it alright if I stay to clean up with the others? And then, a group of us would like to go to McDonald's to celebrate with a milkshake, would that be alright?" I asked anxiously. The one thing I missed from Nafanua's house was the freedom to come and go as I pleased, and I had been trying very hard to make sure I did not fret at the bit too much with Matile and Tuala's rules and curfews.

Auntie's brow furrowed worriedly. "I don't know, Leila, it's getting late and we don't like the idea of you out without someone to look after you. It's not safe. Perhaps it's best if you come home with us ..." her sentence trailed away as she looked to Tuala for affirmation. I had given up on the idea of a milkshake with Simone, when a voice from behind us spoke.

"I would be happy to accompany Leila and make sure she gets home safely, Mrs. Sinapati."

We all turned surprised eyes to see Daniel standing there looking every inch the mature and responsible Head Boy in a black formal *lavalava* and white *elei* dress shirt. Beside him stood his grandmother, regal in her blue puletasi.

Matile seemed flustered. "Oh, well, I'm not sure. You're the boy with the beautiful singing voice tonight?"

I rushed in to capitalize on her fluster. "This is Daniel, Aunty, he's the Head Boy of the school and the House Captain. And this is his grandmother Salamasina. Please, meet my aunty Matile and uncle Tuala."

Everyone moved to shake hands and formalize the introductions, after which Matile and Salamasina chatted about the evening's performance. Uncle Tuala nudged my shoulder with a wry smile as if to say, *nice move Leila, she can't refuse you now that she's met his grandmother can she?*

Simone's cheeky grin seemed to echo the same unspoken message. And, of course, they were right. Within minutes, Daniel, Simone, Sinalei, and I were all walking towards the carpark with Matile's generous farewells in our ears. "Have fun children! Be careful!" I was light-headed. Without quite knowing how it happened, I was going out on a 'typical' McDonald's sundae double date. A bubble of laughter threatened to burst as I reflected on the weirdness of the scene though. Yes, there were two boys and two girls going for ice cream here, but one boy was a *fa'afafine* and one of us could melt ice cream with a thought.

At the car, Simone and Sinalei hopped into the back with unspoken assent, leaving me and Daniel in the front. It felt awkward. A little while ago our hearts had sung in unison for all to see, but now that the music had stopped we were left again with the reality – we were a boy and girl who hadn't actually had a proper conversation for weeks now. I bit my lip in the darkness as Daniel focused his gaze on the road.

"Umm, so tonight was pretty awesome wasn't it?" I tried for casual.

"Actually, I thought it was awful."

His curt response cut me to the quick. "Oh."

He gave me a quick sideways glance. "For me I mean. Not you. You were amazing out there. I've never seen anybody dance like you."

"Oh. Thanks." The silence was suffocating. I tried again. "I don't think anybody was looking at the dancing though. Not when you were singing. You never told me you wrote your own music. Or that you could sing like that." A hint of accusation crept into my voice.

He laughed softly but there was no joy in it. "Leila, there's a lot of things we never got the chance to tell each other. Have you forgotten that this is the first time we've been alone in weeks? The first time we've actually had a conversation in ages? You know, when you're not trying to run away from me or push me away."

I stared at the dashboard and then couldn't resist throwing a barb of my own. "Well, it didn't seem to bother you much. I don't know why you're giving me a hard time about it, seeing as how you seem to be pretty busy and pretty happy with Mele these days."

He jammed his foot on the brake and abruptly pulled the truck over to the side of the road. Simone and Sinalei called out at the sudden jolt. "Hey!" and he ignored them. Instead he turned off the ignition and turned in his seat so he was facing me. So I couldn't evade his eyes. There was restrained anger in his voice.. "What the hell are you talking about? Me and Mele? I don't think so. She's my best friend's girlfriend remember? And besides, why would I even be thinking about anyone else when ..." He broke off abruptly and turned away.

"When what?"

"When the only person I think about is you." He almost shouted the words at me and I shrunk back against their force. "You told me to stay away from you, remember, Leila? And that's what I've been trying to do. But no matter how hard I try, I can't stop thinking about you. I'm turning into a stalker for goodness sake."

I was confused. "What do you mean?"

"I mean that, every day for the last two months, I've been calling your house. Texting your phone. Driving up to Aleisa every other day and not even getting past the front gates, just listening to that woman, Netta, tell me on the intercom that you're not there. You're too busy – studying, working, doing I don't know what. And then last week, when I'm driving back down to town, what do I see? You and some guy going past in his red truck. The same guy that picked you up from school the other day. You told me that you didn't want to be around me because it was 'too dangerous.' Well, obviously it's not too dangerous for him to be around you."

My protest was an indrawn breath. "No, it's not like that. He's a scientist here with a team of researchers studying volcanoes and Nafanua's helping to finance their work. He's been running tests on me, trying to figure out the science of this stuff. He's going to find a cure for me. Make it go away so that I can be regular, normal. So that I won't hurt people." My voice died away. But in my mind I added, *So I can be with you. Kiss you, hug you, love you.*

Daniel shook his head and continued like I hadn't even spoken. "I know that I should just forget about you. That I should just take the huge hint and leave you alone. But then we get pushed into doing this culture item together and I have to sing to you, pour my heart out on stage and I hate it. I hate this. You. Me. Like this. I just don't know what's wrong with me. Believe me Leila, I want to forget about you. The past month has been hell."

I stared at him with shock. And pain. But any reply was halted by a banging from the back of the truck as Simone voiced his impatience.

"Would you two get a move on! We're starving here and sitting in the back of a truck on the side of the road is not our idea of a celebration! What's happening? Your lover's quarrel is getting in the way of party time... let's go!"

Daniel sighed impatiently and swiftly got the truck on and back on the road. His lips were set in a determined angry line and his every change of the gears spoke of his irritation. With me. With everything.

Neither of us spoke again for the rest of the drive to town. McDonald's was packed with SamCo students. Everyone had the same idea as us and the place was rowdy and jubilant. The staff and the air conditioning were struggling to cope with the influx of teenagers. There were whoops and cheers when the boys saw Daniel.

"*Sole* man! Nice one tonight ay!"

He greeted them with a wry shake of his head and a half smile before turning to look down at me. Strict politeness. "So what'll you have, Leila?"

I was trying unsuccessfully not to get too close to him in the jostling crowd and he frowned as a particularly eager customer shoved past me. Quickly, he pulled my hand to move me a little ways behind him, sheltering me with his arm against the throng. A move that was not lost on Simone. He raised his eyebrows at me with a wicked smirk and then yelled at us from the other side of the queue. "You two go ahead with your orders. Me and Sinalei are going to join those guys over there okay?" Before I could respond they had disappeared in the crowd. Leaving me alone. With Daniel – and about fifty other people all wanting to order food. Again he turned to ask me, "What do you want to order?"

In the loud, colorful bustle of a busy fast food restaurant, it was difficult to still be stuck in the quagmire of awkwardness that had held us in the truck. The feeling of his arm casually looped over my shoulder was surreal. Suddenly, I was ravenous. I hadn't eaten all day thanks to the excitement of preparation and now I felt weak with hunger. "I'm gonna get a Big Mac combo upsized and a super sundae with an apple pie. And a diet coke."

He laughed, shaking his head and I gave him a frown. "What! What's wrong? Why are you laughing at me?"

Still shaking his head, he leaned down to tease me. "I thought you only ate leaves and stuff."

I sniffed indignantly. "Whatever. I haven't eaten all day and I'm starving. Dancing is hard work you know."

He smiled again. "Hey don't go getting mad at me – I know better than to get in the way of a hungry girl and a Big Mac. Come on, let's get you fed."

The rest of the evening flew by in a haze of laughter and lightness. In unspoken agreement, we each put aside any more mention of designated 'sensitive' topics and instead focused on food and a light recap of the night's festivities. It was with a sinking feeling that I noticed the time and knew I had better start making my way home or else Aunty Matile would never forgive me. We said goodnight to Simone and Sinalei who were getting rides home with another girl's parents and made our way back to the truck.

The drive back to Faatoia was quiet, but a peaceful kind of quietness. I stole a glance at Daniel's profile in the moonlight, storing him away in my mind. Who knew when I would have another chance to be with him like this? In another week I would be on my way back to the US. To more tests and experiments. The thought of leaving Samoa, leaving the possibility of seeing Daniel was a stab of pain. But the thought of Jason finding a way to cure me was the light of hope in the darkness that I clung to. I smiled to myself as I thought about the possibility of coming back to Samoa a changed person. Able to love Daniel.

"What is it?"

"What's what?"

"You're smiling to yourself. How come?"

"Oh nothing. Just thinking."

"About what?"

We had arrived at the box house nestled in its cheerful garden. Daniel turned in the drive and turned off the engine. There was a rugby game on television. I could hear Uncle Tuala cheering. I knew Aunty Matile would be up waiting for me, unable to sleep until I got home. Cooking probably. A waft of fresh-baked coconut buns confirmed my suspicions.

"I had a good time tonight. With you. The culture show was an amazing experience. One I'll never forget."

"Me neither. I'm glad I was singing to you and not some other girl." He spoke lightly to lessen the cut of his words, "I didn't need to fake the heartbreak and gut-wrenching disappointment."

There was a poignant silence. Which I broke first. "Daniel, I'm going away next week. Back to America. With Jason and his team. They're going to run some tests and see what they can do to help me get over this fire thing."

"Are you sure you should be doing that? What's actually involved? Maybe I've seen too many science fiction conspiracy theory movies, but how do you know you can trust these people? What if they hurt you?"

"No, Jason's not like that. I know him. He's a good friend and I know that I can trust him. There isn't the equipment here in Samoa that he needs to do this. Back in America, things will go much faster and it's way more likely that he can get some answers to this. And then, I can be fixed, don't you see?" I turned excited eyes at him.

"No I don't see. Leila, I'm not so sure that you need fixing."

"What do you mean? Of course I need fixing. You saw me that other night, saw what happened. I don't think you realize how close I come every day to blowing people up, setting everything on fire. My everyday life is like walking on eggshells. I have to watch my every thought, my every move, my every emotion – in case it triggers an outburst. I don't want to live like this."

"But why do you need to resort to a cure? You talk about this like you're some kind of mutant animal or something. I think you're investing a lot of trust in this man. You're going to go with him to America, put yourself totally in his hands, let him do all kinds of things to you – and for what? Maybe there is no 'cure' as you call it ..." his voice died away at my outraged expression.

"What are you saying? Of course there's a cure, there has to be."

"I'm just saying that maybe you're rushing into things with this guy, this Jason. Give it some time. Can't you get somebody you trust in the States to check it all out better first? His lab, his reputation, him? What about your grandmother? She sounds like she's got loads of connections, can't you ask her to find out if this Jason guy is legit?"

I shook my head impatiently. I didn't want to hear this. Daniel didn't know Jason like I did. He didn't trust him because he didn't know him. The night I had spent with Jason, when he had honored my request to be a friend, and all his efforts to help me had created a bond between us that could not be explained. But how could I explain that to Daniel? I turned away from him in the car and bit my lip.

"Leila?" My name was soft on his lips and I couldn't ignore it. "Look at me."

I turned. Daniel leaned forward and brought his hand up to caress my face. I had longed for his touch for so long that I went weak. "I don't want us to fight. It's just that - I don't want you to go."

"What do you mean?"

He shrugged, "I mean, I'm asking you, please don't go back to America. I want you to stay. Here. I don't want you to go."

He was going to kiss me. I knew it. I felt it with every fiber of my being. And I wanted it with every breath, every empty moment that needed him to be complete. But even as my soul hungered for it, I was pulling away. Fumbling for the door handle to get out of the truck. Now. As quickly as possible. Half falling out of the cab, struggling to stand upright, to breathe, to back away. My mind raged with images of *telesā* setting a village alight. Killing people. He looked confused.

"Where are you going? What is it?"

"I can't do this. I can't. I'm sorry. This, us, we can't. It's not right. We're not right." I slammed the car door, grateful for a barrier between us.

"Wait! We need to talk about this."

I was backing away. "No. There's nothing to talk about. I already told you, I don't want to be with you. Stop harassing me like this. I don't want to be with you. Go away. Just go home. You're better off without me, trust me."

And with that, I turned and ran into the house, unwilling to even look back, unsure if I could handle seeing his face one more time. A hasty greeting to Matile and Tuala and I was in the safety of my room, shaking with the effort required not to explode. Not to flash spark. *No, no, breathe. Stay calm. You can do this.*

A shower. That's what I needed. I grabbed that thought with relief and rushed to the bathroom. Only to grit my teeth in frustration at the tiny trickle of water that dripped from the tap. Of course, Samoa and its water pressure problems meant late night showers were impossible. Argh! Back in my room it was a long wait until Matile and Tuala went to bed and I judged it safe enough to creep out carrying my towel. Tonight I needed the soothing chill of my pool. Me and Daniel's pool.

FIFTEEN

I ran through the green night driven by helpless rage and frustration. As soon as I reached the pool, I centered my emotions and let my fists blaze vivid red and gold, wishing there was stone and steel that I could vent my emotions on. I wanted to throw fireballs. I wanted to see the entire forest go up in flames and the night sky choke with grey smoke. For a few moments I battled for control, reminding myself that the green beauty around me didn't deserve to burn just to satisfy my desire to hurt something. Anything.

Instead I knelt beside the pool and submerged my fiery hands, hearing the fizz and hiss as water met fire. I peeled off my shirt and shorts and took slow, hesitant steps into my pool of sanctuary, feeling the rage, the hurt and pain seep away in the water's embrace. I waded in deeper until I was completely submerged, allowing water to lap over my tortured body, putting any threat of fire to rest. Slowly, I swam to my spot beside the diamond waterfall, letting its spray wash away my tears. It had been a long time since I came here to cry, and I had forgotten the peace that it always brought me. I had my back to the forest but, when I heard footsteps in the undergrowth, I spun around in the water.

"Who is that? Who's there?" There was no fear in my voice. Fire had done that to me at least. Banished fear of attackers and bogeymen in the night. I tensed to summon flames but didn't need to.

Daniel stepped quietly into the clearing.

"Hey. It's just me."

"What are you doing here?" my voice was rough as I shrunk back into the black water.

"Looking for you." He shrugged. "I know where you go when you're lonely, Leila, when you're sad. I hoped I would find you here." He spoke quietly in the quiet night. The sounds of evening faded around me as his flecked green eyes caught mine and held me captive.

"What do you want?" again I spoke curtly. The two of us alone with a moonlit pool was far too familiar a scene and I wanted him to leave. Quickly, while reason still controlled me.

"We need to talk."

"No. We already said everything we needed to say to each other. You have to leave. Go away."

He shook his head. "I don't think so. You did all the talking and I didn't get a chance to say what I need to."

"I don't want to talk to you, Daniel. I don't want to be anywhere near you. I thought I made that very clear." Every word was cutting my soul to shreds.

"I don't believe you."

"Excuse me?" Disbelief colored my reply as Daniel swiftly pulled his t-shirt up over his head and waded into the water. I caught my breath at the sight of his torso in all its defined glory. "What are you doing?"

"I'm coming over there to talk to you."

Frantically, I backed away, further towards the waterfall. "No. You can't. I don't want you to. I don't want you anywhere near me, you hear?"

He ignored me. In seconds, he was only an arm's length away, water droplets shimmering silver on his skin as he stood and stared down at me, holding up his hands in surrender. He spoke softly, a calming buffer against my growing hysteria.

"Leila. I just want to talk to you. That's all. Please just listen to me and when I'm done, I'll leave you alone. If you still want me to, okay? I promise."

I looked at the raw, honest plea in his eyes and couldn't refuse him. Not when he stood this close to me and only silken water separated us. Not when all I wanted was to feel his skin against mine. Encouraged by my silence, he continued.

"I know you're afraid to be with me. I know that you're trying to deal with some powerful stuff. I know you think that it's too dangerous for me to be near you. But there's something you need to know. About me." He paused and I could feel the hesitancy in the air as he steeled himself to continue. "I love you. And I can't be without you anymore. I want to be everything to you. But if I can't, then I'll be what you want me to. Your friend. Your debate sparring partner." A crooked smile as he paused before proceeding. "Your designated driver. The guy who picks you up the next time you pass out in the hallway. Heck, I'll even settle for being the guy who gets his eyebrows flamed – just so I can give you my shirt when you burn all your clothes off."

I blushed at that one. Encouraged by my half smile he took a deep breath. "I'll settle for any one of the above. Let me be your friend. Just don't shut me out. Please."

All resolve fled in the face of his naked honesty. "That's the problem, you're always going to be so much more to me than a friend – you *are* everything to me. The past weeks without you have been unbearable. There hasn't been enough air. Enough light. Not enough color. Every moment without you feels like an eternity and I'm drowning. I'm drowning without you. But I can't be with you." I shookmy head despondently. "Don't you see? I could hurt you. That night when we kissed and I blew up, what you saw me do? That was only the beginning of this fire thing. It's gotten way stronger. More powerful. In ways you can't even begin to imagine. The other day I almost made a volcano erupt!" I lifted my hands out of the water and shook them helplessly. "I've been working on controlling it and I have gotten heaps better at it – but whenever I'm around you, I don't know what happens. It's like my feelings for you trigger it and I'm fighting to keep it contained. I'm afraid of what could happen if we're together. I love you too much to risk it. Do you realize I could kill you? I almost killed you that other night!" My voice rose several octaves.

Two steps and then his strong arms swept me into a bone-crushing embrace.

"Daniel – no, I ..."

His lips on mine cut me short and, for a few heart-stopping moments, all rational thought fled as I drowned in his kiss. Hard, searching, breathtaking kiss.

It ended as abruptly as it began, leaving me gasping for air and my head spinning. I stumbled a few steps back away from him in the water as I tried to regain my composure, looking around frantically for any sign of fire attack. Was the water getting hotter? I remembered shrimp boiled pink during my foray in the pool on Nafanua's estate and desperately tried to calm my ragged breathing. Daniel was oblivious to my fears.

"See!" he was triumphant, "I'm still alive. And not even a wisp of smoke or flames anywhere in sight."

I shook my head, emotions and thoughts a swirling mess, still waiting for flames, still searching for rises in the water temperature. "No, it's too risky." Even as I said it, doubts were clouding my resolve. Because he was right. There was no familiar rush of flame and heat. Well, I hastily amended, not beyond what I imagined the usual boy-kisses-girl heat flash to be like. In fact, I was feeling a little cold – half naked in a freshwater spring in the middle of the night. I suppressed a chill in the night breeze and Daniel responded by pulling me into his arms, warming me with his embrace.

"Come here." He rubbed his arms along mine. "You don't feel like a girl about to set the world on fire – you're cold. What were you saying about this being too dangerous?"

I still didn't trust myself to be this close to him and I tried to pull away. "I mean it. We shouldn't be doing this. We shouldn't be together like this."

Again, he pulled me into his arms, only this time shushing me with his fingers on my lips.

"Listen to me. The other night when you – exploded – I'll admit it was scary. But it was also the most beautiful thing I've ever seen. You're not a monster. This power *is* frightening and I can't even begin to imagine what you're going through but it doesn't define you. And you shouldn't let it dictate to you either. Your strength is one of the things I love most about you. I know you can control this. Now, I'm just as in the dark as you are about how to figure it out, about what's going to happen. But I know that together we can do this. I helped you the other night, you reined it in, you spoke and the fire listened. We could be a good team, Leila give us a chance."

"But Daniel, how could you love me?" disbelief colored my voice. "You saw me the other night. It was awful. I could have killed all those people and I ..." my voice dropped to a hesitant whisper, unwilling to speak aloud the unspeakable. "I almost killed people – and I loved it. I loved the feeling of power, that I could create chaos like that. It was evil. *I'm* evil. Daniel, you can't love me. Nobody can." Inside, I screamed *I hate myself, why don't you?* I thought of *telesā* calling down fire to burn a village to the ground. I tried to pull away from his embrace but I may as well have been trying to move the proverbial mountain for all the good it did me.

He looked down at me with one eyebrow arched quizzically. Again he lowered his face to mine, this time to dance his lips feather soft against my forehead, my cheeks, the tip of my nose, a whisper on my lips. A smile before he answered.

"Leila, nobody's perfect. We're all struggling with something. You don't love someone because they're a dream of perfection. You love them because of the way they meet their challenges, how they struggle to overcome. You love them because together you bring out the best in each other. I fell in love with you before you blew up in flames and it hasn't changed. You're argumentative, stubborn, prickly, fiery tempered, and absolutely impossible when you can't get your way. You drive me nuts – and not always in a good way."

Wrapped securely in his broad arms, breathing in the sun-kissed scent of him, and hearing the strong throb of his heartbeat, how much easier it was to believe we were indeed possible. How I longed to be as hopeful as he. As optimistic. And for a few sweet moments as I stood there, I believed in the possibilities. But too soon, cold shards of reason cut through the fantasy. How could I even consider for a moment the thought of being with him when every minute with me was putting his life at risk? If I truly loved him, how could I do that to him?

As if he could read my mind, Daniel released me slightly so he could turn me to face the waterfall, shimmering silver in the moonlight. With one hand on my shoulder, he pointed to the black velvet water.

"Remember how you told me that this pool was the one thing that could cool the fire inside you? How its waters would refresh you and keep you from overheating?"

I nodded mutely, unsure what he was getting at. He pulled away, putting me at arm's length.

"I can be that for you. I can be the waters that keep you ... real. Keep you focused. In tune, in control. We could do this – make it work – together. Tell me you don't want to give us a chance? Tell me you don't want to try? If you can look me in the eye and tell me honestly that you don't love me enough to try, then I promise, I'll leave this alone. I won't bother you any more. And we can go on like this – us – never happened."

My breath caught. Yes I loved him. And I was terribly ashamed to admit that I was selfish. I wanted him more than anything. More than air. More even than the dizzying feeling of power when I erupted in flames. The thought of us continuing as if we had never loved – it hurt like a blade to the heart. I shook my head and whispered so softly that he had to move even closer to hear it, "I love you, more than life itself."

I couldn't argue with him any more after that. He had said everything I ever dreamed of hearing him say. His words knit a blanket of feather soft warmth around me, a security and peace I never wanted to lose. Gently, he kissed me again and this time I wasn't thinking about all the reasons why we shouldn't be doing this. This time I couldn't think of anything but the feel of his lips on mine, his hands as they tugged on my hair, sending wires of heat radiating through me, how good the hardness of his body felt pressed against mine. The kiss ended all too soon though as Daniel released me and backed several steps away.

"We better get you home. We shouldn't be out alone here like this, not if we're going to be doing this."

I was bemused. And if I was being totally honest, I really wanted to keep kissing him some more. "Huh? It's okay, Matile and Tuala are asleep. They don't even know I'm here with you. I don't have to be back for a while yet." I smiled reassuringly at him and made to move back into his arms but he stopped me with a smile.

"No, it's not okay. Come on, I'll walk you back." And with that he held out his hand to help me walk with him out of the pool. Once out of his embrace I had to admit that it was really cold. He reached for my towel on the rocks and wrapped it around me, rubbing my arms and shoulders with it.

"Here, it's kind of chilly now. You alright?"

"Yes, I'm fine." He waited while I dried off and quickly put my t-shirt and shorts back on and then together we walked slowly back along the well-worn path until we were just outside the fence. He stopped with my hand in his and pulled me close to him for a brief embrace. I breathed him in deeply, loving his scent, his warmth, his touch. Everything about him. I knew I would never have my fill of him.

"I'll text you tomorrow, okay?" He left a single quick kiss on my forehead before walking away back the way we had come. I watched him until he was completely out of sight, unwilling to let him go, even with my eyes.

Back in my room, I was awash with delight. I was in love with Daniel. And he loved me. Everything was right in the universe.

SIXTEEN

The next day I knew I needed to talk to Jason. As soon as possible. Yes, I still wanted him to help cure me, but I didn't want to leave Samoa. Not just now anyway. I texted him. Nothing. Called him. Nothing. Where was he? I helped Matile to decorate the church and in between sweeping and arranging flowers, I continued to send increasingly irritated messages to Jason. It wasn't until mid afternoon that someone finally answered his phone. Only it wasn't him. It was Blaine.

"Hello? Leila, is that you?"

"Yes, Blaine? I'm trying to reach Jason. Do you know where I can reach him? What have you guys been up to all day? I've been trying for ages to get through."

Blaine's voice was tight with worry. "We're here at the hospital. Jason's sick. There's something wrong and the doctors are trying to figure it out."

"What? What happened? Is he going to be alright?"

His reply cut me with ice as I felt his fear over the line. "I don't know, Leila. I think you better get over here. We want to get him airlifted out back home, but they said he's not stable enough to be moved."

The next few minutes were a blur as I hastily told Tuala where I was going. "A friend of mine is really sick, I have to be there." Then I was in the Wrangler and weaving in and out of cars, wishing I could part traffic with my thoughts. My hands gripped the steering wheel as I tried to remain calm. The last thing Jason needed was a flame thrower to incinerate his medical team.

The hospital was a weary, miserable place. I ran along the cement walkways, past people sitting on their mats waiting for doctors, past snotty-nosed children playing in the rocky gardens, past operating theaters that reeked of disinfectant that was losing its battle against decay and rot. To Acute 7. Where Blaine and Matthew stood outside a room with two other men in business suits. Blaine was agitated.

"But you're the Embassy, you've got to do something. You've got to help us get him home!"

One of the men shook his head. "I'm sorry but we can't do anything if he doesn't have medical clearance. It's up to his doctors."

"But they don't know what the heck is wrong with him. If we don't get him home, he's going to die here."

I stopped short, unable to breathe at his words. "No! What do you mean? What's wrong?"

Everyone turned at my interruption and the suits looked irritated. Blaine moved to greet me. "Hey Leila. He's bad, really bad. Come on in."

I went to the doorway and peered in, stunned by the sight of Jason lying still and pale, hooked to a mass of machinery. "What's happened to him?"

"Thursday, we were working on collating all our results, getting ready to move out next week, you know, then he was complaining of a bad headache and went back to the flat to sleep. When we got there, he was unconscious and burning up with fever. We brought him straight here and he's been like this ever since."

I walked over to stand beside his bed. The scene was an all too familiar one. The last time I had stood like this beside a hospital bed, I had been looking at my father in a coma. I didn't want to be here. But I didn't want to be anywhere else either, not when Jason was like this.

"I don't understand. Did they run tests? What do they think is wrong with him? Aren't they doctors?" Worry fought with anger in my voice.

"It's an infection of some kind. They think maybe some tropical parasite or bug that's gotten into his bloodstream. They've pumped him full of antibiotics but nothing seems to be working. He's had three seizures already and now, it's like they've given up . Told us we have to wait for more bloodwork results while they keep looking for answers. In other words, he's stuffed. Which is why we're trying to get him moved." Blaine directed a venomous glare back at the two suits that moved uneasily.

"Look, until you can get doctor's clearance for him to fly, our hands are tied. Follow up with them and get that, then we can act. Let us know."

With that weak comfort, they left, relieved to be out of there. Leaving us staring down at a man fighting for his life. Blaine and Matthew went to hunt down the doctors in charge of his case and update his family. Jason and I were alone. I looked at his face, wishing I could see it light up with his sun-filled smile. With a trembling hand, I reached out and gently ran my fingers through his hair, on the side of his face, feeling the slight stubble of three days of neglect.

"Oh Jason, please wake up. I need you. We all do. You can't die. You can't." Tears spilled, and this time I let them as I bent to place a single soft kiss on his forehead. There was an abrupt movement from the doorway and I looked up, startled, to see Daniel standing there, staring at me with a stony, unreadable face.

"Daniel. What are you doing here?"

"I stopped by your house and your uncle told me you were here. All he knew was that a friend of yours was very sick. I was worried so I came straight here to see if there was anything I could do to help." He backed away slowly. "But I see that you don't need me, so I'll get out of your way. We can talk later."

"No wait! Daniel, please."

Quickly, I ran lightly after him, catching hold of his arm in the corridor. "Wait, don't leave."

"Why not?"

I looked at his impassive face and almost faltered. "Because ... because I need you. You're the best part of me remember? We're the team that's going to take on anything the world throws at us – and win. Right?"

He fought an unwilling smile for a moment before sighing and rolling his eyes, pulling me to him for a brief kiss on the forehead. "Okay fine. You got me. I'm not leaving. What do you want me to do?"

With a tug on his arm I pulled him back to Jason's room. "I want you to come and meet my friend, Jason. Professor Jason Williams. Come on." I put added emphasis on the word 'friend,' praying that Daniel would believe me.

There were two nurses with their backs to us fussing at Jason's bedside and whispers of their hushed conversation came to us loud and clear. *E maimauletaimi, e tatauonaave i se fofo...se taulasea, o le mai Samoa.* Startled at our entrance, they quickly left, shaking their heads at us with piteous looks. I stood and watched them leave with puzzlement.

"What were they saying, Daniel?"

He looked uncomfortable and seemed hesitant. "Umm it's just idle talk that's all. They're not the doctors working on his case, so it doesn't matter."

"No tell me, what was it?"

A shrug. "They said that he's been cursed with a Samoan sickness, by an evil spirit. That's why the doctors can't figure out what's wrong. And that's why ..." he broke off and looked down at me with tenderness in his eyes. "I'm sorry, Leila. They said he's going to die. Soon."

"No! I won't accept that. We can't. There's got to be something we can do." I left Daniel's side and went to gaze down at Jason, my voice dying away, "That's it. There is something we can do – come on."

"What? Where are we going?" Daniel was bewildered as he followed me, easily catching up, with his long stride.

"There is something we can do, well, I mean there is someone who can help. Nafanua and the Covenant – they've got cures for everything."

In the car park, I rejected Daniel's green truck for my much faster Wrangler. "Let's take my car." The ride up the mountain road to Aleisa was one of screeching tires and Daniel's terse warnings.

"Watch out, there's a pig on the road! Slow down, there's a speed bump coming up OUCH! Never mind ... You know I would like to live to make it to my next birthday."

I ignored him. Focused on the road. Focused on devising a strategy that would make Nafanua help me, help Jason. After all, when we had last met, the battle lines had basically been drawn in the sand between us. Yes, Nafanua was *telesā*. But she was still my mother, wasn't she? And surely she would at least listen to me? Help me? We drove in through the imposing front gates and I came to a halt. Gripping the steering wheel tightly, I took a deep breath. This was it. I was afraid of what I would find inside, but the thought of Jason, struggling for life back at that hospital, gave me the resolve I needed.

Daniel sensed my trepidation. "Are you sure you want to do this?" I smiled weakly at him and nodded. I had told him my mother and I had parted on bad terms but he had no idea just how bad. He still knew nothing of storm criers, lightning callers, and rain summoners – and if I had my way, that's the way it would stay.

"Yes. I have to. She's made millions with her knowledge of plants and natural healing. I know she can help Jason."

He walked with me up the verandah steps, but I stayed him with a gentle hand. "Can you wait out here? Please? I think it's best if I talk to her alone."

Daniel didn't look like he liked it, but he let me go. "Okay, I'll be waiting right here for you. Call out if you need me, alright?"

I really didn't think he'd be much help against a covenant of angry *matagi telesā*, but still, I was glad I wasn't alone. Steeling myself, I opened the door and went in.

Nafanua was sitting with the others in the front living room - opened bottles of wine, and half-filled glasses proclaiming they were midway through their usual weekend meeting. They didn't look surprised to see me. But then, they didn't look happy either. Sarona's drawl welcomed me first.

"Well, look who's come back for a visit. See here ladies, it's our baby sister, Leila! What a welcome surprise, we didn't think we were ever going to have you join one of our Covenant meetings again, did we?"

There was a painful silence. "I'm sorry to interrupt your meeting but I was wondering, Nafanua, if we could talk? Please?"

My eyes sought hers and found nothing but midnight steel. "Leila, whatever you've come to say, you can say in front of all of us. We are one here, you know that."

This was not going the way I had hoped. I had wanted to speak to Nafanua alone. A daughter to a mother. But it was clear there would be no familial quarter given here. Inwardly, I was shaking, but on the outside I was calling on all my Folger poise. I raised my chin defiantly. "Fine then. I know that we parted on bad terms and I accept that I have disappointed you, upset you. But I've come here today to ask you please for your help."

Sarona smirked and looked around at the others. "Oh, do you hear that, sisters? She wants help. From her sisters. And just what makes you think that you even have the right to ask for help from the sisterhood you have turned against?"

Nafanua stood, silencing Sarona with a single look. Her expression was unreadable, her voice low. "What help do you seek from me, my daughter?"

Encouraged by her reminder that yes, she was my mother, I forged ahead. "Jason is sick. Very sick. The doctors don't know what's wrong with him and he's going to die. But I know that you can help him. All your *telesā* knowledge, of plants and medicines and everything, you can save him. I'm asking you, please?"

A ripple of laughter went through the room as if the women had shared a joke I didn't know. There was disappointment in Nafanua's eyes as she slowly shook her head. "You don't understand anything, do you? You left, turned your back on your sisters. Rejected the gifts you have been given. These are serious crimes."

"I don't understand, what's all that got to do with Jason?"

Sarona interrupted impatiently. "I told you she was a fool, Nafanua. Even now, she cannot even begin to grasp the immensity of the situation, of what we are, of what covenants she's broken." She stood and pointed her finger at me. "You were warned what would happen if you broke covenant with us. But even worse, you shared your gifts with a man. And allowed him to test you like a lab rat. Surely you didn't think that would go unpunished?"

Slowly but surely, like the creeping of a centipede up my spine, I felt, I knew – the awful truth. "You did this? You made Jason sick? Those nurses were right, he's dying because of a curse, a *mai Samoa?*"

Manuia jumped in, waving a languid hand. "Oh don't be so melodramatic, Leila. We're not spell casters and witches from the 18th century. We poisoned him. A simple enough thing when you know as much as Nafanua and Mina do about earth's natural weapons." She smiled at me warmly and studied her hot pink painted nails, "You are right about one thing though – yes, he is going to die. Oh, I'd say, he's got about another forty-eight hours before he limps his way to an agonizing death. No-one can help him now."

"No. You can't do this, surely you're not that heartless?" I appealed to the woman I had mistakenly thought that I knew, "Nafanua, you worked with Jason, he was a friend! He was, is, my friend. He's a good man, you can't let this happen."

"You're mistaken. Again. This boy's fate was not decided by us. It was you who betrayed your gifts with him. It was you who gave yourself up to his Western science. That boy is dying because of you. There will be blood on your hands by tomorrow."

"No …" a sob, half strangled with fear.

I was stunned by the madness of it all. I looked around the room, searching for reason somewhere, for friendship. I had laughed, talked, and danced with these beautiful women. They had taken me into their homes, their arms, their circle, and made me one of them. And yet, in their eyes now, all I found was coldness. I would find no help, no mercy here. I thought of Jason teaching me how to surf, laughing at me as I fell down again and again. I thought of the hours spent laboring over calculus as he patiently explained algorithms again and again. And I thought of his smile as he promised to help me. To be my friend, no matter what. No. I would not let Jason die.

Desperation made me rash, dislodging my fragile hold on control. The familiar searing pain rippled through my fingers as fire made its presence known and I struggled not to scream as my hands erupted into flame. The Covenant tensed and the situation went from bad to worse as I confronted them with the only reaction I knew might get results. I didn't know exactly what I was going to do. All I was sure of was that I would not stand by and do nothing.

I held my fiery hands out in a pleading appeal. "Nafanua, please I don't want to do this …" I didn't get to finish. Before I even sensed movement, Sarona acted.

"You little bitch! You would use fire against us?" From the stillness, a rushing torrent of wind hit me with all the force of a running linebacker, knocking me off my feet, throwing me back, smashing me through the doors and out onto the lawn.

I lay there reeling, gasping for air, my body and mind numb to all else but the bone-rattling pain. My fire had gone out at the unexpectedness of the attack, extinguished just like the blowing out of a candle. Dimly I was aware of Daniel running to kneel by my side.

"Leila! Are you alright? What happened?"

Even amidst my pain, I cursed my stupidity. What had I done? I had brought Daniel here, right into the lion's den. Where six very angry *telesā* could now take their vengeance out on him. I tried to talk, tried futilely to push him away. *"Daniel, go. Get away from here. Before it's too late."* But he wasn't listening. He was lifting me gently in his arms, sitting me up, peering into my eyes.

"Can you hear me? Can you walk?"

From behind him, a triumphant voice. "Ahhh and what do we have here, girls? Leila brought along a friend, how lovely." Sarona stood surveying us, one hand on her hip, a delighted smile on her face as she eyed Daniel up and down, speculatively. "Hmm, nice one – look sisters – isn't he delicious?"

Daniel ignored her, helping me to struggle to my feet, supporting my frame with one arm, anxiously testing whether or not I could walk. I hurt everywhere and I was tempted to call a full body flame up because molten lava was impervious to pain. But I knew we had to get away from there. I had made a terrible mistake coming here with Daniel and I was in no position to take on all six *telesā* at once.

"Daniel, let's go. Quickly."

"How are you feeling? That was a huge knock you took just now."

I was eager to reassure him. "I'm fine. Honestly. I just really want to go. Can you help me to the car please? Now. We have to leave now."

"Oh, leaving so soon Leila? Aren't you going to introduce us to your gorgeous friend? We are your family after all!" Sarona smirked at us and the others laughed from where they stood arrayed on the verandah.

Daniel flushed and narrowed his eyes. I felt him tense and knew all too well what that signaled. His voice was hostile. "Are you Nafanua? Leila's mother? Are you the one who did this to her?"

Nafanua strolled out into the sunlight and regarded us with unreadable eyes. "No. I am Nafanua. And you must be Daniel. The boy my daughter has been pining over for so long. I thought maybe she had outgrown you, but I see that she is still very much enthralled with her childish infatuation."

Nervously, I tugged at Daniel's arm, "Come on. Never mind that. Please just get me out of here."

His eyes were earnest as he refused. "No, Leila, I want to know who did this to you? This isn't right – you could have been killed. And this woman is supposed to be your mother?" He turned and spoke to Nafanua. "I don't understand. What kind of woman would treat her daughter this way? She came here asking you for help and this is what you do to her? I don't know what's going on here but you should be ashamed."

Nafanua arched an eyebrow. "Oh really? There's a lot you don't know. This? This is between me and my daughter. And I would advise you not to get in the middle of a family dispute. It could end … badly for you."

Daniel drew himself up to stand tall in the sunlight. Fire and steel burned in him as he replied, strong and defiant. "That's where you're wrong. I love Leila, and her happiness means everything to me. I don't mean to be disrespectful, but I'm warning you, don't ever try to hurt her again. I won't let you."

There was silence at his words. I had never loved him more than I did at that moment. As he stared with uncompromising eyes at six women with the power to strike him down with a mere thought. I knew that both our lives were on the line and yet I had no fear. Standing there with my hand in his, my heart and soul woven with his, unbreakably.

There was a slight softening in Nafanua's eyes as she regarded us. Then a slight nod, as if acknowledging a good point. "Leila, well done. He is brave as well as handsome and the depth of his sincerity is endearing. But then, how much does he really know about you, hmm?" She walked down the verandah steps and began to slowly circle us, tapping a finger thoughtfully on her lips. "Daniel, has Leila told you what she is? What we all are? Hmm? Has she told you about the work she has done for us? Using her fire to destroy factories. Burn down a building here and there. Terrorize a few people. Hmm? Do you really know what your girlfriend is capable of? I wonder, would you still love her and stand against us so nobly for her if you knew how often she is tempted to set people on fire?"

I caught my breath and hung my head in shame. Daniel's grip on my hand tightened. "Say whatever you like. It doesn't change anything. I told you, I love Leila. Nothing you do or say is going to keep us apart."

Sarona interrupted impatiently. "Oh really? Well, how about this?"

This time I knew what was coming, but I still only had a moment to react, barely enough time to release Daniel's hand and shove him away from me. "Daniel, move!"

This time Sarona summoned lightning. Laughing gleefully as she gestured fiercely, as white light flashed and seared a line – directly down the center of where Daniel and I had stood. The smoking line of black separated us, mocking us both with its divisiveness. Daniel's eyes were wide with horror as he sat on the grass where I had shoved him and stared from the lightning strike to the woman who had called it – and back again. I didn't wait for another strike. I scrambled to my feet and ran to stand between Daniel and the women arraigned in front of the house that had once been my home.

"No! No more. Please. He didn't know what he was doing, what he was saying. He doesn't know anything about any of you. Please just let him go. I was wrong, I made a mistake leaving the Covenant. I see that now. Let us go, give me the antidote for Jason and I'll come back to the sisterhood. I'll do whatever you want me to."

Sarona scoffed, "You are in no position to bargain with us you fool. What makes you think we would want you back? You have nothing we need."

My heart sank. I didn't want to summon my fire in all its unpredictability and, no matter what Nafanua had done, I knew I wouldn't be able to use it against her. But it looked like there would be no other way out of this. I tried not to let my fear show, but still my voice sounded frail in my ears, "I don't want to hurt you, Sarona, any of you. Please don't do this. Just let us go."

Sarona smiled. "Oh, it is not I who will be hurting today, little sister." From far away in the forest I could hear a rushing sound, a wild wind building to a fierce crescendo, drawing nearer and nearer.

"ENOUGH!" Nafanua interrupted, stilling the oncoming wind with a single gesture. She addressed the other women. "Leila has acknowledged that she made a mistake. She is willing to make reparation for it. All of us have made our own mistakes in the past," she narrowed her eyes at Sarona "some graver than others. She is young and yes – she is foolish. But she is learning. And she is still our sister and potentially the greatest of us all. I, for one, am not willing to forsake the gift that she brings to our cause. What say you my sisters?"

Each of the others nodded slowly. All except for Sarona, who merely shrugged dismissively. Nafanua turned back to us. Daniel had risen to his feet and now stood beside me. I longed to see if his eyes were those of the boy I loved – or of a stranger now that he knew the truth about me and my family. But I didn't dare take my eyes off the women who confronted us.

"You and this boy will leave now. It will take me a few hours to prepare the antidote for the Professor. You will return at eight o'clock tonight for it. But listen well, Leila. We do not offer you this second chance lightly. When you return to us, you must be fully committed to our sisterhood. You will cut all ties to your old family and embrace your new one. You will pack your things, you will bid farewell to your uncle and aunt. You will take your leave of this boy, put an end to this relationship, and never see him again. Do you understand?"

I nodded dumbly. What else could I do? I turned to leave but Daniel's voice stopped me. "Wait" he said tersely. He took a step forward and his question for Nafanua was challenging. "All that seems a pretty steep price to pay for some medicine that may or may not work."

Nafanua's reply was lighthearted but there were were biting tree snakes in her words. "You misunderstand me boy – Leila isn't just paying for an antidote, she's buying your life. And the lives of everyone in your family. The lives of her aunt and uncle. You see, Leila knows that we will kill anyone who opposes us. We've done it before and have no problems with doing it again." She shook her head and waved us on our way with a careless hand. "Oh no, luckily for you, Leila's just made a very good bargain."

With that, Nafanua turned and walked with the other *telesā* back up the steps, with Daniel staring after them. I tugged on his arm, desperate to get out of there. "Come on. Let's go."

There were no words between us as he helped me into the passenger seat, as I tried not to show how much every movement hurt me. He must have known though, because he drove slowly back down the Aleisa mountain road, carefully avoiding all the potholes and bumps, giving me pensive looks every so often. I stared out the side window, unseeing of the scenery, my thoughts a shattered mess, Nafanua's directives stampeding through my head. *You will cut all ties with your family ... end this relationship ... say goodbye to this boy and never see him again. We will kill anyone who opposes us ...*

I was so lost in thought that the abrupt halt of the Wrangler had me startled. I looked around. Daniel had pulled over in a sheltered dip in the winding road; we were nowhere near town. "What? Why are we stopping? We're not home yet?"

He turned the car off and took a deep breath before facing me. There was no warmth in his face. "First things first, are you alright? Should I take you to the hospital?"

I shook my head, not trusting my emotions enough to voice them.

"Are you sure?" His voice was tight and angry. "Damnit Leila! I need to know that I can trust you and, right now, I don't even know if you're telling me the truth about how badly hurt you are. Don't lie to me. I'm sick of all the secrets. How bad are you?"

I shrank back against his fury. This was a Daniel I wasn't used to seeing. It was with a small voice that I replied, "I hurt. All over. Like I got trampled in a rugby ruck. I'm going to be black and blue everywhere tomorrow when the bruises start showing. But nothing's broken. And it's nothing that a doctor or a hospital can fix. And that's the truth. I deserve this hurt anyway, I've made such a mess of things, people are dying because of me, people's lives are in danger because of me, I deserve all the yelling and the anger that you've got to give me."

I turned away as I fought to contain the tears. Crying wouldn't help anyone now. But in the next instant, Daniel had bridged the gaping distance between us and was enfolding me in his arms. His voice broke as he soothed me and held me, "I didn't mean to shout at you. Shh, I'm sorry, here I am yelling at you and you're in pain."

His every touch had me cringing and wincing. He backed away in confusion. "What is it? What's wrong? You're not afraid of me are you? I wasn't angry with you, I'm just so frustrated and confused..."

"No, it's not you. It's me – I want you to hug me, but it hurts. Ow!" I groaned as he jumped back away from me at my words. There was nothing but tenderness in his gaze as he leaned forward and held my face in his hands.

"I'm sorry. I won't touch you anymore. I'll just touch the one part of you that isn't bruised ..." and with that, his lips met mine in a single delicate and fragile kiss that left me longing for more.

But too quickly he moved away back to his side of the Wrangler, placing both hands on the steering wheel. "Leila, before we go any further, before we try and figure out how we're going to deal with your psychotic mother and her sisters, I want you to tell me EVERYTHING."

I gulped. "Everything?"

His eyes were stern. "Yes, everything. Start from the beginning. And don't leave anything out. You owe me that much after today."

Glumly, I nodded. I couldn't argue with that. And slowly, haltingly, I proceeded to tell him everything. How the heat flashes had started and then just kept worsening. The pool he already knew about. I told him about the nightmares I would have about Nafanua, even before I had ever met her. How it had felt to meet her that first time and realize I already knew her. I skimmed over the night we had first kissed and my fire had erupted since he had been there too, but at that part of the story, he reached forward and took my hand in his, raising it to his lips. "A night I will never forget ..." he said.

Encouraged, I continued and as I recited my training, my time with Nafanua, her explanation of what *telesā* were and what their function was, her instructions that it would be too dangerous for me to love anyone, and my decision to end our friendship so I wouldn't hurt him – his eyes darkened and his hand tightened on mine. I told him about being afraid of Nafanua but unsure of who else to trust, who else to turn to for answers and help with the frightening changes taking place in my body. My tension eased as I got to the part about the volcano and the night I had met Jason, our friendship and how I had accidentally revealed my powers to him. How I had then confided in him and he had embarked on his quest to try and help me. First by understanding my powers and testing their limitations. Finally, I came to the part about Nafanua and the *telesā* punishing the village, killing people, and burning their homes, which had led to our angry confrontation and my return to Matile and Tuala.

It felt good to get it all out, to finally have all my secrets and fears out in the open. To know that at last nothing parted Daniel and I. When I was done, Daniel's face was thoughtful as he stared out the window, but, thankfully, his grip on my hand had not loosened and I clung gratefully to that assurance that yes, he was still with me and on my side. Then after what seemed an eternity, he turned to me with a soft smile.

"Thank you. For finally telling me the truth. I'm still mad at you for keeping so much stuff from me for so long – and I'm going to make you pay me back big-time for that one!" An almost sly smile at that, betrayed his teasing intentions and he leaned forward to capture my lips again. This time, the heat that flared between us was enough to send ripples of red energy fizzling through the cab and Daniel had to duck as sparks glanced off the side of his face, "Ouch!" Quickly, I backed away, deep breathing to calm my pulse and assert control before I blew us both up.

"Sorry, sorry. Are you okay? I didn't mean to do that, you just always make me want to explode." I winced at the double meaning in the words, and he laughed the golden laugh that always made my world lighten.

"Yeah, I tend to have that effect on girls everywhere." Laughter aside, he turned serious again. "I'm fine, I've had worse burns from welding. Leila, I don't want you going back to those women. You know you can't. They're just going to use you and your powers. Make you do stuff you don't want to."

"But I have to. You heard them, not only is Jason going to die, but they're going to go after my family next. And you. And your grandmother. I don't have any other choice." I shook my head. "No Daniel, there's nothing else we can do."

"That's where you're wrong. Look, let's take this one step at a time. The most important thing right now, is saving your friend. We can worry about the other stuff later. Let's go. We don't have much time. They said he's got 48 hours left." He started the Wrangler and reversed, efficient urgency in his every move.

"Where are we going?" I longed to find hope, some kind of escape route from this nightmare, but I didn't see any other way out.

"My house."

I was still confused. "Why?"

"Your mother's not the only person who knows how to heal people with plants. We're going to see my grandmother, ask her if she can help us."

That's his brilliant plan?! The woman hates me! "Umm, I don't think that's a good idea, I don't think that's going to work."

But Daniel's resolve was unshakeable as he sped down the mountain road, driving like Michael Andretti on crack. "Of course it will. Grandmother will know what antidote your friend needs and then you won't have to give in to those psycho witches." He winced at me, "Sorry, I know one of them is your mother. Grandmother might be able to buy us some time to figure out what to do next."

I gave up arguing because I could see he was convinced his grandmother was my lifeline. I didn't want to remind him that she had warned him to stay away from me because I would just bring him heartache. Pain. Trouble. I groaned and shut my eyes as I faced the truth of her prediction. Because here we were. Faced with heartache, pain, and trouble. The old woman had been right and I dreaded her reaction when Daniel asked her for help. Could this day get any worse? Remembering the coldness of her reception that long-ago day in her garden – I knew it could.

SEVENTEEN

If I could have had my way, we would have driven forever. Away from here to the furthest reaches of the Mojave Desert. Or to the coldest wastelands of Siberia. Anywhere, just so long as we were together and out of reach of even the memory of *telesā*. But too soon, we were pulling into the driveway and parking beside the familiar weatherworn welding shop. Daniel's movements were brisk and authoritative as he helped me out of the jeep and walked us into the house. He left me in the kitchen and went in search of his grandmother. "Mama? Where are you? Mama?" Still sore from the earlier encounter with Sarona, I gingerly sat down at the kitchen table and tried to prepare myself for what I was sure would not be an easy meeting.

I didn't have long to wait. I could hear Daniel's voice as he greeted his grandmother, and the next minute they walked into the kitchen. Clearly the old lady had been working in her garden as she came in still wearing muddy boots and with a woven hat secured to her head with a colorful scarf. She looked worried and barely nodded at me as she made her way to the sink and hurriedly washed her hands, still talking to Daniel over her shoulder. "What is it son? What's wrong? Are you in trouble? Tell me."

Daniel's voice was patient and reassuring. "I'm alright, Mama. Please, just sit down so that Leila and I can explain. Please."

Unwillingly, Salamasina sat down, choosing the seat furthest from mine. I gave her a weak smile, which she ignored. Daniel sat beside me and took my hand in his underneath the table. I held on to it gratefully as Salamasina turned glaring eyes at me. "What's going on? Why is she here?"

Daniel and I looked at each other, unsure which of us would speak first or where in this saga we should start. He was about to begin when suddenly, a look of horrified realization came over his grandmother's face and she stood and launched into a fury of words – all in Samoan. Angry words tripping over each other and all directed at Daniel. I was lost. Bewildered, I looked from her to Daniel, and was even more confused when Daniel whooped gleefully and started laughing, shaking his head. "No, no, Mama. You've got it all wrong. It's nothing like that. Mama!"

Now both Salamasina and I were baffled as Daniel fought to contain his laughter. He reached over to give his grandmother a warm hug, which she accepted unwillingly, still speaking a hundred words a minute, none of which I could understand.

"Daniel, what's your grandmother saying? What is it?" I hated to interrupt them, but I was worried that if she got any angrier, she would self-destruct.

Daniel laughed some more. "Mama thinks that we have come to tell her that you're pregnant. And she's angry with me and telling me off for being a disobedient son, a foolish irresponsible boy who has not treated you with enough respect."

I was horrified. Waves of shame battered me. "Ohmigosh. No." I appealed to her with frantic earnestness, "No, I'm not. It's not possible. Me and Daniel, we're not … umm … we haven't …" my voice petered away as I wished I could just rip the earth open with a quake and sink into oblivion.

Taking pity on my awkwardness, Daniel stopped laughing and spoke to Salamasina with calm sincerity. "Mama, I swear, that's not it. I wouldn't do that. Me and Leila, we love each other, but I would never go against what you and Papa have taught me." It was as if the two of them were alone in the room as he shrugged and said simply, "Leila is my life. Her happiness means everything to me. I would never take her virtue from her."

There was silence. I stared at the floor, rendered speechless by the fervor of Daniel's declaration. I had never heard of abstinence being equated with 'virtue' and respect before and the unexpected sweetness of its expression pierced me like nothing else. Suddenly, it hit me. There was so much more for me to learn of this boy who I loved, so much more for me to discover. And the thought that I may not have the chance to – because of my mother and her sisterhood of *telesā* – yanked the breath right out of my chest. Daniel was right. We could not give in to them. Not without a fight. My eyes pricked with unshed tears as I looked up and smiled weakly at Daniel and Salamasina. The old woman spoke first and her tone was somewhat mollified.

"Oh. I apologize for being quick to make assumptions, Leila. About my son and about you."

Daniel nudged her. "That's okay, Mama. We're sorry if we gave you a heart attack."

Salamasina's tone was questioning. "But if that's not the 'serious matter' you wanted to discuss with me, then what is it? What's wrong?"

Eager to change the embarrassing subject, I jumped in. "I was hoping that you could help with your medicines and natural healing remedies. My friend Jason is very sick in hospital. He's dying and the doctors there don't know what's wrong with him. Could you please help him?"

"Well of course I'll try. But I'm not a miracle worker. What makes you think that I can find the answer if the doctors cannot?"

I struggled to find the right words to answer her, but Daniel jumped in first. "Because we already know what's wrong with him. He's been poisoned."

Salamasina shook her head in disbelief. "With what? How do you know this? And why don't you just tell the doctors?" Her eyes narrowed as she stared first at Daniel and then at me, sensing there was oh so much more to the tale. "Who did this? Who poisoned your friend?"

There was no easy way to say it. "My mother. Nafanua."

I expected even more confusion but, instead, Salamasina faced me with an almost resigned look of awareness. Our eyes met and held. "Of course. This is all making sense now." She didn't even look at Daniel, just issued him with a curt request that expected no argument. "Daniel can you excuse us please? Leila and I are going to take a little walk in the garden. We need some time alone. To talk."

She stood and beckoned imperiously for me to follow her outside. I gave Daniel a helpless look. He rose to his feet uncertainly, "But Mama."

Salamasina silenced him with a weary smile. "My son, I know. This is the girl you love. Believe me when I tell you that I understand – there is *nothing* I can do or say to change that. Now Leila, come."

Together we walked into the garden. Evening was approaching. The kind that fell like gossamer silk, stardust and moon song making wispy trails from ocean to land. In spite of my apprehension about what Salamasina would say, the calm peace of the garden spoke to me as plants always did. Soothing my troubled soul. Calming my frightened heart. Salamasina walked to the furthest reach of the garden and stopped beside a luxuriant froth of jasmine bushes. I was still limping from my bruises and so she waited until I stood beside her before she spoke.

"You are *telesā*." There was no question in her statement. It seemed ridiculous to even try to deny it.

"Yes. But how did you know?"

She waved aside my question impatiently. "Did you drug my son?"

"What?" I was horrified.

"You heard me. Did you drug my son, emption him to love you?"

"No. I would never do such a thing, to anyone. I met Daniel before … before I knew what I was, before I met Nafanua and learned about all this *telesā* madness. I loved him before and then when it happened, I tried to stop, I tried to push him away from me but it was too late. I already loved him so much." My voice broke. "I'm so sorry, I tried to keep him away from me, truly I did. I never wanted to hurt him. I never wanted to hurt anyone. Please believe me. I love him and I would never do such a thing to him."

She stared impassively at my tears. "I had to ask. *Telesā* are users of men. You know this. They are incapable of love. Well," she amended "most of them anyway. When Daniel first brought you home, I knew you were no ordinary girl. And when you told me who your mother was – well, that just confirmed it. I tried to warn him, tried to stop him forming a relationship with you, but it was futile. And I wondered if it was because you or Nafanua had been using *telesā* ways on him. I have been giving him my own protective remedies to drink to counteract anything, but still, I worried that Nafanua had managed to come up with some way of getting around my defenses."

I stared at her in shock. Who was this woman? And how did she know all this stuff? But I was not the one asking the questions here. Salamasina continued, "Now tell me, why has Nafanua poisoned your friend?"

I ran through a quick summary of the past few weeks, giving Salamasina the bare bones of the story, telling her only that I had shared my *telesā* gifts with Jason and he had been trying to help me get rid of them. Which had brought the wrath of the Covenant upon him. And me.

Salamasina gave me a wry smile, "You think that there is a way for you to 'cure' being a *telesā?*" She rolled her eyes and shook her head at me, "Ah, the foolish ignorance of youth. This poor man Jason, he didn't know what he was letting himself in for. Yes, I will help you with an antidote."

I wilted with relief at her words. "Oh thank you."

But there was no warmth in her next question. "But in return, you need to tell me everything. Starting with what kind of *telesā* are you?" There was steel in her words. "Are you *matagi* like your mother and the rest of her pack? Are you Air?"

"No. I'm Earth. *Fanua afi.*" I stumbled over the pronunciation, but Salamasina understood me enough and her reaction was instant. A look of unbridled horror laced with fear and she stepped back away from me. As if afraid I would fry her right there and then. I cringed at her revulsion.

She shook her head fiercely. "I don't believe you. *Fanua afi* is a myth. An old *telesā* story told to frighten small children."

I shrugged tiredly. If she didn't choose to believe me, that was fine by me.

"Prove it."

"Huh?"

"Prove it. Show me. Now." She stepped back further away and waited expectantly.

I shook my head. "No, I won't do it. The fire is unpredictable at best. If I'm not careful, it can run totally wild. I'm tired and messed up right now, if I let it out, then I can't be sure that it won't get out of control. Please don't ask me to call it."

But Salamasina would not be dissuaded. She folded her arms and stood there defiantly. "You want me to help save your friend? Then summon fire and prove to me you are really *Fanua Afi.*"

I closed my eyes in the dying day. Fire came quickly. Easily. Eager to wipe away a body of flesh and blood that was battered and weak from a long and challenging day. First there was the inevitable brief flash of pain, quickly followed by delight. Bruised muscles and torn sinews gave way to lava that bubbled with strength and power. I stood molten red and gold on the grass, trying not to let fire's joy brim over too much, trying to keep it restrained. Salamasina stared at me wide eyed and stumbled back weakly to sit on the garden bench. "Aue, it's true." Her eyes brimmed with tears and she sunk her head into her hands, "No, it can't be." She looked heavenward, as if praying, appealing to some faraway entity, "My son, not my son, please ..." her voice died away as she stared at me with the eyes of one drowning in hopelessness. I hated to come any closer to her, still unsure of what my fire would do.

"Salamasina, are you alright?" I asked anxiously but she did not respond. With silent tears streaming down her cheeks, she sat lost in a daze. I raised my voice back at the house, "Daniel! Come quick, something's wrong with your grandmother."

That seemed to snap her out of her daze. She shook her head and stood up, wiping away the treacherous tears, "No, I am alright. Just shocked that's all. I'm fine."

Daniel appeared in the back doorway, stopping at the sight of me in flames, side by side with Salamasina. "Leila? Mama? Is everything alright?" There was an edge of fear in his voice which cut me. Did he think I was hurting his grandmother? Salamasina waved out to him with a forced smile.

"I'm fine son. I asked Leila to show me her gift and it caught me off guard. But everything's alright." She turned back to me, "Thank you Leila, for indulging me with a demonstration. Can you ... umm...turn it off now? Make it go away?"

I nodded but then stopped short, suddenly awkward as I remembered I had just fried all my clothes and would be left standing naked in front of my boyfriend and his grandmother. *Ouch.* "Umm, is it alright, please can I borrow a shirt or something to wear for when I stop burning?"

Daniel flashed me a grin, "Just hang on Leila, I'll grab a *lavalava*. Don't want you to go flashing Mama and totally freaking her. She might think you're a woman of loose morals. A skanky ho." He turned to go back inside but not before Salamasina's prim reprimand.

"Daniel, don't be cheeky eh! There is no need to speak with such disrespect. Go, get Leila something to wear."

He disappeared into the house while Salamasina turned back to me. "There is much you need to tell me, about your mother and her sisters and their plans for you. But we don't have much time. We must prepare an antidote for your friend and we must work quickly if we are to have any hopes of saving him. But when we're done with that Leila Folger, you will be honest with me and tell me everything else I want to know, is that clear? Now come."

I would never have dared to argue with her. The woman was intimidating – even when I was in fire form. I nodded and followed at a safe distance behind her as she began walking towards a little shed at the furthest reach of the fenced garden. My curiosity got the better of my hesitancy, however and I ventured a question. "Salamasina, how will you know what antidote we need for Jason? I mean, don't you have to examine him first, try to figure out what they poisoned him with?"

She barely gave me a momentary glance as she stopped to unlock the padlock using a jangly bunch of keys. "No, it's not necessary. *Telesā* have many concoctions for causing sickness, but there are only a mere handful of poisons designed to be fatal and only one of them ensures a drawn-out death. When *telesā* want to kill someone, they don't usually mess around, they'll just give them the instantly fatal choice. They must really want to punish your friend because what they've given him causes several days of intense suffering." She paused to give me a look laced with compassion. "I'm sorry, Leila. I'll prepare the antidote but you must be aware that it may already be too late for him."

Fire burned brighter as I fought to contain the rage that leapt to the surface at her words. Rage that wanted to destroy Nafanua and her entire sisterhood. I clung to the small measure of hope offered by Salamasina's words. "Thank you. I know it will work. It has to. Please."

Daniel surprised us both then as he came up behind us carrying a red floral *lavalava*. "Here you go, something to wear. What else can I do to help, Mama?"

She refused. "No, I have all the ingredients I need right here and it will only take me about twenty minutes to prepare the measure your friend will need. Leila, why don't you get covered up and come help me? Daniel can get us some dinner perhaps, I'm sure we will all be very hungry once this is all done."

I couldn't help thinking that Salamasina just wanted Daniel out of the way so that she could interrogate me further but I would have walked through Arctic ice barefoot, anything to get a cure for Jason. The old woman went into her medicine shed and I motioned at Daniel with a jerk of my head. "Turn around."

"Why?"

"So I can kill these flames and put some clothes on."

He folded his arms and still stood there with his head tipped to one side. "Well, go on – kill the fire – and then I promise I'll give you the *lavalava*." His tone was teasing.

Mine was threatening. "Turn around, give me the *lavalava* and I promise I won't kill you with my fire. And don't look."

He laughed. "Fine. No need to get so aggressive. I promise, no looking." He turned away and held out the *lavalava* with one hand, throwing one more jab over his shoulder. "It's not like I haven't already seen you half naked, you know."

I would have flushed red if I had been in flesh form. As it was, my flames hazed brighter and errant sparks spluttered dangerously close to Daniel's feet, making him dance a side-step out of the way. "Hey, watch it! I said I wouldn't look."

"Sorry. Accident." I mumbled as I focused on trying to still the flames, a very difficult thing when Daniel was standing right there reminding me about the nights he had found me swimming in 'our' midnight pool. The time he had joined me in the black water, held me, kissed me. *Damnit, stop it Leila! You'll never turn this thing off if you keep this up* ... Several deep breaths, focusing on the quiet beauty of the garden in the moonlight and my fire flickered and dimmed, spluttered and hissed. And I was left naked and shivering. Quickly, I reached out and grabbed the *lavalava* from his outstretched grip, wrapping it hastily around me. "Got it, thank you."

Daniel turned and before I could move to join his grandmother in the workroom, he pulled me to him and moved us both out of sight. Into the jasmine-fragranced darkness. "What?" my query was stilled as he enveloped me in his arms, gently running his hand through my hair to tilt my head back so he could bring his lips to mine. He was shirtless and I could feel every inch of him through the thin fabric of the *lavalava* that separated us. I clung to his warmth, his hard strength as he reminded me that I no longer faced my nights alone. His kiss spoke of the crashing surf on the distant reef. Of the silver splash of mermaids dancing on a crested moonlit wave. And I drowned in it. When he finally pulled away, there was a look I couldn't recognize in his eyes. Raw, ragged, and urgent. His hand came up to caress my face, lingering on my lips. "Leila ... I ..."

"Leila! I'm waiting, I need your help here." Salamasina's imperious voice broke us apart. Daniel released me with a quick grin.

"You better get in there."

I nodded and moved away, but my eyes told him I didn't want to. *Focus Leila. Jason needs you remember?*

The workroom was a cluttered space where many different fragrances battled for supremacy. Salamasina stirred a small pot over a single gas burner. She pointed to a cluster of bottles each with a different colored liquid. "Pass me the purple bottle."

"What's in it?"

She carefully measured two teaspoons of the liquid into the mixture in the pot before answering, "Distilled essence of the tulia flower. A powerful neutralizer for *ti-fatu loa*. Which is what I'm sure that Nafanua used on your friend."

For the next ten minutes, Salamasina and I worked together over the antidote. I followed her instructions, cutting and stirring. Only when the antidote was complete and we waited for it to cool did I venture to ask her the question that had been burning at me.

"Salamasina, how did you know? About Nafanua, about me being a *telesā*?"

There was a tense silence before she answered. She gazed at me with a stare that seemed to try and pierce my very thoughts, as if trying to determine what I would do with her answers. "My mother was *telesā*. Back in Tonga."

I was stunned. "There are *telesā* in Tonga?"

"Of course. There are *telesā* in many places throughout the Pacific. My mother was *Vasa Loloa*, water. I was raised in her sisterhood, taught their ways until I was twelve. Until they were certain that I had no earth gifts. And then they gave me away to a family in a coastal village." She spoke the words simply, but even now, many years on I could feel the pain in her words.

"Did you ever see her again?"

A shrug. "Sometimes they would pass through our village but she never came to see me or ask after me. But it was alright. She gave me to a good woman who raised me with her other children. I was always gifted with plants. And healing. And I had learned many medicine secrets of the *telesā*, which I used to help my family and my village. So I had love and respect. And then when I was seventeen, I met Tanielu – Daniel's grandfather. And I was no longer alone." A soft smile transformed the severe face, and in the gas light I saw the beauty of the love they had shared. "We never had any children of our own though and so when Daniel's mother – Moana – brought her baby to us, seeking a home for him, we were happy to have him and to love him. He doesn't know that he is not our blood grandchild. And I would ask that you respect my wish to keep that information between us. For now at least." For a moment she was lost in the past before she gave herself a mental shake and returned to the problems of the present. "So yes, I know a great deal about *telesā* and their ways. You know that what Nafanua and her sisterhood have done is an abomination to the true *telesā* calling don't you?"

I shook my head and she continued. "*Telesā* are women blessed with gifts from earth but they have always used those gifts only to safeguard a particular area and to serve the people living there. *Vasa Loloa* to guide people to the best fishing spots, and protect the fishermen. The strongest among them were meant to be the oracle of warning for times of tsunami and storm surge, to keep people safe. *Telesa Matagi* are to summon rain for crops to grow, bring water to a parched land, call winds to drive the canoes to new lands, lightning for fire, for cooking and for clearing forest to build homes. Ancient *telesā* lived in harmony with earth and humans. And in return, people honored them. Paid them tribute. Heeded their counsel about the best ways to care for the earth and her gifts."

In confusion I interrupted her, "But that's not what Nafanua told me. *Telesā* were rulers, powerful forces to be feared and reckoned with, I don't understand …"

"There will always be those who use their gifts for evil. It has always been that way. Nafanua is a very old and very powerful *telesā*. She has long bullied and suppressed *telesā* in Samoa who did not adhere to her way of thinking. No-one in her sisterhood can come close to matching her in gift strength I don't think. Have you ever seen them use their powers?"

I nodded. "I've only ever seen two of them call lightning though. Nafanua and a younger one called Sarona. The others have summoned rain and wind but nothing like my mother and Sarona have."

"Yes, that is usually how it is. The Covenant Keeper of a sisterhood doesn't ever like to have *telesā* who are too powerful in their covenant. You understand how a covenant works?"

"No."

"*Telesā* are best as solitary creatures. They are not known for their unity and loyalty to one another. Think of all the stereotypical worst traits of women – backstabbing, manipulative, and catty – and then imagine them exacerbated by *telesā* powers. I grew up within a sisterhood, so I know first-hand. To reduce the likelihood of *telesā* warring for territory, a single *telesā* who is unusually gifted will gather around her lesser *telesā* and weave the covenant that binds them together. The followers are bound to honor their leader and she can draw on their accumulated gifts as her own, thereby multiplying her powers many times over. In exchange, the Keeper is bound to protect them and can never raise her hand against them, or else their covenant is broken and they are all weakened as a result. It provides a form of protection for all parties. The Keeper cannot harm any other lesser sisters, which keeps them safe from her and they in turn cannot rise up against her, which cements her leadership."

"I see, kind of … but they don't live forever do they? Eventually a Covenant must die or something?"

"That's true. *Telesā* live long lives but they are not immortal. They may not be quite human in the sense that we understand the term, but they're not like vampires or anything ridiculous like that. *Telesā* will age eventually and, when a leader ages, her powers weaken. Either she will step down and pass the covenant on to a younger sister or else she will have it taken from her in outright battle or some other form of subversive rebellion."

Salamasina checked the antidote and pronounced it ready for use. She poured it into a slim phial and handed it to me. "If he cannot drink it then it needs to be administered intravenously. Inserted into his IV bag. All of it."

"And then?"

"And then all you can do is wait. And pray. Now come, let us go in and Daniel can go with you to the hospital."

Before we went into the house though, Salamasina stopped me with a firm hand on mine. "Leila, I ask you not to tell Daniel anything about my Tongan *telesā* connections. He does not know. And it is not time for me to tell him. Let the only *telesā* he knows - be you."

I nodded and we joined Daniel in the kitchen where he had chop suey and rice waiting. I couldn't eat anything until I had taken the antidote to Jason though so Salamasina phoned Matile and Tuala to let them know my whereabouts and to get their permission for me to stay late at the hospital with my sick friend, promising them that Daniel would ensure I made it home safely. Daniel got me a t-shirt to wear with the *lavalava* and we were in the car driving to the hospital. I was anxious. It was already 9.30pm. What if we were too late? What if I was making the wrong decision? What if Salamasina's antidote didn't work? That would mean I had held Jason's only hope in my hands earlier that afternoon with Nafanua's offer and then dashed it to pieces with my refusal. Daniel sensed my agitation and, at the hospital, he held my hand in his as we made our way to Jason's floor.

Blaine and Matthew were there, falling asleep on benches outside Jason's room. Both men jerked awake at my greeting. I introduced them to Daniel. Neither of them had anything hopeful or positive to report on Jason. He was still unconscious and his vitals were steadily weakening. The doctors had given him another antibiotic an hour before but didn't seem very hopeful about his chances. Blaine confided that Jason's parents were flying in and would arrive the next afternoon, but he didn't think that they would be in time. To say goodbye.

"Can I see him? Alone? Just for a moment, please?"

"Of course, go on in."

Daniel stayed outside with the other two while I went in quietly. Jason lay as I had left him earlier that day. I had to move fast before a nurse came in and questioned what I was doing. I washed my hands at the tiny sink before carefully unscrewing the protector cap on the IV bag insert. I poured the antidote in with shaking hands, watching the clear liquid run into the IV fluid, sending with it all my prayers and hopes that it would work. I bent to whisper in Jason's ear,

"You need to fight this, you hear me, Jason? I know you can. I'm so sorry I got you into this. I'm fighting for you, do you hear me? I'm not going to let Nafanua get away with this. I promise you. I will set the earth on fire if I have to."

And then I slipped out of the room, answering Daniel's questioning eyes with a slight nod. I didn't want to leave Jason's side, but there was one more thing that I needed to do. I asked Daniel if I could use his phone and walked outside into the corridor to make the call I had been dreading.

- *Nafanua? It's me, Leila.*

- *Where are you? You're late. You were supposed to be here at eight to get the antidote. If you leave it too late it won't work and Jason will die.*

- *I'm not coming.*

- *What do you mean? We had an agreement.*

- *No, you made an offer, which I'm declining. I don't want your antidote. And I'm not coming back to your sisterhood. I don't want to be one of your telesā. I hope you can respect my decision.*

- *You fool! You're going to regret this a million times over before the week is out. Don't you see, I am offering you the opportunity of a lifetime? To belong to the most powerful sisterhood this land has ever known. To be a key part of the new Samoa.*

- *You mean you offered me the chance to be a killer like you. And your insane sisterhood. You're supposed to be my mother. Love me, care about me, want the best for me. Instead you try to kill my friend? And threaten the lives of the boy I love and the only real family I have?*

- Leila, listen to me, there is so much more you don't understand, so much I can teach you, you cannot turn your back on me now.

- No. You listen to me. I was lost for a little while, but now I'm clear. I know who I am. And what I'm not. I'm not your daughter. I'm not a psychopathic telesā killer like you and your sisters. I'm Michael Folger's daughter. I can set this world on fire and I will use all my gifts to stop you and your sisters if you dare come near any of my friends or family again.

When I pressed the cut-off button I was trembling and grateful for Daniel's embrace as he came up quietly behind me. He cradled me in his arms. "So you did it. You made the break and threw down the gauntlet."

I shivered as I remembered the gleeful fury of Sarona's attack that afternoon. "I hope I made the right choice. What if the antidote doesn't work? What if they do it? What if they hurt you and Salamasina?"

He shushed me with a soft kiss. "Hey, you made the only right choice available to you. Think about it. If you had gone back to them, they would have eventually used you to do far worse things. Can you imagine what kind of a weapon you would be in their hands if they could get you to join them? No, you couldn't give in to them. We just need to wait now and trust that Mama's medicine works. Then we'll worry about tomorrow and what it brings, okay?" He bent to look direct into my eyes, "As long as we're facing this together, we will be alright. I'm not afraid, as long as I have you."

I couldn't argue with that. And so, even though fear still tiptoed with icy feet through my chest, I allowed Daniel to hug and kiss my worries away and we went back to the ward to sit and wait with Blaine and Matthew. For Jason to wake up. Or to die.

I must have dozed off, because the next thing I knew, Blaine was shaking me awake. "Leila. Hey Leila!" His voice was urgent. Daniel and I were both slumped on the waiting bench, Daniel with his arms around me. We both jerked awake at the same time. "What is it? What's wrong? Is it Jason?"

"He's waking up. Come see."

It was just past midnight. I leapt to my feet and rushed into Jason's room, where several nurses were fussing over a very groggy but very awake Jason. My breath caught in my throat, "Jason?"

In the midst of the buzzing medical team, he heard my voice. His head turned and his face lit with a pale smile – a mere ghost of the usual sunburst grin – but a smile nevertheless. "Leila? Boy am I glad to see you." He looked at the nurse taking his temperature and jerked his head at me, "See that gorgeous girl over there? That's a face I never thought I would see again. Not in this lifetime anyway."

The nurse frowned warningly at him and then back at me. "Well you're still not one hundred percent clear yet so don't go getting all excited about that face. We need you calm and still and rested so we can get you better. And that means your visitors have got to leave."

Jason ignored her and reached out to me with a shaky hand. "Come here."

I moved to stand beside him and put my hand in his. He felt cold and I smiled at him with as much warmth and relief as I could muster. "I'm so glad you're awake. We've all been so worried about you." I tried not to cry. More than anything, Jason needed positivity and strength.

"Don't go yet. Seeing you is making me feel heaps better." He appealed to the grouchy nurse. "Please let her stay a while. She lights up my world you know."

I grimaced at his attempt at a joke. But he wasn't finished. "You should see her set things on fire with a single touch."

The nurse was not amused and pursed her lips in disapproval. "Setting you on fire is the last thing you need right now Mr. Williams. Your visitor will have to leave soon." And with that she stalked away.

"Jason, stop it. You shouldn't be cracking jokes at a time like this." I was painfully aware of Daniel's looming presence just outside the door and tried to pull my hand back. But Jason's grip tightened. He raised my hand to his lips and kissed it. There was nothing but seriousness in his blue eyes as he spoke to me softly, excluding the entire room.

"I wasn't joking. Leila, they tell me that I've been dying for the last three days. And trust me, I felt like it. But you know the one thing that kept me hanging on? The one thing I kept fighting for?"

Dumbly, I shook my head, battling tears. He continued, "You. And my promise to you."

I shook my head, trying to cut him off, trying to stop the words before they couldn't be unspoken. "Jason, no ..."

"No, please, let me finish. Let a critically ill dude speak. Please?"

How could I argue with that? Especially since it was my fault he was lying there half dead anyway.

"Leila, you asked me to be your friend. And nothing else. And I am. But nearly dying does something to a person y'know? It makes him realize that life is short. And you have to grab at every moment, every happiness with both hands. Tight. And not let go. So, yes, I'm your friend, and I'm one hundred percent committed to helping you deal with your problem. But you gotta know, I'm in love with you."

His words hit me with a hammer blow and I struggled for a way to make him take them back.

"Jason no, you don't know what you're saying. You're sick. You need to rest. Listen to your nurses."

But he would not be swayed from his declaration. "Leila, I've never been more sure of anything in my whole life. I've loved you from that first night you bewitched me with your fake bimbo-ness. And then when I watched over you as you slept during that storm, then I was sure."

And finally, with his declaration fully revealed, he was spent. A wave of exhaustion swept over him and he sank back into the pillows, closing his eyes. From behind me, I was dimly aware of Daniel slipping out of the room. The control-freak nurse chose that opportunity to jump in and shoo me away. "Out, out. He needs to sleep. All visitors must leave. NOW."

I backed away from the bed and Blaine and and Matthew followed me out. The two men were flushed with excitement and buzzing with plans to call and update Jason's family.

"He looks like he's gonna be okay. Isn't that awesome, Leila? I thought for sure this was going to be his last night on earth." Blaine shook his head in wonderment and I smiled weakly at him but all my breath was focused at Daniel who stood still in the corridor with nothing but blankness on his face. Staring at me. As if I was a stranger he had never met before.

The two men finally noticed him and their chatter died. We all stood in an uncomfortable silence for the briefest of moments before they both took off to Skype Jason's dad the good news. Leaving me alone with Daniel. Who didn't speak a word. Slowly, we walked back to the truck in the car park and still neither of us spoke. It was deserted, with only a few stray dogs sleeping in a huddle beside a rock wall. Daniel opened the passenger door for me but before I could climb in, he caught me still with his hand on mine. I stared up at him, trying to read him in the darkness, wishing he could read my heart and soul. And see his face imprinted there.

"So, the antidote worked."

"Yeah, it seems like it." I fought unsuccessfully to keep the joy from my voice. But it was impossible. Jason was alive. We had thwarted Nafanua's crazy attack on him. I didn't kill him. I wanted to scream it from the rooftops. But I didn't want to hurt Daniel.

"I'm glad." He spoke the words with simple sincerity. "I know he means a great deal to you." He brought a hand up to cradle my face, looked me in the eyes and said again. "I'm glad."

I was weak with relief. He wasn't mad. "Really? Even though … umm …" I hated to say the words. So he said them for me. With a knowing grin.

"Even though the guy's crazy in love with you? Yeah, I'm still glad the antidote worked. Now if he hadn't been sitting on death's doorstep? Let's just say that I wouldn't have been so patient about standing by and watching some genius Professor hold your hand and profess his love for you. Or kiss you. I might have given in to the temptation to smash him. Or something like that." His dancing eyes laughed at me.

I winced at the thought, and Daniel responded by pulling me closer to him and wrapping his arms around me. All teasing was gone as he said, "Seriously? I don't like it that Jason is in love with you. But he can help you in ways that I can't. And he's your friend.' He paused and looked at me questioningly, "That is all he is, right? Unless you do, have other feelings for him?"

I hated the hint of doubt in his eye. I didn't love Jason. At least not like that. Did I? My mind flashed back to the storm-filled night we had spent together. Jason half naked in Nafanua's kitchen, resplendent in the firelight of my hands. How he had wanted to kiss me. And how I had wanted him to. No! I slammed a door on my thoughts. I loved Daniel. He was looking at me, waiting for my response. Impulsively, I reached up and pulled his head down closer to mine and kissed him with every desperate emotion inspired by this rollercoaster twenty-four hours, trying to convey how much he meant to me. To show him that Jason really was only a friend. Trying to ignore the little voice inside that asked me, *Who are you trying to convince here? Daniel? Or yourself?*

Daniel kissed me back with a fierce urgency I had never felt before, one that had me struggling for balance. In one fluid motion, he lifted me up so that I was sitting perched on the car seat with my legs linked around his waist. His mouth left mine and I moaned in protest, but it was so that he could burn a pathway of kisses down the arched curve of my neck. His mouth whispered fiery secrets against the base of my throat, his hands slid one spaghetti strap of my tank top off one shoulder and then the other so he could kiss a trail of fire along my naked skin. My hands pushed away his shirt, hating anything that came between us, wishing I could incinerate the clothing that contained us both. But before I could act any further, Daniel pulled away, leaving me flushed and breathless.

"Daniel?"

"I'm sorry." He gave me a rueful smile, carefully pulling my tank top straps back onto my shoulder, before disentangling himself from my embrace. "I ah … shouldn't have done that. I'm sorry." He ruffled his fingers through his hair in that nervous gesture I knew so well.

"I'm not sorry." I slipped off the seat and moved to take him in my arms again. He stood stiffly and did not hug me back. "I love you. All I want is to be with you. What's wrong with that?"

An awkward shrug. "Nothing. But what I said back at the house? About respecting you enough to not put your virtue in question? I meant it. Just now, that – us getting carried away – it won't happen again. I promise. I'll be more careful. You can trust me. Okay?"

He waited for my response and seemed to think it would be a happy one, so I gave him a plastic smile and nodded. But inside I felt deflated as little bubbles of excitement fizzed and burst. I **wanted** him to get carried away with me. I **wanted** this to happen again and more of it. I **wanted** him to rip my clothes off and cover my entire body with his kisses. And here he was promising me that he never would?! *Great. Sure, that's totally what I want. To be able to trust you to not get turned on when you're with me. Thanks.*

Unaware of my disappointment, Daniel continued, "We should get going. I need to take you home." Without waiting for a reply, he unclasped my hands and went around to the driver's seat. The drive home was quiet as we drove along empty streets. At home, Daniel opened my door and then stood and gazed down at me, his face unreadable. In the moonlight he looked tired. Drawn. But he tried to smile as he said, "What a day huh? Nothin like almost getting fried by a psychotic weather witch to liven up your afternoon."

I nodded glumly, my excitement at Jason's recovery was subdued now as I had to face the reality of what would come next. Of wondering what Nafanua and the *telesā* would do next. "Daniel, what are we going to do now? I mean Jason's going to be okay and the sooner Blaine and them get him transported back to the US and away from the *telesā* the better. But where does that leave everyone else?" I looked over his shoulder into the house where I knew Matile and Tuala would be waiting up for me, worrying about me. "How am I going to watch over them? And your grandmother? And you? What are we going to do?"

He quieted me with a quick hug. "I told you, everything will be okay. We've got tonight and tomorrow at least, until the *telesā* find out that Jason's been healed. We'll figure it out tomorrow. You need a good rest tonight – what's left of it anyway. I'm going to ask Mama for her advice. She's the wisest person I know and she'll help us find a way through this. Come round tomorrow, after church and we'll deal with this. Okay?"

It was difficult not to be soothed when six feet and two hundred pounds worth of muscle had you secure in his arms. I shut my eyes and breathed in deeply of his scent, memorizing the feel of every rock hard curve and sinew, treasuring his closeness, this feeling. Like together we really could take on the *telesā*. And win.

He stood and watched me until I went in the house. And then from the window, I watched him drive away. Then and only then, did I go to explain wearily to Matile and Tuala why I was late – minus all the *telesā* bits of course. And once they were appeased, I tumbled into bed. Asleep before I could even remember that I was supposed to be scared. And worrying about a solution. A way out of this nightmare.

Daniel was right. Salamasina was a very wise woman and she probably would have been able to help us find a way to deal with the *telesā*. But our greatest mistake, which we would have much cause to bitterly regret, was thinking that we had time.

To sleep. To talk. To plan. To prepare.

To live.

EIGHTEEN

The next day began like any other Sunday. Tuala snapping at Kolio about the slack way he made the *umu*. Again. And Matile hurrying me awake to go check the state of the flowers in the church. Again. Just in case some nutty flower thief had absconded with the floral arrangements during the night. And then it was rush back to the house and get dressed. With Tuala yelling at the dog to *Get out of the umu you stupid beast!* And Matile scolding him for being mean to her dog. Again.

But today I was grateful for the routine. The ordinariness of the day. It went a long way towards distracting me from the previous day's horrors. In church, I secretly texted Blaine to check on Jason. And was thrilled to hear back that, yes, he was showing nothing but improvement. And the doctors had pronounced it safe for him to travel. And his parents were arriving that afternoon and would probably take him back with them on tomorrow's flight.

I sang the final hymn with genuine gratitude and thanksgiving. *Aleluia!* Jason was alive. And by tomorrow he would be winging his way home to the States with his family and forever be safe from Nafanua and her sisters. The thought alone gave me hope that a similar solution could be found for me and Daniel. And all those we loved. Because it was true.

I realized it as we drove home. As Tuala sang along with the radio and Matile groaned and rolled her eyes at him. And I hid a smile. I loved them both. In their home I had finally found the closest thing I had ever had to a family, the closest thing to regular parents.

After lunch, Matile refused my offers to help with the dishes, instead waving me away, "You go have a rest before your dinner with Salamasina and Daniel. You were up late at the hospital last night. Go, sleep. Your uncle and I are going to afternoon church and won't be back until late. You will have the house to yourself. Sleep and enjoy the peace. We will see you when you get back from your dinner outing."

In the bedroom, I sent a quick Sunday email update to Grandmother Folger. As usual, censoring out about ninety percent of my actual life here in Samoa. A wry grin as I pressed SEND. If she only knew the half of what was really happening here, the poor woman would probably have another stroke. And then send a team of Black Ops out to extract me. I checked my watch. Three o'clock. I had about an hour before it was time to go to Daniel's. I hadn't been planning on it, but Matile was right. I was tired. I grabbed myself a big glass of lemonade from the fridge before I went to the room. Drank. And slept.

I awoke to a nightmare. Vision hazed, nausea threatened. I shook my head, trying to clear it of the cobwebs, the tangle of mist-laden vines that clogged it. I regretted it immediately. Another wave of nausea overwhelmed me and I leaned forward to retch. Jerking back as I swallowed water. I coughed and spluttered.

"Ugh." A grimace at the sour taste in my mouth and I prepped for the possibility of another spew. It didn't come. Instead, a knife-like pain cut through my head, jerking a moan from me before I could stop it. "Ow arrrgh."

I tried to raise my hands to my head, but something held them captive behind me. I jerked against the restraint uselessly. Wet. Water. I was standing in salt water and tied to a post of some kind. The water was cold and stopped just at my chin. I looked around. It was a beach I didn't recognize. A rocky shoreline jutted. The dim light didn't give away many clues. Where was I?

I could hear the ocean, feel it lapping around me. What had happened? My last memory was of downing a big glass of Matile's freshly squeezed lemonade, hoping its sweet coolness would help me sleep. Grimacing at the unusually bitter aftertaste. Then ... nothing. No – wait. Blackness. But not before faces came into view. Smiling triumphantly. Nafanua. Sarona.

The realization hit me. I had been drugged. The bitches had somehow laced my lemonade with something strong enough to knock me out so they could bring me here. Where was 'here'? I strained at the bindings that held my arms at my back and the sound of my struggle brought voices.

"I think she's awake. Get Nafanua."

The voices came closer and with them came light. I looked around me for clues as to my whereabouts. Anything that would give me answers.

"Don't bother wasting your energy. There's no way you're getting loose from there."

That was a voice that needed no introduction. Sarona. I glared upwards. She stood on the rocky shelf a few meters away holding aloft a fiery flare. Her eyes sparkled with malice. Her voice was gleeful. Instinctively, I thought about flames. Heat. Anger. But nothing happened.

She laughed. "Oh, are you trying to knock me out with a fireball, silly girl? Not going to happen. You see, one very important piece of information about your 'gift'? It doesn't work when you're in water. The only *telesā* who has any power at all in rivers and oceans is *Vasa Loloa*. And oops. You're not one of those. Tell me Leila, do you know what happens when lightning strikes someone who's standing in water? Do you want to find out?" A lazy wave of her hand and the skies crackled threateningly. A voice from the darkness behind halted her.

"Sarona! Stop that. We have a plan to follow and that isn't part of it." Nafanua walked out of the forest darkness and joined her on the rocks. The other *telesā* joined them. Sarona wasn't fazed. A careless shrug and a roll of the eyes.

"Fine. But I don't see why we need to use these methods anyway. You know my feelings on the matter. We should bring her over here so we can 'persuade' her to co-operate. A few choice samplings of my lightning and she'll be begging to join us."

My glare dared her, begged her to release me. To raise me up out of the water so I could show these mistresses of air who really possessed the choicest gifts of Fanua. I called out to the gathering of women. "Yes, Nafanua you should listen to her. Get me out of here, and then we will hear pleading for mercy." I taunted them. "Are you afraid of me? A child? You *telesā* who have ruled here for how many hundreds of years? Come on, let me go!"

Nafanua held out a hand for silence. She looked tired. "Don't be foolish. We are not going to hurt one of our own. No. That is what men are for." She turned to the other women with an imperious gesture. "Bring him out."

A coldness of dread pierced me. No. This couldn't be happening. Please, don't let it be …

It took two *telesā* to drag Daniel's inert shape out of the bush. Manuia and Fouina strained with the effort to carry him. His head hung limply and his legs dragged over the cutting rocks. They cast him on the ground and he didn't move. At that moment, the moonlight peered through the clouds and I could see clearly. He was half naked. His chest and back were covered in cuts and blackening bruises. Blood trickled from the side of his mouth and his hair was matted at a deep wound at his temple. He was breathing but that was the only sign of life. I screamed.

"Daniel! No Daniel." I strained at the ropes, cursing and shouting. "What have you done to him? Daniel? Please answer me. Daniel!" I paused, turning pleading eyes at Nafanua. "Please, Nafanua, don't do this. Don't hurt him any more. Please."

All the women smiled. Sarona spoke scathingly. "Pathetic. See sisters?" she turned to the others. "This is why we don't give ourselves to men. See what happens? It makes us weak."

She looked back at me and laughed. "You – you are supposed to be the most powerful *telesā* that has walked this land in over three hundred years and look at you. Reduced to tears and begging, for what? For this?" She nudged Daniel in the ribs with one perfect foot. There was no response. She smiled at her sisters again, "Now, let's see what she does when I do this."

She flicked her wrist. I felt the energy coming before I saw it. The way it ripped through the air, crackling and spitting as it came. The lightning bolt sat perfectly in the palm of her hand and she paused deliberately for a moment, holding it aloft as she gazed over the water at me with a maniacal glint in her eye. Then she stabbed at Daniel as if with a knife. Only this knife carried with it megawatts of power. Gut-wrenching, electrifying power.

I screamed again and this time, my scream was merged with Daniel's shout of agony as he jerked and writhed on the ground. "Arrrgh!"

"Stop it! Please, stop it. You're killing him. I'll do whatever you want. Just stop it please. Daniel!"

I had never wished so hard for fire. I had never prayed so fervently for the gods to hear me. I begged the earth to hear me. But the ground was wet, cold, and silent beneath my feet. I kicked and strained, but my pitiful strength was no match for the bondage of the *telesā*. And in that moment – as I watched the one I loved light up in electrifying pain – I realized. I didn't want to be a 'regular girl.' I didn't want to be just Leila Folger. I wanted to be the chosen one of Matavanu. Pele incarnate. Because never again did I want to stand by uselessly and watch while he suffered this way. Sarona paused in her lightning strike and looked down at Daniel as he clawed his fingers against the rock, trying to kneel.

I stopped crying. I stopped struggling. When I spoke, it was with clarity and calm strength. I ignored Sarona. "Nafanua, call off your dog. I am ready to be what you want me to. I am ready to do whatever it is that you want. Let him go."

At my voice, Daniel turned his head and my heart tore to see the confusion in his eyes. His voice was ragged. "Leila? What's going on?"

I smiled, with my voice full of tears. "Daniel, it's okay, everything's gonna be okay. I'm sorry. I'm so sorry I got you into this. Please forgive me."

Sarona groaned, "Oh please, enough. You two are sickening. Silence fool." She gestured to call down another flash of lightning – but not before Nafanua grabbed her hand.

"Enough Sarona. See?" she pointed at me, "Leila's ready. We don't need this boy anymore. Let him go." Nafanua called to the others. "Cut her loose. Get her out of there."

Sarona's face clouded over in disbelief. "Are you crazy? We can't let him go, not until she's done what she's supposed to. Besides, he knows too much about us anyway. Manuia and Fouina, take him to the boat. And make sure you keep giving him reminders of who we are and what we are capable of."

The women half lifted Daniel again and began dragging him to the water's edge where a large double hulled canoe swayed slightly in the tide. This time he tried to struggle as he looked back over his shoulder at me. "Leila. Let me go. Leila! Don't you hurt her. Leila!" He shoved against Manuia's restraining arm and tried to free himself of Fouina's grip but a single jolt of her lightning response stopped him in his tracks and he slumped weakly to his knees. Working quickly, the women got him onto the boat and began paddling some distance from the shore. I shouted his name, but this time there was no response.

Sarona smiled and spread her arms expansively. "Now, see Nafanua? Isn't my plan so much better? Now we can cut her loose and not have to worry that she will try any silly fire tricks on us." The smile faded and she addressed me with ice in her tone. "Now you listen very carefully, Leila. Manuia and Fouina have strict instructions. If you defy us, if you try to escape, if you try to attack any of us – they will slit that boy's throat. And throw his body to the fishes. Show her your knives ladies."

Moonlight glinted on silver blades as the two *telesā* on the boat waved cheerfully at me. Sarona spoke again, "Now, do we have an understanding, Leila?"

I nodded, my eyes only on Daniel as he lay unconscious on a creaking wooden canoe with two insane women bearing knives.

Nafanua tried to reassert some authority on the scenario. "Alright, enough of the theatrics. Get Leila out of there so we can set the plan in motion."

I took a deep breath and tried to calm the frantic beating of my pulse, the shaking of my hands. This was no time for panic. Daniel needed me. *Focus, Leila. Think.* Fotu and Mina made their way through the water to where I stood, cutting the ropes, and pulling me back to shore with fingernails digging into my arms. I stood on the sand, wet and bedraggled, with my thoughts running a million miles a minute. *Think.* I needed a plan. Daniel needed a plan. Before I could take a step forward, however, lightning sparked and I was hit from behind. Sarona laughed, even as Nafanua called out "No!"

I had never experienced *telesā* lightning while in my flesh form. Excruciating didn't even begin to describe it. It seemed as if every fiber of my being was being shredded apart, as if a thousand hot knives were stabbing every available inch of flesh. The pain drove every sane thought out of my mind and all I could do was sink to my knees, convulsing and writhing against the agony.

As soon as it had begun, it ended, leaving me a shattered husk. Dimly, I could hear the women's hushed tones as Sarona laughed some more and Nafanua rebuked her. "Sarona, the girl needs no more persuading. That's enough. She may have been an unwilling sister – but she is *telesā* and deserves to be treated as such."

"Oh please, you think we don't know about the sisters you have put to death in the past? The ones who dared to oppose you? Nafanua, don't pretend to be so nobly committed to sisterhood now – just because this girl is of your blood. Oh, and speaking of your blood, does she know how you disposed of the boy child?"

Nafanua stood rigid with barely-contained fury. "Don't. You are forbidden to speak of it. Stop it Sarona. Stop it I say! I am the Covenant Keeper here."

Sarona's eyes danced gleefully in the moonlight and realization dawned on my pain-fried brain. There was something going on here that didn't involve me. Sarona was challenging Nafanua for leadership of the sisterhood and I was just a bystander in a power struggle that had roots in several generations.

Still lying on the ground, shaking my head to clear away the clouds of pain that still lingered, I seized on the thought triumphantly. *This is it. This is my chance to escape, to save Daniel. Divide and conquer. Let the bitches turn on each other.*

Nafanua and Sarona stood facing each other with the other *telesā* gathered in a semi-circle around them. I lay in the center, like some chewed-up piece of mouse that cats were spitting over. Sarona turned her gaze away from Nafanua and again addressed me. "Ohhhh, so she hasn't told you then, has she? Tell me Leila, what happened to your twin brother? How did he die?"

I shook my head slowly, every word hurt to utter. "I ... don't ... know."

"This is priceless. Leila, *telesā* are forbidden to have male offspring. Did you know that?"

My eyes told her no.

"Do you know why they are not allowed to have sons?" She didn't even wait for a reply this time. "Because it is forbidden for our gifts to be wielded by men. Makes sense really. *Fanua* is our mother. Man is her child who continually turns against her so that is why women are needed. To keep things balanced. If men could have our gifts … well, the thought of what they would do with them is too awful to imagine. But sometimes, there is an aberration and one of us gives birth to a boy and so that boy must be disposed of. Leila, you know your twin was a boy. Do you know how he died?"

I swallowed and shook my head, dreading her reply.

"Nafanua killed him. She waited until your father had left the house and then she took a pillow and smothered your brother. While he lay beside you." Another smile in the white gleaming night. "But you don't remember that, do you? You were just a baby, a tiny defenseless, weak baby. And so was he."

I shook my head, shifting my gaze to Nafanua who stood silently to my left. "No. You're lying. I don't believe you. Nafanua, tell me that's not true?"

She said nothing and that was answer in itself. My world reeled again and I slumped to sit on my knees, laughing joylessly.

"Of course it's true. I don't know why I should even be surprised. You're *telesā*. You've done nothing but lie to me from the beginning. You're murderers, you run around killing people with the insane idea that you're saving the earth."

I looked up at Sarona. "Thanks for that. You've done me a big favor. You see, I was still clinging to that tiny little bit of hope that Nafanua was really a decent person. Misguided perhaps, but still with some fragments that I would be proud to call my mother. Well, that's all done with now."

But Sarona wasn't finished. "Oh, but you don't know the half of it, Leila. You want to hear the really interesting part of this sordid infanticide story? Your brother was *telesā*. You and he were complementary halves of a truly perfect whole. He was *Vasa Loloa,* ocean. Potentially, the most powerful one to ever be born. Tell her

Nafanua, tell her how you knew that. Go on."

She didn't wait for Nafanua to respond, rushing on to reveal everything. "I was there, you know, throughout your mother's pregnancy. Yes, we were 'sisters' even then. Even before her body started swelling with child, the ocean moved to him. When we walked by the shore, the ocean would rush to bring her gifts. Casting oysters rich with pearls at her feet. The water would spin and dance, scattering foam patterns of silver mist. Dolphins came as close as they dared to dance in the shallows, calling to her child. Every night she longed to go swimming and she would never swim alone. Fish would come and swim in circles around her. Stingrays, eels, even sharks – they would keep their respectful distance but they would come. There was love in the water. We had never witnessed such a thing before, to carry a child with gifts strong enough that they called from the womb! Oh, Nafanua was so excited about the possibilities. About the child that would be born. The powers she would have – because of course she never dreamed for a minute that the child would be a boy."

Another malicious laugh. "And then came the night you were born. She was on the beach, giving birth in the shallows, wanting you to immediately embrace the ocean that would lift you up to be a shining messiah for us all. You came and Nafanua rejoiced. Here now was the *telesā* that would bring this land to a remembrance of the respect they owed to us. But something was wrong. The birthing was not done. Another child was born. A boy. And he bore the mark of *Vasa Loloa* – the wave crest on his left hip. All water *telesā* have them somewhere on their body. Just like all *matagi telesā* bear the lightning mark on their bodies. But you? You had nothing. Nafanua refused to believe it at first, but there was no mistaking it."

Her eyes took on a faraway look. "We carried you both into the ocean that night. I held your brother in my arms, just like this. It was amazing, I released him into the water and he laughed. This funny little gurgle filled with so much joy. And then, they came. The dolphins. They had been waiting for him. One lifted his head up out of the water, another supported his little body and he waved his arms about and just laughed in the moonlight." She shook her head at the memory and my breath caught in my throat as I thought of the brother I never knew, a baby swimming in a black velvet ocean shimmering with silver. "But you, they ignored. And Nafanua had to catch you up before you drowned. We took you both back onto shore before your father came back with the midwife, before he could suspect Nafanua's disappointment. It was too late to kill him that night. Your father had already seen him." A shrug of disgust. "Men, they are so pathetic when it comes to new life. Probably because they can't give birth. Your father was so excited. He had hoped for one healthy child and instead was given two! By his beautiful, loving wife. Such a stupid man." The entire circle of women cackled with laughter at that.

"Don't you dare speak of my father that way, he was worth a thousand of you." Without thought, my right hand ignited with a fire ball, but Sarona was quicker. Lightning ripped through me again, only long enough to have me shuddering on my knees. Then she called out to the two women on the boat.

"Fouina, this fool needs a reminder why she has to show us respect. Cut him, now!"

"No!" I shouted and, as I did, Fouina and Manuia pulled Daniel to an upright kneeling position. One held up his head while the other swiftly slashed a knife across his upper chest. Even from this distance, the red spurt of blood was clearly visible in the moonlight before they tossed him down again in a ragged heap.

I was frantic. "No, please, I'm sorry. I'm sorry, I won't do that again. Please, don't hurt him. Please." I shouted out across the uncaring ocean. "Daniel? Daniel!?" Back to Nafanua, "Aren't you supposed to be in charge here? Since when was she running this show? Do something. Say something. He's going to bleed to death if we don't do something to help him."

Nafanua interrupted then. "I think we've all heard enough family history for one night thank you Sarona. We are done here."

"Oh, but I don't think we are. I think she wants to hear everything, don't you Leila? After all, isn't that why you came to Samoa in the first place? To know your beloved mother, to find your family" an expansive sweep of her arms at the circle of *telesā* "and to discover your beginnings? So you could, umm let me think, in the words of that oddity - a gifted white man, 'Know thyself ... and to thine own self be true'!" Sarona circled slowly, enjoying every minute of her performance. And against my will, I was caught captive. She was right, because, here at last, on this night, I would finally find everything I had been looking for – the truth. And the longer I could distract this psycho from Daniel, the more chance I had of saving him. I sent a quick glance sideways to where Daniel lay on a moonlit ocean. *Patience Leila, patience, be strong, breathe, you will need all your control if Daniel is to live through this night.*

"So there you were, one big happy family in that little house beside the sea. Oh that week was hilarious. Nafanua kept taking you to the water, trying to see if somehow, something of *Vasa Loloa* had rubbed off on you.

But alas, nothing. Not a single smidgeon of anything. Not even a hermit crab scuttled to your beckoning fingers. And you had nothing of *matagi* either. Such a disappointment … tsk, tsk. Imagine her disappointment. A *telesā* with a gifted son that she didn't want, a daughter with no visible traces of any gifts at all and a tiresome husband who was enthralled with the both of you. Oh, now don't misunderstand me, it has been known to happen before, at some point to all of us. I think we've all given birth to daughters who were useless. No gifts at all. Right?"

She turned for affirmation to the others, everyone nodding in assent. Everyone except for Nafanua, who stood like stone, impassive and immovable. "It's not unheard of – the father's genes being too distasteful – and so *Fanua* chooses not to instill any of her gifts in the child. But no matter, there were always any number of villages that would gladly take the offspring of *telesā* because they knew such children would always be wise with plants and healing things. So after a few weeks, Nafanua was beginning to accept the reality that you were one of those. You see, we didn't know then that your brother was your complement opposite, that *Vasa Loloa* was really the control for your fire, the neutralizer if you will. But then, there's never been an earth *telesā* that we have known, just in legend, so how could we know?"

Confusion had me reeling. "I don't understand. Are you saying that my brother, my twin – he was the answer to this fire thing? He was the one who could cancel this thing from erupting all the time?"

Sarona waved her hand, annoyed with the interruption. "No, no, he was more like the soother. The calming influence that could make sure you wouldn't blow yourself up or someone else, whenever the time came for your gift to manifest. Your power is one that requires some gentling because of its unpredictability so, clearly, *Fanua*, in her wisdom, only ever gifts it in pairs. In twins, so that one can calm the other. That's why Nafanua couldn't sense your gift in those early days. Your brother's water gift was meant to subdue your fire, probably to make sure you didn't explode in the womb, or kill your own mother during the delivery process." A shrug, "Hmm, lucky for Nafanua. Besides, your powers are not much to write home about, clearly, your brother got all the power in the family." An airy flick of her wrist. "But we knew none of this back then. So when the time was right, Nafanua killed him."

The words alone sliced pain through me. Pain that Sarona ignored as she continued. "She was planning to give you to a family at Lefaga, since you were supposedly ungifted but she was careless. She underestimated your father. She had gotten sloppy with giving him his usual love potions. You see, he was suspicious of your brother's death. He just about walked in on Nafanua carrying out the act and she wasn't very good at concealing all the evidence. It didn't help when she didn't summon enough emotional distress at the funeral like a real mother would have. He asked a few too many questions of people. The storytellers and 'Christian' gossipers, people like your aunty Matile. Somehow he found out a little too much about *telesā*, witchcraft I think he called it. He confronted Nafanua about their son and since she was planning on leaving him anyway, she told him the truth. He left that same day, taking you with him." A begrudging admiration crept into her voice. "Have to say, that was a bit clever of him. A bit spirited. Unexpected really. Men are not known for running away from us. But Nafanua was not amused, were you sister?"

Again, Sarona did not really expect an answer. "Oh, the rage of a *telesā* denied is legendary. It did not matter that Nafanua had not wanted you for herself, that she was going to discard you anyway – no – what mattered was that this man, this creature, had bested her. Not only had he shaken himself free of her bewitching beauty, but he had dared to take her daughter with him. Ha! The resulting tantrum was the greatest hurricane Samoa had seen in over 50 years. But there was nothing she could do. *Telesā* cannot reach across oceans to the land of the free and the home of the brave. And so Nafanua forgot about you. What was one more ungifted child after all? Oh you did not know that either? Did you really think that, in all her lifetime, your mother has not given birth to other children beside you and *Vasa Loloa*? Oh yes, there have been others. But none of them have been gifted, none of them. It has been her greatest shame, hasn't it Nafanua? That a *telesā* as powerful as she, the Covenant Keeper of our *matagi* sisters has never been able to have a child with any gifts worth talking about. Yes, Leila there are a few of your blood sisters scattered about these islands, most of them much older than you of course. Finally, after so many years of waiting and hoping, you were supposed to be the child she had prayed to the gods for but such a disappointment. *Fanua* works in mysterious ways – she gives Nafanua the greatest gift child – but he is a boy!"

"And then, after eighteen years, imagine our surprise when you show up. Looking for answers, looking for the past. Oh Nafanua knew you were here, almost the minute you arrived. Samoa's a small place, you know. She knew you were here and where you were staying but had no interest in you. Just another daughter. But then, we started sensing things. There were signs. Matavanu stirring, which brought that seismological team here to study her. Some of us began having dreams – that's how *Fanua* likes to communicate with us sometimes. Dreams, visions if you like. At first we thought they meant a new *telesā* had been born. We've been scouring the country for babies with unusual gifts. Unexplained ocean happenings. Nothing. Then we followed up with all the ungifted daughters we had placed in various villages. Just to be sure, perhaps one of them was a late bloomer? Nothing. Which led Nafanua to check in with you. Not really thinking we would have much success, mind you. I suspect she harbored some curiosity about the daughter that the one man who had left her had taken."

A question thrown to Nafanua. "And revenge maybe, Nafanua? Have you been carrying some latent rage towards this girl's father perhaps? Hmm? Some desires for revenge, maybe?"

Against my will and, in spite of all the truths that had been thrown at me in the past few weeks, the news that my mother had not ever wanted me – had never planned on keeping me – hurt. Pinpricks of hurt stung at my heart. I turned to look at this woman who was part of me. Had I ever really known her? Were the past months all a lie? At any time, had she ever really cared about me? I thought of the endless hours of lessons, her patience with my clumsy efforts to make fire do my bidding. Patience I had mistaken for genuine concern.

I turned pain-filled eyes at Nafanua. "You asked me to give you a chance to be my friend and I did. I trusted you. Did the last few months mean nothing to you? And my dad, he loved you Nafanua. He never stopped loving you. The woman he thought you were. Without your potions and herbs, he loved you. He was a good man and you didn't deserve him. Did you ever feel anything? For him? For me? Or was I just a tool, a toy with a part to play in your grand plans?"

Nafanua's fierce gaze softened and she shrugged helplessly. "Leila, you are my daughter and nothing will change that. But we cannot change the past and must not dwell on it. I'm sorry you can't understand this. I am *telesā*. We all are. I warned you. This attachment you have for this boy, it is foolishness. It will only make you weak and lead to sorrow. For him, for you. You are *telesā* and there is no future for you and this boy. Surely you must see that. Your covenant with your sisters must come above all else. We are *Matagi* and you are *Afi* but you are still our sister. We need you and you need us."

Sarona scoffed and rolled her eyes. "Oh please, Nafanua. We don't need this child. And have you forgotten what she has done? You are our Covenant Keeper and it is your responsibility to enforce our laws. She broke silence, she shared *telesā* knowledge with a man. Not only that, she allowed him to take specimens, blood samples, DNA, so that he could study it and then use it to try and cure her. What sacrilege is this?"

The other women in the circle nodded in agreement.

"And then, when we offer her a second chance, she has the audacity to throw it back in our faces. She gets a Tongan *telesā* reject to give her an antidote for the scientist and thinks she can live happily ever after with her little boyfriend!" I looked around at the others and saw in their eyes that anything we had shared in the past would mean nothing now. I had broken their trust by asking Jason to help me and loving Daniel certainly didn't help my case either. No, there would be no mercy from any of them.

I appealed one last time to Nafanua. "I understand your anger with me and I'll do whatever I need to make things right with my sisters. But Daniel is no part of this. Let him go. Please."

Nafanua shook her head. "Quiet. Enough of this. Sarona is right. You broke our laws by sharing *telesā* knowledge with this boy and with the professor. They both must die. But Leila, you can spare them. We are willing to let them both live if you release the volcano. Take out Apia and the surrounding villages. And the main town in Savaii as well. Do this for us, do it now and Daniel will live. And so will Jason."

I tried to stall. "Alright. But you have to release Daniel first."

Sarona screamed at me in answer. "You are in no position to issue ultimatums here girl!" Again she summoned lightning before I could even process what she was doing. Again agony ripped through me, shredding all rational thought and as soon as her attack paused, I tried to hit her with a ball of fire. But I was in no state to hurt anyone and it was a frail attempt to fight back, which she deflected easily with a rushing wind.

"Is that the best you can do? And you really thought you could take us on with *that* kind of power?" She shook her head in disbelief. "We're not playing here, Leila. And I am tired of you thinking that we are. Nafanua, we discussed this. The Covenant has already agreed what must be done." She turned to the women in the boat. "Kill the boy. Now."

I screamed. "Nooooooo!" But the universe did not listen. In some grotesque silhouette in the moonlight, Manuia grabbed a handful of Daniel's hair in her fist, jerked his head back and stabbed her knife deep into his chest.

"Now, throw him to the sharks."

Time and space slowed. For me, everything faded as the two women heaved Daniel's body over the side of the canoe. He slipped into the black water with barely a ripple. And then he was gone. Gone.

Do you know what death feels like? As a million and one sparks of life flicker, dim, and then are extinguished? Neurons die like butterflies scattering on the wind as they flutter their last breaths. Your lungs release their final gasp of CO_2. And your heart shudders to its concluding beat. And as consciousness slips away, you realize, death is sweet. Nothingness is joy. Better than living. Better than breathing. When you are without the purpose for your existence. Nothingness is joy.

How do I know this? Because when Daniel disappeared into the ocean – I died. The madness around me carried on, but I was no longer present. Not really. I saw and heard but it meant nothing to me. Sarona laughed. And Nafanua reprimanded her for 'jumping the gun.' Manuia and Fouina brought the boat back to shore. And I sat and felt nothing. Daniel was gone. There was nothing left to feel.

The *telesā* dragged me away from the shoreline, further up onto the rocks to a vantage point where we could look across the distance and see the lights of Apia flickering. They threw me down roughly and the rocky plain was sharp and cut my bare legs. But still I felt nothing. Nafanua and Sarona continued with their arguing.

"You dared to defy me, to reveal covenant information about my past without my permission. Just what was your intention?"

"The girl deserved to hear the truth. You wanted her to join us and yet she was ignorant about her past, about her mother. How long did you plan on lying to her? There are no secrets in the sisterhood, Nafanua."

"Oh yes, I forgot how important honesty and trust were to you." The sarcasm in Nafanua's voice was a whiplash, but Sarona did not back down.

"This is not about you and I, Nafanua."

"Oh, isn't it? You think I don't realize what it is you are trying to do here? All this? The theatrics and the drama tonight? I know it's all a play for my position. Don't deny it. You have felt threatened by Leila's presence right from the start, from when you realized her gifts made her the most logical choice for the next Covenant Keeper. That's what this is about. The decision for leadership."

Finally, Sarona's composure was jolted and she snarled, "There is no decision making to be entered into. All our sisters know that I will be the next Keeper, that's the way it has always been and will always be." She gestured wildly at the other *telesā*. "They all know it. And you know it, Nafanua, this girl cannot be one of us, no matter how much you want her to. Her loyalties lie elsewhere and she cannot be trusted. You are letting your emotions as a mother interfere with your judgment. How ironic, you condemn Leila for allowing her feelings for that boy rule her and yet, here you are, placing your daughter above the will, above the good of the sisterhood."

The gathering of women shifted uneasily on their feet and looked everywhere else but at Nafanua. The thought came to me idly that none of them wanted to risk getting involved in the showdown between the two most powerful members of their sisterhood. No, they would watch and wait. And then run whichever way the winds took them. Some sisterhood they were turning out to be. I wished they would hurry up and kill me. I didn't know much about the afterlife but I didn't want to run the risk of losing Daniel in the crowds over there.

Nafanua scoffed at Sarona's accusation. "Don't be ridiculous. All I want is for our Sisterhood to fulfill its mission as protectors of this land and the best way for us to do that is by enlisting Leila and her gifts."

"And if she won't use them willingly? What then, huh?" Sarona grabbed a fistful of my hair, roughly pulling my face back to the night sky. "Look at her. Does this look like a *telesā* who feels passionately about protecting the earth? Does it?"

Manuia stepped forward authoritatively. "She's right, Nafanua. We can all see it. We have kept silent, watched you train her, shared our knowledge with her, but it's been obvious to all of us. She is not of us and never can be. Maybe if she hadn't met that boy Daniel, things would have been different."

My eyes flickered a little with recognition at his name. *Daniel, where are you? 'As long as we're together, everything will be alright.' Daniel, how can I still be living, breathing – when you are not with me?*

Fouina chimed in, "I agree. The bond between them has been inexplicable. Even you yourself could not break her obsession with him, Nafanua, not with your potions and plants." She hesitated, a troubled look on her face, "It was so ... unbecoming of a *telesa*. And yet, so in-human as well. Almost as if there was something else at work between them. I can't explain it."

Sarona rolled her eyes and snapped derisively, "Oh please, Fouina what is this? A Twilight moment? Get real." She turned back to Nafanua. "The fact is that Leila does not qualify to join the Sisterhood. And she has broken a countless number of our rules. There is only one option available to us. We must kill her. Right here. Now." She looked around the circle for confirmation and there were unwilling nods from all of the women.

If I'd been capable of emotions, I'm sure I would have felt the slightest bit miffed at losing the most important popularity contest of my short life. As it was, I only welcomed the announcement with relief. I was so very tired of this. But my death wasn't going to be as simple and straightforward as Daniel's.

Nafanua hissed. "No. You will not assign death to my only gifted daughter, do you hear me? I am the Covenant Keeper and you cannot do this without my permission. You are all being blinded by this fool's jealousy of her competition. Don't be so short sighted. I've told you, Leila's fire is the gift we have been waiting for. Don't throw it all away."

She looked around wildly but found no support. In one deft motion, she pushed Sarona away from me and sank to her knees beside me to whisper fiercely in my ear. "You saw what just happened to your boyfriend? We will do the same thing to Matile and Tuala. And that old woman – your boyfriend's grandmother? We will find her and we will kill her too. Call the volcano, now. This is your life on the line. Do it."

Sarona was disbelieving. "Nafanua can't you see this girl is not capable of what you are asking her to do?"

I gazed at Nafanua from my numb daze. I wondered if she was worried about them killing me? Or just really eager for me to summon a volcano? But then, did the difference really matter? Probably not. I slumped back down and waited for the death strike. Wished for it. Prayed for it. But even so, I wasn't ready for it when it did come.

Sarona stabbed with a lightning bolt, but not enough volts to kill. Just enough to serrate my every nerve with the kind of pain that took on a life of its own. I hadn't meant to scream, but agony ripped from me anyway and from far away I could hear myself begging. For mercy. For death. But that had never been Sarona's plan. No, again and again she sent lightning rippling through me, juddering my teeth, yanking every fiber of my being through a meat mincer until I couldn't tell where light ended and darkness began.

For a moment there was a reprieve as Sarona paused in her attack and I could hear voices.

Nafanua. "Stop it. You're torturing her. Stop it!"

Sarona taunted. "Oh, what's the matter Nafanua? Can't you handle it when someone else is administering the torture? You didn't seem to mind that time I was on the receiving end of lightning – remember that time when you and the sisters decided I needed some humbling? Hmm? Oh no, you didn't have a problem with it then. Or how about that time you ordered death for that little upstart *telesā* from Aleipata? The one who didn't want to leave her mommy and daddy and join our sisterhood? Oh no, you had no trouble with killing wayward *telesā* then."

Nafanua's voice was strained. "Those times were different. This is different."

"No, the only thing that's different is she's your daughter. And you want us all to ignore centuries of tradition and sacred rules just so that you can have her be your little pet. Go on Nafanua, do it! You know you want to strike me. Go ahead."

Nafanua stood with head bowed. Sarona called to the others to join her. "Come on, let's finish this." One by one, each of them added their lightning strike to hers so that the entire rocky shore was lit up in startling, blinding light.

This increased attack jerked me to an upright kneeling position. I turned my head and begged Nafanua to end this. "Mother, please. Just kill me. Please. I'm begging you."

Nafanua turned her head slightly towards me, a soft smile on her face, far gentler than any I had ever seen.

"Leila, I may not have loved your father. But always remember, I loved *you*."

Before I could register her intention she stepped directly into the path of lightning that seared through me. Sarona and the others were so shocked their onslaught faltered slightly. Nafanua used their momentary pause to her advantage. Eyes closed, hair flowing in the swirling tempest, she raised her arms to the heavens. A jagged flash lit the sky and thunder shook the very ground we stood upon. She turned white eyes towards the line of women, eyes that bled with white fire, uttering words I could not understand. The very air shivered as electricity ripped through it. Searing the nearby trees. Striking the *telesa* straight on. Knocking them all to the ground. All except for Sarona. She stood and laughed, appealing with widespread arms to all around her.

"May the earth and all my sisters bear witness, Nafanua has become the Covenant Breaker and we are no longer bound in sisterhood. What was sealed is now broken. What was done is now irrevocably undone."

She turned to face the woman who had raised her and nurtured her gifts since she was twelve years old. "Is that the best you can do? You are tired and weak, you old woman. I knew I was right to take the lead. You are not strong enough to do what needs to be done any longer."

My mother did not reply. She was gathering the currents around us, drawing electromagnetism down from the atmosphere for another attack. Again, she sent a charge of lightning blazing towards the women she had spent several lifetimes with. Again the women were knocked back on their knees. Fouina and Manuia screamed as their skin caught fire and they ran blindly towards the trees, beating at the flames. But still Sarona shrugged the attack off easily, blocking with her own lightning charge. With bated breath, I realized what the others had known all along. My mother's powers were eclipsed by another. Salamasina's words resounded in my mind, *when a leader ages, her powers weaken. Either she will step down and pass the covenant on to a younger sister or else she will have it taken from her in outright battle.*

Nafanua spoke, "We were wrong, Sarona, I was wrong. This plan is not the way. Let us stop this and reconsider."

Cold dread gripped me. There was a note of pleading in my mother's voice. She knew she could not win. And so did Sarona. She laughed and then slowly, almost lazily, she beckoned and the heavens obeyed.

Before I could think. Move. Or breathe. White light shot from Sarona's upraised arms. So bright and blinding that I could not see. I heard my mother scream. A scream that was drowned by the thunder. I opened my eyes to see my mother consumed in white fire. Her every particle seemed electrified in a grotesque beauty. Then there was nothing left where she had stood. Just a smoldering pile of ash.

It all happened so fast. I tried to breathe as I lay there on the ground, looking at the remnants of the woman who had borne me. Smothered my brother. Lied to me. Manipulated and used me. And then, at the very end, died for me. Images flashed. Nafanua brushing my hair and putting a scarlet hibiscus behind my ear. Her proud pleasure at watching me dance. Laughing at my attempts to make fire do my bidding. I thought I had wanted death, but now? Now, I wasn't so sure.

I stumbled to my feet. Sarona still stood across the lava rock expanse, asking her fallen sisters if they were alright. I stared at them. The women who had killed the man I loved. I gazed past them at the crashing ocean that was Daniel's final resting place and somehow, it spoke to me on a salted wind. It spoke of my father's love for me.

Would he want me to give up on life so easily? A white seabird knifed through the air, over and above me it wheeled. I stood and watched it dip and soar. Its plaintive cry resounded through the charred air. It spoke of Daniel's love for me.

Leila, you need to live. To fight. You need to use your fire to protect Salamasina, Matile and Tuala. Will you let them do to them what they have done to me?

I listened to the voices of the ocean. And rage came. It simmered and boiled. Like the volcano that long ago had formed this lava field. Closing my eyes, I whispered to earth. To her black soil that pushed up gardenias and other green things. Deeper to bedrock. Granite hard and immovable. Then deeper still, to flowing molten red rivers. That twisted and rushed. *Hear me*, I whispered. *It is I, Pele. Hear me and come.* And far, far below my feet – earth listened.

I opened my eyes to hear Sarona's mocking cry, "Oh look, it's the daughter of the traitor, the pathetic fire girl. What are you going to do, little girl? Cry more of your useless tears?" she turned to laugh with her sisters. "Or maybe you will blow smoke at us? And spit steam? Ha! If you did not remind me so much of your mother, I wouldn't even bother killing you."

She looked bored as, with a flick of her wrist, she sent a jagged spear of lightning my way. Which I easily deflected with a thought. A fiery thought that wrapped around the spear and choked it to a halt.

I smiled at Sarona's puzzled furrowing of her brow. I felt the heat coming. Eagerly. And it felt good. I knew I was going to enjoy this. I took several steps forward, gingerly stretching out my bruised legs. Again, Sarona threw her lightning. This time I didn't even need to look. Fire caught it without even being told. Only this time I threw it back. With an extra measure. Me being generous.

There was a muffled oath as Sarona was jolted back by my unexpected 'gift.' Her sisters looked bewildered as she yelled back at me. "What are you doing fire girl? You don't seriously think you can match us? Your mother couldn't – what makes you think you can?"

I didn't answer. Not right away.

Because the fire was here. The ground beneath my feet heaved and a jet of orange red lava spurted forth like a geyser. As it caught me, I allowed the fire to consume me, welcoming the now-familiar explosion as every fiber of my being opened its doors to the inferno.

The whole mountainside shook. *Mafui'e*. Earthquake. My earthquake. I slowly stood on tiptoe and spun, danced a pirouette. Loving the flames as they danced with me.

Across from me, the *telesā* were struggling to stay on their feet as the earth shook violently.

"Sarona, what's happening?" they asked her fearfully. But before she could answer, I called to them.

"Tell them, Sarona. Go on. Tell them what's happening." I laughed. And the lava laughed with me. I drew patterns in the air with it and slowly started it spinning towards the assembly of spirit women. Lazy circles. Graceful, delightful circles of flame. And molten rock.

Sarona did not answer. Instead, she summoned her lightning with a thunder clap that shook the sky. That went through me harmlessly. She sent raging wind, gale force. Hurricane wind.

"Oooh, trying to blow out the fire?" it was my turn to mock her now. "Please do continue to fan the flames."

Next was water. Rain came from nowhere. Buckets of it, drowning tons of it. But nothing can stop a volcano. Nothing. I beckoned and the lava stream lifted me, raising me high above the now-cowering women. All except for Sarona. Still, she tried to use her storm to subdue me. Useless. She screamed with rage as her water showers merely fizzed in a hiss of steam.

To give them credit, the *telesā* did try to subdue me. With their storms and water and electricity. One even threw trees at me. But nothing can stop a volcano. Nothing. Sarona called her winds to lift her up to where I stood on my platform of fiery rock.

"What are you doing? What are you?!"

I paused then. Surveying my handiwork. The entire mountainside was a raging river of red. The *telesā* were completely encircled by the lava. I smiled before replying,

"Why, haven't you heard? I'm Pele. The creator and the devourer of lands. And you – you and your sisters, you bore me."

With a flick of my wrist, a ball of flame hurtled towards Sarona, knocking her off balance, sending her tumbling to the circle of rock where the others had been shaken to their knees. I looked down at them, idly considering my options. I wanted to kill them. Obliterate them in a fury of fire. I didn't want even ashes to remain. My mind danced dangerously near to the memory of what they had done to ... NO, I would not, could not even think of him. I would not be able to bear it. I had to stay in the *now*. This moment right here. Hmm, what should I do with them? But as I paused, Sarona turned to scream at the *telesā* closest to her – Fouina.

"I call on your life force with the ancient right of the Covenant Keeper!"

"No!" she had a look of horror on her face as she tried to back away. But there was fire at the rear and she had nowhere to run to. What was Sarona doing? As I watched, she uttered a wild chant of words that made no sense to me but that sent the others into a frenzy of panic.

Manuia yelled, "Stop it Sarona, you can't do this!" She went to pull at Sarona's arm but she was no match for the younger, stronger *telesā* and Sarona dropped her with a single lightning strike. She then turned back to Fouina, finished her incantation and just like that, Fouina exploded in a blinding flash of brilliant light – a light that seemed to linger now on Sarona's own form. Mina was next and finally Fotu. Sarona took them all in some bizarre *telesā* spell, sucking their life force dry. And just like that the *matagi* Sisterhood that Nafanua had spent her life building was gone. Sarona's callous treatment of her sisters stunned me. But I had little time to ponder on it before she was borne aloft again on a swirling wind. This time, her lightning strike was powerful enough to hurt. It scissored through me, carving a tingling path through the lava, like a stab wound through the gut. It caught me by surprise and I stumbled back unsteadily on my mid-air platform. Sarona smiled triumphantly and hit me again. *Ouch!* Who knew that anything could actually impact on lava? A different strategy was called for. *Focus, Leila. Remember your lessons with Nafanua. Remember, lightning is just another form of energy, and you are the mistress of energy.*

Sarona thought she had me as I reeled for balance. She flew in closer for another shot, hoping for a death strike. But this time, I was ready. Instead of flinching against the lightning, I welcomed it, seeking out its components with my mind and when it hit, I was ready – to convert it. Absorb it. Make it my own.

Before Sarona could realize her attack had failed, I threw a non-stop rage of fire balls at her that threw her to the ground in a battered heap where she was still. Sarona was finished.

I should have been happy. Triumphant. But all I felt was empty. Alone. I manipulated the river of fire to set me down gently on the sandy beach where I had stood and watched Daniel die. It didn't seem right. I was the most powerful energy force on the planet but even I couldn't bring the one I loved back to life. Or turn back time. Silken waves lapped the shore and the moon cast her black diamonds on the waters. It was beautiful. I breathed in the salt air and allowed myself to feel.

The pain of heartache and loss cut me. *Daniel, I love you. How will I live without you?* I walked slowly into the ocean and, as the waves embraced me, my fire hissed, spat, and died. I dived and swam out to where I had last seen the boat, hoping for something, anything, of Daniel. But there was nothing. The sea refused to give up her secrets. I was *Fanua Afi* after all and *Vasa Loloa* owed me nothing. The salt of my tears mingled with the ocean. Exhausted, I turned and swam back towards the shore, fighting not to give in to my soul's desire and just shut my eyes and sink beneath the waves. Death called me with its sweet promise and it was difficult not to answer her.

I was a few meters away from the shore when I saw it. Away to my far right. Flashes of silver as a multitude of something leapt and splashed. *What the ... !* Fish? No, dolphins! I stood in hip deep water, transfixed at the sight of at least six dolphins wriggling, splashing and churning the shallow water. And just beyond them, lying on the sand, with the waves washing over it, was a dark, still shape. A body. My heart leapt and caught in my throat, "No, Daniel?"

I ran. Through the water, out on the sand and along the beach until I collapsed beside him. Yes, it was Daniel. I hardly dared to touch him, to gently turn him over so I could see what the ocean had left me of my love, unwilling to confront the evidence of the *telesā* attack. He was almost naked, his shorts in ragged tatters. I had never seen a more beautiful thing. Yes, there were cuts and blackening bruises on his face, his body. And the knife wounds were a violation on a glorious tapestry.

But he was my Daniel. And he was breathing. Slow, barely perceptible breaths, but he was alive. How was this possible? How could this be? I had seen them stab him. Watched him disappear into the water. And now, several hours later, here he was, looking like he was asleep in the moonlight. The thrashing sounds in the water sounded more urgent as if calling to me. I turned to look, in time to see the pod of dolphins, leaping, dancing, jumping over each other in an almost frenzied joy. Their piercing clicking sounds intensified. What were they trying to tell me?

Stop it, Leila, now you're losing it. They're not talking to you, you idiot. Focus. Daniel needs to get to the hospital. Now.

I shook my mind away from silver dolphins and moved to carefully drag Daniel further up the beach. I had to get him away from the waves, put him somewhere safe while I went to get hold of a phone. It was no easy thing to move him, especially considering the beating my body had taken tonight. But finally I got him to a sheltered spot under a cluster of trees where I collapsed beside him in a breathless heap. Which is when I saw it. A white birthmark on his exposed right inner thigh, that glowed a burnished silver in the moonlight. A very clear – without doubt – mark of a cresting wave, *"the mark of Vasa Loloa – the wave crest....all water telesā have them."*

"What?" I sank back on my knees in shock, my gaze moving instinctively back to the ocean. Where silver dolphins still played. Carefree sentinels, watching over him. Waiting to see what I would do, how I would take care of him.

"Leila?" My name was a weak whisper in the night as Daniel stirred. He was waking up. I moved back to his side, remembering just in time that I was in flesh form – and missing my clothes. *Oops.* Frantically, I looked around. Leaves, coconut shells, some broken bottles were the sum of all my wardrobe options. *Argh.*

"Leila? Is that you?" His query came stronger now, he was trying to sit up. This was no time for modesty. I gathered my long hair and brought it to cover my front, never more thankful than now that it came to my waist, trusting in the night to conceal the rest of me. I bent over him.

"Hey, it's me. I'm here, baby. I'm here." I whispered softly against his cheek and tears came unbidden. "You're okay. We're both okay."

He reached up and gently caught my tears with his fingers. "Don't cry. You're the fire goddess remember? You don't cry."

I grinned and choked on a sob. "Yeah I do. Fire goddesses always cry when the one they love comes back from the dead."

"Who said I was dead?" He shook his head and the movement made him wince. "Ouch. Last thing I remember they were zapping you with lightning and I couldn't do anything about it. I couldn't help you. Some boyfriend I turned out to be."

"Are you kidding? I'm the girlfriend with a psycho family who stabbed you and threw you into the ocean for the sharks."

Bewilderment furrowed his brow. "They did? I don't remember that. So where are they?"

I shrugged. "Gone. All of them." I didn't want to dwell on what had happened. On what Nafanua had done for me. There would be plenty of time for that later. And time to figure out what to do about Sarona. I looked back to the rock field where it had all taken place and was disconcerted to see that Sarona was gone. With bated breath, I quickly scanned the area all around us, but in vain. No sign of her. What did that mean for the future? I didn't have time to think about it though, Daniel wanted answers.

"How did you do it? What happened? How did I get here?" He half sat up and looked around and then hastily averted his eyes. "Umm, Leila?"

"Yeah?"

"Did you know you were naked?"

"No I'm not!" I folded my arms over my curtain of hair. "I'm covered. A bit. We just escape from the jaws of *telesā* death and the first thing you do is notice my lack of clothes? Stop looking at me."

He laughed and brought his face level with mine. "I'm not. Looking at your body, I mean. Because I'm too busy looking into your eyes. So I can make very, very sure – that this is real. That you're real." His eyes turned serious. "I thought we'd lost each other tonight." His lips captured mine and into our kiss I poured all the sweet relief and joy of finding him alive. When he finally pulled away, it was with his crooked smile that I loved so much. "Yes, you're definitely real." A quick glance downward. "And you're very naked."

"Daniel! You promised."

"Sorry. I can't help myself..."

"Don't look. Or I'll never speak to you again." He just laughed at the weak threat. I looked around and spied a ragged piece of cloth half buried in the sand amidst other debris. I sent a silent prayer of thanks out to whoever was dumping their rubbish on this beach and pulled at the flimsy piece of fabric. It was half of an old *lavalava*, enough to drape around my hips. My hair would have to be enough for the top. Somewhat dressed, I went to help Daniel stand.

"Come on, let's get out of here. You're hurt and I want Mama to take a look at you." *Because you're supposed to be dead ...* my brain screamed silently. Slowly, we made our way along the beach towards the distant road. Daniel limping and half leaning on my shoulder. Every part of me ached but every part of me rejoiced. The sisterhood were defeated. Jason was alive. Daniel and I were alive. And together.

At the spread of black rocks where fire had met lightning, I paused for a moment. Dustings of ash swirled in the wind. Remnants of Nafanua and her sisters? I wasn't sure how I felt about her sacrifice for me. Yes, she had chosen me in death. But I would much rather she had chosen me in life.

Daniel looked down at me and his voice was soft with concern, "Are you okay?"

I nodded. "Yeah. Fine. Let's go."

Once more, I looked back at the black ocean. The dolphins were gone. Like they had never been. Was it all just a wild dream? A fire- and trauma-induced fantasy? I snuck a glance back down at Daniel's hip. No. The crest birthmark was still there. Defiantly silver.

What did it all mean? I thought back to the night in Salamasina's garden when I had revealed my fire gifts to her. Her reaction. The glimpses she had given me into her past. She would know what this birthmark meant. Surely. The question was, whether or not she would be willing to share the answers with me.

But for now, Daniel walked beside me. And I knew that the covenant of love between us was unbreakable. For now, that would be enough.

The End.

Watch for the second book in the 'Telesā series by Lani Wendt Young.

When Water Burns

The promise of the day ahead was a fiery lightness that lit up my every step. A whole day with Daniel. Just us two at the beach. It would be the first time I had seen him since he had finished getting his full body tattoo done. The requisite two weeks of isolation and healing time was completed and I was eager to be with him. Texts and phone calls were a poor replacement for the real thing. Daniel's smile. His laugh. The crinkle of his green eyes as they would dance teasingly at me. I wanted to soar and sing with the anticipation alone of the picnic we had planned. I had cajoled the sour Aunty Matile into teaching me how to make her banana muffins – and then earned her sniff of disdain when I 'polluted' her recipe with handfuls of chocolate chips. It was a wickedly delicious recipe and the first sampling bite had me smiling. Yes! *Not bad Leila* I muttered to myself as I assembled ham sandwiches and packed everything into a cooler with sliced fruit. Daniel was bringing Diet Coke and some of his grandmother's coconut buns. I was checking off my beach supplies when I heard his truck pull up out front.

A foolish smile was plastered on my face as I ran to the door. A quick good bye to Matile who was still ignoring me and the evil chocolate chips. And then a breathless halt on the verandah at the sight of Daniel coming up the steps. A wry smile as the thought crossed my mind – would this boy ever have an 'off' day? A bad hair day? A fat day? An I'm-so-ugly-I-don't-want-to-go-out-day?

He stood there smiling at me and I hoped he couldn't hear my thoughts that screamed of delight. Love. Bliss. Adoration. *Ugh*, I was sickening. But look at him, who wouldn't be a mass of mush at the sight of him?

Khaki shorts, white t-shirt, dark sunglasses raised over his sea green eyes. My gaze went to his legs where the bands of black patterning peered from his shorts.

I could not shake the worry about all the possible things that could go wrong with a body length tattoo. Catching the direction of my gaze, he stopped in his tracks to bend down and fold up the hem of his shorts. "See? I told you they were fine. So, what do you think?" He mocked striking a supermodel pose. I pretended to look pensive, hands on my hips and shaking my head.

"Hm, I'm not sure. I need to get a better look. Can you please turn around and pull your pants down so me and the whole world can get a better look at your bum?"

He pretended to look shocked. "Hey, don't even joke about it or else I will!"

I laughed and my happiness surprised me with tears that I had to blink away. The joking faded, his eyes softened and he quickly took the final steps towards me, pausing to look behind me to ensure the coast was clear before taking me in his arms. A whisper in my ear – *is this okay?* I didn't care whether aunty Matile was watching, I held him close, breathing in his scent and hiding my slight tears in his sleeve. My voice was a hushed whisper of awe. "Oh Daniel, it's so good to see you. I've missed you so much."

There was answering emotion in his reply. "Me too."

I could have stood there in his arms forever but a minute was all I was going to get. As swiftly as it had begun he released me and bent to take the bag and the cooler to the truck.

"Is this everything?"

I contented myself with the reminder that we would have the whole day together far away from everyone as I followed after him to the truck.

"Yup. That's it. Did you get all the drinks?"

His quick grin gave me chills. "Yes, three Diet Cokes for the coke addict,"shaking his head. "You know that stuff is like nuclear waste, don't you?"

I groaned, slamming the door with an extra flourish, rolling my eyes. "Yeah, yeah so you keep telling me. I like my insides polluted with nuclear waste thank you very much."

He laughed. And his laugh had me sighing with contentment. It had been too long since I had laughed with the one I loved.

In the car, Daniel turned on the radio as we started the forty-five minute drive to the beach on the other side of the island. Samoa's musical answer to everything – Bob Marley wailed *No woman, no cry*...

He turned to me with a mischievous smile. "Bob sure got it right didn't he?"

"Huh?"

"Women. Always making us cry."

I just rolled my eyes at him. He laughed and started singing along with the chorus, "No woman no cry, little darling, don't dry your tears…"

I shook my head but didn't disturb him. I could listen to him sing forever. Even if it was a song that was making fun of me. The drive to Lefaga beach went quickly and it wasn't long before we were pulling off the main road and down a bumpy sandy track towards the ocean. Once in sight of the sea, we turned and started driving slowly along the parallel road past village houses and beach *fale*. Still he didn't stop the truck, not until we had come to the very end of the track did he pull up beside a thicket of mangrove trees.The nearest house was a half mile away and the little slip of sandy beach was completely empty. We both got out of the truck and I turned shining eyes towards Daniel as he began unpacking our cooler from the back. "It's beautiful Daniel. And totally private."

He shrugged as he heftily put the cooler on his shoulder "Yeah, but the problem with that is there's no water, no taps for us to clean off afterwards but you said you wanted to rough it today. So here you have it, nothing but sand, sea and sun and bugs and mosquitoes and dirt and sweat. Ugh."

I laughed at his lack of enthusiasm. "Oh, don't be such a spoilt baby. It'll be great. Come on." I took his free hand and pulled him with me towards the beach where we found a shady spot for the cooler under a tree.

He unrolled the mat and stretched back on it with a pleased sigh. "Ah, that's better. This is how I like the beach, looking at it from the shade."

I ignored him as I rifled through my backpack looking for a hair tie. Daniels truck had no air conditioning and it was a relief to peel off my sweaty t-shirt, leaving only the black bikini top and cut off denim shorts.

"Are you coming in?" He wrinkled his nose and shook his head. "Nah. No thanks. You go ahead. I'll hang out here."

"Aw come on!" He shook his head in refusal again. I didn't push the issue though, knowing his sensitivity about his mother and her drowning. "Okay, I'll just have a quick dip to cool off. Don't eat all the muffins before I get back...or else." With that mild threat, I waded out into the azure water, lugging an inflatable tire Daniel had brought and launched myself into the silken warmth of blue. "Yoohoo! This is beeeyootiful. You're missing out!"

But Daniel was now dozing in the shade and there was no answer. I swam further out until the water was too deep to stand and then pulled myself up on to the tire and lay back to soak in the sun. Could there be a day more perfect than this one? I luxuriated in the chance to just be with Daniel, hang out and do normal things with him. We had spent so little time together where we were not either fighting for our lives or fighting over whether or not it was safe for us to be together. I was determined that today would be the first of many days that would be blissfully ordinary.

I don't know how long I floated along like that, lulled by the warm sun and the gentle sway of the ocean, but when I felt a slight shiver down my spine, I sat up. *Uh oh.*

The current had taken me further out than I had expected, further out than my second-rate swimming skills felt comfortable with. I was now closer to where waves crashed on the reef than I was to the faraway shore. I could no longer make out Daniel's shape underneath the trees.

Dammnit, good one Leila. I sat up and started paddling my way back to the beach, kicking with my legs to help spur me along. That's when I felt it. An ice cold tingle of my skin a sharp contrast to the silken blue warmth of the water lapping around me. I felt a presence. A something - threatening, darkening coming towards me. My heart pounded as I clutched the inner tube tightly, wishing I was safe on shore. *Stop it Leila, just quit it, youre being ridiculous.* But not even my grandmother's favourite phrase could stop the rising panic that had me turning wildly in all directions to see what hidden threat had me silently screaming.

I couldn't see anything. The sun glinted on the diamond water. The golden line of sand beckoned. A soft breeze played in the coconut trees lining the shore. I looked back at the ocean, scanning the blue for anything out of the ordinary. All seemed well – on the surface. Then from far away, Daniel shouted, and the fear in his voice confirmed the wild panic within me.

"Leila! Leila! Don't move. I'm coming. Don't move!"

Daniel was running along the beach towards me, then several splashing steps into the water and he dived. Strong and sure he surged through the water with quick even strokes. He was a powerful swimmer and amidst my ragged breathing of fearfulness, I heard myself exclaim in surprise. "Damn, he's a good swimmer." He was like liquid in the water, the gaping distance between us was nothing to him and his pace never slowed. It seemed like bare moments and he was beside me in the water, one arm looped around the inner tube while he half-turned to look out over the ocean.

"What is it Daniel?" I grabbed onto his shoulder, feeling foolish in my inexplicable fear. I longed for him to laugh, to brush away my concerns as nothing but foolish imaginings. Instead, his reply was quiet and low, his eyes darting in all directions, searching.

"Just keep still. Very still. Try not to move. It's circling."

"What is? Daniel – tell me – what is it?" My question was a piercing whisper. I didn't know why I felt the need to whisper. And I already knew the answer to my question, only I was hoping that I was wrong.

"Shark. A big one."

He spoke the words I knew he would, but every fibre of his being was focusing on the water, as he twisted his body this way and that, eyes darting back and forth.

I choked back a sob. As if being quieter would somehow make us invisible to the most deadly hunter in the ocean. As if. I'd seen Jaws. I knew what was coming. I didn't need the theme music. The pounding of my heart was crescendo enough. I threw a searching gaze back to the shore. Was there any way anyone could help us?

The deserted beach stretched away in the blue-gold afternoon. My earlier thrill at having the day to ourselves now mocked me. We were alone. In the ocean. Too far out from the shore thanks to my day dreaming. Alone without any weapons of any kind. Not that weapons ever seemed to help shark attack victims in all the horror movies I'd seen. Funny. They'd never seemed that scary when one lived in the suburbs of Maryland and only sniffed the ocean twice a year. Now? Here I was with the love of my life about to get torn to pieces in the water. I started to shake, my teeth chattering as if we were in the midst of the arctic instead of the glorious Pacific. Daniel threw me a concerned glance, unwilling to take his eyes off the waters around us.

With one arm guiding the tube, he shielded me with his body, muttering under his breath as if talking to himself. "He's trying to decide. What angle he'll come in on. Which side will be the best point of attack. Trying to figure out which of us is the weaker. Hmm…should I take out the stronger element first? Or pick off the smaller prey? Circling. Doesn't want to let us too far. But still not worried. Knows he's got the advantage no matter what."

In the midst of my terror, I paused as confusion added itself to the mix. What the hell was Daniel talking about? Was he losing it? I grabbed his shoulder.

"Daniel? What are we going to do?" I could barely make sense because my teeth were chattering so much. I was cold in the midst of a screaming hot day. I tried to think about flames. And rage. But I knew from past experience that all the fear in the world could not make me summon fire when I was in the ocean. We were going to die. Daniel was going to die. And useless, hopeless me was going to let it happen. His voice in my ear disrupted my thoughts.

"Leila, listen to me. I need you to slowly and carefully paddle to shore. Do you hear me? Don't splash too much. Just move real slow through the water on the tube. I'm going to draw him off. Go now. Go!"

Before I could process the full import of his words and argue with them, he shoved the tube away from him and towards the shore. From nowhere, a massive wave lifted the tube and started it rushing through the water without me even beginning to paddle. I threw a terrified glance over my shoulder back to where Daniel waited in the water.

He had his back to me as he tread water and for the first time I saw it. Clearly. The dark shape in the water. Moving almost lazily as it knifed towards him. And still he did not move.

"Daniel!" the scream tore from me without thought. "No!"

He turned his head, green eyes speaking to me across the water, as he stretched out his arm towards me. Another impossible wave seemed to emanate from where he swayed in the water, rushing me further away from him and to safety. *What's happening? Where are these waves coming from?*

Vainly I tried to halt the current but it swept the inner tube along relentlessly. There was only one thing to do. I heaved my body off the tire and splashed back into the ocean. The tube swirled away in the foam, happy to be rid of my dead weight. I had no plan. No brilliant ideas. I just knew that there was no way I was leaving Daniel out there to face a shark alone. But now the water wasn't my friend. I was no match for the strange current that only seemed to have one goal. To sweep me along to the shore – no matter what. Even if it meant taking me upside down with a mouth full of water.

I managed to choke out his name once before the sea swallowed me, churning me like a washing machine. Just when I thought I couldn't hold my breath a moment more, I was right side up and gasping for air. All thoughts of the shark fled as I battled the current just to stay afloat, splashing and kicking, sucking in air and water in huge mouthfuls. My grasping hands met with the runaway tire. I clutched it gratefully, my lifeline. Hanging on tightly, I took several breaths of air before wiping the hair out of my face.

I cleared my vision in time to see Daniel begin swimming towards me. Midway he stopped and shouted, "No! Get away from her. You can't have her!"

He reached out in my direction again, yelling "Go Leila! Get out of here!" As he did so, another impossible wave seemed to issue from his outstretched fingers. It rushed at me, carrying me with it. I turned my head to look back at him, in time to see a dark shape close in on him. From far away I heard myself screaming. I saw Daniel spin around in the water, then he dived and the water was still. And eerily silent. No Daniel. No shark. No nothing. Just me. Hanging on to a tire. That was now scraping me along in shallow water, coral nicking at my feet. And still the current wouldn't let me go. Not until it had deposited my stunned self on the shore.

"Dammnit!" Viciously I kicked the tire away from me, ignoring the sting of salt on the cuts on my feet. I dived back into the water and began swimming out to where I had seen Daniel disappear. But again, a determined wave appeared from nowhere and shoved me back to shore. I battled it uselessly. Frustration at war with fear.

"Dammnit, dammnit, dammnit! What's going on?!" I screamed at an impassive ocean. "Why are you doing this to me?!"

I stood in the shallows, hoping. "Daniel. Daniel?" my scream died away to a whimper. "Daniel? Please…come back."

I knew I should be running back to the car. Driving to town. Going to get help. But I couldn't make myself move. I had left him behind once. I would not leave him behind again. Irrationally I thought that as long as I kept my eyes on the ocean, there would be hope for him.

The minutes ticked by. Five and then ten, then twenty. I dropped to the sand, numbed beyond belief. Daniel was gone. The afternoon was fading.The last crimson rays of sunset threw their bronze spiderweb arcoss the ocean. It was the most perfect of days. And I felt nothing for it. I knew with dreadful certainty that there was no way he could have held his breath for that long. Even if the shark hadn't finished him off, the water would have. Not even a splash or red water to mark his last dive. In a haze I thought dimly – *how inconsiderate of that shark, it didn't even leave me a piece of Daniels finger to remember him by*. Then I knew I was approaching hysteria. A finger? My Daniel was gone and I wanted a bloody piece of his flesh to remember him with? I was cold. So cold. I could not believe that here I was again, sitting on a lonely beach looking out at an ocean that had taken Daniel from me. This was beyond unfair.

And then there was a splash and Daniel surged up and out of the sea several feet away from me. He was a glorious sight. With his arms stretched wide, raven red head thrown back, silver droplets on gleaming skin in the approaching dusk he was a water god. A silver dolphin. He shook his head sending diamond spray scattering. His eyes caught mine and his face lit up in a joyous smile. Again he dove in to the water and power stroked his way swiftly to my side. In less time than it took to exhale, I was in his arms.

And he was warm. And real. And solid flesh and muscle against me. And his kiss was hot and salty. I drowned in it. And the waves lapped us in their embrace. I felt a peaceful calm sweep over me as once again the sea felt like a friend. Safe.

Effortlessly, Daniel lifted me and carried me out of the water gently setting me down beside our picnic gear under the trees. He wiped wet strands of hair away from my face and wrapped a thick towel around my shoulders, rubbing my arms in response to my shivering.For several minutes neither of us spoke. Just breathed. I ran myfingers over his face, through his hair, along his tattoo, glorying in his perfection. My eyes drank him in, unwilling to believe that he was alive. Complete. Unhurt. Well, almost unhurt. There was a welt of matted red along the side of his bronzed chest.

"Daniel you're bleeding. We've got to get you to the hospital."

"Nah, it's nothing. He didn't bite me, I got this from his skin, the impact when we collided. Agh, did you know that sharks have skin like toxic sandpaper?" He shook his head with a faint grimace as he gingerly felt his wound.

I jerked out of his embrace and leapt to my feet. What was I thinking sitting here lapping up his hug when he'd been injured? I grabbed the First Aid kit from the car and applied a dressing to his cut, ignoring his assurances that he was fine. Not until he was bandaged and we were both dressed in dry clothing, not until I was really sure that he was alright – did I ask him the questions that had been bubbling underneath the surface.

"Daniel, what happened out there?"

He sat beside me, staring out at the fast sinking sun and his voice was carefully neutral. "I'm not sure."

"I mean, what was that? You knew that shark was there? How? And when we were out there hanging on to the tire, you talked about it, like you could read its mind or something." Saying it out loud only made it sound all the more implausible. I laughed weakly, waiting for him to dispel what were surely just fanciful notions.

He shook his head. "I don't know. It doesn't make any sense. One minute I was half-asleep and then the next I could feel this thing, this presence and I just knew right away that you were in danger. Once I got into the water, the thought came so clearly to me – a shark. A big one."

He stopped and looked away, out over the waves crashing on a faraway reef. I prompted him. "Yeah, and then?"

"Then what?"

"Then you were talking about its thoughts. You were freaking me out, what was going on out there?"

He said nothing. Shrugged. I persisted. "Daniel, say something. What just happened? Those waves that came out of nowhere, pushing me to shore? Did those come from you? And then when that shark attacked you, how did you get away from it? With only that 'sandpaper scratch'? This is crazy, you were gone for over twenty minutes, I thought you were dead. It was just like…"

His anger halted my tirade. "Like what Leila?! What?" Roughly he stood and walked away from me, down towards the ocean, throwing curt words over his shoulder at me. "Just leave it okay? Leave me alone. I don't want to talk about this. Just leave it."

There was barely controlled rage in his voice and it stunned me. I let him go, watching him stand at the water's edge while a dying sun bled with orange-red light. I didn't know what had happened with him as that shark had tried to attack us, but of one thing I was sure – whatever was going on with Daniel – it had everything to do with his crested wave shaped birthmark.

"The mark of Vasa Loloa…all water telesa have them."

'When Water Burns' coming in 2012.

About the Cover Model – *Ezra Taylor*

Ezra Taylor is a rugby union player who was born in Brisbane, Australia and grew up in West Auckland, NZ. He is Samoan with Kiwi, Scottish and English ancestry. He represented New Zealand at the U-19 and schoolboy levels in rugby union and made his professional debut for Otago in the 2006 Air New Zealand Cup. He has played rugby for the Highlanders, Queensland Reds and European club Connacht of the Magners League. He has also represented Samoa, playing for the national team – Manu Samoa. Ezra Taylor is married to NZ Tall Ferns basketball player,Natalie Purcell.

I have taught English literature in secondary schools in Samoa for ten years and know there is a gaping chasm in the Young Adult market for fiction with Pacific Island themes, characters, places and values.Our youth need books that they can see themselves in, that they can relate to, that will assist in lighting the fires of creativity and a love for reading. Ezra was an ideal choice to represent Daniel because he is a dedicated, successful Samoan athlete who values his family above all else – making him an excellent role model for Pacific Island youth everywhere.

Thank you Ezra, for helping to bring Daniel to life.

ACKNOWLEDGEMENTS

Every book is borne from the creative fire of the writer who dared to envision it and represents the love, sweat and tears of many people. I am only able to write because of the patient support of my husband, Darren. He fashions powerful, beautiful things from steel with blue fire – thus making it possible for me to sit at my laptop and tap out fiery things of my own.

My five fabulous children were the first ones to read snippets of *Telesā* and fuel my writing with their enthusiastic enjoyment of it. I am especially grateful to my daughter Sade Aroha who gave so willingly of her ideas so that *Telesā* could take flight. I look forward to the books that Sade will write one day– they will surely eclipse mine in every way.

As a self-confessed hermit, I would never have left my cave for the release of my first book '**Pacific Tsunami Galu Afi**' - if not for the gentle, yet firm insistence of my very wise and very talented publicist, Pele Wendt. She dragged me kicking and screaming onto Facebook, forced me to join the social media party on Twitter and gave me many lectures on how to build a 'writer's platform.' If not for her creative vision, it is doubtful that anyone would be reading this book right now. (Or know of it's existence.) Thank you Pele.

I thought that because I was an English teacher that I had written an error free book but copy editor Anna Thomson very generously showed me how wrong I was! Elizabeth Macdonald also lent her editing magic to this book. Thanks to their expertise, *Telesā* is a much better book than it started off as.

Launching a book successfully requires the energy, expertise and enthusiasm of a passionate team. Much gratitude to Renate Rivers for making a photoshoot with Ezra Taylor and Flora Rivers happen. Huge admiration for the photography genius of Tim and Efi Rasmussen. I continue to be amazed with your work. Thank you to marketing and media consultants, Henry Tunupopo and Nydia Chu Ling for being so generous with your creativity.

Jordan Kwan's masterpiece of a book trailer has been a powerful tool, taking **Telesā** to the world. Thank you Jordan for bringing my book to life on the big screen, even if only for a few minutes!

I continue to be grateful to Mr Hans Joe Keil for his ongoing encouragement of my writing. If not for him, I would have taken far longer to discover that - yes, I am capable of writing and finishing a book.

I thank my parents for their love and encouragement and my siblings for all their support. A special thank you to my big brother Dr.Cam Wendt who's addiction to X-Men comics gave me almost limitless options for my imagination to take flight. (Even if I had to be that annoying kid sister who took his comics without permission.)

To all those who believed in my writing choices – I give my gratitude. Thank you for not looking horrified or disdainful when I shared my book ideas with you.

It is an exciting time to be a writer and I am grateful to have the opportunity to be living my dream.

You can read more writing by Lani Wendt Young and stay updated on the **Telesā** series at her website: Sleepless in Samoa. Here, you can read about the **Telesā** writing journey, the search for the cover model (and peruse all the photos that didn't make the cover), find out what music inspired the book, get recipes for all the delicious Samoan foods that Leila enjoys, check out Pacific tattoos (and the people who rock them), learn more about the tropical haven that is Samoa, marvel at the stunning creations from leading Pacific design store Plantation House (that feature in Nafanua's stately colonial-style home) and see how a slightly demented Domestic Goddess stays sane while writing full-time *and* trying to be nice to her Fabulous Five children.

http://sleeplessinSamoa.blogspot.com

Contact the author - LaniWendtYoung@hotmail.com

Made in the USA
Las Vegas, NV
12 March 2021

19458801R00243